THE TIES THAT BIND

by

C. P. MANDARA

I0520535

Published by Chimera Books
ISBN 9781780806808 (Updated)

This novel is fiction - in real life practice safe sex.

'I've already told you: the only way to a woman's heart is along the path of torment. I know none other as sure.'
Marquis de Sade

CHAPTER ONE

Cocoa

Mark couldn't sleep. It wasn't your normal, run-of-the-mill insomnia, either. This time the stress payload he was carrying was nearly impossible to shift. Submission! The dirty old bastard wanted to see him brought low, but for what? His breathing hitched and he could feel the sweat breaking out on his forehead. That damn phone call had broken his cell. He'd been so shocked at Redcliff's request that he'd dropped the thing. Get a grip, he cursed, feeling his fingers shaking around the pan of hot milk he had simmering on the range.

It was three a.m. in the morning and he was making cocoa, of all things. Apparently, the stuff helped you sleep. Something about milk and an amino acid called tryptophan, but he wasn't convinced. This was his third mug and the cloying chocolate was beginning to make his tongue curl in distaste. He didn't want to think about Redcliff and his insane request, but typically that was all his subconscious wanted to focus on, and he was beginning to realise that he'd need chemicals in order to get the asshole out of his system. For a man who always prided himself on his exemplary control, resorting to sleeping tablets was the absolute last straw. It would be almost as if Redcliff had won before the battle even commenced. So cocoa it was.

What did the man want? Not money, as he'd originally thought, but he most certainly wanted something. He'd put too high a price tag on his daughter, though. Mark's body was not for sale. He'd travelled the submission route a long time ago and it was an experience he didn't care to repeat. Once upon a time he'd had barely a penny to his name and once upon a time, he'd have done nearly anything to succeed. That was many years ago, though. He'd chosen his path and he'd known the consequences.

Back in his teens, when he'd dropped out of college due to lack of funds, he already knew where he wanted to be and, more importantly, how to get there. The trouble was, he'd needed money and plenty of it in order to achieve his dream. He'd been frequently propositioned by women, even back then, but he'd always refused them. Mark hadn't been bothered by the fairer sex at all in his youth. Sure he'd had some fun with them, but he was far too focused to let them take up much of his time. When they got all whiney and needy, as most of them did, he got rid of them immediately and moved on. All of them had swiftly gotten the hint, except one.

He let his thoughts trail back to Sophia. She'd been his ticket to ride. He owed

2

her everything that he was today, but she'd demanded an astronomically high price in return. Sophia had been twelve years his senior, and back then the age gap had been insurmountable for him. She'd been a woman of the world, well travelled with a high-profile career, and she was frequently spotlight fodder for the paparazzi. The pair of them regularly met on his early morning run around Hyde Park, but although she smiled at him, he never gave her more than a cursory glance in return. Over the years he'd discovered that smiling at the wrong woman was dangerous, and he knew without a doubt that Sophia was not someone he wanted to mess with. She had an unshakeable air of confidence about her, eyes that spoke of cunning intelligence, and a beautiful body that was built for fucking. He knew she wanted him. Every time their paths crossed, and it was more frequent than it should have been, he could feel her lingering glance upon him, and the turn of her head as he jogged past. Here was a lady who was used to getting what she wanted. It was too bad she'd picked the wrong man to throw her lures at. He was simply not interested.

Sophia had been smart enough to bide her time and wait. She'd had him under surveillance, although he hadn't known that at the time, but when he dropped out of college, she'd known what kind of trouble he was in. Even then, she hadn't pounced. The woman had watched him apply for a ton of jobs, none of which he acquired due to his lack of experience, and then she had let the despair of soaring rent prices and stacking bills creep upon him. Her timing, when she finally did approach him, could not have been more perfect. He was nearly on his knees with despair, but little did he know that in a few days' time, he'd be on his knees with a whole lot more than just depression on his mind.

The woman entered his life by brazenly blocking his exit out of Hyde Park's Queen Elizabeth gates one day. She'd stood stock still in the widest stance she could manage with her legs shoulder width apart and her hands on her hips. He could have run around her, but it was clear she wanted to speak with him and knowing he would probably run into her sooner rather than later, he figured he'd stop and put an end to the silliness once and for all. Feigning a politeness he did not feel at her intrusion, he asked, 'Can I help you?' If his tone was a little clipped, it was simply too bad.

'No,' she'd answered him with a calculating smile, 'but I believe I can help you.' He'd looked at her darkly then, shaken his head and made to walk past her, but she'd held out one arm, stopping him in his tracks and said, 'Here's my card. Just read my offer. That's all I ask.' He had taken the cream vellum business card from her proffered fingers, which had been expensively embossed with gold swirls, without really thinking about what he was doing. Before he could give it back she had neatly sidestepped out of his path and continued on her way, leaving him to stare at the twisted wrought-iron flowers, leaves and spirals that decorated the length and breadth of the magnificent gates. It had taken him several seconds to gather his wits and continue onwards. When curiosity led him to examine the card, the front was fairly harmless and told him that she held the position of Chief Financial Officer at a prestigious law firm in Chelsea. He remembered whistling. Whilst he was no expert in salaries, he knew enough to know that the woman was loaded. Turning the card over in his hands, he hadn't really expected to find anything on the reverse, but there in scripted handwriting was just one word. Sex. It accompanied the figure of one thousand pounds. His jaw had hung open all the way home.

He hadn't accepted her offer at first, but neither had he thrown the card away. You had to be pretty desperate to accept an offer like that and he had been sure there would be a job for him just around the corner. There hadn't been. Two weeks later he had no money, no food and two days until his landlord threatened to evict him. His level of hopelessness had spiralled to such a degree, that he decided a one-night stand with an attractive lady couldn't be all that bad. Still, he'd sat outside her office for two hours before he'd summoned enough courage to walk in.

It was clear Sophia had been almost as surprised as he was, with regards to his presence in her bureau. She'd almost taken a step backwards when she found him propped upon a black recliner, waiting for her. Her gaze had quickly hardened to a pinpoint stare as she'd coolly assessed him.

'Your offer expired a week ago,' she said, and her tone was not friendly.

Mark had given her a lazy smile, one that belied his racing heartbeat and sweating palms, and had simply said, 'Then write me another.'

She stared at him for the longest ten seconds of his life, before answering. 'Meet me back here at seven p.m., sharp. If you're late, the offer is null and void.'

He hadn't been late.

The milk slopped into his powdered cocoa with a lot more force than necessary and he had an Icelandic geyser moment, where it whooshed out of the mug, did a double backflip and then landed with a wet splat against the flat surface of his ceramic hob.

Goddamn. Jumping backwards to avoid the scalding hot liquid, he could at least be thankful that he hadn't managed to burn himself. What was wrong with him today? But the question wasn't even worth asking. He knew exactly what was wrong. Redcliff had dropped a bombshell and now his ordered little world was fraying around the edges. He didn't need a trip down memory lane right now. That part of his past had been over a long time ago, but he took a moment to wonder if the old man knew about it. It was doubtful. It wasn't the sort of thing you spread around in general conversation and he couldn't imagine Sophia having talked. She had far more to lose than he, should the details have been leaked.

Mopping up the mess of spilt milk and chocolate, he let his gut instinct take over. Clearly Redcliff wanted something. Mark had no doubt that he'd love to have his hide bent over double and spanked raw, but that wasn't the main reason for his little request. There was something bigger at stake here. Money, power, control - it might be any of those things that the old guy wanted, but Mark's submission would be secondary to the equation.

The trouble was, Mark knew how men like Redcliff operated. The word 'no' was not in their vocabulary and if one avenue of attack failed, he would most certainly have a back-up plan. It was the back-up plan that concerned him. No way in hell was he willingly going to agree to flatten himself out at Mr R's feet, but if a few wheels turned in the right direction and a few palms were greased, he might just find himself exactly where he promised himself he would never be again. Whilst Sophia might have pushed him to his limit and beyond on more than one occasion, Redcliff would be looking for more. He would want blood, sweat, and tears. Let's face it; the man was clearly unwell. He wouldn't be winning any 'father of the year competitions' in the near future, and if he was capable of doing that to his daughter, hell only knew what he had planned for him. Rolling his fingers around his two throbbing temples, he decided that at the very least he'd have to upgrade his security. Then he needed to come up with a plan. He, like Redcliff, was not the sort of man to fall at the first hurdle. He would have Ms Redcliff, one way or another, and it would be on his terms or not at all.

CHAPTER TWO

Salted Caramel and Frozen Cheesecake

Soft groans of torment could be heard from inside the queen-sized bed. Arms thrashed wildly upon the heavily starched white sheets and legs flailed about helplessly, but whether the occupant was having a dream or a nightmare was uncertain. Dark, chestnut hair spilled out in all directions, unkempt and tangled from a fitful night's sleep, and tempting, naked patches of tanned flesh frequently spilled from its generous confines.

From behind his screen on the observation deck, Vince grabbed his bowl of cornflakes, dug his spoon in deep and decided that even at the ridiculous hour of five a.m. he loved his job. There were many perks to being a security officer at the Sandringham Apartments. You got a comfy leather chair, twenty-six days annual paid holiday and as much tea and coffee as you could handle. You also got paid to watch some of the most beautiful women on the planet earth in all states of undress, quite legally, and for as many hours as you could handle. All he had to do was make sure none of them had any fun. His orders from the top were few. The women were allowed no unauthorised visitors, but more importantly, they were not permitted to orgasm. It was his job to review the security footage of the building on a daily basis, and report back any infringements of the rules to his boss. Unfortunately for him, his life had been very boring as of late. The girls could all have been auditioning for the role of Mary Poppins, because every single damn one of them toed the line to the letter.

No masturbation, period. Not in the bathtub, not in the shower, not sneakily under the covers in the bedroom and not even hiding behind the sofa. They filed and painted their nails, they primped their hair, they trimmed and plucked, pouted and painted themselves in all kinds of make-up, but they never had any fun on his watch. This was all very well, but he signed up for this gig to watch women orgasm. He got a hefty bonus if he caught one of the girls playing the disappearing finger trick. Four months had gone by with nada to report. Nothing, zilch, zero and zip. Either he was going blind, or these girls were giving the late departed Mother Teresa a run for her money. It wasn't that he needed the money. Zystrom paid him well enough without bonuses, but a little entertainment every now and again wouldn't go amiss. So when he caught the merest hint of under-the-cover duvet action, he nearly fell off his chair.

Staring at Miss Morreau intently, Vince ascertained that her hands were moving underneath the sheets and, well, wasn't that a turn up for the books? Giving a little muttered, 'Way-hay,' he got his face up close and personal with his eighteen-inch monitor. Too close, as it happened, because his breath fogged up the glass. Backing away a touch, he felt his jaw drop open. Miss Morreau's sheets had just slithered to the floor and both her hands were firmly between her legs. 'Yes, yes, yes,' he hissed through his breath. His day had just taken on a rosy hue.

Marianna was simultaneously having the best and worst dream of her life. Reliving the events of Wednesday night, one moment she was awake and tearing at the sheets, and in the next she was thrashing about in the throes of sleep. Everything was coming back to her with startling clarity.

She was dressed in a teal outfit of see-through, diamond-shaped netting that displayed all of her assets in their entirety, every time she made a move. She was not wearing a shred of underwear. Breasts, nipples and a pair of reddened ass cheeks were on prominent display to any and all that cared to watch. As to her hands, they were fastened behind her back in a box-tie held tight by a leather thong, and her lips found themselves clutching a bright red ball gag. If that wasn't bad enough, someone had attached a clear Perspex tray to her abdomen, anchored upright by two clamps on the outer edge that were attached to her nipples by long silver chains. This meant any weight placed on the tray was borne by her poor, tender teats alone. Add nine small ceramic jugs of sake to the tray, and the result was a walking disaster precariously perched upon five-inch stilettos.

In her dream the floor moved in beautiful shades of turquoise green, interspersed with shoals of goldfish and bubbles. Unfortunately, walking in high heels on a constantly moving floor made her horribly dizzy. The nine flasks of warm, Japanese wine she carried on her tray were also excruciatingly heavy, and whilst the pain brought sobs to her throat, it also sent lightning bolts of desire straight through her. Her predicament was the sweetest of torments one moment and the most all-consuming agony the next. It was no wonder her feet were almost jogging forward, in her eagerness to be rid of her heavy load.

Wednesday Evening 10 p.m. - Atlantisse Bar, London.

Approaching the table she lowered her limbs gracefully, so that her tray was at a comfortable level for the seated patrons to grasp their beverages. She had been taught well and her years of schooling were beginning to come back to her. Fight through the pain, lock it away and let the endorphins take over. As long as she kept moving, everything would be OK. If she stood still for too long, she would end up screaming. The gentleman to her left must have guessed at her pain tolerance, for he gave her a sympathetic wink and quickly whisked his drink away. Marianna would have given him a smile of gratitude, but her gag made that impossible. She dipped her eyes by way of thanks and hoped he understood. Another jug was removed, a hand crept up the inside of her thigh and two fingers tickled her sex. They fluttered along her clitoris as lightly as a butterfly, and flew away just as quickly. A hand then slapped her ass and told her to hurry up along the line before the wine cooled. She shot up with a yelp, watched in horror as seven jugs wobbled around dangerously, and breathed a sigh of relief as they settled. She didn't want to think what might happen if she dropped them. The men and women in this room would have punishments in store for errant behaviour the likes of which were unimaginable. Marianna did not want to be at their mercy if she could possibly avoid it.

Squaring her shoulders and lifting her head, she felt her chestnut hair sweep gently around her chin. Damn Dev and Stephen for pulling her neat chignon to pieces. She hated wearing her hair down when in a submissive role. It was part of her body armour, the harsh lines of an up-do gave off a regal, don't-touch-me air and that had all been lost in an instant. Marianna was positive she now looked like a walking billboard for a brothel, and there would be no need for flashing red lights. Her eyes were drowning in desire.

Two more flasks left her tray in fairly short order, but they came at a high price. One hand grasped at her right ass cheek and squeezed tightly, whilst a single finger circled the tight little nub of her left nipple and that light touch was the cruellest of whispers across her skin. She almost screamed behind her gag. Then she lost count of the damn flasks. There were hands all over her, fisting themselves in her hair, tugging at her dress, squeezing her breasts and pulling at her teats. The sensory overload was almost crippling to one who had been denied any kind of stimulation for so long. Her body responded by arching itself into their hands, and begging for more of the same.

In short order, two men had bent her low over the long glass banquet table and, after spreading her legs as wide as they could possibly go, had sat down on either side of her and let their fingers have free rein. Both men were tall, well-built, stocky fellows and there was no way she was going to mess with either of them. She kept her eyes forward and her head lowered.

Taking a firm hold of the soft waves of silky hair at the base of her neck, one of the men twisted her face sideways upon the table so she was forced to look at him. Well, she was looking at the middle of a very elegant, tailored dinner jacket, in any case. 'I'm Raynor,' said the first, introducing himself. His accent had a Germanic twinge and she would have placed him as Dutch. 'My partner in crime over there is Huss, and he likes ass play, so I'd brace yourself if I were you. He's going to stretch both of your tight little holes until you can't remember which day of the week it is, and after he's done that, he's going to see if he can completely wreck your calendar with his multiple orgasm technique. How many was it last time, Huss?'

Huss, who was currently working over her clit with fingers that were far too dextrous and skilled, made a grunt from behind her. There was a pause as he decided upon his answer. Marianna mewled pitifully as his fingers stopped in mid-flow. 'I think maybe four, but it could be five. I lose count when I get excited.' His fingers then continued on their beautiful journey, graduating from the lightest of touches to a modest spiral.

'She's breathing quite heavily, Huss. I'd say you're on the right track, old chap.'

If Marianna had been able to speak, she'd have agreed with Raynor. Huss had very talented fingers and if he kept up the twirling pace he had set, she would be screaming in less than... goddamn. Raynor pressed his hand firmly into the small of her back as if he'd known what was about to happen, and then her body started to buck and tremble. She began dribbling and screaming the place down.

'Thank God this one's been gagged, Huss. How come you're so good at this shit, anyway?'

It could have been Marianna's imagination, but Raynor sounded slightly miffed.

'I press buttons for a living,' replied Huss.

In response to that little gem, Raynor lowered his face to the table, caught Marianna's eye and raised his eyebrows. 'He always says that, but I don't believe him, do you?' Marianna just stared back at him helplessly, especially since Huss had decided that her body did not need a rest and his fingers continued on their immediate quest for climax number two. Raynor continued, 'If he was just good with his fingers I might believe him, but you haven't seen what he can do with his tongue.' He smiled. Marianna tried to smile back with her eyes, but it was a difficult thing to master with your lips viciously strained around a bright red ball.

When Huss inserted a thick finger inside her pussy and began pumping it back and forth, she was lost and her eyes fluttered closed. Raynor didn't care much for that and he kissed them gently open again, whilst his hand in her hair tugged slowly, tilting her head back. 'Uh, uh, uh,' he said, shaking his head. 'I'm a watcher. I love to watch women when they come, so you're not allowed to close your eyes for me baby, or I'll have to spank that delicious ass of yours. He palmed her bare ass and scraped his fingernails along her right cheek. Smiling as she squawked around her gag, he nodded slowly. 'Been a naughty girl, have we?' Running the other hand through his long, platinum blond hair, he appeared to consider the matter. 'Tell you what, as it appears it's already had a good going over today, I'll let you off just this once, but you close those glittering green emeralds again and I'm going to find a crop. You don't want me to do that, baby, do you?' Marianna tried to shake her head, but his grip on her hair was fierce. 'No, I didn't think so.' The look in his eyes was flinty and hard. It screamed 'do not mess with me', and, oh boy, Marianna was not about to. 'Now you look at me and focus, because I want to watch every time Huss manages to hit gold before the dessert course is served.' To emphasise his point he used the middle and index finger of his right hand in a 'V' which he pointed at her eyes and then swiftly moved them across to his. Marianna nodded emphatically. The message had been received loud and clear.

Huss currently had two fingers plunging inside her and Marianna felt her body jolt with each long thrust of his hand. With the other he continued to manipulate her clit with consummate ease. She could only wonder at what kind of buttons the guy pressed in his favoured career. Perhaps he designed video games, or there was always the possibility that he dropped neutron bombs, but whichever it was, he'd gotten in plenty of practice over the years. His fingers were as explosive as dynamite, and just as deadly. As the thought bloomed in her head, it took a mere two seconds for her body to process it before it decided to blast into orbit itself, because a third finger had begun squeezing its way into the tight confines of her nether regions and the exquisitely full feeling his fingers produced made her claw at the table, almost panicked at the second ride she would have to endure in such quick succession.

With her body bucking and shaking uncontrollably she found it almost impossible to look at Raynor, but did her utmost to keep her eyes from ramming themselves shut, all too aware of his dark grey eyes boring down upon her. Trying to ignore the soft little flicks of Huss' fingernails against her sensitive clit, she whimpered madly against the soft rubber ball in her jaw and felt the sides of her lips chewing at the leather straps. Her eyes were nearly rolling in her head. She couldn't take much more of this. It was nearly impossible to keep her eyes open during orgasm, she could literally feel her eyeballs bulging out of her head, but somehow she managed it.

'That's it baby, show me those glorious eyes. Enjoy riding those fingers, slut, because each subsequent orgasm is going to get more and more painful until you're sure you can't stand the thought of another.' Raynor hoisted his body up on the table and picked up a lock of her hair, twirling it in his fingers. He then pulled the strands upwards and she was forced to follow his eyes. 'But you'll take everything that Huss can dish out, won't you, slut? You wouldn't want either of us to have to complain to your owner, would you?'

Marianna's hips were swishing left and right with a mind of their own and they had an objective: avoid the terrible fingers at all costs. Huss was obviously wise to this game because his hand stayed stuck to her clit like a leech and no amount of movement on her part was going to shift him. Her sex was becoming sore to the slightest touch, throbbing and pleading to be released, and her eyes

9

were beginning to water. The worst part of the ordeal was that her 'watcher' missed nothing.

'Feeling slightly sensitive, are we? Do you need a little pain to take your mind off some *pressing* concerns?' He raised his eyebrows at her and waited for a response. Marianna just stared at him for several long seconds. She couldn't have articulated words at this moment in time even had she not been gagged, and thinking was proving exceptionally difficult, too. Her body was screaming. Her mind wasn't far behind. Finally she managed to nod her head, not really sure whether she wanted pain or not, but thinking it might be a better alternative than withstanding another round of Huss' fingers inside her, relentlessly pulsating and pushing without pause. She then nodded vigorously. Any distraction from her pounding sex would be most welcome.

'Mistress Faith, we have need of your talents,' called Raynor, although his eyes did not leave Marianna's for a moment.

Apparently they did not need to, for a seductive, throaty voice called out, 'Flogger, paddle or crop?'

Raynor gave Marianna a saucy grin. 'Which one would you prefer, slut?' He let his finger trace a soft path over her swollen, crimson lips, and smiled when she made insensible noises at him. Grinning wickedly he raised himself up and spoke over her head. 'She can't decide, Faith, so you'd better give her a taste of all three.' Marianna made louder noises, but Raynor effectively muffled them. He'd decided that he liked the taste of her sparkling vanilla lip gloss very much and the substance was going to be his, every last drop of it.

As half of her face was being sucked off around the limiting confines of the ball gag, she lost concentration for a minute and tried to close her legs, anything to stop the relentless fingers of the gentleman behind her. A sharp slap of a hand on her buttocks startled her and her body shot upright, the plastic tray at her waist dragging painfully at her nipples. Then Raynor's hand pushed her back into the cool glass of the table top.

'You must not close your legs at any time,' he said, shaking his head slowly and wagging his finger at her, 'or I will be forced to find the widest spreader bar available in which to tether your ankles apart. Do I make myself clear?' Marianna looked up at him pleadingly, the pressure on her extremely sensitive clit nearly unbearable. Whilst she did not want her legs restrained, knowing that the bar would give Huss even greater access to her sex, she didn't know how much longer she could stand the pressure of his fingers without going mad. It wouldn't be too much longer, she suspected.

Straining her legs wide and concentrating on keeping both eyes peeled on Raynor's, she felt her thighs begin to tremble violently. Was it possible she was going to have her third climax in less than five minutes? The abrupt thud of the flogger upon her shoulder blades brought her back to the land of living. She sent up a silent prayer of thanks.

There was a chuckle from behind her. 'Mistress Faith at your service. I'm going to slowly work over that delightful body of yours until everywhere looks just as red as your ass. You're going to remember me for the next few days, every single time you move.' The flogger thudded down again as if to emphasise the point, and it did so with quite a bite. Whilst Huss' fingers did not stop in their detailed exploration of her clit, the sensitivity had lessened somewhat and her trembling ceased.

'Huss, you've got your work cut out for you now,' grinned Raynor, and he gave his companion a cheeky wink.

Huss snorted in response and pulled his fingers from Marianna's pussy, proceeding to take them a little higher up into the valley of her ass. 'I haven't even started yet,' he grunted. The fingers swirled their moisture around Marianna's tight little hole and pressed for entry. There was another grunt. 'She's tight, this one.'

'So are you, Huss. You've yet to buy me a drink, asshole.' Raynor raised his glass of Boërl & Kroff, which was finished bar one last sip, and gave his friend a grin.

'Speaking of assholes...'

Marianna could feel the warm breath of Huss' mouth on her backside, and then the soft pressure of his hands as he sought to prize her ass cheeks apart. Her breathing quickened exponentially. The flogger thudded down, confusing her thoughts, but it was lighting up nerve endings everywhere it touched. The pressure on her backside increased. As the mountainous valley was slowly parted she couldn't help but hold her breath, anxious to know what the man was going to try next. On the one hand she was grateful that the pressure on her clit had stopped, but on the other, it appeared that things were quickly going from bad to worse because a long tongue had sneaked out and begun weaving a circular path around her sphincter. Raynor's fingers then replaced those of Huss', and they were nearly as talented. When a tongue dived in and began circling her rear entrance Marianna banged her face down on the table repeatedly in horror, her gag saving her from too much damage, but the message was clear. She was now launching herself into orgasm number three and it was so painful that her scream was clearly heard even though her mouth was firmly plugged.

'Faith, we have a disobedient little pet here. One who can't obey simple orders. Dispense with the flogger and bring out the crop, would you, dear?' Raynor curled a finger under Marianna's chin and tapped her nose in a warning gesture. 'Now you've displeased me and I intend to make sure you don't repeat the same mistake again. He yanked her upright by a hand in her hair. She moaned in protest, but it fell on deaf ears. Huss also complained as his fingers lost their tight purchase on her ass, but he too was ignored. 'You will keep your eyes on me or suffer the consequences,' said Raynor.

The blond stranger stared at her for what could have been a minute, maybe more, before he finally made a move. He released one of the clamps from her nipple tray. There was a second of silence before Marianna went berserk, howling, whimpering and struggling madly to free her arms from the firm restraints they had been placed in. It was an instinctive reaction and she should have been able to control it, the trouble was it had been such a long time ago since she felt such intense pain that she didn't know what to do with it for a minute.

'Silence!' The loud, resonant tones of Raynor's voice managed to still her body into instant submission, before Mistress Faith's leather crop sneaked slowly up between her breasts to gently rub its tip against her throbbing nipple, immediately freezing the air in her chest. She held herself so tightly she found she couldn't suck the precious substance into her body or exhale it. With her eyes shrinking back inside her head, she remained as still as a statue and found herself twice as cold.

Satisfied that she had managed to get herself under control, Raynor smiled. 'You will obey me, or there will be consequences... *severe* consequences. Between the three of us we intend to make sure that you come at least five or six times. There is, of course, a reason for this.' Raynor straightened his black bow-tie, unnecessarily, and brought his fingers to his lips, making a grand show of sucking them. His fingers lingered inside his mouth, as if he was a connoisseur of the female essence, and though his eyes were inscrutable at first, gradually he appeared pleased. This she gathered from the slowly forming smile that began to transform his features.

'You taste delightful. So wet, so hungry, so needy.' Raynor's emphasis on the world 'needy' was not lost on her. 'We mean to see that you are fully sated before you go back to your Master, and more to the point, we intend to make sure that you will be of little use to him on your return. Huss, my dear friend, is going to make sure your clit is so sensitive that it will be impossible for you to have any further fun this evening. All you have to do is stand there and take whatever we give you until I have decided that we have indeed wrung you dry and no more orgasms will be forthcoming from that lovely body of yours. Do you understand me?' He tilted his neck to the side and looked at her thoughtfully.

Marianna's eyes nearly jumped out of their sockets with that awful revelation. Alas, she obviously didn't bob her head quick enough because the crop flew backwards and there was an awful second of mesmerising shock before the tip connected with a sharp thwack on her engorged and throbbing teat. This time her eyes did burst out of her head and the accompanying noise she made was quite impressive.

'Do you understand me?' The repeated comment had her nodding her head furiously. 'Good. I'm glad we've got that out of the way. Huss, you may continue where you left off.' Raynor indicated with a swipe of his finger that his friend could once again get up close and personal with her derriere.

'I'm going to use fingers this time, so you'll feel something a little wet and cold on your ass at first, but I promise you'll enjoy it.'

That was what Marianna was afraid of. Three orgasms down and her body was of a wobblier consistency than a jellyfish in a tsunami. When Huss began to smear a generous helping of what she assumed was lubricant around her sphincter, Marianna nearly lost it. She'd just had the multiple orgasm session from hell and it appeared that it wasn't about to end anytime soon. Working in the fluid with deft little slides of his fingers, Huss burrowed his face in her sex and began a very gentle series of lapping strokes. It was agonising in the extreme. The urge to close her legs and squeeze them tightly shut was uppermost in her mind, for her clit was now so highly sensitised that even the lightest touch was painful. It was only the presence of Mistress Faith with her crop hovering in mid-air and the knowledge that Raynor would wreak vengeance upon her for the slightest infraction, that kept her eyes forward and her legs wide open. Her ordeal would have to be over soon, wouldn't it? Surely there would come a point of no return? Alas, they were not yet at that point, and Huss' talented tongue and fingers were probing in all the right places and with just the right amount of pressure. The lubricant had now warmed up nicely and a single finger slowly worked its way into her ass, maddeningly wandering back and forth.

'Do you like that, slut?' Raynor didn't miss a thing. The heat in Marianna's cheeks had just doubled and her eyes had taken on a dreamy expression. As she nodded her head in an almost euphoric state of bliss she absently wondered how mad Matthews was going to be, when he realised she had been wrung out to dry. Then again, maybe he wouldn't care. It wasn't as if she couldn't deliver the goods, she just wouldn't be yelling the place down. When two fingers replaced one in her ass she almost swooned with pleasure.

'You do like that, huh? Keep that up, Huss, but a little harder and a little faster. We'll have her exactly where we want in no time.' Marianna drowned in the pale grey of Raynor's eyes. Her focus was all over the place, her clit had a damn pulse all of its own and her body was on the orgasm train to heaven again, God help her. I can't do this, she thought helplessly, I can't come again... But Huss' tongue on her clit and his fingers thrusting away powerfully in her ass had her undone, tied up in knots, inside out and back to front. She didn't know which way was up. She'd given up trying to breathe and her eyes were rolling in her head as orgasm number four smacked her upside the head and into next year.

Oh, oh, oh, oh... That was the only word her brain could manage to whisper and it repeated itself over and over. Climax number four had proved to be the strongest of them all. When she finally rode the last waves of her crested cloud joy quickly turned to despair. The tongue was greedily lapping up all of her ejaculate, and she could feel her thighs sticky with the stuff, but she knew her respite would not be a long one.

'Huss loves to taste the ladies as much as I do.' Raynor gave her a crooked smile. If you taste good, and believe me you do, Huss will spend some time between those thighs cleaning you up. Rest assured, he will be tackling orgasms five and six in short order, though.' Raynor scooped up a long line of dribble from her jawline and put it to his lips. 'Hmm. Even your saliva tastes wonderful. Fancy that.'

There was a popping sound as Raynor's finger worked its way loose from his mouth and he used the wet digit to circle Marianna's freed nipple, which was standing proudly to attention. She mewled pitifully in protest, but he paid her little heed. 'For such a petite little thing you have the most generous pair of tits I've seen. He cupped them in his hands and gently kneaded them with his fingers. 'Does that feel good?' he whispered.

Marianna wasn't sure if it was Raynor's hands on her breasts that felt good, or Huss' tongue on her sex, but she nodded heavily in response. Then he slapped them gently from side to side, noting that her pupils immediately dilated in pleasure. 'You like a bit of rough with your pleasure, don't you?' She moaned softly and that gave him all the answer he needed. His soft little smacks continued, and her breasts bounced from left to right with a beautiful swaying action.

When Huss' tongue came back to continue its previous onslaught Marianna had a battle on her hands to stop herself from diving under the table and bursting into tears. It was too much. Her body was shaking in agony. The thought of another orgasm was going to make her violently ill. She was going to embarrass herself and her Master by giving her safe signal. All of the girls Matthews owned had a standard safe signal and it would be well known in the places he frequented. Three nods of her head was all that stood between her and walking out of the giant glass fish tank she currently found herself in. *You can't leave*, a little voice inside her head whispered, *because if you leave there is no going back*. When Huss' fingers began plundering her ass once more, intense though the pleasure was, she was sure there would be no way that her body could summon up enough enthusiasm or energy to excite the swollen, pulsing, weeping, crying, sore organ that her clit had become. She was wrong. Mistress Faith fired the crop at her freed nipple and Raynor removed the clamp from the other. The ball gag shot forth from an explosion of air from her silent scream and her legs went out from under her. She nearly flattened Huss as she fell heavily to the floor.

Blood roared in her ears, colours swam in her vision and her body was uncontrollable. On the floor she was a tangle of disjointed, trembling limbs that couldn't have stood up had her life depended on it. A few soft sobs left her lips when she managed to get her breath back, and they gathered in intensity and volume quickly. The storm gates had opened, but there was nowhere for her temper to be unleashed. When a pair of hands stroked her back gently and moved under her armpits, pulling her upright, she screamed and shook her head. 'No more. No. More,' she tried desperately to articulate. Her head nodded once, then twice, but before she managed to get out a third nod she found herself gathered to a familiar chest.

'Shhhhh,' whispered Matthew's voice in her ear, and suddenly she was scooped up in his arms and held tightly. When she chanced to look up into his dark eyes she nearly had heart failure at the stern expression that resided there, until she discovered that the source of his displeasure was not her, but rather the two men behind her.

14

'Gentlemen, thank you for taking such good care of my sub, but I believe I'll have her back now if you don't mind.' His tone was brusque, his gaze was hard and his fingertips were thrumming upon her backside. Turning around he made to walk away, but after a careful moment's consideration, turned over his shoulder for one last parting shot.

'You pull that stunt again, Raynor, and I'll make sure you're barred from this joint and any others you might want to frequent, permanently.' He didn't need to say any more. Raynor was well aware of the power he wielded, as were the rest of the members of the room who had now gone silent. There was barely a sound in the vast hall as Mark made his way over to the banquet table and sat himself down. Signalling one of the waiters, he decided to take the focus away from himself and Marianna, and procure some dessert in the process. A few soft words was all it took, and then the bar suddenly became a buzz of activity as everyone braced themselves for the next round of entertainment. He swiftly removed the buckle that held her gag in place, before making short work of unfastening the leather thong that held her arms together behind her back.

'Marianna?' Usually one word was enough for their heads to come snapping back up, but the woman had buried herself so tightly against his chest that he wondered if she was trying to tunnel through to the other side. He gave her another minute before he repeated her name, but this time he gave her blistered rear a squeeze for good measure. With a little squeak she finally raised her head and looked him in the eye. 'Do you want to safe word?' Tearful eyes looked up at him and he could see she was carefully considering his proposal. Her thinking would be somewhere along the lines of 'I know I can't face another orgasm, and the chances are he's going to put me through one.' As it happened, her thinking would be dead on the money, but it wouldn't be as bad as she feared. She still had to make the decision for herself, though.

Her eyes looked up at him beguilingly, almost pleading for him to make the decision for her, but that he would not do. 'I saw the two nods, Marianna. I know you were close to safe-wording. So, do we stay or do we go?' The pad of his thumb brushed along her jawline, back and forward, as he held her gaze. He knew she was uncomfortable, for she kept trying to turn her head away, but he wouldn't let her. 'Answer the question.' The girl was torn by indecision, weighing up her options left and right, and having no clear answer in sight. She knew there would be repercussions if she went, but she had to deal with some fairly serious problems if she stayed.

Sucking in a breath, Marianna pushed a handful of her long chestnut locks behind her head and whispered, 'I'll stay,' before adding, 'but I'm not sure I'll be much fun.' She couldn't resist a giggle at that remark. He laughed with her.

'Good decision, Marianna. You'll be right as rain in no time, don't you worry.' He couldn't help another laugh as he saw the rueful expression she directed his way. He'd tackle her little problem in a minute, and it was only a minor one, but at the moment he thought he'd take her mind off her body with some idle chatter. It would help her calm down a bit before he administered her 'medicine'.

15

'So, what did you think of my friends, orgasm one and climax two?' Mark gently manoeuvred her body so she was propped upon his knee and reached along the table for a napkin. 'You're dribbling a little,' he said, trying to keep his lips compressed together. He pressed it into her hand.

Marianna dabbed gently at the corners of her mouth, which were slick with drool, and tried to get her breathing under control. Just sitting on Mark's knee brought tremors of excitement to her body, and she really didn't want to feel anything remotely sexual at the moment. Raynor and Huss had made her want to take to her bed for a week, and the 'no orgasm rule' really wouldn't have been a problem for a change. 'They're friends of yours?' She wore a somewhat incredulous expression upon her face.

'Hardly,' came the ironic reply, 'with friends like that, who'd need enemies? As it happens, I took over their numerous failing business ventures a little over two years ago. I managed to get them into profit, and they have never forgiven me for the fact. Every time I bring a girl here they do their little orgasm trick, assuming I'll be able to have no fun with her for the rest of the evening. Well, admittedly they got me the first time, but I've become wise to the ploy ever since and I have damage control in place.' He winked at her. 'How many times did they manage to make you come, out of curiosity?'

'Five times, I think, but they were hoping for six.' Marianna pouted.

'And here you were telling me that you had a lot of catching up to do and couldn't wait to get back into the swing of things...' Mark raised his eyebrows in friendly challenge.

'Hmph. I didn't want to catch up quite that quickly. One orgasm every half an hour is enough for any girl. Five orgasms in twenty minutes is a little excessive and I don't want to be greedy...' She fluttered her eyelashes at him and writhed on his lap.

'Squirming already, Miss Morreau? I had thought you might need a little break, but I'm all for getting straight back into...'

'Noo,' she mewled, as his fingers began to rove in delicate lines up the insides of her thighs. 'I swear, there is no way you'll be able to make me come this side of tomorrow.' She bit her lip and looked at him pleadingly, and hers were eyes that had no equal in this room. Her words had little effect on his fingers, which continued their nefarious journey with little twists and swirls, taps and flourishes. When they got to the uppermost crease of her thigh, Marianna found herself gritting her teeth. What should have been delightful anticipation had turned into apprehension and anxiety.

'As the time is now eleven o'clock that doesn't prove an awful threat,' Mark sighed theatrically before continuing, 'but I'll take that bet and you'll be required to pay in one way or another if I manage to *come* up with the goods.' He grinned wickedly.

'Do your worst,' came the reply of one very confident submissive.

Mark smiled. He'd knock hers off her face soon enough. Lowering his head to her ear he whispered, 'Oh, I intend to, but this time it will be much better than my worst. It's going to be my most awful performance to date, I expect,' and with that he captured her lips and inhaled the trembling, weak, soft mass of limbs she had become. The woman was quickly lost under the artful sway of his talented lips and did not even notice the single wayward finger as it reached for her clit.

He ignored her cries of protest. The object of the game wasn't to torment her, though. He just wanted to assess how sensitive she had become. Judging by the immediate bucking of her hips and the strangled gasp that left her lips she was sore, very swollen and perhaps even a little bruised. If they continued with their games tonight she would not be playing tomorrow. As it happened, that wouldn't be a problem as he already had plans. So, he would allow her a long and luxurious day of bed rest tomorrow in order to recuperate, as by the end of this night she was most certainly going to need it.

He leant down to whisper in her ear again. 'Relax, I'm not going to hurt you. I know you're sore. I'm going to take care of it.' He reached into the back pocket of his trousers and pulled out a small tube. Unscrewing the cap, he applied a small sliver of fluid to his fingertips. As gently as he could he applied it directly to her clit. 'Shhh,' he murmured, feeling her body shake, 'it's all done.'

'What is it?' she whispered.

'It's a numbing agent: Benzocaine to be more precise. It's going to make that little nub a lot less irritable, which is good, because I want to be able to touch you shortly.' His fingers reached up to her neck and he caressed her pulse point with his thumb, letting the soft heat of his lips work their way up to her ear. Upon hearing her soft sighs, he smiled. She was a resilient little thing. Then the lights dimmed and the room went silent.

'What's happening?' Marianna nuzzled her neck into his face as if encouraging him to continue. He obliged her and it was several seconds later before his lips were able to gather enough enthusiasm to tear themselves away from her.

'Dessert and an additional entertainment course, if you can call it that. They always bring out a slave who needs punishing with the coffee and the petit fours. I'm not sure why they bother; dessert is usually enough of a distraction in itself, but I guess they like to cater to all tastes.'

Marianna barely heard a word of what he was saying, for a row of naked, marching maids appeared out of nowhere and began to clean the table with clear plastic spray bottles and linen dishcloths. At least, she assumed they were maids because the only article of clothing they wore was a tiny, frilly lace cap on the top of their heads. That did not mean that their bodies were not adorned - they were, just not with clothes. Her eyes searched along the line and sucked in every little detail with awe.

The women's nipples had been rouged and tightly clamped with long chains of silver from which dangled a teardrop-shaped pearl as a weight. This ensured each stood to proud attention. Every single mouth had been closed shut with a black piece of duct tape and each set of buttocks had been soundly spanked, judging by the glowing hues which varied in colour from salmon pink to the darkest crimson. None of the girls would be sitting down any time soon, but Marianna guessed that was the idea.

The nipple clamps were not the only additional accessories the maids wore, for around each waist was a thick black leather belt, and another similar belt came down vertically, making a 'T' shape. Three silver padlocks, two to the side and one at the front, ensured that the maids would not be receiving any pleasurable attentions from the patrons of the bar. Both their sex and back passage were locked up tight. Marianna shuddered and found herself ridiculously wet. Why the thought of wearing a chastity belt should turn her on she had absolutely no idea, but the idea was ridiculously appealing.

Mark, of course, missed nothing. 'Shall I get you one? It would certainly solve the panty problem. You wouldn't be wearing any naughty undergarments over that thing, I can tell you.' He playfully raised his eyebrow at her and squeezed her thigh.

'Very funny,' she whispered, but was annoyed to find her voice reedy and breathless. She knew without a doubt that the man could do all that, and much worse. Whilst she'd had a backseat in the Zystrom office, she'd had a bird's eye view of all the goings on. If you managed to work there long enough your eyes went into permanent shocked-wide-open mode, and sometimes it was really hard to shut them again.

'I'd make sure there was just one key, sweetness, and I'd be the one to hold it. Wouldn't that be fun? We could even take the cameras out of your place because with one of those beasts around your waist, you wouldn't need them. What do you think?' A very prolonged silence greeted his question.

Meanwhile, the maids were diligently applying themselves to the task of cleaning the tables. Breasts bounced this way and that, and each was careful to ensure that no part of their bodies touched the table. They had been well trained. They scrubbed furiously, with both arms outstretched and their legs spread wide apart. There were plenty of wandering fingers that trailed up and down their naked flesh, teasing and tormenting, but none of them made it inside the ingenious design of the belt, though several tried.

'Well, what do you think?' Mark repeated, sensing that Marianna's attention was elsewhere.

Marianna was not at all sure what to think. Was Mark playing with her? She'd learnt the hard way that you never made the mistake of underestimating the man. Thankfully the arrival of the dessert course gave her a reprieve and the question would hopefully remain unanswered, if luck was on her side.

The blushing pink bottoms of the maids wiggled and jiggled as they made their way back to the kitchens and caught the eye of every red-blooded male in the room, let alone the females, most of whom were also dribbling. If they weren't, the arrival of thirty naked male chefs would probably do the trick. Marianna's jaw dropped open and it was almost as if the ball gag was still inside her mouth. There was a tick in Mark's jaw and a twinkle in his eye as he closed it for her. 'They'll be leaning over you and serving up your dessert in a moment,

Miss Morreau, so you can save the drooling for later. With any luck they'll think you're orgasming over the dessert course or I might have to lay you across my knee and spank you right here and now.' She squeaked as he grabbed hold of her ass and gave her thigh a playful swat.

Even with the threat of a public spanking Marianna couldn't resist checking out the delicious rippling abs of the men as they walked towards them. Oiled up and ripped as they were they could have graced any number of women's magazines, but when her gaze inevitably dipped below their waistline she gasped. 'They're wearing the same kind of devices as the girls?' While the male slaves were similarly attired to the females, with little more than big, poufy white chef's hats and tight silver clamps around their nipples, they also wore what must be the equivalent of a male chastity device. A clear, contoured cage covered each of their cocks and a thick circle of clear plastic wrapped around the circumference of the top of their testicles. Due to the size of the cage, none of the men would be able to achieve an erection anytime soon, and more than one cock was straining for escape.

'Not quite the same; the equipment differs somewhat,' said Mark, who was most amused by Marianna's shocked expression.

'Do they hurt?' she whispered.

'They shouldn't, as long as they're fitted properly, but they take some getting used to,' Mark said with a lopsided grin.

'And can they still get an erection like that? Those little cages look so small...'

Mark nearly laughed out loud. Marianna appeared to be fully over her earlier incident, her attention now wholly absorbed in the plight of these slave-boys who were currently preparing to do damage with chocolate sauce and raspberries, if he wasn't much mistaken. He nuzzled against the back of her neck and answered her question. 'Yes, they can still get hard, the device is able to move away from their bodies, but they're certainly not going to have any fun while wearing one. Anyway, I think that's enough questions for now. If you interrupt the dessert description I am going to buy the sturdiest steel chastity belt money can buy, and I will lock you away inside it for a week without relief.' His teeth nipped at the soft skin of her neck to emphasise his point.

There was a general clatter of squeaky wheels as the slaves each picked up a shiny metal dessert trolley that had been lined up to the side of the bar. Each trolley was filled with all manner of interesting looking implements, from what appeared to be large, squirty aerosol canisters to blow torches. There were plenty of different sized pots and containers, and even a saucepan that had been carefully placed upon a food warmer that was being gently heated by the flickering light of a candle below. As the trolleys wheeled along slowly, under the powerful arms of the naked chefs, the smell they diffused in their wake was divine. Marianna wasn't exactly sure what she was inhaling, but at a guess she'd go with cinnamon, raspberries, caramel, almonds and chocolate. Now that the burning sensation of her poor little clitoris had died down somewhat, she found herself mightily glad that she'd decided to stay. Dessert, it appeared, was going to be something spectacular.

'I daresay that would be a walk in the park, compared to the last eighteen months or so,' she said, trying unsuccessfully to hide a smirk upon her face.

Mark turned her round on his lap so she was facing him and the expression he wore upon his face looked downright feral. He leaned forward so the hot breath of his mouth tickled her ear and then he let her wait a few seconds as his tongue traced the outline of her lobe before he decided to grace her with a reply. 'You've just earned yourself an appointment for a fitting with several padlocks, young lady. Don't expect to backchat your Master unless you're willing to suffer the consequences.' She tugged her ear away from his mouth and giggled. He rolled his eyes in disgust. This one might be new, but she'd learn quickly enough. 'And I daresay you'd be wrong,' he said, replying to her earlier question with a voice that was dangerously slow and dark. 'This time you'll have me to contend with and I will make sure I torment your body to the limits of its endurance... whilst denying you the privilege of relief. If you thought your earlier episode tonight was unbearable, Miss Morreau, then I assure you, you have yet to tangle with me as I mete out a lesson.' His eyes sparkled dangerously. 'Now be quiet before I toss you over my knee, spank every last sound from your body and make you come at least another five times.' He raised his eyebrows and dared her to challenge him.

Marianna pursed her lips with an exaggerated flourish. She knew when she was beaten, and seeing as how she was in enough trouble already, thought the better of pushing her luck. The trouble with Matthews, she thought, was that you never knew exactly where you were. One moment he was wonderfully considerate and caring, and the next he turned into a rampaging beast. What was even worse was that she didn't know which persona she liked the best.

It quickly became clear that dessert in Atlantisse was no ordinary affair. There were no plates or cutlery in sight, and it appeared the course would be served directly upon the table. The deliciously bronzed slaves had an array of metal spoons in their hands and were dripping, dotting, swirling and swooping lines of molten chocolate into an intricate pattern on the clear glass in front of them. Lines of golden caramel followed and were swiftly decorated with a smattering of chopped macadamia nuts. Marianna looked on with fascination, at both the wonderful pair of naked buttocks bent over the table directly in front of her, and at the exquisite design beginning to take shape and form on the glass surface.

The slaves talked as they worked and described each item or ingredient they were using for their avid audience. Phrases such as, 'crème anglaise made with Tahitian vanilla pods with a light dusting of cinnamon and cardamom' left their lips and then a brief history followed, for those that weren't salivating so much they could still pay attention. Marianna, for instance, had no idea that vanilla pods were harvested from the vanilla orchid, which was the only orchid plant to produce an edible fruit. Due to its unique shape, the vanilla orchid could only be pollinated by the Melipone bee. Nowadays they were pollinated and picked by hand and then specially cured for consumption in a process that could take around fourteen weeks, and when you took into account that the beans or pods had a nine-month ripening period, you could appreciate what a painstaking process it was.

'You're lapping all this up then, Miss Morreau, or are you too busy staring at the pair of tempting cheeks in front of you?'

Marianna, who was most annoyed at having her dessert description interrupted, managed to keep a deceptively bland face and simply said, 'I'm taking notes, yes.'

'You'd better be. There'll be a questions and answers session later to see if you've been paying attention.'

Now that she was sitting face forward upon his lap once more, she felt his arms reach around the netted teal diamonds and curve under her breasts. There his fingers gently stroked her flesh, but stayed just shy of her nipples. It was a tormenting caress designed to do little more than distract her, but Marianna tried her hardest to pay attention to the immense creation being built up around her. 'Salted caramel nougat, raspberry reduction and seventy percent cocoa, coupled with chilli infused Madagascan chocolate cigarellos,' were just some of the words she was finding it increasingly difficult to process. Mark's fingers had now moved upwards and begun to circle the incredibly tender little buds of her nipples. To say they had not yet recovered from the exertions of the evening would be a grand understatement. She jumped up off his lap and yelped, but his firm hands pressed her back down again and he used a lighter touch. This time, even though they were still extremely tender, it was at least bearable.

The slaves were now smothering individual raspberries, which had been steeped in claret, in little puddles of warm chocolate and caramel, before dotting the length and breadth of the table with miniature wild strawberries. For the finale tiny steel circlets were unearthed with loud sucking noises from white plastic cool-boxes, and they each issued vapours of smoke as they were carefully positioned into place.

'Baked cheesecake?' Marianna, who had now just about managed to accustom herself to the constant attention of Mark's wandering fingers, tilted her head sideways as she examined the last addition to the dessert table.

'Try again, Sweetpea. That's nitrogen gas, and they're frozen not baked, which means we have hot chocolate sauce to play with and ice-cold cheesecake. It's an interesting contrast of temperatures, but I'm sure you'll enjoy them. Just not as much as I'm going to enjoy them,' he added with a knowing wink.

Marianna wasn't at all sure she liked the look Mark Matthews was currently wearing. It was one of those looks that said 'I know more about what's going to happen next than you do, and that's probably for the best, because if you knew what was going to happen next you'd probably make a break for it.' Already, numerous suspicions were beginning to form in her mind and she suspected things were about to get very... messy.

'Now, let's see if you can guess what the next treat they bring out is. If you can, I think there may be a reward in it for you,' and with that, Mark's fingers moved dangerously close to her very overwhelmed clitoris.

'Rewards like that I can do without,' murmured Marianna as she squirmed on his lap, trying her best to scoot out of the way of his marauding fingers.

'Ah, but that's the rub, or not as the case may be. If you manage to get the next dessert course correct you get to forgo your next orgasm of the evening.'

'I cannot believe I'm having this discussion after having been celibate for most of the past two years,' she said, with a pained expression on her face, 'but I'll take you up on that challenge and hope for the best. I'll have you know I'm a dessert connoisseur.'

Mark snorted. 'You'd never guess, looking at that body of yours. You are wasting away, young lady, and I intend to feed you up. With food and sex, as it happens. You'll soon get your appetite back for orgasms, you'll see.' His eyes twinkled as his devilish expression said it all. 'Now pay attention.'

Concentrating on the naked men around her, or trying not to concentrate on the naked men whilst looking closely at what it was they were carrying, Marianna desperately tried to ascertain what was currently being waltzed around the table. More steel circlets followed, and were laid out between the swirls and curls of chocolate and caramel with exacting precision. This time the contents were not smoking and she could only guess at what they contained. It didn't take her long to find out. When the sound of hissing filled the room her head span around in panic, but only to find that the blowtorches were being primed. That was when she breathed a long and slow sigh of relief. To her knowledge there were not too many desserts that required a fiery blast of heat to finish them off. Turning to face Mark she whispered, 'Crème brûlée,' and gave him a wide smile of satisfaction. The blowtorches would be used to caramelise the sugar to a hard glaze, thus giving it its trademark crunch.

'You seem very confident,' he said, tipping his head to one side as he studied her expression. 'A little too confident, perhaps, because you are of course aware that they use blowtorches to brown meringues as well as caramelised sugar?'

The smile was wiped off Marianna's face in an instant. Having been fairly sure of her guess she was now facing the prospect of another round of dancing fingers, and she wasn't at all convinced she could handle them. As if to emphasise his point, Mark's hand began to slide down her inner thigh and sank deep into her quivering flesh. She bit her lip. The little circlets were removed, the blowtorches were aimed and the flames licked out bright blue tongues of heat as they were carefully swept from side to side.

Marianna still had absolutely no idea what the dessert was. A beautifully tanned back and muscled pair of buttocks were blocking her vision, and they, in combination with Mark's slowly moving hand, had her eyes unfocused and her attention vague. Fingertips were running up and down her pussy, barely there caresses which slid over her flesh with lazy strokes and the occasional bold step. They dipped into her sex to find her hot, wet and weeping, before returning to her mouth in order to have her suck them clean. Fingernails scribed little patterns upon her flesh, lips suckled at her neck and teeth nipped at the delicate spot between her ear and jaw. She squirmed and groaned madly as her eyes rolled, and never once did the very expressive fingers go anywhere near her throbbing button. It should have been a good thing. Her clit was still pounding from its earlier attentions, but now it was engorged with fresh blood and pulsing for a different reason entirely... It was, unbelievably, greedy for more attention, and the speed with which Mark had achieved her arousal was disturbing in the extreme.

The slave finally moved away, but Marianna had no idea what the hell was on the table and she could not have cared less. The fingers were delicately running up and down the lips of her labia and for the zillionth time that night, she was yet again a woman in heat.

'Ah, congratulations, my dear, it is indeed crème brûlée. What a clever thing you are!' His fingers immediately stopped their wanderings and Marianna wanted to stamp her feet in protest. The only reason she did not was because she knew exactly where that would get her with Mark, which was absolutely nowhere.

Turning her head around and shaking out her glossy chestnut waves she decided to put a brave face on the situation. 'Oh, lucky me.' Her smile was a weak one, her skin was hot and her body was pulsing with newfound energy. Why Matthews had this effect on her was anybody's guess, but he was much better than caffeine, that was for sure.

'Take off your dress.'

Marianna knew a command when she heard one, but even so, her lips pouted in protest and she gave him big Bambi eyes as her face looked up into his. She didn't voice her objections, for that would be stupid and give him an immediate reason to punish her, but there was plenty of pleading going on within her expression.

'Nearly all the women here are naked, Marianna. You're a submissive who's had to endure plenty of training in order to get used to being naked. What you're wearing now only accentuates your nakedness. It most certainly doesn't hide it, and whilst I should not have to explain myself to you, in this one instance I will. You've had a rough night, and I can be kind on occasion.' He gave her a knowing look. 'You need to get out of that dress, Marianna, because you are shortly going to be featuring as my dessert plate. If you would like to be able to wear it on the ride home, it might be prudent to remove it now. I am, of course, perfectly happy to take you home without a stitch of clothing to your name and I suspect the taxi driver would probably pay *me* money to see your...'

The speed at which Marianna began to remove her dress was nothing less than astounding, especially considering that her heartrate had already had a good workout this evening. 'For God's sake, slow down, Miss Morreau,' said Mark, who held his hands up as twin stop signs at the faster-than-a-speeding-bullet striptease. 'I want to be able to enjoy the exquisite experience of your beautiful body being disrobed, rather than be elbowed in the face...' He leaned back and frowned at her, but his eyes had their trademark sparkle of merriment, dancing happily within them.

Marianna's hands, which had been frantically gripping the material and shoving it upwards as if someone had liberally doused her dress in hydrochloric acid, hovered in mid-air and paused. There was a moment's indecision, as it took a few seconds to process that he was not intending to carry out his threat, and then she dropped her hands back to waist-height and threaded her fingers through the sheer netting that adorned her body. So, the monster wanted to play. She could play. She'd waited a long damn time to play, in fact.

The beautiful teal dress weaved, shimmered and slid across her body like a second skin as her hands manipulated the fabric, making it glitter like a thousand princess-cut diamonds. In her head someone had plunged the room into darkness and turned up the stereo full volume. It was a thumping base beat that pounded all around and her hips gyrated to the music. The garment twisted and rippled, her fingertips reached through the silk netting and sought the smooth fabric of Mark's trousers, scraping her fingernails up his thigh before turning around and raising the dress, little by little, over her reddened ass cheeks. She tugged hard enough to make the pert globes wiggle and then pressed herself back into his body, grinding into the soft cashmere wool of his sweater and rubbing sinuously along the hard planes of his chest. The sequins rose higher, her hips flew and her back arched against him. She tilted her head back to entwine her face with his, rubbing along his smoothly shaven jaw and purred in his ear, 'Are you enjoying yourself yet?'

Turning around again she faced him and began to work her dress back up over her breasts with slow, lingering sweeps. A single finger dived through the netting and she let the smooth lacquer of her nail varnish caress his lip. They opened at the gentle pressure and a warm breath of air escaped before he captured her digit in his mouth. He bit down, enough to capture her attention, but not enough to hurt. Upon releasing it he said, 'This is all very nice, Marianna, but it's not going to be anywhere near as good as smearing deliciously warm crème brûlée all over your beautiful body and licking it up. So get naked, Precious, and sit that pretty little backside into a generous portion of chocolate sauce and frozen cheesecake.' He stood up, towering over her generous five foot nine inches and with a hand on either side of her dress, plucked it from her body and threw it behind him. Before she could protest at such cruel treatment befalling one of Chanel's finest creations, he had picked her up and... squished her down on the table.

Marianna's eyes blinked rapidly for a few seconds and her mouth gaped open so wide you could almost have fit a football through it.

'Cold, by any chance?' Mark kept a straight face, but she wasn't fooled for a second. The man was expecting her to rant and swear at him, but she was going to do no such thing. She already had punishments enough to worry about, thank you very much, and she refused to add to them. Even though her backside had just squashed an extremely cold, frozen cheesecake into an unrecognisable shape and her thighs were wallowing in warm sticky custard, she was not going to say a word. But oh God, that cheesecake was cold!

'Lay back, pumpkin. You're my dessert canvas and I want to paint you with all the wonderful little treats that have been laid out for me.' Mark had just taken what looked like a mini wooden spatula from one of the many slaves who were busy handing out all sorts of implements, and Marianna wasn't sure she was going to like this very much. Sitting a naked backside down on crème anglaise was one thing, smearing your whole body and hair in it was quite another entirely. Slowly closing her jaw, which had just managed to come under her control once more, she sneaked a peek through her lashes and studied his expression. One look at him told her there was little room for leeway. The eyebrows were raised, the jaw was taut and the steely brown eyes said that this was not a question up for discussion. Wincing inwardly, she counted to ten and slowly began to lower herself backwards towards the glass. It would be the crime of the century to destroy the artwork the naked chefs had presented upon the tabletop, but that didn't seem to concern Matthews in the least. All he had on his mind was food. Men were all the same.

On the downward descent she closed her eyes. Her hands slid on squidgy, wet, warm, ice-cold and crunchy - all these feelings and textures were hers to explore and endure. Matthews, damn the man, was laughing, which told her that the look she was wearing was probably not one of her prettiest.

'Relax, Marianna. Believe it or not there's a really good reason I am going to get you horribly sticky and messy. Do you want to fathom a guess as to why?'

She did not, but his gaze continued to feast down upon her until she became so uncomfortable she couldn't help but blurt out an answer. 'You're going to use me as fish food and dunk me in the aquarium?' Her reply was somewhat dry. The frozen cheesecake was not. It was beginning to melt against the small of her back and it was a most invigorating experience.

Mark grinned and looked up at the immense aquarium that decorated the whole wall to the back of the bar. The fish had become quite excitable as the night wore on, much like the patrons of the bar, and were darting around with considerable enthusiasm, blurred colours weaving in and out of the seaweed and rocks. 'Nice idea, but wrong guess.' Moving his Perspex stool closer to the table, until he was resting between Marianna's legs and his face was just inches from her sex, he blew a little tickle of warm air upon her swollen clit.' She groaned in heat and he couldn't resist a wolfish grin. 'The messier you get, young lady, the more time it will take me to clean you up.' He picked up a dollop of caramel sauce and let it dribble from his spatula to land in little ribbons upon her immaculately smooth pussy. 'There are no showers in this building, sweat pea, and there is only one way to get clean. If you can hazard a guess as to how you'll get clean, I might try my best to ensure that you have only one orgasm, rather than several.' He picked up a chocolate cigarello and twirled it around in his fingers before sucking softly at the tip, letting the heat of his mouth melt the soft and wondrously smooth chocolate. Then he transferred his makeshift pen to her abdomen.

'Oh God,' whispered Marianna, now desperately wishing she had uttered her safe word when the opportunity had presented itself.

Mark teased her, swirling the chocolate tip around her navel, watching as her flesh quivered in need. 'What shall I write? Hmm...' The cigarello hovered in mid-air for a moment as he considered his canvas, and then it teased her bottom lip. 'Suck, precious, for I have a feeling I am going to need a lot of ink.'

Obediently Marianna sucked the chocolate into her mouth and he helped its progress by thrusting it gently inside her, letting her get a taste for the dark yet beautifully sweet flavour. He let her have a good suck and when he pulled it out again she whispered, 'It's spicy.'

'And here was me thinking you weren't paying attention earlier. Yes, they've introduced a little chilli to pepper the strong taste, and I think it works quite well. There are parts of you that might disagree with me later, but that's by the by. Now... as to writing...'

He plucked the cigarello, which had diminished considerably in size, from her lips and trailed a long line from her chin down to her stomach. He grinned when she wriggled. 'Ticklish? My, oh my, Miss Morreau, you're going to have quite an amusing evening tonight.' The pen poised itself just under her breasts and then began to write in the swirling script of an artist.

'I must answer, without fail, every single question my Master poses. Failure to do so will result in being made to come at least another twenty...'

'All right, all right,' said Marianna, now more than a little breathless. 'You are going to lick me clean, but I think I should warn you that there are a lot of calories in that stuff, if you're considering decorating me all over in it.' The chocolate quill had begun to focus on her breasts and drew sensuous circles around the soft flesh in a spiral shape, getting smaller and smaller until they reached the unbearably tender point of her nipple. She whimpered and squirmed as the cigarello teased and tormented the hard little nub, nearly out of her mind with lust.

'Wrong answer. I'm going to lick some of you clean, but there's a reason our naked chefs are still in attendance. When I have licked, sucked and nibbled to my heart's content, I'll let someone else have a go and watch you writhe and scream from a respectable distance. Actually, probably not so respectable, but you'll be too busy enjoying yourself to notice. They're well trained. We could even try two at once. Think you'd enjoy that, Miss Morreau?' He brought the chocolate stick up to his lips and took a bite, tilting his head to the side as he savoured the experience. As the silence stretched he raised an eyebrow at her. 'OK, twenty orgasms it is then. Let's start now, shall we?'

Marianna nearly shot up off the table as she realised her mistake, but a single hand on her hipbone held her fast. 'Give me an answer and we'll half the total.' Caramel eyes bored into hers and refused to let her look away.

She swallowed convulsively and for a second her voice caught in her throat. The threat of twenty impending orgasms forced her to push past her reticence to speak and she opened her mouth, which issued nothing more than a mere croak.

26

Closing her lips and swallowing she tried for speech a second time, because she had no doubt that the man was more than capable of making good on his threat. Mark Matthews was capable of an awful lot of things, and she'd seen far too much for her to take his threats lightly. 'Yes, I would like that.'

'I thought you might.' His mouth bent down over her breast and he sucked the point of a nipple into it. Her hips would have flown off the table again had he not kept his restraining hand firmly against them. As her body shuddered beneath his teeth as they nipped at the murderously sore tips, she watched his face and the evident enjoyment displayed there. He liked watching her reactions. The man in front of her was extremely skilled at reading people. You always had to be on your guard around him. 'So we're down to ten orgasms. Shall we have another question and answer session or are you happy with that total?' He let his tongue lap at the agonised nipple.

'More questions,' she somehow managed to gurgle, feeling little trickles of frozen cheesecake dribble out from underneath her. She'd soon be resting in a puddle of her own making, if Matthews continued on his path of torment, and once the floodgates opened she wasn't sure anyone would be able to stop them. Having been absolutely certain that she never wanted an orgasm ever again only about five minutes ago, she realised that hormones were a difficult thing to control.

'Why did you apply to work in my office?'

Marianna's head spun and her whole body was a dizzy mass of endorphins. 'Money,' she whispered.

'Five orgasms and counting,' he said, with a wry twist of his lips. 'Memo to me: bury your ego firmly underground before asking questions you might not like the answer to.' There was a pause and a click of his tongue before he continued. 'I'm curious, Marianna, did you actually want to fuck me, or was the money enough?'

Marianna found her tongue finally. 'The money was not enough and there isn't a man alive who could make me repeat the experience I've had under your hands for the past several months.'

Mark couldn't help but smile at that. 'Well, consider yourself utterly fucked then,' he added, and while he didn't raise a smile at his own joke, the protégé beneath him did. 'And what is so funny, pray tell?' His stern tone and steely gaze should have quelled her facial features into submission, but she had a grin on her lips a mile wide. 'Spit it out, Marianna.'

'How in hell's name do you intend to give me two and a half orgasms?' The giggles had started, and now they were in full flow there was no stopping them.

Mark closed his eyes and rubbed his fingers against his temple. He took a deep, calming breath and decided that the human resources people were going to get some abuse. Seriously, where did they find these women?

'You won't have to worry your pretty little head about it, Miss Morreau, because your smart mouth has just doubled your total once more to a glorious five.'

That quickly wiped the smile off her face. She opened her mouth and prepared to utter remonstrations against her newly heightened sentence.

'Uh, uh, uh,' said Mark, shaking his head at her. 'That would be a really foolish move. There's only one person who's allowed to utter naughty words around here, and that's not you, in case you were wondering. Do you really want to go back to the figure of ten? I'll make sure you suffer through each and every one of them, and will personally watch and count them. We will probably have to stay here till around four in the morning to achieve them all, but I'm game if you are.'

His piercing gaze tore straight through her, but she had to settle for an inward curse, and she made damn sure it was a good one. Even now, just the weight of his stare made her wet and there was plenty more than just a set of pretty caramel eyes to contend with. The man was a horror movie dressed as a fairy tale. An animal that needed constant feeding, except with sex rather than food. Her gaze reflected her frustration at being so expertly manoeuvred, but she curtailed her acidic response and smiled prettily. 'Whatever pleases you, Sir.' She pouted as if to indicate she was ready for all he might care to dish out.

'The answer requires a "yes" or "no", Marianna. "Maybe" simply won't do.' Mark dipped his finger in a swirl of molten chocolate and smeared it across her clit. Repositioning himself between her legs he let the tip of his tongue flick lightly against her clit. It was nothing more than a butterfly caress, but she felt her body arch as his tongue descended in little flutters.

So much for the numbing cream, she thought. Everything was very much wide awake and in full working order, already gasping for more. Feeling her hips tilt towards his face of their own accord, she groaned before grinding out between her teeth, 'One or two might be lovely, but I think I'd pass out before ten, Sir.'

Mark licked his lips, now covered in chocolate, and savoured her taste for a long moment before he gave her a glance that was far too astute. There was the merest glint of white teeth as he opened his mouth to speak, 'Oh, I don't know, Marianna. I have a feeling I'd be able to find something or other to keep you awake.' He placed two fingers on the glass table and slid them, little by little, through a path of creamy custard. With no further preamble he flipped his hand over and thrust the two fingers, now closed tightly together, towards her sex.

He entered her with a single thrust and buried his fingers to the hilt. Then the infernal man wiggled them. Matthews had such deliciously long fingers, Marianna wondered if she might come there and then, but they abruptly stopped their movement. 'Sure you want to stop at just two? You might live to regret that decision.' This time, thankfully, he didn't require an answer, but employed his beautifully talented fingers to a greater purpose.

Marianna was nearly delirious. The whole experience was as surreal as a Salvador Dali painting. She was stretched out on a glass table, without a stitch of clothing to her name, in front of a few hundred people. She wasn't the only one. There were several more women in just such a position as she, splayed out wide and being covered in various different colours and textures of creamy goo.

They were being licked, sucked, nibbled, suckled and some parts of them appeared to be being swallowed whole. The entire room was now a zoo of rabid males, and it appeared someone had unlocked the cages and freed the animals. The room reeked of sex and sugar. Marianna's nose had tuned in to the sweet smells, and she inhaled tantalising breaths of vanilla and chocolate that sent her senses reeling, which drifted across the table with each swish of Mark's fingers. He had a twofold use for the slippery custard he was painting against her sex; it made a great lubricant and apparently tasted rather pleasant for his mouth lingered against her... lapping at her body with the gentlest of touches. For the girl who thought she never wanted another orgasm again in her life less than a half hour ago, she was now on fire. This new ordeal was hell on wheels and having witnessed all the artistic delights that now graced the table, she desperately wanted to taste them. Her mouth was watering for a morsel of syrupy sweetness. There was always a chance Matthews might have to tie her down in a moment, because if she saw him dipping his finger in the salted caramel with no intentions to share, she would not be responsible for her actions.

'And now for a spot of crème brûlée, I think,' said Mark, who had his little wooden spatula in hand and was carefully scooping up a generous portion of warm pudding. Bringing it up to Marianna's face, he let her watch the little wisps of steam that rose from his prize. He waved it in front of her nose and she whimpered. 'Want some?'

'Yes please,' she said vehemently. It was about time. Being teased with sugar was evil in the extreme.

'Then I shall fill you up until you can take no more, Miss Morreau.'

Marianna did not like the downward turn of his eyes, and she also did not like the direction the crème brûlée was headed in. She whimpered in protest as her taste buds suffered the woes of denial, watching the mouth-watering creation head south and far, far away. Her fingers clawed into fists as she briefly wondered what the punishment would be for flipping herself over and hogging everything on the table.

'Do not even think about it, Sweetpea. I assure you the ramifications of such an act would be grave indeed.'

Marianna banged her head down against the glass with a little more force than necessary and groaned as she felt the custard being fed inside her, spoonful by warm, sludgy spoonful, and she wanted to howl at the unfairness of it all.

'Don't fret, pumpkin, you'll be getting a taste of it in a minute because after I've filled you up to the brim, I'm going to make you come and then I'll feed you the leftovers, if there are any.' He gave her a wicked grin and patted her stomach soothingly as he filled her sex full to bursting with everything the table had to offer. Spatulas and spoons scraped gently against the inside of her pussy walls and with each further delivery of liquid goo, the tension in her body escalated. It got to the point where she was sure that she couldn't be made to take another spoonful, but still he continued. When he finally let his implements fall it was a strange, full feeling that encompassed her body and made her go weak all over.

'Now, it's time to make that cream just a little bit creamier, Miss Morreau.' Mark's hands reached up her body, leaving smears of chocolate and custard in their wake, and he rubbed the pad of his thumb roughly across her lip, before slipping it into her mouth. 'Suck, sweetheart, and I promise I'll let you swallow in a minute.' She needed no further encouragement. His thumb was coated in raspberry sauce and tiny morsels of gooey nougat; that was about the extent of the ingredients she could pick out. Everything else blurred into the most fantastically decadent, melting extravaganza on her tongue. Her mouth curled greedily around him and sucked tightly. Meanwhile his lips descended to her nipples, and he gently stroked them with his tongue. As his teeth grazed a proud point she gasped and gave a tormented cry of pleasure, her body arching up off the table. Repeating his tactics, over and over, he then added his fingers for good measure. As soon as they hit her clit she was a mess. Everywhere was a seething mass of over-stimulated nerve endings that wanted to do anything except feel. Alas, they didn't have the luxury of that choice and it was just as well, for the impending release was gearing up to rival an antimatter explosion.

While Matthews had his work cut out trying to get her body anywhere near an orgasm, he certainly seemed to be heading in the right direction. The things he could do with that tongue... He knew exactly where all the sensitive spots on her body were. Her neck, behind her knees and her abdomen were treated to the lightest of kisses that tormented in the extreme. One hand had its fingers tangling in her hair and stroking her scalp, and with the other he continued to maintain the pressure upon her clit, using the rest of his fingers to caress the smooth expanse of her mons. She wanted to scream, but the sound seemed to have been tied up inside her with a tight knot, and she could not edge it past her throat. Fingers, tongue, lips, hands... they pulsed, tugged, stroked and feathered all over her body, and watching his deep brown eyes stare into hers as he assessed her reactions made her doubly aroused.

'Three,' he whispered in her ear, and she wanted to ask him what that meant, but the knot remained and the burgeoning flower of desire continued to grow. It was expanding at a magnificent rate now, and as the petals unfurled the tightness in her chest began to increase. Turning her head to the side, to avoid the knowing eyes boring into her skull, she came face to face with another woman in much the same throes of ecstasy as she, for her eyes were lidded and her pupils heavily dilated. Her blonde hair had once been artfully arranged on her head, but judging by the wisps that flew all around her face this wasn't her first orgasm of the night either. Looking up at Marianna the woman smiled as a male head dived straight between her legs, and let out a shuddering breath of excitement. Her hands slid in the melting mess on the table and her beautifully long fingernails were covered in dribbles of chocolate. She appeared not to care. Her facial features began to tighten and then her glossy red lips pulled into a taught line as her eyes began to flutter closed. When her hips began to arch Marianna did not need to hear her screams of excitement to know what had happened.

The word 'two' directed her attention back to twin orbs of deadly flames, for Mark was not impressed with her lapse of concentration. 'Look at me as I count you down,' he ordered. Marianna couldn't even focus, her eyes were swimming with dancing lights and colours, but she tried her best to placate the beast in front of her and placed her face in front of his. 'Your attention should be solely on me and my fingers. Where are they, princess?'

His voice was a dark growl that reverberated around her eardrums. Thankfully she didn't need her eyes to answer that question. 'Some are inside me,' she managed to choke past the tightening rope in her chest.

'Some are, yes,' he purred, 'but not all. Where are the rest, Miss Morreau?'

As if to make sure she was paying attention he tapped the remaining fingers for effect. Even though it was a light touch she nearly came there and then. 'On. My. Clit.' The words were bitten out in pained, staccato bursts and she could feel tears of frustration leaking across her cheekbones.

'Good. You are paying attention after all.' The fingers inside her flicked back and forth at lightning speed, and the ones on her clit also increased their pace, adding a little pressure for good measure. 'One,' he whispered, and she barely heard him, but her body responded to his command as if he'd shouted it at the top of his lungs. Limbs twisted and flew in all directions as if she was having a seizure, and her heart had decided it was suddenly made of elastic, for it swung around wildly in her ribcage and threatened to burst through her chest. On the 'one' her body had disintegrated into tiny little fragments that would take forever to put back together and she was lost in a sea of bright light. Her entire body shook and trembled as if having been ravaged by shock, but that was not enough to stop the beast. The man never knew when enough was enough. He turned to one of the male slaves, who was obediently waiting for orders with his body prostrate against the cold plastic floor and his head pressed down so that his forehead touched the floor. Mark tapped him lightly on the shoulders and said, 'Make sure you get her to orgasm at least twice, and take as much time as you like.'

As the oiled, naked slave rushed to do his bidding, leaping up from the floor and curling his hands behind his back automatically, Mark took a second to admire the athletic form Atlantisse kept their staff in. To get a physique in the kind of condition that had abdominal muscles rippling all over and thighs bulging required a lot of training and dedication. These gentlemen were worked daily and hard. The workout they received in the evening was another matter entirely and, he suspected, a far more enjoyable one.

The slave, with direction from Mark, concentrated on her breasts to begin with, giving her a slow and sensuous tonguing. Mark, meanwhile, dug his spoon into Marianna's pussy and was delicately scooping out a generous portion of cream. He brought it to his lips, inhaling her essence, before sucking the contents into his mouth. The newly created concoction tasted divine. He had a feeling he was going to enjoy every last drop of it.

As the slave set about arousing her for yet another round of orgasmic theatrics, he contented himself with twirling his spoon deep inside her pussy. He did it because he knew it would annoy her, and if there was one thing Mark liked, it was getting an emotional reaction from his submissive. Actions and reactions gave him an idea of exactly how to control his charge. He hadn't spent years working with hundreds of women without knowing when and how to push the right buttons. A few seconds of the gyrating spoon and he decided to take pity on her trembling thighs.

'Would you like to taste yourself, Marianna?'

The spoon rested on the top of her silky smooth mons and he noted her pulsing clitoris beneath it. She was going to have to wait a little while before it would see any more attention. He dragged the spoon slowly up her stomach and watched as it dipped at her navel, smiling as her muscles automatically contracted even at the light pressure he wielded. He let it do a figure of eight around her breasts, which were still lightly bouncing up and down as her ribcage sucked in desperate gulps of air, and then he placed the spoon at the entrance to the slave's mouth, who had pulled away from his attentions at her breasts, to allow the spoon to continue on its current trajectory.

'Eat,' Mark commanded, and smiled as the man did exactly that. He patted him on the head. 'Good boy,' he said, as he watched the slave swallow. Out of the corner of his eye he watched Marianna's face colour in a deep blush. A little bit of humiliation went a long way, it appeared, for the blush began to extend down her face to her throat. Miss Morreau was feeling the heat, it seemed. 'Did she taste nice?'

The question wasn't entirely rhetorical, as while he knew the slave wouldn't answer him, he was allowed to nod or shake his head. In actual fact, he did more than that. He licked his lips and nodded his head enthusiastically. Mark smiled and said, 'Good. Get back to work.'

'Please,' Marianna pouted, trying to catch his attention and failing the first time around. Mark was far too absorbed in watching the man's lips pull at her distended, rosy nipple. Both areola and nipple were heavily engorged and sensitive, for she squeaked and tried to pull away more than once.

'Relax,' he ordered. 'Take deep breaths and relax your body. Then you'll be able to enjoy his touch.' She closed her eyes tightly and tried her best to do as he'd ordered, but he knew it would take a little time and probably a distraction or two before she began to loosen all the tight planes of her body.

'Please,' she whispered again.

'Please what?' He was expecting her to ask the man to stop.

'Please let me taste.' Her throat gave a croaky rasp and her lips parted in a soft little moue.

'Ah, you're upset that I'm hogging dessert all to myself,' he laughed, reaching for his spoon and burrowing inside her, in order to feed her the most generous portion he could find. 'Do you have a sweet tooth, Miss Morreau? Is that why you're begging me for a taste?' He didn't wait for an answer, but slowly traced the metal spoon around her lips, leaving dribbles of cream in its wake. Each time she reached up to grab the spoon he held it aloft just high enough that she could not grasp it. After several teasing swoops at the spoon with no success she let her head drop back to the table in defeat. 'Patience, Miss Morreau, is a virtue I'm told.'

She just looked at him pleadingly and he laughed, before taking pity on her plight and letting her lick the spoon clean. 'Would you like some more?' He tapped it against her cheek as he awaited the reply.

'Yes, please,' she whispered, and that's when the fun started.

He slipped a plain black satin blindfold over her eyes and whispered, 'Do not move.' She struggled a little with the order, mainly because the slave was attending very carefully to her breasts, but after a few warning clucks from his tongue, managed to keep her body relatively relaxed. 'Each move you make will earn you another orgasm. I should think that is incentive enough to keep still?' The girl wisely kept quiet, although he suspected there were a few curse words she might have liked to utter had she not known there would be repercussions for them.

Mark began to dress her in coiling ripples of caramel and chocolate, and then with dollops of warm crème brûlée, followed by very warm raspberry sauce. He used her body as an artist would use a canvas, and painted away with the spatulas, spoons and brushes he had been given. He swirled colours together, mixed them and moved them around her body to create a cohesive pattern that was slowly going to cover her entire body. He painted her underarms with custard, and warmed up the cigarellos until they were melting all over her body. He dripped the warm chocolate over her nipples and sex, knowing it would harden later and drive her mad. To help it set he used generous helpings of the frozen cheesecake, which he liberally smeared between her thighs and between her breasts. He continued to feed her at intervals and couldn't help but smile at the mess he'd made of her. Her face was a mass of sticky rivulets of running cream and chocolate. Once the stuff started to melt there was no stopping it. His own caramel-covered fingers ran up her neck, leaving sticky prints, and he reached with his spoon to deliver yet another mouthful to her greedily waiting lips. She sucked at the spoon and then her face contorted in horror as she realised he'd fed her the ice-cold cheesecake.

'Shouldn't be so eager or so greedy, Sweetpea,' he purred in her ear as he slithered the rest of the contents down the curve of her neck until it rested in the hollow of her throat. She screamed and shot up, but he was ready for her and pushed her back down, licking the offending concoction away with a few swipes of his tongue. 'Another orgasm for Miss Morreau. Congratulations, pumpkin.' He stepped back and indicated to the slave that he should get between her legs. 'Make her come at least twice,' he said. Immediately assailed by another scream and two pairs of frantically waving limbs he frowned and tore her blindfold off, so she could witness his disapproving look. 'Fine, if that's the way you want to play, so be it. I don't mind fighting dirty.' He shook his head and picking up a spoonful of custard he whispered, 'Close your eyes, pumpkin,' before smearing a long line of the sticky vanilla cream over them. Now there would be no peeking and she would be immersed in darkness for the remainder of her ordeal, upping the intensity somewhat. Then, easily locating another three available slaves, he smiled at them, winked and said, 'Do your absolute worst.'

Present Day

When Marianna finally awoke from her dream it was to find herself rubbing her clit furiously and tumbling headlong into a delicious orgasm. She'd just relived the whole of Wednesday night and it had been one of the most amazing nights she'd ever experienced. It had taken her nearly two days to recover. And then it hit her. She'd just brought herself to orgasm without permission. There were cameras in her room. Christ. Her body wasn't under the duvet, which had long since sunk to the floor, and if anyone had spotted her blunder she would be liable for instant dismissal. Shit. She couldn't have come this far only to fail at the last hurdle, surely? Could she be fired for doing something in her sleep? She closed her eyes tightly and recited every single swearword she could remember. Well, there was nothing for it. She would have to go into the office and act like nothing had happened. There was always a chance it might have gone unnoticed.

It was with shaking hands that she picked up today's pair of panties, knowing they would reside around her ankles most of the day. If she still had a job.

CHAPTER THREE

Another One Bites the Dust

'She's been screaming her head off for an hour, Michael. Can I knock her out, or at the least move the woman somewhere far, far away, preferably underground?' There was a long sigh at the end of the telephone receiver and it was clear that the owner of the voice was in a testy mood.

'K, darling. It's unlike you to be so squeamish. What's up?'

The blonde on the other end of the receiver sighed again. Michael's voice was not one of sympathy and it was clear that her sentry duty was far from over. 'Your son is putting muddy footprints all over my brand new silver travertine tiles. He's already necked most of the alcohol in the house and has now taken my remote control prisoner.' She added a little growl for effect, to let him know she was not at all pleased at the turn of events.

There was a slight pause as her complaints were considered before all of them were rebuffed as she had expected.

'You have a cleaning lady who will be in first thing tomorrow to clear up the

34

footprints and any other mess he might leave, paid for by me I might add, and I'm more than happy to get you a delivery of whatever tipple might take your fancy. Of course, you realise you can't drink anything with her in the house and nor can you watch TV, so I fail to see your point.' The voice had taken on a bemused tone. 'It's the screaming that's getting you down, hmm? And here I thought you enjoyed that sort of thing.'

The blonde heard a burst of uncharacteristic laughter erupt from her handset and nearly fell over from her position, leant casually against the granite kitchen countertop. As it was, several cookbooks fell to their demise and a jar of chrome utensils quickly followed suit.

'K, dear, are you OK? It's nearly all over now. We'll have him right where we want him in just a couple of days. The girls are in place, and there's the added bonus of having both Isabelle and Jennifer as an incentive to get Mark to co-operate. I think the man has a conscience, but we'll find out shortly, darling.'

'What are you planning to do with them?' Scuttling around on the floor, she banged shiny serving spoons, spatulas and ladles back into their container loud enough to create pretty impressive backing for a drum and bass album.

'Something diabolically nasty, what else? I want to watch him squirm and I want him to know exactly what I'm capable of. When you take on someone of Matthews' calibre, you make sure he understands you the first time, because there's no way you'll get hold of him a second time.'

The banging stopped abruptly and a smile flittered across K's face, her bright red lips uplifting in sudden comprehension. 'Oh goody, we get to play with them, too?'

Michael Redcliff cleared his throat and smiled to himself. 'Yes, dear, that was the plan. Have you cheered up a bit now?'

'A little,' she admitted, her voice having taken on a soft, dreamy quality and her thoughts were suddenly whisked to far more pleasurable pastures.

'Good.'

'But what about the damn screaming?' she groaned, coming back to earth firmly with a bump.

'Do you have your cell phone handy?'

K finally managed to get herself upright and set the utensil jar safely back on the counter. She pulled the receiver away from her ear and looked at the phone as if it had sprouted purple fur and claws. Rolling her eyes, already wondering where this was leading, she put the handset back to her ear. 'Of course I have a cell phone, but I'm on the home phone at the moment. You want me to call you from my cell?'

'No darling. I want you to record the delightful Isabelle's screams. A little bit of sobbing and begging wouldn't go amiss, either. Let's stir Matthew's up and get him a little jumpy. Make the recording around a couple of minutes in length and then send it to me. I'll need to deliver it from an untraceable account. We don't want to give the boy any ammunition he can use.'

'OK, give me ten minutes and I'll get it to you. Out of curiosity, though, why aren't you keeping her at yours?'

'Ahh, that's because there's always the chance that Matthew's may be really stupid and have the authorities come barging in here. I'm the only link he has. He doesn't know that you're my sidekick. You won't even be up for consideration. He gets very protective of his staff, I hear, and has gone to some great lengths to "save" them in the past. It helps that he's got a soft spot for Isabelle and a hard one for my daughter.'

'But Isabelle isn't one of his girls, is she?'

'She is now.'

CHAPTER FOUR

Signed, Sealed and Delivered

Do not break down. Do not cry. These were only some of the words Jennifer Redcliff was repeating over and over in her head. She wasn't the type of person to become a 'victim' but the events of the past week to date were about to get on top of her in the worst way. Have to get out of here. I have got to get out of this mess. Want to break down. Do not break down! As her cage roiled violently within what she assumed had to be a large lorry, she closed her eyes tightly and buried her head in her hands. She was so damn groggy she could barely think straight, and fighting the darkness that wanted to consume and devour her was a losing battle she did not have the energy to fight. Do not give in. Do not roll over. Wake up. Wake up. Goddamnit, wake up! It was a fight she couldn't hope to win. Drifting back into the calming swell of unconsciousness, she could only wonder what awaited her at the other end of this crazy ride.

When Mark Matthews had told her she would be spending most of the journey asleep she had assumed he meant naturally, as in an exhausted slumber. It hadn't worked out quite that way. Someone had thrown a blanket over her cage and two sets of hands, possibly three, had hoisted her outside. The cage swung violently in their hands and they were not gentle. Pricking her ears up, she used what little of her senses were left to her, but there wasn't much to hear. The sound of a large rumbling engine drowned out everything else and she knew that was inevitably where she was headed. Onwards to the abode of Leyland Forbes, wherever that might be, and it was unlikely that anyone would tell her. She was nothing more than chattel to any of the employees here. Albrecht had more respect for the animals than the human slaves they housed, as Jenny had found to her chagrin. The King of wacky bondage, that's what they'd said. The man would probably do something utterly bizarre with her body and then deliver her back to Albrecht. Oh God, that couldn't happen. She could not go back to Kyle, not after what had transpired. Someone would have to commit her to the nearest mental institution if she ever came face to face with that man again.

A painfully sharp prick took her by surprise and she bumped her head into several wire bars above her as she tried to avoid the vicious object that had been sunk into her upper thigh. No such luck. There was another second of pain as someone slowly depressed what had to be the plunger on a hypodermic needle. Jenny shrieked out her displeasure at such treatment, but the shock collar she wore gave her a vicious bolt of current, and all she managed to get for her troubles was a stream of male laughter and a couple of slaps upon the top of her cage. Someone said, 'Calm down in there,' and she only just managed to stem the growl that wanted to erupt from the deepest part of her lungs. Another said, 'She'll be calm enough in a minute. I don't think she'll give us any trouble on the journey down.' This was met with more laughter and Jenny had a hard time controlling her anger, not that there was the slightest chance she would find a vent for it. The sound of retreating footsteps and the rustle and slam of a corrugated loading door indicated that she had been sealed inside the vehicle, and then her whole world went black. The engine shifted up a gear and there was a brief pause, probably as the driver or drivers were getting ready to move out. Jenny waited for her eyes to close and sleep to overcome her, for that was what she assumed they had drugged her with. Damn. That would make it two times this week that she had been sedated.

As the truck roared into life and took its first shuddering sways forward over the gravel, Jenny felt her head spin. The stuff didn't act anywhere near as quickly as they had you believe in the movies. It was frustrating because there was nothing more Jennifer Redcliff wanted at this point in her life than complete and utter oblivion. When it finally came for her, it wasn't a moment too soon.

When the sedative finally started to wear off Jenny was unamused to find herself still in transit. Whilst her cage had been anchored to the floor by means of several long nylon straps, she had not been, which meant that every time they went round a corner she ate metal bars. You'd think there was some kind of race in progress judging by the velocity the bends were being taken at. As she was slammed into the side of the crate for what must have been the twentieth time, she felt the air leave her body in a rush before she was rudely deposited back in place as the lorry evened out its weight once more. *Breathe. Keep breathing. One small step at a time.* Hah. She was in a cage for Christ sake! She could barely move. It was most certainly time for a hissy fit, if she could summon up enough enthusiasm. Actually, scrap that, she thought, for it would most certainly involve tears and noise and the collar around her throat wouldn't allow such niceties. Matthews would get her out of this. He wasn't a complete bastard. He would work something out and they could take it from there. She'd do his housework, she'd play his naughty games and the first opportunity that presented itself for escape, she'd take it. Jennifer was nothing if not resourceful. Where there was a will, and there certainly was a will, there was a way. She might play his games for a couple of weeks or so at first, though, because the man had created a nasty itch within her body that was going to require some impressive scratching. Sharing his bed for a little while was not going to be a hardship, unless she was much mistaken. So, the good news was that she might only have to endure this hell for a few more days before she could get out of the rabbit hole and enter some kind of normality. One where she could clean her teeth at night, eat decent food, take a warm bath, and have the occasional conversation. Jenny had no idea how much you could miss the sound of your own voice when you were continuously refused the use of it. She was seriously beginning to go some kind of crazy inside her own head.

Finally there was a squeal of breaks and the truck lurched to a shuddering halt. The smell of gas suddenly flooded the van and it was not pleasant. Doors slamming indicated that her drivers were exiting the vehicle and she hoped to hell this wasn't a rest stop. She desperately needed to get out of this cage. Everything was stiff and sore from being cramped up in such a tiny space, and she needed to stretch out all her aching limbs. As per normal, no one was particularly bothered about her wants and needs. The sound of crunching boots over gravel and banging could be heard, brass doorknocker type banging, she thought. Then there were voices. Unfortunately they were far too muffled for her to pick out anything more than a few words here and there. *Early, scheduled, water, wait, girls* and a string of other unfathomable sentences whistled past to remain forever a mystery. They appeared to be having quite the conversation, but none of it could be understood from her position, huddled on the floor of a large metal container. In the end Jenny gave up trying to listen and banged her two feet against the bottom of the cage in protest. It didn't make much of a sound, and the floor was hard, so when she was completely ignored she didn't try to repeat the gesture. She was just going to have to wait patiently in silence, because there was no other option available to her.

When the loud rumble of the door finally sounded Jenny wanted to scream in jubilation, but remembered just in time that wasn't such a great idea. Keeping her lips firmly closed she blinked her eyes against the bright light filtering through the vehicle, even though her cage was still covered by a blanket, which thankfully diffused its harshness. The straps anchoring her cage were removed in short order and she felt herself being lifted in the air once more, the cage swaying to and fro. The only vantage point available to her was the ground below and she took in everything she could, which wasn't much. Fine gravel stones, all uniform white in colour, decorated the ground beneath her and the occasional flowerbed could be spotted as the men marched her smartly along the driveway. After a minute or so a set of large white marble steps came into view, and as the men began to ascend them her cage jolted back and forth uncomfortably. Then she passed over tiny, glittering tiles, arranged in a fascinating mosaic pattern, and found herself frustrated that she could not make out the pictures beneath her due to her limited vision. That was a crazy thought, because she had problems enough without worrying about the floor design, but there it was.

Finally, and in a none-too-gentle manner, she was deposited upon the floor with a considerable thump. Her teeth rattled inside her head, but thankfully no permanent damage had been done.

'Sign here, please.'

The voice was rough, had a cockney twinge and rang out clearly in what must have been a vast hall. Listening closely, Jenny heard the sound of scratching and guessed it was a fountain pen on paper, perhaps, or just a plain boring old biro. It appeared someone was signing the receipt of her delivery, if she was not much mistaken.

'She'll need some water. We had to wait for hours for her to sleep off the sedative.'

The rough, rasping voice was already fading into the distance. He had obviously fulfilled his purpose with that last sentence and was now off home. Jenny would have liked to tell him that she required a great deal more than just a glass of water, but sensibly she held back. Things were bad enough as it was, and she didn't feel the need to add to her woes right now with a bolt of electricity.

'Get me a bowl of water, Laeticia.'

Now that voice was a different kettle of fish entirely, thought Jenny. Refined, cultured and snobby, it was an imperious and authoritative command that had been smartly issued. It was a voice that said 'do not mess with me or there will be consequences'. She was thoroughly sick and tired of those kinds of voices and most glad that she was hidden away under her blanket, where she curled herself into a tight ball and tried to remain as quiet as possible. With any luck they might think she was asleep and leave her alone for a few hours.

That hopeful thought was quickly and cruelly dashed away as the blanket above her was lifted in a flurry of air. There, above her, stood a portly gentlemen dressed in the liveried garb of a servant, and his beady gaze devoured her naked form before his stare turned to one of derision.

'Oh, you're one of *those*.' He sighed. 'Sometimes we get cute little kitty cats and puppies, but not today it seems. His gaze then wavered to her back. 'What on earth...?' His mouth hung open and there was a rather unpleasant slackening of his jaw. Gathering his wits, he snapped his teeth shut and said, 'Well, his highness is not going to be very happy with you. I'm not sure if he'll send you back or demand a refund, but you should know he will not be best pleased.' His thin mouth compressed into a tight line and he picked up a telephone and began to speed dial his recipient. The call was picked up in a matter of seconds.

'Your package has arrived... She's been marked... But it's all over her back... Surely you can't use her... Of course. Absolutely. I'll have her delivered to you in a few minutes, in that case. My apologies, Sir.'

Jenny heard all of what he was saying somewhere in the back of her head. She was paying just enough attention to figure out that she wasn't going to be immediately sent back to Albrecht, and that was probably a good thing. She thought 'probably' because she really had no idea what these people had planned for her, and whether it would be worse or better than her previous few days at

Albrecht. Scrap that. Surely it couldn't be any worse? While these thoughts flickered through her head in an absent matter her attention was wholly on her surroundings, having been revealed in all their immeasurable glory as the blanket had been stripped away. The house, if it could be called such a thing, was of palatial proportions and there was wall-to-wall magnolia as far as the eye could see. That didn't mean there was a sea of cream to be seen - far from it. Fluted pillars decorated the wide, wooden entrance doors, and smaller plinths bearing all sorts of trailing horticulture offerings, such as grapevines, ivy and jasmine were positioned carefully around the room. Then there were olive trees, fan palms, orange and lemon patio plants - the whole place was draped in greenery. Looking up towards the ceiling confirmed what Jenny had already suspected: a glass roof. This was someone's idea of a reception/greenhouse. It smelt heavenly. No expense had been spared upon the décor, either. Beautiful gilt friezes topped by carefully wrought cornices surrounded the upper edges of the walls, and the walls themselves must have suffered under the weight of art that had been hung upon them. Heavy gold frames surrounded Monet-style artwork, and bright colours exploded everywhere. Fields, flowers, bridges, windmills, sail boats, sunsets, sunrises... all this and more could be found as you trailed your eyes slowly around the periphery. One of the pictures looked suspiciously like Van Gogh's *Spring* but was probably just a very clever reproduction. If it wasn't, Leyland Forbes had one hell of an insurance bill.

'Your water, Sir.'

That snapped Jenny's attention back to the land of the living and it was to witness a pretty little employee, dressed smartly in a black, shoulder-length dress, hovering next to Mr Snarky with what appeared to be a chrome dog bowl.

'Thank you, Laeticia. Leave it in front of her cage.' He waved his hand at her in an absent manner, as if to shoo away an errant fly, but it apparently had the desired effect. The girl all but ran from the room. Then Mr Snarky slowly walked towards her, snapped open a couple of clips on her cage, and lifted a small square opening just large enough for her head to squeeze through. With his foot he slid the bowl closer towards her. 'Drink,' he ordered.

Jenny looked up at him, looked down at the bowl, and considered her options. So much for a glass; these guys were just as crazy as the Albrecht crew, it seemed. 'You can drink water, or you can be force fed other fluids, and I hasten to assure you they won't taste as good as water... so I'd drink if I were you. It might be a very long time before you get another opportunity to replenish yourself.' Jenny had already decided she was going to drink, she was damn thirsty, but the threat was an added incentive to dive straight in. Lapping at the bowl in front of her, she felt Snarky's hand come down to pet her head. As she continued to drink he gave her long smooth strokes against her hairline, as you would if you were stroking a favourite pet. It was downright annoying, but there was little she could do about it.

When she had finished the contents of the bowl, carefully licking around her lips to get rid of stray drops of water, he stopped his petting and slowly moved around the cage, examining every inch of her.

'You're new. Ponies are usually much skinnier when they've been at the stables for a few months. That will work in your favour here. His highness likes a bit of meat on his subject's bones. Nice tail,' he commented, before Jenny yelped as it was given quite a hefty tug. Her head shot back inside the cage so fast that the little opening slammed shut in protest. 'You're still a little frisky, I see. Well, you have quite the programme ahead of you tonight, Petal. Would you like to know what's in store for you, or would you prefer that I kept the details a secret?'

Jenny wanted to slap him. She was desperate to know what was about to happen to her, because being forewarned, in her opinion, was forearmed, but she had no wish to get another dose of voltage through her steel collar, so she sat quietly and fumed.

'It must be terribly frustrating not being able to talk. You look like someone who likes to talk.'

Snarky was apparently trying to get a rise out of her. She had news for him. She raised her head, batted her eyelashes and gave him her most insincere smile. He got the message. 'Ahh, so you can play. Good, that will work in your favour. Most of the ladies beyond are actresses, and if they're not they certainly know how to use their bodies and facial expressions to their best advantage. That's all they have available to use, by the way. None of them are allowed to talk when Mr Forbes is in residence.'

Snarky looked at his watch and clucked his tongue. 'Well, your café stop is up. We need to get you ready for your first performance of the evening. That means a wash, buff and polish, as his highness is nothing if not a stickler for perfection. We'll have you looking a million dollars in no time.' He gave her a little frown, which indicated that she looked anything but that aforementioned figure at this moment in time. 'Ah, here they are now.' For the first time since she'd laid eyes on him, Snarky smiled. 'Here are your porters, Petal. They will carry you off to the ladies quarter. Be a good girl and behave yourself, won't you?' He tapped the cage twice with his hand, as if to emphasize his point. Then two gentlemen, dressed from head to toe in black, picked up the handles to her cage and she was once again airborne.

As she rocked to and fro, between the swinging handles, Jenny watched the floor spin in dizzying circles beneath her. The porters set a brisk pace that had her wishing her final destination was fairly close by, because if it wasn't, she was soon going to decorate their floor with bodily fluids. Trying to take her mind off the rolling nausea sweeping across her in waves, she studied her surroundings once again. Beneath her the floor was solid wood and made of antique oak, if she wasn't much mistaken. They had entered what must have been a hallway because the room was narrow and long. A few pieces of Regency furniture adorned the walls at thoughtfully placed intervals and the owner's passion for art had been given as much free reign in this room as the last, except that angels and cherubs, rather than flora and fauna, graced the walls. She had little time to examine it further for they were approaching the end of the corridor and a grand staircase loomed into view. From a central base two tiers spiralled off to the left and right, for as far as the eye could see. The wooden balustrades were highly decorative and the stair spindles had been painstakingly carved to reveal leaves, flowers and beautiful detailed scrollwork. Leyland Forbes wasn't afraid to splash the cash.

The staircase went up and up, and it seemed to be an endless climb. The porters obviously had their own woes in the form of heavy breathing and frequently changing hands as they continued the journey, shifting the weight of the cage to manage the climb as best they were able. When they finally reached the top both of them grunted with effort as the cage stabilised in their hands. Jenny was no less happy. Metal bars dug into her skin and her head swam. The guys then banged their way through several sets of double doors and they finally took a door off to the right. The sound of running water, hairdryers and the insistent snip of scissors could be heard. The floor underneath her and the walls above were made up of large slate tiles. She had reached her destination. This was confirmed when her cage was set down gently upon the floor. The porters took one look around and left as quickly as they had entered. Jenny only wished she could have done the same.

Turning her head to absorb what could only be described as an immense dressing room, Jenny tried desperately hard not to stare at the vast array of naked women that lounged and posed in every conceivable position upon whatever was available to lean against or sit on. Everyone in the room was female, and everyone, without exception, was devoid of clothing. Even though she had become used to seeing the naked female form at Albrecht, seeing so many women *au natural* in the same place was a bit disconcerting. As her jaw slowly started to drop she kept her head moving, afraid that if it stopped she might never be able to move it again.

A series of mirror tiles ran along the middle of the room, framed with gilt butterflies. Some had escaped the confines of the frame and flew in disarray all over the room. It was beautiful and startling. The wings glittered with every move of her head. If that wasn't distracting enough, fountains of water erupted from several outlets towards the top of the wall and created a cascading, waterfall effect. The warm lights above created a soft halo effect that swirled with the heat of the room. Several girls were soaping each other under the bountiful supply of water, with sponges and hands. The sweet smelling scent of something exotic lingered in the air. Mango, pineapple, lime and coconut all seemed to blend together in harmonious notes. Jenny inhaled deeply. She would have happily sold her soul for a drop of that shower gel. Albrecht had almost stripped her sense of smell from her. She had become used to the mud, slop, straw and sweat, just as the ponies had warned her on her first night in the stables.

Her eyes still moving, she noticed the chrome stools lined up against the opposite wall, directly in front of the long butterfly mirror, and all were filled

42

with women having manicures and pedicures, while their hair was being simultaneously styled and trimmed. It was a little surreal that even the hairdressers and manicurists were baring all of their lovely assets for everyone to see. Were they, too, going to be part of the show later in the evening? Time would tell, she guessed.

There was plenty of attention to detail. False eyelashes, glitter, lip gloss, lacquer, gel, blusher, sparkling hairnets, curlers and eyeliner were only some of the tools being used to make these women as beautiful as they could possibly be, and in all honesty, they were hardly needed. Sleek curves, high cheekbones, toned thighs, long necks, full pouty lips and golden tans that would have taken six months on a deserted island to achieve, because there were no bikini lines to be found anywhere, were in plentiful supply. All of the women in the room could have posed for Playboy, without exception, and Jenny found herself feeling quite dowdy and self-conscious in comparison.

The lack of verbal communication was also unsettling. All the ambient noise in the room was amplified to unbearably loud proportions due to its disappearance. The spray of water, the shaking and spraying of aerosol cans and the quiet hiss of hair tongs all seemed immediately overwhelming. No one paid the slightest bit of attention to her. Here she was, a creature in a cage complete with tail, collar, and shiny chains and this was apparently not in the least bit strange to any of its occupants. She didn't even receive a glance, which all added to her already devastating feeling of insignificance. Gone was the pampered little rich girl, and in its place was a mere shell of the feisty, fiery young lady that she had once upon a time been. Staying strong required so much damn effort and she honestly wasn't sure how much bravado she had left in her. Albrecht had stripped her down to something less than human and she wondered if she'd ever be able to rebuild herself - if she ever got herself out of here. *When* not *if*, she quickly corrected herself. There would be no future for her at Albrecht. She'd go mad. The house pet of Mark Matthews she could deal with, she'd have him twirled around her finger in no time, but life in the stables with Kyle was not an option. She just had to trust that Matthews would sort things out.

When a face appeared directly in front of her and began rattling a key in the padlock on her door, Jenny jumped. The lithe blonde women in front of her smiled apologetically and offered her hand in order to help her out of the cramped space. With contortionist moves she had no idea she was capable of, somehow she managed to make it out of the box with little more than a few scrapes here and there. The woman helped right her to an all-fours position and, bending down to her level, brought a finger to her lips, warning her not to speak. Jenny simply nodded. She already had inducement enough not to speak, so the woman needn't have worried. Stroking her back in a series of soft, comforting lines, she then made a show with her hands, two of them breaking apart, that she would be taking something away. When Jenny felt the plug in her ass move she knew what was happening. The horsehair tail attachment was being gently removed. Things were looking up, apparently. The blonde then deposited the tail back in her cage and gave a mild tug at her leash, indicating she should move forward. Led along by a long silver chain to the waterfall-style shower, her temptress did not stop until they were both submerged under its spray. Given half a chance Jenny would have made it there before her. She had been longing for a decent shower for over a week. Unable to help herself, she pushed her face upwards and embraced the tumultuous downpour as it exploded over her body.

Oh God. She could have nearly orgasmed then and there, because the water was warm. Plumes of beautifully hot steam surrounded her and she wanted to revel in the blissful feelings that encircled her. She hadn't realised how much she had taken the simple pleasures in life for granted, but bathing was most certainly one of her favourites.

With her hair now slick against her head, the blonde reached for a bottle located in an alcove set into the slate wall. Squeezing a generous portion of the liquid into her hand, she scooted down so she was at the height of her new charge and began soaping her hair with delicate, circular motions. It felt heavenly. Closing her eyes, Jenny let out a pent up breath she hadn't realised she'd been holding and felt herself relax, just a mere loosening of her limbs, but it was the first time she had felt safe in days.

The blonde bent to her ear and murmured very quietly, 'I know you can't talk, but while we're under here, I can.' Her long fingers expanded their reach and began to massage her scalp, forcing Jenny to swallow a groan. 'Sorry,' the blonde whispered with a little laugh. 'I'll lay off the pressure.' True to her word the insistent weight of her fingers stopped, and Jenny almost wanted to groan again in protest.

'Leyland is very excited about having you in the building. He's had pets here before, of course, but never a pony. He can't wait to get shots of your ass all plugged up with that magnificent tail.' There was another laugh and her hands, satisfied that they had done a reasonable job at shampooing, started to explore Jenny's body. 'Just paw at the floor if I do anything you don't like, OK?'

As two hands cupped her breasts and busied themselves rubbing shampoo soapsuds around, Jenny didn't waste much time thinking about pawing, or anything else for that matter. A familiar ache reignited itself between her legs and her lips parted on a soft gasp. The hands paid no heed. They tugged at her nipples, rolling them in smooth fingers until Jenny squirmed in heat beneath them.

'Oh, that's nice, huh? I'll be sure to tell his highness, when he's in need of the "perfect shot". They always want you revved up before the cameras start clicking.' Her hands rolled over her ribs, feeling their way down each bone until they reached her waist. Then they reached back up and began to lather some more soap into the small of her back and buttocks.

'I'm Adele, by the way,' the blonde introduced herself, 'one of Leyland's regulars, and I'll be guiding you through the processing stage.' Adele's fingers smoothed the slippery soap into the crease between her buttocks, rubbing gently, before she carefully began to slide her fingers around the circumference of the butt plug, lubricating the base with great care before she began to pump it slowly in her fingers.

'I've always wanted to be a pony-girl, but Leyland refuses to let me go. He says the training will take far too long.' Her breasts brushed against Jenny's back as the plug pumped inside her and the throbbing between her legs increased. Why was that so damn pleasurable?

Adele's voice continued to murmur quietly at her ear, 'The uniform is awesome. Teeny, tiny little straps, jingling bells, plugs, clamps and tails. When I see one of you girls in your gear I'm a walking advert for an orgasm.' Adele reached for the other plug in Jenny's pussy and gave it a light tug, laughing when it popped out easily. 'Ah, you guys are always so wet. They tell me it's the training. Is that right, Petal?'

Three of Adele's fingers thrust straight into Jenny's core and she almost had to bite her hand to stop herself from squealing. After two days in the latex suit she was hornier than ever. Someone had once said the average man thought about sex every few seconds, and she was beginning to sympathise with them. Her body was turning into that of an oversexed rabbit who'd overdosed on Viagra. Each day she wanted more and more, and she wondered if she might implode at some point. Her hormone balance was off the scale. What were these people doing to her? She was going to become an addict in short order, and hell only knew what would happen then!

'I'm going to get a harness for your fat little plug in a moment and fuck you with it, if you'll let me?' Adele hammered that point home with a few little thrusts of her butt plug, in case Jenny was in any kind of dilemma over the proposition, which she wasn't. 'I promise to make you come, sugar. What do you say?'

Jenny watched the tendrils of frothy soap swirl about the floor as they headed for the small holes of the stainless steel drain beneath her. Her head was spinning in a similar fashion but her body knew exactly what it wanted. It was helped along the right path by Adele's sexy but insistent voice.

'Gotta nod your head if you want it. If not I can just towel you down and take you back for a nap.'

Jenny's head couldn't help itself. It nodded frantically. She badly needed an orgasm and there was no way she was going back in that cage if she could possibly avoid it. Being a prisoner was one thing; being behind bars was another entirely.

Adele's tinkling laugh penetrated the outer reaches of her eardrums and her backside got a soft, wet swat with the flat of a palm. It felt horribly good. 'Atta girl. Let me go get my harness. I'll be right back.'

Left to her own devices under the pounding water, Jenny shook her wet hair out. She tried to wipe the water out of her eyes, but it wasn't easy when both hands and feet were in chains. Whilst her restraints weren't particularly heavy, they were noisy, cumbersome and most frustrating. Thankfully perseverance won in the end, and she blinked open her bright blue eyes to find Adele's pussy in front of her, complete with a black leather harness featuring a strap-on belt and one shiny silver plug attached to the front of it. She couldn't help but blink very wide eyes at the contraption, before looking slowly up at her soon-to-be domme with an expression of unmistakeable hunger.

Had Jenny taken a moment to glance around the room she would have noticed that nearly all of the other occupants had stopped what they were doing in order to watch and stare. Only the most professional of the beauticians and stylists continued with their ministrations, and even they were watching the antics out of the corner of an eye with every opportunity that presented itself. Thankfully she was far too absorbed with what was going on right in front of her to notice any such thing, and as such remained completely oblivious to all of her avid onlookers. Had she noticed them things might have played out slightly differently, but then again... probably not. The fires had been fanned and the flames were already hot enough to melt mercury. Adele's next words sealed the all- too-tempting deal in an instant.

'Suck me, Petal. Get me nice and wet so I can show you a good time.' The plug rubbed gently against Jenny's lips and dragged them downwards as it enticed her to do its owners bidding. Opening her mouth to take it inside, she pouted when the prize was immediately withdrawn. Adele wanted to play, it appeared, and she teased her mouth with light touches and strokes, but pulled back when she got too close. 'I'm not burying it inside you until you suck me, Petal. Come on filly, you can do better,' she cajoled, and that was all the incentive Jenny needed. She chased the damn plug around the shower like a bitch in heat, little good that it did her. Hampered by the chains, Adele outmanoeuvred her at every turn. The plug scraped against her cheeks, caressed her neck, squeezed between her legs and tickled her sex, but it never found her mouth. Finally, panting in defeat, Jenny sat on her haunches and lifted pleading, beguiling eyes up to her temptress, knowing this was a battle she could not hope to win.

'Ah, so humble in defeat, little filly,' she murmured. 'You are adorable, but you're right. I want something. I want those hooves up beside your ears, and I want you to beg me for the privilege of sucking the metal cock that will shortly be plundering your insides. Can you do that, Petal? Can you stick that little tongue out, whimper sweetly, and paw those hooves at me? Because I want to see desire, lust, frustration and a little humility in those eyes.' Her lips formed a slow, knowing smile and the plug, slick with water, wormed its way between Jenny's legs once more to rock her body back and forth upon its girth.

Her breath catching and eyes closing gradually in defeat, Jenny wanted to be strong. This was another ruse that was being played with her body and another mind that knew exactly how to manipulate her. Why the hell was she so weak when faced with these silly little games? Fight it, she pleaded with herself. Don't do this...

'It's OK, Petal. You can go back to your cage, if you want.' A hand reached down to pet her soggy head and a delicate hand slid down her face in a gentle caress. The kindness was her undoing. Actually, it may have been the threat of the cage but Jenny didn't care about the reasoning behind her actions. Her body just wanted relief. The relief and pleasurable blankness a sixty-second orgasm would give her. It would be worth the few seconds of shame she would have to endure in order to achieve it. It would have to be.

Keeping her eyes closed Jenny sat up on her haunches, raised her face out from the spray of the shower and counted slowly to ten. She needed those precious few seconds to get a grip on her trembling limbs. As soon as she had enough strength to move her hands she brought them upright to her face, trying her best to quell the shaking that would not go away no matter how fiercely she clenched them. Knowing there was no hope of stilling the tremors she gave up, and curling her hands into little paws, she clawed frantically at the air.

'Cute, but that's not going to cut it, Petal. Open those eyes and look at me.'

God, what was it with these people and the need to see your eyes all the time? Jenny wanted to flash her eyes open and glare at the women, but her short stay at Albrecht had taught her one thing, if nothing else. You could not win these games. Your best shot was to try and obey to the best of your abilities and hope you were treated nicely. It was that thought, uppermost in her mind, that had her eyelashes fluttering open and a shy smile present on her lips. She blinked a few times, to let the water run from her eyes, and then she slowly dragged her tongue out from the confines of her mouth. It hurt to do so in ways that were not physical, but were equally painful in her mind. Her hands pawed up at the air again as the look was completed.

'Oh God, you look adorable.'

Thankfully those were the last words Jenny had to endure before her mouth was offered the hard steel of the dildo and she could concentrate her attentions on a simple task. It was easier to *do* than *think*. Thinking hurt so damn much.

As if to make up for her nasty demands, Adele was unbearably gentle and the absolute antithesis of Kyle. Her soft, barely there touches quickly had Jenny weak at the knees. The plug brushed at her lips, again and again, slowly lubricating itself, before she was allowed a proper taste. Finally, when she could bear no more of the teasing, her head swooped in to swallow the beast. There was another pat upon her head as Adele worked the plug into her mouth, twisting from side to side to ease its journey.

'You have no idea how hot you look, down on all fours with your mouth full to bursting.' Adele pushed her crotch forward into Jenny's mouth and groaned. 'If Leyland won't let me be a pony, I wonder if he'd consider buying me one. I'd love having you around the house.' A wicked grin was bestowed down upon her but Jenny could do little to acknowledge it, and smiling was most certainly out of the question. Adele seemed determined to work the entire plug into her mouth and the last inch or so was proving difficult to take.

A single finger lifted her chin and extended her neck upwards. 'You'll be able to take it all in if you raise your head, filly. You want to please me, right?' Featherlike caresses skimmed her eyebrows and two hands cupped either side of her jaw as the plug twisted and turned inside her. Jenny couldn't even nod her head in agreement, because the plug had anchored itself firmly in place and breathing was becoming rather difficult. 'Just a centimetre to go, filly, you can do it,' her antagonist encouraged and surprisingly, Jenny reached forward to automatically obey. Stretching her jaw to the limits of its endurance, she forced the thickest part of the plug past her lips and felt her teeth scrape down on the narrower, smooth ring beneath it.

'Good girl. What a good girl.'

More wet pats could be heard on the top of her head. Plumes of water beat down on the small of her back and aggravated the waterproof dressing there, but she could not have cared less. There was one thing and one thing only on her mind. Adele must have been satisfied with her efforts for she popped the plug back out of her mouth with a single twist. Jenny flew backwards and sucked in a huge lungful of air, but she wasn't given the chance to think.

'Turn around. Show me that beautiful backside, Petal. Wiggle it and show me how much you want it to be filled.'

Jenny's conditioning was beginning to kick in, because her body wanted to be used so much it instantly obeyed. Shimmying this way and that for the amusement of another, she only hoped that the promised gratification would not be long in coming.

'Wiggle those ass cheeks slowly, from side to side, and spread those legs. Let me see exactly what I'm getting, Petal.' Adele's knees brushed against hers from behind and Jenny let out a mewl of surprise. Then the plug pushed forward and tapped at its firmly embedded neighbour and she could only groan in torment.

'Mmm, don't worry sweetheart, we won't forget about that hole, but first I'm going to see how wet you are for me. Do you like girls, pretty little pony, or is it only men who get you all juicy and flustered?' Her hands massaged her shoulders and then they traced a slow path along her shoulder blades. A sharp smack against her buttocks followed and Jenny was so surprised she opened her mouth on a gasp and found it instantly filled with a torrent of water. She had little choice but to swallow, for the spanks began to rain down in earnest.

'We need to get these pink and perfect for the shoot. There won't be a girl alive in that room who hasn't had a sound spanking, and whilst your tush is probably pinker than most, it won't hurt to give it a top up, will it, Petal?'

Jenny nodded in agreement, although she had barely listened to a word the woman said. The spanks flew down and all Jenny wanted to do was beg for more. The pain was exquisite. Her backside was so tender that each smack made its presence known by exploding like a firecracker. Then the tapered end of the plug moved downwards and Adele's heavy breasts were pushing against her back. They were moving on to bigger and better things.

'Time for the finale, Petal. We need to get a glorious rosy glow upon your *other* cheeks, and that only comes courtesy of a damn fine orgasm. You see, for your first appearance tonight you're going to be airbrushed up as a carousel horse. You're going to be delightfully naked, but body paint will be used to make you look nice and pretty. You'll still get all the trimmings you've been used to, so don't worry that you're not going to enjoy the experience. Everything that can be clamped will be. We also have a lovely gold bridle with your name on it and the shiniest black leather saddle you have ever seen, lined with twenty-four carat gold and decorated with rubies, emeralds and the like.'

Another couple of hard spanks slammed into her backside as Jenny gargled on yet more water, desperately trying to process what the woman was trying to say. In the end she gave up, feeling the beautifully thick plug journey downwards, teasing the folds of her labia before gently working its way into her gaping pussy. She swallowed another mouthful of water before she shook her head and clamped her lips together, feeling her arms tremble beneath her. Adele continued on, oblivious to her struggles.

'We've decided that your base colour will be black, so when we leave your sex, lips and nipples bare they will really stand out against the colour, especially when we rouge them up a little. Over the top of that the rest of your body will be decorated in carnival colours. Think bright purple, green and blue. We'll give you a bright red blanket to wear under your saddle so you're nice and comfy, because you'll be going for quite a ride this evening. The standard rules for carousel poles won't apply for the ingenious little set up we have, but I'll let you discover the ins and outs of that later. All you need to concentrate on right now is my fat little cock and how good it feels inside you.'

And that was exactly what Jenny did. The plug was slipping inside her, working its way deeper and deeper and all Jenny could think about was her burning need to come. Finally, when it reached its maximum depth, there was a sharp grunt from Adele and a long pause.

'Can you feel that, Petal?' Jenny nodded. Oh boy, could she! 'Good, I want you to feel me and I'm going to make sure you feel me, because this thing is going to be slamming into you so hard they're gonna slip on the vibrations next door. But first, we're going to take it nice and slow, so I can tell you all about the rest of your evening here at Leiceston Hall. We're all very excited to be a part of this. Leyland only host's events like this maybe once or twice a year, and when they get in full swing they are a thing of beauty and awe.'

Adele had a hand on each shoulder and she'd began pumping herself slowly against Jenny's body, grinding her breasts into the small of her back and letting the tips of her fingers run up the insides of her neck. As she moved backwards her nails scraped against the delicate flesh there, and this drove Jenny wild.

'Leyland's invited a whole army of photographers in tonight. He knows he's only got you for a limited time, so he's making the best of it. They're going to photograph you from every single angle possible and he'll be able to use the prints to paint from later. Your pretty little face is going to create a stir in these parts, I can tell you. His favourite pastime is painting women in the throes of orgasm, so if you want to create a good impression you might want to employ

49

your very best acting skills at the point of no return. If you don't look like you're enjoying yourself you just get to do it again, in any case.'

The plug was moving a little faster now, and the wet, slithering tendrils of Adele's locks dragged over Jenny's shoulders. It felt strangely erotic. The soft squelching sound of the plug was increasing in tempo, but was going nowhere near hard or fast enough for Jenny, who wanted the impact of Adele's body thundering into her, connecting with her prickling backside. Hadn't Mark said to her that she would begin to crave the pain? She had a suspicious feeling that the man knew exactly what he was talking about.

Mark Matthews. As her body surged back and forth a pair of deep mahogany eyes danced in front of her. In the last few days he'd gone from hated enemy to possible rescuer. Her only chance at rescue, she suspected. If he managed to pull some strings she'd go from pony-girl to house-slave. Oh God, was that any better? The plug twisted and pulled at her insides. She threw her head back and let out a silent moan. Who was she kidding? Life with Matthews would not be hell. She practically lost her lower jaw every time the man appeared before her. Serving him in the bedroom would not be an onerous chore. Serving him outside it was going to be interesting, but that would be his problem. Her cooking and cleaning skills were non-existent. Having been a girl long obsessed with sex, she guessed that Matthews might just about have the stamina to keep up with her demands, which were increasing daily. Being out of the reach of her father would be worth just about any sacrifice, and she hazarded a guess that with a little effort and enthusiasm on her behalf, which she would not have to fake, he would be wrapped around her little finger in no time. The trouble with that scenario was she knew, without a doubt, that her father was not going to let her go that easily. He'd spent his life watching her suffer, and when the tables had finally been turned he'd tried to get his own back in the most spectacular fashion. So what was her old man's end game? He sure as dammit had one, and she knew from previous experience that he was a wily old bastard. Someone had something he wanted and she was a mere pawn in a rapidly unravelling thread. Unfortunately, at this moment in time she had little choice but to play her part and see where the piece of string led. She would just have to hope that she could extricate herself from the resulting mess.

Adele grabbed a handful of her cropped hair and pulled her head backwards, over her shoulder. It refocused her attention sharply. 'Is that nice, Petal?' The plug was lunging long and hard now, and Jenny could do little but nod enthusiastically. It was very nice, but it could be nicer and a couple of fingers on her clit wouldn't go amiss. Wisely, she kept her mouth shut.

'Good, because I was going to keep going regardless. Now, where was I? Ah, yes, after the carousel shoot we'll be moving over to the tanks. Leyland has commissioned the biggest aquarium that can be found in a private residence, and it is taking pride of place in his ballroom for the next couple of weeks. Some of the girls will be immersed underwater for days as he goes about his filming, photography and artwork. You're only going to be in there for an hour or two, but oh my, you have the most amazing costume coming your way.'

The plug then began a much more promising rhythm and Jenny began to feel the sting of each slap of Adele's hips as they began to pound in to her. Her headspace was rapidly overloaded with swirling colours and rushing endorphins, and it was a struggle to listen to what Adele was saying. Trying to lock the important details away in the back of her mind, she let the words run over her and attempted to absorb what she could.

'The whole tank is going to be full of tropical human fish. You're going to be a little lionfish. Do you know what they look like, Petal?' Adele had to repeat the question twice because her fingers had started to creep their way down Jenny's inner thighs, tickling and tormenting the sensitised flesh on their way to silkier, wetter pastures. Jenny finally managed to shake her head in response, a receptor somewhere in the back of head acknowledging the question, even if the rest of her didn't want to.

'A lionfish is stripy and has lots of colourful spines along its back, and beautiful spikey fins. You'll be covered from head to toe in liquid latex, and as per most of our designs, certain parts of your body will be left bare or adorned with additional toys. In this case it will be just your breasts and sex, because you'll be breathing from an artificial gill that is going to keep your mouth occupied for most of the shoot. Your arms and feet will have webbing attached to them, enabling you to move through the water, although your chains are going to hamper your progress somewhat, but there's little that can be done about that. You'll just have to figure your way around them. Fins are going to be attached to your body by means of neoprene and Velcro and some impressive tail spikes will be added upon your plug. They're going to be heavy, I think,' Adele paused a second, to give her butt plug a couple of pumps, in time with the rhythm of the one around her waist, before continuing, 'but in the water they will be much more manageable. When you move, those fins are going to torment the areas that have been left bare, and even if they don't, you'll have to contend with a tank full of predators who will be anxious to have their wicked way with you. There will be some other fish to contend with, but you need to watch out for the divers. You'll be spending most of your time trying to keep out of trouble because once the men inside there get hold of you, they're going to torment you to the best of their abilities. I'm not sure how many women are going to be joining you, but it will only be a few. We'll just have to hope you're fit and ready to swim a little. It's going to be a little bit tricky with your chains, though, so I suspect you're going to be a favourite with the boys.'

Great, Jenny thought. Her day was getting better and better. She was going to be painted in goo, covered in spikes and dropped to the bottom of a large tank of water. As if that weren't bad enough she was also going to have several sex-crazy ocean fiends chasing her around for a spot of the good stuff. Oh, and let's not forget that people were going to be watching and filming every move she made.

Adele's fingers were beginning to nip the flesh on Jenny's inner thighs. Not hard enough to hurt, but she used enough pressure to let Jenny know she was there. 'Do you want to feel my fingers on your clit, Pretty Pink? Mmm? If so, be a good pony and open your legs good and wide for me. I've had enough of your pussy; now I'm going to service your ass.'

Jenny had no idea if she'd managed to comply with Adele's wishes. Her brain was mush as soon as Adele had run her first fingernail up the wet trails of her labia, to tap softly upon her clitoris.

'Legs, Petal. Spread 'em. I want to watch that gaping pink hole weep for me while I lube up my plug.' There was a sharp slap to her backside, and that was all the impetus Jenny needed to obey the earlier command. She stretched her legs to breaking point as her backside squirmed from left to right, feeling her butt plug being pulled from its rather secure anchor point. With a soft pop Adele freed the offender and swapped it for another. 'This one's a tiny bit bigger, sweets, but it's made of rubber, so it'll be a little more comfortable. Coming around this baby will have your face lighting up like the red carpet run at the Oscars. It is going to blow your mind. OK, this harness has space for two plugs, so I'm gonna do both of your holes at the same time and you're gonna love it. Guaranteed.'

Jenny turned her head around a fraction to watch Adele as she smothered the smaller plug with a generous helping of lubricant, using all her fingers to smear it around carefully. Jenny's stomach clenched in desire at the sight; she couldn't help herself. Her body was now thoroughly revved up and aching for release. All she could think about was being taken by those plugs and having her body rocked senseless. She ached to come so badly she could have kissed Adele's feet.

When her tormentor was finally satisfied that her plugs were suitably slick and fastened in the right places she gave a soft command. 'Eyes forward, Petal. I want you to feel me, not watch me, remember?'

The twin plugs, both steel and rubber, nestled at her entrance as the order was waiting to be obeyed. It felt exquisite. The teasing little circles had her panting for breath and Jenny was anxious for the fun and games to begin. Turning her face to stare at the shower wall she let herself smile a slow, secret smile. Now she could close her eyes and no one would be any the wiser.

'Keep those eyes open, Petal. I'll know if you close them.'

Jenny's eyes shot open, but whether it was due to the mind-reader slamming into her behind or the two plugs surging forward seeking darker climes was anybody's guess. It was going to be a tight squeeze when they were both buried to the hilt, but she had no doubt that Adele would achieve her aim. The plugs twisted and turned, slowly thrusting in and out and Jenny couldn't help pushing back against them. She wanted to be filled, to have that delicious feeling of being broken open and torn apart, and craved the white heat that only a delayed orgasm could bring.

'Dip your head to the floor and rest your head on your hands, Petal. I'll be able to work them in easier that way and it'll give me a little bit more access.'

Adele's voice purred gently, fingernails scraping down her back as she pushed gently against her shoulder blades. Jenny got the message. She felt her body bend, as her mind wanted to break. Sucking in air, she concentrated on breathing. In and out. The simple act of breathing had never seemed so hard. Jenny couldn't help but wonder how the hell she was going to get through the evening.

I don't think you're cut out for submissive duty, although your body might beg to tell you otherwise.

The mahogany eyes were back. They swam before her, merging in to one another and blurring, before separating again to frame that perfect, beautiful, masculine face. She had news for him. If the sex was always this good she could probably cross the divide, heaven help her.

The hands upon her shoulders dipped to her waist, pulling her back onto the plugs before pushing her off again. They started with a slow and easy rhythm, but quickly progressed to a heavy thud that had her senses reeling. The plugs had nearly found their mark. The pain spiralling through her head as her sphincter was stretched was all consuming, but as soon as the thought crossed her mind fingers were moving down to her sex. They toyed with the folds of her labia and then stroked downwards, circling the base of each plug as it rushed forward for entry. It was a tantalising, teasing stroke that had Jenny gasping for air and throwing her head back, spattering the walls with water.

'Give it up, Petal. You can't fight it. Just let it wash over you. Practise that face for the cameras. Lose yourself in pleasure and if you're lucky, you may never find yourself again.' Adele's fingers found her clit and twirled around faster than a figure skater's spiral spin. When she added a touch of pressure to go with the revolutions Jenny felt a couple of tiny convulsions shimmer through her body.

'Yes, that's it, filly. You're nearly there. Pull that head up off the floor and open your eyes wide, Princess.'

Jenny somehow obeyed, though her head spun. The plugs had finally hit home, they were plunging back and forth with a wicked rotation and her back was already arching as her hands scraped along the slate tiles of the floor. As her lips opened a loud shriek of pleasure left them, and her body began to spasm wildly. Neck arching and eyes bursting open with the full force of her orgasm, she felt a thousand white lights flooding the room. Shaking her head in a dazed fashion, her body still rocking back and forth riding the plugs, Adele's voice broke through her consciousness.

'You weren't supposed to use flash, you idiots. Oh well, I hope you got some good shots. Leyland wants these up in the bathroom.'

CHAPTER FIVE

In Place

'The recording was excellent, dear. How's our screamer?'

'Asleep, thank God.'

'Not much longer now, K. I've got everything set up just as you described. You're very particular, aren't you?'

There was a tinkling laugh over the telephone. 'I've been waiting for what seems like forever to put Matthews in his place, as have you. It will be nice to watch him suffer. Very, very nice.'

'How did you hear of his fear of heights?'

'I'm not one hundred percent positive, but one of your girls says he avoids looking out of the window at all costs, which is kind of ridiculous when you consider he has a penthouse apartment and an office on the top floor of a skyscraper.'

'Well, we'll use what we can. If he appears nonplussed, no matter. There'll be plenty of other things in our room to entertain him. It will be a test of his endurance, and I'm interested to know how long he can hold out. He's young, relatively fit, and he's not new to the life of submission.'

'Are you worried his cronies will get to him before you finish what you intend to start?'

'No. He's not going to know what hit him. I will get exactly what I want, but I have a feeling we'll need to take shifts. He'll not give up his freedom without a fight.'

'I assume you're filming everything?'

'K, dear, you know me too well. The place has hidden cameras all over it. It's going to entertain me in my old age.'

A soft sigh of contentment left her lips. 'We can watch it together, darling.' There was the sound of creaking leather as she stretched out her arms and legs.

'K, you're not wearing my favourite catsuit, are you?'

'I might be,' came the seductive purr.

'Then you can get your ass over here now and let Kyle do some babysitting. Just make sure he knows not to touch the damn girl. We'll leave the theatrics for later. It'll be much more fun if she doesn't have a clue what's coming.'

'If *they* don't have a clue.'

'You underestimate my daughter, K. I wouldn't make that mistake if I were you.'

CHAPTER SIX
Spray Paint and Saddles

The orgasm had been at least sixty seconds long and the post orgasmic smile of bliss did not leave Jenny's face, even as she was yanked away by Adele's hand wrapping her leash tightly around her fingers until it was almost a choke chain. Scrabbling along the slate tiles with a grin upon her face that was undaunted by all the staring faces that seemed to be drinking in every move she made, Jenny tried hard to cling on to the euphoric, languid state that her body now found itself in. The silence had resumed and she found herself thankful for the fact. She didn't want to hear another single detail of what might be befalling her body before the night was out. Judging by Adele's previous comments, it was probably better she didn't know any more than absolutely necessary.

When Adele suddenly stopped walking in front of a set of elegant, vintage French drawers which had been painted white and decorated with shiny gold handles, Jenny nearly went into them head first. Sucking in a breath, and shaking her head from side to side as if to clear it, she noted it was decorated in a shabby chic effect and there were several similar pieces around the room to complement the look. The top drawer was smoothly slid open, and Adele pulled out a couple of soft, cream towels and began towelling her down, starting with her feet and working her way upwards. Alas, the silence was not to last.

'You're lucky that you have no hair and no nails. You get to skip the beauticians and manicurists entirely. There's really not much they can do with you.' Adele's voice was a low murmur; pitched softly enough that only Jenny would be able to hear it. Lifting her legs up one by one and navigating the chain that connected them, she began vigorously rubbing at Jenny's skin, paying particular attention to her backside.

'We need these buttocks nice and pink, but you already know that,' she said.

Jenny nodded. She'd already figured that much out from earlier. Stifling a groan, she felt her skin prickle beneath the towel and a small flurry of liquid heat shot between her legs. Again? She'd only just come. This was getting ridiculous.

'It's cute that you can't talk, but a little annoying too,' said Adele on a sigh. 'I'd love to know what happened to your back. Normally Leyland would have returned you in a heartbeat after having discovered something like that, so you're lucky you're a "speciality" of sorts. Thankfully he can work his way around it or I suspect he would have demanded that Albrecht send him another.'

Jenny didn't care how Leyland felt one way or the other, but Adele had just begun to rope the towel between her legs and was pulling it back and forth with a brisk flourish that had her stiffening her back and groaning out loud.

'The secret around here is to always look half-starved for sex. That keeps Leyland smiling and we keep the boss happy at all costs.' The towel softened then, slithering up over her body and gently down under her stomach. Her breasts were almost lovingly caressed and gently squeezed by the towel, before deft fingers gave her hair a quick rub. Her towelling-off session was over all too quickly. Squeaky clean, pleasant smelling and almost ready for round two, Jenny couldn't help but wonder what was next on the agenda.

Adele got to her feet and towelled herself down, paying particular attention to her blonde locks, as she squeezed and blotted them dry. She then grazed the towel against her nipples, making them stand on end and carefully dried between her legs with gentle swipes. Hanging the towel upon a hook by a set of double doors, she pressed an intercom button to the side of them.

'The pony-girl is ready for her body art session. Do you want me to take her up now?' There was a long pause and Jenny felt herself counting the seconds down in her head as she studied the grain of the slate tiles below. Finally a male voice crackled onto the line.

'Yes, we're ready for her. You'd better bring her in. It'll take a couple of hours to finish her from top to toe, so we'd better get started.'

'I'll meet you in two minutes. Can you release the door for me?'

'Sure thing, Adele.' There was a pause and then a soft click as the locking mechanism of the door came undone. Jenny's leash was picked up once more, and there was a rustle and clunk of metal chain as she scrambled to keep up with the long, shapely legs in front of her. The doors opened to reveal wooden floorboards that were slightly scratchy underfoot with the odd piece of antique furniture that she had to dodge around. The ceilings were impossibly high, especially from her vantage point of being only centimetres away from the floor. The walls were full of yet more artwork, this time paintings of people from the past one hundred years or so - ancestors perhaps? Jenny couldn't help but feel they were all looking down upon her. Large glowering eyes stared out from Victorian gilt gesso frames with a whole array of different stylised borders, and fingers pointed from ebonised oak surrounds. It made her so uncomfortable that she found herself staring hard at the floor, not daring to look upwards.

'Intimidating, aren't they?' Adele looked over her shoulder and gave Jenny a knowing wink. 'You get used to them after a while. They've never whipped anyone to my knowledge, so I wouldn't get too concerned.'

Her attention back on the corridor in front of her, she strode on ahead with a soft little laugh, giving the metal chain of Jenny's leash a friendly yank. Her head held high, her body completely naked, she walked with a confident stride that said she was very comfortable in her own skin. She was a woman who was proud of her body and more than happy to show it off. Jenny wasn't. Even now she wanted to gather up all her available hands and cover up what she could. Knowing the action would be futile; she continued forward on her hands and knees and tried to ignore the various metal banging and clanging that accompanied her every move.

'We're nearly there, Petal. Try not to put any dints in the floorboards. You've got a thing or two to learn about grace, haven't you? Submissives are supposed to use their wrists and elbows, and wiggling your ass while you crawl shows good form. I know there's nobody watching us at the moment, but practice makes perfect.'

Adele let Jenny's leash slither slowly to the floor. She then got down on her hands and knees and did exactly what she'd described. It was a slow, seductive, side-to-side crawling motion, where her ass swung to and fro and her fingers barely touched the floor.

'See? If you want to make your life easier in this new world you've found yourself in, then take it from me that you need to use your body to each and every advantage. Sway, wiggle, taunt, tease, lick, blink, gasp and moan at every opportunity. Wrap the men around your fingers. Make them mindless with your every move. Make them feel. The more desirable you make yourself, the higher calibre of bidder you will attract and, generally, the better your life will be. Make them jealous of every male look that comes your way, use all that testosterone to your benefit. So come on, show me, and for God's sake lose the self-conscious waddle. Your life now has a capital "N" for naked imprinted upon your forehead and you need to get with the programme. Use those assets. Show me...' Adele beckoned her forward with the crook of a finger, her glossy, French-manicured nail oddly compelling. 'Lose the inhibitions, be proud of that body and make my eyes fly out of my head.' Adele's lips pouted prettily and she raised her head in challenge, but Jenny had already heard all she needed to hear.

There was a sparkle in her eyes and a tilt of her head as she almost glided across the floor. Looking directly at Adele she blinked slowly, twice, and let the flutter of her long eyelashes reveal the bright blue irises beneath. Her full lips opened softly and she licked slyly at them with her tongue. Then she wiggled her ass. A gentle sashay from left to right, she used her hips to swing her backside from one end of the room to the other. As she came within inches of Adele's face, she smiled ever so slightly and bared her most coquettish expression for full effect.

It was met with a satisfied smile. 'That's exactly it, Petal. Knew you had it in you. Now remember that look for later. This is an evening that every man here will remember for years. Make sure your face is uppermost in their minds. Well, that's enough from me for now. See the open door at the end of the corridor? Your make-up artist is ready and waiting to transform you into something incredible, so get ready to party, Petal. It's going to be one hell of an evening.'

Jenny stared at Adele's retreating figure behind her and then at the innocent-looking room in front of her. The door had been painted white and the room inside was brightly lit, for there was a large crystal vase located just beyond the door that sparkled all the colours of the spectrum. The glass table it rested upon had been polished to such a high sheen that the thing reflected every single one of the vase's facets. The walls were a soft pastel green, there was an old fireplace above which hung an enormous art deco mirror, and two upholstered carver-style armchairs resided either side of it, presenting a rather cosy look. Jenny would have given away a pair of her Jimmy Choo 'Damsel' sandals in order to sit down on one of them. Sighing, she took another fleeting glance behind her and discovered that she had been left to her own devices. Should she make a run for it? Before the thought had even taken hold she realised what a stupid one it had been. There were staff everywhere, doors that had internal locking systems, and probably hidden cameras as well. Add to that the fact that running in chains was going to be precarious at best, she guessed it was time to accept her fate and save her battles for those she stood a chance at winning. Sucking in a deep breath, she crawled forward and let her head slowly pan around the room.

The first thing that struck her as odd was the plastic sheeting, liberally covering most of the floor space to the left of her. The second thing would be the two naked girls lying on the floor with their legs spread wide open. The third would be the guys between their legs, holding what looked like a shiny silver gun. If that wasn't weird enough, one was being covered in purple spray paint and the other was getting a brilliant orange coat. The paint was being sprayed everywhere, and she meant *everywhere*. The two women appeared to be enjoying the experience for the expressions they wore could have melted stone.

'Ah, you must be Petal. We've been expecting you. You're the last of the girls lined up to get a full body spray for the carousel ride. Why don't you hop on in the bathroom with Georgia and she'll prime you for the artwork. I'm afraid it might sting a little, but that can't be helped. We're using alcohol-based paint because Leyland's very particular that there are no smudges, wrinkles or rings in his "muses". The stuff we use can be worn for hours, but you're having a change midway through the evening, I hear. You'll get scrubbed down and repainted in liquid latex for part two, and boy are you gonna love that. It will feel like you're wearing a second skin, but we'll talk more about that later. Georgia!' As he shouted out the name an elfin-looking waif with shockingly purple lips and hair popped her head around the bathroom door. 'This one's a real-life pony. Time to get her greased up, but don't enjoy yourself too much, eh? We're on a schedule here.' He gave her a wink. 'You've got twenty minutes and then I want her out here, OK?' He pointed to the plastic mats below, just in case she hadn't got the idea.

'Yeah, yeah, hotshot. I know the drill. I can have plenty of fun in twenty minutes anyway, so hold your horses.' The purple princess didn't smile but it was clear the sarcastic barb hit home. She waggled five elegantly long purple nails at him and with a brisk nod of her head to the left, indicated that Jenny should follow her into the bathroom.

Jenny was feeling heartily sick and tired of bathrooms but she ploughed on forward, namely because there was no going back. The door behind her had clicked closed by a hovering attendant and there was a snick as the locking mechanism caught. Must be great fun to live in this place, she thought, rather sourly.

58

'OK, we need to get you in the tub. It'll be easier to clear up the mess that way. Can you manage by yourself with those restraints or do you need me to help you?'

Jenny did not waste precious energy sighing. She simply eyed the claw-footed tub and began to scramble her body into the contraption. If she scraped the enamel and left black smears everywhere it was hardly her problem, was it? What was with the uber clean police anyway? She'd just had a shower. Did she really need a bath as well? This was all going a bit too far...

'Nice look,' said Georgia, who wore a smirk on her face that said she knew exactly what Jenny was thinking. 'I'm not bathing you, Petal. I'm shaving you. The paint application is much better if you're completely hairless.

Jenny raised her eyebrows at her. Bar her head she was already completely hairless. What on earth was the woman going on about?

'And there'll be no time to prep you before the liquid latex, so I need to remove every last hair from your body, except your head. I'm talking face and arms for the most part, as I know the rest of you has already been done. Latex paint can only be removed by pulling it off the body, a bit like that PVA glue they used to have when you were kids; you know the stuff?' When Jenny didn't nod in response it didn't deter her. 'Anyway, if I don't remove it, when you pull the latex off, that'll remove it, and it's not pleasant. So we do it now. Just sit in the tub and I'll wax it off. Then we can cover you in some lotion to help make the paint application a bit smoother. There's a little stool in there you can perch on, so you shouldn't be too uncomfortable. I'm just going to check and make sure the wax is warm enough and I'll be right with you.'

While Georgia rustled about behind her, Jenny continued to haul herself into the large enamel tub, banging and clanging her numerous chains about. They were beginning to get rather irritating, but she suspected that would be the least of her woes before long. Someone was going to wax every single last tiny hair from her body. What did these people have against hair for Christ's sake? Finding the small wooden stool that was set in the centre of the tub, she awkwardly managed to perch herself upon it and centred herself as best she could. She had an awful moment where she considered whether her eyebrows would be staying or going, but she guessed if they were going there was little she could do about it. The scent of melting strawberry wax infiltrated the bathroom and she shifted awkwardly on her stool, feeling her naked buttocks stick uncomfortably to the wood.

'OK, tilt you head to the side and we'll start with your face.' Warm goo hit Jenny's cheek and the torment began.

By some miracle she got to keep her eyebrows, but twenty minutes later Georgia had gone over her with a fine tooth comb and pulled, plucked and tore rather sizeable wax strips from every area of her body that might have foolishly dared to grow an offending follicle. Her skin prickled and there was a residual burn on her face, arms and buttocks, which was where most of the unwanted hair had been situated. Ridiculously the cumulative little tears of numerous wax strips left her sex wet and her libido ravenously hungry. As she slid along her slippery wet chair she was nearly panting in heat.

'Time for the lotion. This is just vitamin E cream, but it will help the paint stay on a bit better, and it's not bad for the skin either. The good news is that I get to rub it everywhere. The bad news is that I might not have enough time to get you where you want to go, so you need to concentrate and try real hard to come quickly, because believe me when I tell you that those little airbrushes being sprayed all over your most intimate parts are going to drive you crazy. Let's hope you're not ticklish, or your life will be hell for the next couple of hours.'

Georgia squirted a generous amount of the unscented liquid in her hands and began slathering it all over Jenny's body. It was wonderfully cool and soothing after the waxing and for the first few seconds she did nothing but bask in the pleasure of someone's hands wrapping themselves all over her skin.

'You're going to need to help me if you want that little treat, Petal. Do you want a special treat? You have been a very good girl, sitting here so patiently with barely a whimper. It's only fair you're rewarded, right?'

Jenny mewled in agreement and got a condescending pat on the head for her troubles. She didn't care. She wanted that damn orgasm bad.

'Hold out your hands and I'll give you some cream. You start rubbing it into your legs and feet, and I'll start rubbing somewhere much more fun.' Georgia giggled, before helping Jenny to stand up and waddle out of the bath. She then squirted some more cream into the cupped hands that Jenny had formed for her. 'Perfect. Bend over and start working that into your skin.' Her bright purple hair swayed against her face and a long purple nail pushed it back behind an ear. When Jenny went to do exactly as ordered there was a clucking sound of disapproval, which made her jump.

'Legs spread wide, Petal. You should know that by now. Whenever you're given an order generally people want access to your delightful charms, so be sure to make it easy for them, OK?' Jenny was rewarded with a slap on her backside as she performed the requested manoeuvre. 'That's much better. Hands, arms, legs and feet, sweetie. I'll do the rest.'

Bending over to concentrate on her feet, Jenny heard the sound of the moisturiser bottle being squeezed once more. Rubbing the thin fluid into the backs of her feet and ankles, she felt a pair of wet hands begin to massage her buttocks. Groaning, she almost forgot what she was doing for a moment. 'Keep rubbing and keep moving, Petal. Else you'll lose your treat.' The hands generously coated the round globes of her backside before dribbling a lone line of liquid between them. Jenny concentrated on the porcelain-white tiles beneath her and tried to remember to breathe and rub at the same time, meanwhile the cold liquid began to trickle between her legs.

'Leyland has invested in hundreds of bottles of lubricant for tonight's proceedings. He's always the ever-thoughtful host. After several orgasms some of the participants find it hard to work themselves up, so plenty of lubricant ensures his guests are never disappointed. It's also necessary for lots of anal fun, as I'm sure you're aware by now.' The gloopy cream was being circled around Jenny's sphincter and she was aware of absolutely nothing bar Georgia's fingers. 'He always keeps his guests entertained. There'll be plenty of fun and games at tonight's proceedings, most of them at your expense, but that's half the fun of it, isn't it? I can't wait. I'm going to be buried in one of the glass tanks.'

The expression on Georgia's face was almost reverent as she contemplated the evening ahead. She looked as though an invite to Leyland's house was akin to meeting the Dalai Lama, and it was an impressive expression to master. Although Jenny couldn't summon up quite the same amount of enthusiasm, there was a definite tingle in her loins at the thought of the acts that might be performed upon her body later, and it had little to do with the fingers currently exploiting some very sensitive holes upon her person. Actually, on second thought it had something to do with those fingers, but they weren't entirely responsible.

'I hope you don't get dizzy,' said Georgia as her hands smoothed the lotion gently between her legs. It took Jenny several seconds before the question actually managed to compute itself in her head. 'The carousel doesn't go around very fast, to make sure the onlookers cop a good view. Oh, and most of the audience will have a spanking paddle or two, so it will need to be slow enough to allow them to get the odd smack in. But however you look at it, you'll still be going round and round for quite a while. Do you get dizzy?' Georgia forked her index and middle finger around Jenny's clitoris and squeezed it gently. Her question was met with a loud gurgle. 'I'll take that as a no, then. Hope you're not afraid of heights, either. Some of the girls are going up high, though I have a feeling you're one of the underwater ladies.'

Jenny tried nodding her head but the effect was lost as Georgia's clever fingers began to alternate between sliding back and forth, and dipping inside her.

'Still rubbing that lotion in, Petal?'

She groaned in response. You were expected to move when someone had hold of your clit and was steamrollering it into next year?

'Georgia, we need Petal out here now!'

'Sorry, Len, we were just coming!'

Jenny had no idea about Georgia, but she definitely was, and she'd just swallowed a mouthful of moisturiser as her hand banged in shock against her mouth.

Less than two minutes later Jenny found herself lying on her stomach with her every movement a rustling symphony against a large white plastic sheet. The thing stuck to her rather unpleasantly, and her underside felt hot and sticky. On the plus side, the interconnecting chain that held her restraints together in the middle had been removed. Someone had said something about 'special dispensation', but Jenny didn't care about the whys and wherefores; the extra freedom it granted her arms and legs was wonderful. Her remaining collar and chains had then been covered in a layer of plastic tape to protect them and she was instructed to remain perfectly still. But that was the least of her problems. There was a guy behind her spraying fire into her skin. OK, so it wasn't quite fire, but it certainly stung.

'Make sure you keep your eyes closed, Petal. This is isopropyl alcohol and there's going to be some overspray floating around. Believe me when I say your eyes won't like it.'

The warning was actually unnecessary, as Jenny had her eyes tightly closed, but it was always nice to know someone was spraying neat alcohol at your skin. Her back was being coated in fine mists of paint and it was an unusual experience, to say the least.

'Your base layer will be black, so there will be two of us using single action airbrushes, and that should have you covered pretty quickly. For the detail work we'll need something a little finer, and I'll work with a dual action and some detail brushes. If Georgia hasn't already told you we'll be spraying virtually all of you, and this includes your eyelids, lips, behind your ears and the soles of your feet. The only bits that get to escape the black paint are a heart-shaped portion around your ass, a similar area around your tits and a small oval that will frame your sex. It's easier to see if you're wet if you remain "pink" so I'm told. Personally, just about all of Leyland's punters check anyway, for their own amusement mostly, but I'm just following orders. What I'll do to keep those areas clear is put a bit of sticky plastic over you. Then I can just tear it off when we're finished. First one's going on your ass, now.'

True to his word, a thick cold piece of plastic was applied to the lower portion of Jenny's backside.

'Now spread your legs as wide as you can and then I can pop the second piece on.'

Jenny felt her face flame in mortification and for a moment her body thought about stalling, but there was no such room for error in this place. Her legs were simply grabbed at the ankles and stretched.

'Next time do as you're told, filly. We have spanking privileges too, in case you were wondering.' A swift slap was delivered to her upper thigh as if to confirm his remark.

When her legs were spread wide enough for their satisfaction, they were slowly lowered back to the floor once more and another giant sticky plaster was applied to her sex. It was not a particularly pleasant feeling. She squirmed and felt the plastic sheet grab at her skin, crunching sounds being made as she wiggled about. Len was obviously satisfied that his work had been done, for he quickly took a step back and prepared to join his partner in crime. The sound of two compressors could then be heard and the stinging sensation upon Jenny's back intensified. Squinting her eyes tightly shut she tried to close her legs back together, but the plastic sheet made the action difficult.

'Keep those legs open, Petal. We'll need to spray between them shortly.'

The spraying went on for some time. It tickled her skin relentlessly with its feathery light touch and she had to work hard to stop herself from squirming all over the place. At the slightest movement Len was good to his earlier word and was happy to give her a short sharp slap for her troubles. This just increased the torment. Georgia's orgasm seemed like a million miles away now, and she was already revved up and rearing to go again. Would this madness ever end, she wondered? Biting her lip hard, yet again, in order to stop herself from rearing up at the airbrush as it hit the top of her buttocks, she wondered how on earth she was going to get through the evening ahead. She hoped to hell it was going to be fun in parts, because after two days of the latex suit all she could think about was sex. It was almost like someone had painted the three-letter word inside her head, and had added an audio track for good measure. Sex, sex, sex. It was delicious and crazy, but what was worse was the knowledge that she was almost looking forward to the antics ahead.

'Draw your hands to your ass and pull apart those pretty butt cheeks for me. I need to paint between the beauties, and as you're going to have black hands in a minute anyway, it makes sense for you to do it rather than me.'

Jumping a little as the question snapped her out of her current daydream, she quickly proceeded to do exactly as asked and was rewarded with a pat on the head. Sighing inwardly, she almost wished she had been tardy so she could have had a smack. Shaking her head, she rolled her eyes upward.

'That's your back finished. Now see if you can get up without messing up any of your artwork.'

Another silent sigh and Jenny tried her best to peel herself off the plastic sheet she was now firmly glued to. Finally managing to get up on all fours, she was ordered to remain in that position while the paint dried for a few minutes. Taking a glance over her shoulder she couldn't help widening her eyes, as there was nothing but a black canvas where her skin should have been. It was a weird sensation. They were dehumanising her again, she guessed, and by the time their get-up was complete she would probably be horrified, but it was somehow arousing at the same time.

'Flip over on your back.' Len wasn't much for talking. He barked out occasional commands but seemed completely absorbed in his work. His colleague kept giving her breasts and sex the odd sneaky stare when he thought no one was watching, but it was clear that this was just another job to the guy in charge. Jenny couldn't help but wish they would paint her face first, so the furious blush burning up her cheeks could be hidden from view. No such luck, of course. They began tackling her from the feet upwards, and the soft spray of paint was infuriatingly arousing, even there. Watching the airbrushes as they swayed from side to side and listening to the soft hum of the compressors, all Jenny could see was her body disappearing from view. It was almost like they were repainting her latex catsuit back on her, but without the added benefit of its thin rubber coating. This evening she was going to be completely naked, her charms accentuated by cute little heart frames, and then put on display in front of hundreds of onlookers in full pony-gear regalia. Her mouth went dry at the thought.

'Spread those legs wide again.'

The simple command was far worse this time, because she could see the pair of them looming in front of her and was well aware they knew just how aroused she was. Her nipples pointed upwards, proud as traffic cones, and her clit pulsed like a jackhammer. How utterly humiliating.

'Nice to see you're having fun, sweetheart.' The comment was probably one of the nicer ones she had received today, but as per normal it came with consequences. 'Unfortunately we're going to need them a little wider than that. There's little point being self-conscious around us, because before the night is through you're going to be exposed in much worse positions than this, I'm afraid.' Not waiting for her compliance, he grabbed her ankles and pushed them as wide apart as they would go without snapping a limb in the process. Jenny squeaked in protest. 'You had your chance. Either you do as you're told immediately or you risk the consequences. Remember that, or you're going to suffer.' Jenny watched as a Q-tip was coated in black paint and drawn up the left crease of her inner thigh to fill the gap where the airbrush couldn't reach. Her clit swelled, throbbed, and drummed out a heavy metal protest as she gave him her most beseeching stare. 'Don't even think of giving me that look. You've had your fun for now. Be a good little girl and someone might take pity on you this evening, although I wouldn't count on it.' As another section of plastic was applied over the mounds of her breasts, Jenny felt her stomach clench as they caught the tip of a nipple. She made a stuttering sound. It was to be the first of many...

Two hours later and she was blacker than a coalminer. They had got the damn paint everywhere, just as they'd previously predicted. Then, to add insult to injury, they'd got out several tiny little paintbrushes and proceeded to paint in the detail work to get a three dimensional veneer in place. They'd done a damn fine job. There was pretty gold latticework around her breasts, sex and ass. The swirling brushes had been very busy and exceptionally skilled. Sparkling gems were pasted in long glittering lines from her neck to her ankles, with only the area on her back escaping their attention, due to the saddle she would wear, she guessed. Black eyeliner had been pencilled inside the pink waterline of her eyes and swirling gold highlights applied to make sure her eyes didn't disappear into her face with her new monochrome paint job. This gold artwork continued around the line of her gems and spun in slow, sweeping arc's around her body. She felt like a Christmas tree bauble. The tiny brushes had been a worse torment than the airbrush, and their soft bristles made her twitch and wriggle, earning her several sharp slaps for her troubles.

The two of them then worked ankle-high leather pony boots onto her, complete with gold lamé cuffs and what felt like solid gold horseshoes. When she tried to move her legs the boots were so heavy they formed a better restraint than the rustling silver chains that sat atop them. Similar style mitts were attached to her hands, although thankfully the horseshoes were of a lighter design. Then a wig made of long glossy black hair that tapered into ringlets was carefully glued onto her head and arranged around her face, before being meticulously combed through. Oddly enough, it felt nice to actually have hair again, even if it was acrylic and slightly itchy to wear.

Finally a glimmering gold bridal was fitted carefully around her face, and though thankfully there was no bit in sight, there was a very impressive headpiece attachment which sprouted several plumes of gold feathers and an array of dazzling, shimmering gold wire and faceted jewels. When it was snapped into place it was heavier than she had expected, and it would take some degree of concentration to keep her head held aloft if to be worn for any length of time.

When a red blanket was draped into place, and a black leather saddle that still had the just-out-of-the-box highly polished sheen to it was tied to her waist, Jenny felt every inch the spectacular show horse that had taken over three hours to create.

'Just your tail to go, Princess, and then it's showtime!'

Well, not every inch, apparently...

CHAPTER SEVEN

Ankles and Panties

Marianna had officially put a smile on Mark's face this morning, which was a damn good thing, because the Redcliff saga was starting to eat away at him and he needed all the distractions he could get. The woman had proved herself marvellously up to the task, because she crept into the office after a couple of days off, and when he said crept he meant pink panther style, which must have been nearly impossible on her five-inch heels. Employing her stealth tactics to the max she quickly hung her mac on the coatrack and with her head lowered and her leather Chloe handbag as high as she could hold it, made an impressive dash for her desk at the back of Zystrom's headquarters. Mark couldn't help chuckling to himself. If she was under the impression he had a very short memory, she was about to be disappointed. His alcohol intake last night had been moderate, and his faculties were still firing on all four cylinders so far today, or as much as they ever were, in any case.

He watched her bag drop quickly under her desk and she almost drag-raced the coasters of her chair forward in her hurry to get herself under the desk. This was priceless. Was she that disturbed by his demands on Wednesday night? Giving her a few minutes to get her breath back and make herself comfortable, he contemplated his next move.

Kayleigh chose that moment to enter with his coffee and he watched, somewhat absently, as she laid the silver platter down on his desk and knelt upon the floor awaiting his dismissal. He took a moment to wonder if she could be trusted. Now that he realised Redcliff had his sights upon his person, he would not be at all surprised if he'd placed some of his own personnel strategically within Zystrom. He already had Khalil on the case, checking out each one of his team individually, but it would be like trying to find a needle in a haystack. He might manage to out one or two, but the chances were that one would be buried so deep there'd be no chance of finding her.

'Kayleigh, if I said the name Michael Redcliff to you, what would it mean?' Mark's eyes were beadily watching the girl's reaction. He intended to pull this stunt with each of his submissives and see where it led. Khalil could do his part from behind closed doors, and Mark would do his, but hopefully with a better success rate.

'Never heard of him, Sir.' There was barely a flicker of her eyelids and her body remained in its relaxed pose of obedience. Mark was well aware of all the obvious signs of lying, and either she was well trained or this one could be crossed off the list. There were no sudden head jerks when the question was mentioned, and no change of breathing, because her shoulders hadn't risen any higher. Her voice remained measured, no fidgeting or shuffling was apparent, and the blink rate of her eyes was neither rapid nor non-existent, and that was always a good tell. He'd cross her off the list. If Khalil found anything in his prying, then they'd try other tactics, but for now she was not under any further suspicion.

'Very good, Kayleigh. You are not to mention our discussion, if it can be called that, to anyone. Dismissed.' Kayleigh knew better than to give him the questioning look that was lurking beneath the surface, but he knew she was now curious enough to pop back to her desk and Google the hell out of *Redcliff*. It wouldn't do her any harm, but to be on the safe side he'd better get all the girls in this morning and try his tactic, before someone let the cat out of the bag and gave them due warning.

Sliding the silver tray, with its softly bevelled edges towards him, he picked up the Wedgewood cup and saucer and stirred its contents around with the spoon provided. There really was no need, he took no milk or sugar with his coffee, but it was a force of habit that was hard to break. The spoon twirled round and round as he mulled things over and organised his entire day in his head. When he had reached a conclusion he gave a delicate little tap to the side of his china cup and laid the spoon to rest. He'd start with the disciplining of Marianna, which would be fun, progress to catching up on all things business related, which wouldn't, and then end the day on a high note. He'd just treated himself to something very expensive, and would take delivery of it this evening. Whether it would be worth the money was anybody's guess, but he had a feeling he'd be in for an entertaining time.

Twitching his lips and smiling to himself he pushed back his chair and got to his feet. Looking at his watch he realised that if he wanted to complete everything that needed to be done today, he had better get started and what better to way to start the day than by reprimanding a delightfully feisty employee?

'Marianna. I think you have forgotten something.'

He loomed over her desk, giving her the full benefit of his dark and brooding stare, before placing two wide-stretched arms out on either side of her. He filled her space, purposefully crowded her in, and watched her head reel back in panic.

'Sir,' a very small voice whispered, 'I haven't forgotten.' He watched her swallow carefully, before she rolled her chair back slightly to allow him to witness the pair of delicate lace panties that rested above the tight ankle straps of her black spike heels.

Mark smiled for a moment as he admired the pretty black piping and ribbon that decorated her relatively modest lingerie. The see-through thongs and diaphanous G-strings had obviously been abandoned for the time being, whilst her panties were to be on display to all and sundry.

He stared straight at her for several seconds without saying a word. She managed not to squirm under his intense gaze, but her facial muscles stiffened to the point where the woman looked painfully rigid. He finally put her out of her misery. 'Ah, but Marianna, you have. Can you remember what I said Wednesday evening, back at your apartment?'

Marianna lifted her eyelids upwards and let her gaze connect with his, perhaps hoping that staring at his face would help jog her memory. She didn't manage to hold his brooding look for long though, and as her eyelashes fluttered downwards she whispered, 'Not exactly, no.'

'Hmm, I'm not entirely sure you're telling me the truth, Miss Morreau, but we'll give you the benefit of the doubt and let you rectify the situation. Does that sound fair?' Mark didn't care one little bit if it sounded fair or not, but he was prepared to play the good guy for the time being.

'Yes.' It was a feeble little whisper.

'Good.' His voice nearly drowned out hers and the next sentence he uttered was even louder, enabling most of the office to eavesdrop in upon it. 'I distinctly remember telling you that when you arrived at the office you would bend over and push your panties down around your ankles. Which meant that when you entered the door to this building that would be the first thing you'd do. The fact that the whole office will witness your humiliation was to be part of your punishment. I did not say, nor imply, that you could hang your coat up, waltz around the interior, grab a cuppa and then sneakily remove your panties under the privacy of your own desk. So if you're hoping nobody in the office is going to witness your little *faux pas* you're about to be disappointed, Sweetpea, unless you want to defy me, and I'll sort that kind of behaviour out in my special room for naughty girls. The choice is yours, Marianna.'

She chewed on her lip prettily and he didn't miss the nervous tremor that went through her shoulders, but she was smart enough to play ball.

'Did you want me to go outside and start all over again?' Her bottom lip wobbled.

Atta girl, Mark thought, as he slowly nodded his agreement. She'd just made her punishment ten times worse, because now everyone would be watching and waiting for the exciting little performance that was about to play out. 'After you've completed your task, you may come and see me in my office. Now stand up.'

Marianna slid her chair back and stood, watching as he came around the desk and then got down on one knee before her. 'Let me help you with these, sweetness.' Hooking each of his hands in the respective leg holes, he let them slide up her calves and caress her legs with slow and lingering fingers. Letting his nails softly graze the skin of her outer thigh he smiled as she sharply sucked in her cheeks.

'I see you've recovered from your exertions of a few nights ago.' He tipped his head back to watch her trembling fingers flick a lock of hair from her face. It was strange, but considering he'd only taken an interest in this one just a few days ago, the effect he had on her was quite literally astounding. As his hands dragged the silk material higher he heard her panting for breath with halting, faltering gasps. 'Just a little higher, Marianna, and you'll be back to square one.'

They both knew that wasn't entirely true. The stakes had changed and the air was charged with sexual tension. As the panties finally managed to rest around her hips once more, Marianna let out a long breath and her eyes gazed off into the distance.

'Has anyone ever left your service before, Mr Matthews, Sir?' Her voice wobbled and wavered.

Mark slowly got to his feet and bending his neck to the left, watched Marianna wince as she heard it crack. He then lowered his gaze until his eyes were level with hers and they had locked their prey into place. 'Not willingly, no. Are you going to be the first, pumpkin?' He brought his right hand up under her skirt, gripped her sex in the palm and lifted her a clear two inches off the floor. She shrieked. He let his middle finger press on what must have been a rather swollen clitoris, and was rewarded with a curdled yell. 'Well, are you?' His finger swayed from side to side, tormenting the little nub through the now wet fabric of her panties.

'No,' she sobbed. It was swiftly accompanied by a, 'Please put me down, Sir.'

His stare lingered. He drank in the heat that resided in the deep emerald depths of her eyes and watched the pulse in her throat as it ticked away. Reluctantly he lowered her to the floor. 'Be a good girl and be quick, Marianna. I'm not sure you'll relish a spell in the naughty room today.' With a quirk of his eyebrow he watched her swallow awkwardly, before she managed to gather her wits together and scamper from the room. Her handbag remained wedged under her desk, completely forgotten in her hurry to escape him.

Mark felt the corner of his lips twitch in amusement but he did not allow himself a smile. The stresses and strains of getting Jennifer Redcliff out of the precarious predicament she now found herself in were beginning to wrest large, splintering cracks into his brain, though damned if he knew why. He had long ago given up caring intimately about women. It was crazy that he should feel anything but contempt for the little socialite who'd managed to dig herself a hole so deep it would take nothing short of NASA to blast her way out of it. He could procrastinate about the whys and wherefores as much as he liked, though, and the end result was no different. He did care. He had a vested interest in the girl that even he couldn't understand, and freeing her from her current situation was his top priority at the moment. He could think about his motives, pure or otherwise, after the deed had been accomplished. If it could be accomplished. Who was he kidding? Where there was his will, there was always a way.

His attention was brought back to the here and now by the soft ping of the lift's arrival. Miss Morreau had indeed taken him at his word and had not dallied around below decks. He clapped his hands swiftly in the air, twice, to alert the office to the spectacle that was about to befall them, though it was hardly necessary. All eyes were glued to the shiny metal doors that were slowly peeling apart, unaware of the turmoil that surrounded the girl within. Marianna would probably be shaking by now, unprepared for the scene that was about to unfold. Really, she could almost be compared to a complete novice, for she had practically been celibate for the past eighteen months. Being thrown in at the deep end was a bit mean of him, but it was always best to let the girls know where they stood sooner rather than later. He did not tolerate disobedience, and the lesson would be firmly etched into her brain after today.

As the lift doors glided open with a whoosh of air, everyone zeroed in on the hapless victim who appeared to be holding on to the front buttons of her coat for dear life. There was little of the 'tough girl' demeanour left in her, if she had managed to retain any of it on her journey into work this morning. He watched her close her eyes as a leg moved forward, leaving the bright lights of the lift behind. Those eyes stayed closed for the longest time, and he almost thought she was going to perform blind, before her lashes managed to recover themselves and wide pupils, now so large they were almost black, filled her face. The room was so damn quiet you'd have thought there was an examination going on, but not even a rustle of paper could be heard. Every face in the room was peering above its computer screen and waiting with dark anticipation for the inevitable performance to begin.

Not daring to break the silence, Marianna simply bent over double and let her hands reach inside her skirt.

'Not so fast, Precious,' said Mark. 'We want a good show, a striptease, without the entire strip but with lots of tease. So turn around, bend over, hitch that skirt up slowly and drag those panties down as if you're trying to gain the attention of the sexiest man in the room. That's me, by the way. Work it, baby. Work it hard. You're aiming for a round of applause, if you manage to get it right.'

He made a twirling gesture with his finger, spinning it around in circles, and Marianna got the message loud and clear. Giving him a look that might have spontaneously combusted a lesser mortal she slowly let her coat drop. Slithering elegantly down her arms in pretty little folds until it fell softly to the floor, it was to be immediately discarded.

Marianna's face then took on a flinty look and it appeared she had accepted or at least acknowledged that there was no way out of his little challenge, so she was prepared to play her part. Squaring her shoulders, it was almost as if she was preparing to do battle. Judging by the myriad of evil looks in the room, she probably was.

When the coat pooled at her feet it revealed a delightfully tight, asymmetric dark wool dress that clung to her every curve. Patterned in sloping bold stripes it made quite an impact, especially from the side, which was the view now coming into line as she made her way back around the room, so she would be facing the lift doors once more. When her profile came into view Mark noted that she had forgone the opportunity to wear a bra, which made his cock pulse and his eyes dance. The woman was at least trying to play by his rules, though she had a lot to learn.

When her back was turned towards her avid audience she paused for effect, before dipping and undulating her body slowly towards the floor. The movement was graceful, athletic, and hellishly sexy. To make sure everyone had an ideal view of some of her primary assets, she widened her stance and let her hands grip her ankles. Mark swallowed tightly. Why did these little scenes always backfire on him?

When her fingernails finally began to flutter against her heels she brought both hands back up her legs and slowly gripped the hem of her dress in her fingertips. She paused for effect, and when satisfied she had made them wait long enough, the dress began to move and change shape. Inch by inch the dark black material slid up the silky expanse of her thighs and, if he wasn't much mistaken, there were a few lusty sighs in the room. If his girls were enjoying themselves he really didn't stand a chance. Her skirt moved slower than dial up broadband, and that was saying something. When he'd told her to work it he hadn't actually expected much of a show.

Her nails were a glorious, unashamed red today and they reflected the bright halogen lighting of the office with little streaks of white. Moving a little faster at last, they began to reveal the underside of her ass cheeks that were once again prettily ensconced in her monochrome panties. The white material hugged the curves of her ass tightly, and as the dress rolled higher the slight quiver of her cheeks was anticipation of an intensely painful kind. This was made all the worse by the knowledge that he would not be sampling her delights today.

Firstly, she looked desperately tired. He'd noted it in her eyes when he'd bent over her desk. There were smudges of black that she'd tried to artfully conceal with makeup, but not much made it past his perceptive glance.

Secondly, as a matter of principle he would never take a girl after his having to correct or discipline them. That in itself was the worst form of punishment; arousal with no chance of relief.

Thirdly, he had plans for this evening. Big plans. As he fully expected it to be a rather long night he'd need all his stamina for later. So with that in mind he guessed they'd both have to suffer, although thankfully the length of her suffering would far outstrip his.

The dress had risen above the edge of the black piping of her panties and a tiny little bow quivered between her ass cheeks, almost as if it knew what was coming. Mark shifted uncomfortably, feeling the hard surface of the plastic desk grind into his backside. It wasn't the only thing that was hard, by a long shot.

The red nails threaded their way through the waistband, stretching the tiny trails of hidden elastic and then they tugged gently downwards. The beautifully perky and rounded globes of her ass bounced a little when Marianna tried to get them past the widest curve of her hips in the awkward bent-over position she was in, but perseverance won out and the panties finally cleared her curves. They struggled for a couple of seconds on their downward journey, but it mattered not. No one's attention was on them anyway. Everyone had their eyes glued to Marianna's gaping sex and the delicate, glistening moisture there. The bright lighting effectively illuminated her arousal at being publically humiliated and Mark suspected that the rest of the girls were equally as wet, from the squirming and fidgeting he could see going on. Spread wide as she was, there was little that was not on proud display for all to see, but if you were to be taught a lesson it was always good to have the experience properly cemented in your mind.

'Pull your cheeks apart, Marianna, and let us feast our eyes on those beautiful assets you have there. We don't want to miss anything.' Mark smiled to himself as a definite groan could be heard, but to her credit she didn't miss a beat as the sodden panties swooped downwards and headed towards the floor, because her hands were already moving to complete her task. Resting tightly on either side of her backside, she pulled them carefully outwards to peel back her cheeks and fully expose herself to her audience. There was a smattering of applause and a couple of the girls let out whistles of appreciation.

'Right, fun's over you lot. Back to work or I'll crack the whip, and I'm not speaking rhetorically.' There was an immediate shuffling of feet and papers as everyone returned to their seats and settled back down. 'Marianna,' he then barked, 'stop dithering around on the floor and get your delightful ass in my office. Now.'

Mark had already turned around, but some of the girls who lingered to watch Marianna's recovery got a good giggle when she tried to upright herself, having forgotten the additional restriction of her newly and ingeniously cuffed legs. She nearly fell straight back to the floor in an inelegant tangle of limbs, but with frantically windmilling arms, disaster was avoided by a hairbreadth escape. It was a frantic struggle and whether the panties would ever be usable again was anybody's guess, but on the plus side, at least she hadn't hurt herself.

'I'm waiting, Marianna, and I am not a patient man.'

Mark's voice had already faded into the distance. Looking down at the mess between her ankles she made a groan of despair. It didn't take a genius to deduce

71

that walking was going to be nearly impossible when trussed up like this, but it wasn't as if she had a choice, so putting her best foot forward she waddled as quickly as she could to the Master's evil lair. It was not a pleasant walk, and it was accompanied by more than a few sniggers from the girls, who were all peering above the tops of their computer screens to witness her walk of shame. Marianna made sure to concentrate her gaze straight ahead and not catch any of the eyes that were dancing with malicious mischief as she walked forward. Yes, they'd see her flaming cheeks, and yes, she had her panties around her ankles, but she wasn't going to give them any more than that. Hopefully. She wondered why Matthews wanted her in the office. Hopefully it had nothing to do with her misdemeanour this morning. Already feeling desperately aroused, she would probably get down on her knees and beg to have sex, if it wasn't already on the cards.

Right now she had the beast to contend with, and he didn't seem in the best of moods. Finally approaching his office door she shuffled inside, pushed the door to behind her and awkwardly got to her knees. Dipping her head towards the floor and folding her hands behind her back, she waited to be acknowledged.

It was well over a minute before he spoke, and she could feel her heart thundering in her chest before he finally graced her with his voice.

'Can you go and fetch me the Rogers file I've left on your desk, Sweetpea?'

Gah! Marianna could have happily slapped her boss as she once again struggled to her feet to waddle straight back out the way she had come and repeat the horrid experience for the entertainment of her sniggering audience. The man had done it on purpose, that much was for certain. She wanted to stomp her heels as loud as she was able, but realising that would just draw more attention to her predicament she held her attitude in check and bit her tongue. She did curl her hands into little fists, but that was the only outlet her anger was allowed. Making a beeline for her desk and striding as fast as her swishing panties would allow, she snatched up the required file and turned around without missing a beat.

Eyeing the dark mahogany of Mr Matthew's door once more, she dearly hoped she would not be seeing it again today.

'Marianna, what does the name Michael Redcliff mean to you?'

She was just sinking to the floor, yet again, when she frowned and sucked in a breath. Her knees connected with the hard tiles beneath her and her hands once again snaked around her back. 'Isn't he the one who made all of his money from oil, Sir?' She was a little breathless, and when she raised her head to answer his question it was to find his stare hard and intense upon her.

'Yes, that's the one.'

The stare continued and it was clear he wanted her to elaborate on the answer. Studiously keeping her eyes on his face, although they wanted to look anywhere but, she managed to draw enough breath to answer, 'Well, not an awful lot, Sir. I know the name of his company, Synstyte, but that's about all. Did you want me to do a bit of research?'

'No. I've got someone else on it. I'm just covering all bases. On another note, is there anything you feel the need to tell me today?'

Marianna fidgeted furiously with her fingers behind her and suddenly found the mahogany slab of his desk very interesting. There was a little chrome desk tidy, a few papers with charts and figures strewn about, a cup of coffee that was no longer warm judging by the lack of rising steam and a rather boring telephone handset. Reply to the question, she told herself sternly, when she wanted to do anything but.

'What kind of something would that be?' she asked carefully.

'Oh, I don't know,' said Mark, running a finger slowly along his lower lip. 'How much fun you had last night perhaps, what you ate for breakfast, or maybe something else entirely.' He shook his head and looked at her with a most amused expression.

Marianna knew the game was up. One indiscretion in nearly two years of service and she had to get caught. Unbelievable. Her hands trembled violently. If she'd thought the walk of shame was bad, it was nothing compared to what the punishment might be for an unauthorised orgasm. Her eyes stared wretchedly at the floor and her inner voice chanted, 'Please don't sack me,' over and over again.

'I was asleep,' she whispered miserably.

'So I was told. I do hope it was a good dream.'

When Marianna looked upwards to catch his gaze she found it was not a lenient one. It was clear she was in trouble. Panic began to well up inside her but it mingled rather strangely with what could only be classed as anticipation. Why she had ever wanted to be one of Matthews's favourites was beyond her. The stress of the position was going to give her a coronary.

'It's such a shame, because I had fully intended to go easy on you today. You've had a fairly busy week and I thought that kind of deserved a reward in itself. However, it looks like I'll have to take care of business and punish you now, doesn't it?'

Marianna nodded her head mutely. She was still too traumatised to speak at the mention of her failure.

'What will my punishment be?' she managed to murmur, though her voice was reed thin and stuttering wildly.

'All in good time,' said Matthews, with a stern look that did not appear promising. He propped his feet up against his desk and sighed loudly. He took a sip of cold coffee, grimaced and then proceeded to gulp the remaining liquid down. It seemed caffeine was more important than interrupting their session for a fresh cup, and that was worrying enough in itself.

'What are you going to do to ensure this kind of thing never happens again, Marianna?' He frowned at her and let his stare penetrate through her entire body, making each of her limbs weak and useless as he did so.

Her brain working frantically, she tried to come up with a reasonable answer.

How did you stop yourself orgasming during sleep? Chain your hands to the headboard, perhaps? Drug yourself into a stupor? As Mark's piercing gaze continued to sear her body, liquefying all moving parts to a consistency closely matching jello, she finally came up with an answer. If she was going to be punished, she figured she might as well be punished in style.

'How about I purchase a set of thick flannel pyjamas, Sir? Or, perhaps I should invest in one of those fluffy velour onesies with the zip up the middle? What colour do you think would suit me best? I think I'd look cute in pink...' She didn't get to finish her sentence.

'Marianna,' he barked, slamming his coffee cup down so hard in its saucer she was sure he had broken the thing, 'it seems you have managed to find yourself a slot in the naughty room after all. Be a good girl and go fetch the key from Cynthia.' He smiled darkly, allowing Marianna the opportunity to wish she had never been born. Why the hell couldn't she keep her smart mouth shut?

Mark's voice continued. 'Normally, when one of my employees earns themselves a place in my special room, I endeavour to make them crawl when I send them for the key. It lets them reflect on their punishment for a bit longer, which can only be a good thing. However,' he paused, and gave an exaggerated growl of displeasure, 'today I'll allow you the privilege of walking. It's far more fun to watch you waddle. Be quick.' He shooed her from the room with a quick wave of his fingers.

Whilst Marianna got precious little time for reflection on her short journey to Cynthia's office, even with her annoying shuffle-around-the-panties dance, she did note one thing. He, who laughs last, laughs longest.

CHAPTER EIGHT

A Friendly Warning

Mark had wandered over to his filing cabinet and was just pulling out some paperwork when the door to his office opened silently. Without turning around he said, 'Sophia, for heaven's sake what are you doing here?'

There was the sound of a clucking tongue behind him and a sharply indrawn breath. 'How do you do that, Matthews?' The voice sounded annoyed. 'How do you always know when I'm in the room, even though you have your back to me?'

Mark rolled his eyes to himself at her question. It was one that had been asked more than once. There were three easy tells to spot Sophia in a room. The first and most obvious was wafts of Amouage Reflections for women. She'd worn the same scent ever since he'd first met her and the smell of jasmine instantly made him think of her. He mused that smell was such an evocative sense. Nothing brought Sophia back to memory as quickly as Amouage could. If you discounted that tell, then the sharp click of marching heels was another good giveaway and if that failed, then his sixth sense usually cut in. Whenever she was around his skin seemed to prickle and it was probably remembering times long past. Of course, if he was in a busy room he could just watch all the male heads turn as they directed their gaze upon the intimidating flame-haired titan, who still looked as beautiful now as she had all those years ago. Hers was a presence that demanded attention and it was rare that she wasn't surrounded in droves by the opposite sex. The woman could work a room from top to bottom in a matter of minutes with her vibrant personality and mischievous tales. Once upon a time he'd hung off her arm and listened to every word.

Letting his eyes linger on Marianna, who was now waiting patiently on the floor with the key to his 'naughty room', Mark wondered what on earth the woman was doing here. She should be thoroughly engaged elsewhere at this moment in time, and more to the point, doing something she loved. It did not bode well.

'She's a beauty, isn't she?'

Mark tilted his head to the side, to indicate that he'd heard Sophia's question. It took a long moment before he could summon up the enthusiasm to face her. Finally he turned around and sauntered up to her, giving her a brief kiss on each cheek. 'She's actually a little more attractive when her ass is not sticking up in the air.'

'I can imagine.' There was a soft peal of laughter and his former Mistress curled a lock of her shoulder length red hair in her fingers before flicking it over her back.

His body wanted to react to the artful little flirt, but he refused to give it permission to do so. 'What are you doing here, Sophia?' Mark gave her a searching look. 'Shouldn't you be working Kyle over back at yours? Isabelle did drop him off, didn't she?' The woman couldn't have gotten herself lost, because he'd personally given her the directions to enter into her satnav.

Sophia's face became immediately serious and that was not a good sign. 'The girl was a no-show. That's why I came today. I thought I'd better let you know, and as I was in the area, thought it best to let you know in person.'

Mark swore. 'She should have been with you yesterday afternoon at the latest.'

'That's what I thought. I've tried contacting her via the number you gave me, but it goes repeatedly to voicemail. So I think you'd better check up on your girl. I've made enquiries and no one can get hold of her.' Sophia looked at him, chewed her lip for a second and then frowned.

'And what else have you learnt, dearest Sophia? You're wearing that look that says you know something I don't and you're wondering whether to tell me. I know your minions are even better at searching out little morsels of information than mine, so spill, darling dearest.'

She raised her eyes slowly back to his and smiled. 'Usually I make you work for things like that,' she replied softly.

He gave her a wry smile in response. 'Once upon a time you did, yes, but you and I know those days are long gone, Sophia. If you want to keep your secrets, that's fine with me.' He made to turn back around, now ready to dismiss her, but her hand on his shoulder stopped him.

'Wait,' she whispered. 'You need to be careful. Redcliff is not a man you mess with. If you take him up on his offer you are going to suffer, and more than that, you aren't going to make it back to your little empire the same man that you were before.'

'Well, I wish someone had given me that kind of friendly warning before I met you, darling dearest.' He smiled good naturedly at her pout and continued, 'And I'd already figured that out, so don't worry about me.' Again he made to turn around and again she stopped him. 'You do that one more time and I'm not going to tell you a few very important things that you need you know. Stand still, Goddamnit.'

Mark pursed his lips and battled the grin that wanted to escape. He managed to control it, but couldn't help a cheeky reply. 'Yes, ma'am.'

She rolled her eyes at him, but the look she was wearing was a friendly one. 'Listen up. I know you're aware Jennifer Redcliff is not the flesh and blood of her father. What you don't know is that Kyle Levison is Redcliff's son. Whilst the father and the daughter may not be related, the gruesome twosome share the same genes, and they're not of the Levis variety. Redcliff has not admitted to the parentage but he is well aware of the fact, which means he's keeping an eye on the boy. I'd hazard a guess that he's tapped Isabelle's phone and knew exactly what she was up to. That means Kyle is now probably somewhere very safe and...' Sophia gave him a little grimace.

'Isabelle isn't.' Mark finished the sentence succinctly. He did not want to think about the turn of events that had just spun out in his mind. He especially didn't want to think about what Kyle might do to Isabelle given half a chance.

'I know you have a soft spot for the lady, but I'd advise you to cut all ties and stay as far away from her and Albrecht as you can. More than that, I'd recommend you leave the country for a couple of months, although I know you won't.' Sophia bit her tongue, indicating that she wanted to say something else but thought better of it.

'Out with it,' Mark ordered.

Sophia pushed a handful of her thick red locks over her shoulder and her lips twisted. 'I have it on good authority that Miss Redcliff's mother did not just disappear, as the papers reported. Redcliff disposed of her. In a particularly nasty way.'

'You're talking rumours and conjecture, Sophia. Come and talk to me when you have something that holds a little more weight.' He shook his head, annoyed now.

'Let's just hope it isn't your coffin, Matthews. He's more than capable of such a deed and you won't realise what an idiot you've been until he ties the noose around your neck. I have a bad feeling about this. Redcliff is clearly unstable from the reports I've heard and if he can do what he did to his so-called "daughter", then the man is capable of anything. He now has you firmly on his radar and he will be happy with nothing less than blood.' The look she gave him was searing.

Mark shook his head. 'You can't think he wants to kill me. The old guy is not that crazy.' He gave her a mocking look.

'There are far worse things than death, Matthews, and you'd do well to remember the fact.'

CHAPTER NINE
The Carousel

There were cameras everywhere. Massive black lenses glinted in the bright light as they angled themselves for the best shot, and there was plenty to choose from. If the cameras pointed up towards the ceiling they found numerous lithe girls in flight, encircled by steel wire and spinning around a large central chandelier in an exotic aerobatic mobile. They had been draped in a few sheer pieces of organza and silk, which fluttered and flickered as the air currents caught them, while soft orange light had been directed down upon them, so the material appeared to be aflame. Some of the girls had been positioned swooping down with their arms positioned upwards behind them, others were in the throes of a backwards somersault or were reaching, arms outstretched as if to break through the roof canopy. That was not what caught Jenny's eye, however. Every single orifice the girls contained had been plugged with a perfectly crafted and delicately veined artificial penis. Some were buried deep inside the girls, others were so large that at least half of them remained on display outside their victims, held in placed by the numerous wires that ran around the artful merry-go-round. The oddest thing, to Jenny's mind, was that there was not a single movement from any of the participants as they spun around and around. Either they had been exceptionally well trained, were bound even tighter than she thought, or they had been drugged with some kind of relaxant. However Leyland had managed to achieve his airborne sculpture, it was one of the most beautiful things she had ever seen. The girls truly did resemble birds in flight, swooping down for prey or reaching for the unattainable - freedom, perhaps? Alas, she couldn't look at them for long if she didn't want to make herself ridiculously dizzy, so Jenny lowered her gaze and began to absorb the artwork that decorated the ground floor.

Vertical glass tanks, polished to a high shine, lined the circular ballroom and all appeared to feature a headless girl, for each body had been encased in a vat of pale white sand - just as Mark had recounted earlier at Albrecht. When she examined them more closely, every girl had a feature pressed tight to the glass that was highlighted with dazzling, halogen spotlights. There were delightfully pert ass cheeks which had just been soundly spanked, and these competed with beautiful pendulous breasts and enormous aureoles, the nipples of which stood proud and to attention, mostly due to the tight clamps that were imprisoning their poor buds. Hands could be seen pressed against the glass in gestures of supplication or surrender, there was a pair of knees that exhibited impressive carpet burns, the soles of a pair of feet and even a beautifully concave, flat stomach could be found if you searched around from cage to cage. All their mouths had been tightly gagged with a flesh-coloured ball gag that bore a wide, painted smile on its surface. It gave the girls a rather peculiar air of happiness that was accompanied by copious dribbling. These girls were also as still as statuettes, for while glittering diamond nets carpeted their glossy hair in various intricate styles, rope had been weaved between their tresses and pulled up to a panel resting just above the crown of their heads, thus making sure they could not move an inch out of place. Ouch.

Jenny shuddered, but the bondage she had just witnessed was by far the most innocuous. If you looked just a little bit higher the artwork got considerably more interesting, or distressing, in her case, because she had no idea what exactly would befall her in her little sojourn at the hands of the notorious Forbes.

Having been painted from head to toe in the eye-wateringly stingy black paint, Jenny had then found herself in hoof boots and mitts in fairly short order. The gold horseshoes that each sported felt like they were made of lead. Her headdress was also heavy and jingled every time she moved, not that she could actually single out the noise, because by the time the two paint boys had finished she sounded like she should have been pulling a sleigh. There were delicate little gold clamps on her nipples, complete with gold teardrop-shaped weights that sported three little bells each. More gold bells had been threaded through her impossibly long black tail, once again anchored firmly in her ass, and her glitzy gold bridle had them strewn in plentiful abandon everywhere. To top it off, she had a bright red blanket on her back strapped in place by a heavy black leather saddle around her midriff. All in all, she felt like she had gained twenty pounds, although she was certain she had probably lost at least three since her episode at Albrecht had begun.

Being led around by her bridle, a gentleman in a pinstriped suit walked alongside her at a brisk pace. With the crippling weight of all her adornments hanging heavily upon her, all she wanted to do was lie flat on the floor and plead for mercy, but that wasn't going to be an option and it probably wasn't worth the spanking or caning her backside would have to cash in order to test the theory. Struggling along on all fours, she tried to keep up with the gentleman who had been given her reins, but it was a nearly impossible task. Thankfully there were plenty of distractions to take her mind off her numerous and varied discomforts.

Her eyes were unable to resist looking upwards once more, although she wished they wouldn't. Square steel platforms were suspended from the ceilings and each square featured a single female occupant dressed in nothing more than a pair of killer heels. The colour scheme for the heels varied in shades across the spectrum, but each lady was of the extremely curvy variety and sported heavy breasts that swayed and bounced with each little movement she made, and there was lots of movement. The girls were anchored on three moving steel poles that rose from the centre of the platform. Two were fed directly between their legs and a third was a double-jointed, angled pole that reached inside their mouths. They appeared to spin round and round as the central pivot below them turned gently, little tendrils of their long hair fluttering behind them as the steel pole glinted in the harsh light. The platform also acted as a swing. Hung from two lines of thick steel cable it could be swung forward and back, and from left to right. If the poles were anchored with thick rubber plugs, and Jenny heartily suspected they were, the girls were in for quite a ride by the end of the evening as they wriggled their way all over the place. The lust that sparked from each girl's eyes was a sight to behold.

Although their faces had been made up to the max with bright red lipstick, eyeliner and plenty of blusher, it was the fake eyelashes that really drew attention. The absurdly long, feathery lashes accentuated each and every slow blink and gave them a sultry, almost wanton look of desire. Their skin gleamed with iridescent gold glitter and oil, and the thick red lips pouted prettily around their phalluses. Having examined them closely, Jenny decided she did not want to spend the evening up high. Especially as she was now witnessing how the next set of volunteers were strung up.

A selection of men and women hung centre stage from the middle of the vast hall, strung up with what appeared to be electrical cable. It had a neon purple tinge to it and crackled with each movement that the roped ensemble made. She guessed that the theatrics were just for effect, but wouldn't have put money on it. Crazy things were happening everywhere, and she was about to be nothing more than a tiny little part of the staged performance.

The cable was circled around the group, ensnaring legs, torso, arms, neck and everywhere in between. Although each participant was tied to the other, the only way they could lessen the strain of their cable was to tighten the strain of their fellows. Trying all sorts of tactics to lessen the grip of the rope she found them standing on their tiptoes, bracing themselves with their fingers, or curving their ridiculously supple bodies into impossible shapes. There was a lot of movement going on up there and the occasional worrying spark, which flew across the room with a startling burst of energy and speed. Her eyes could have goggled at the phenomena going on above her for some time, but her bridle was yanked abruptly, indicating she should come to a stop, and there in front of her was a contraption that was going to make her heart stop.

It was an old-fashioned carousel, of course, but not just any carousel. All the usual features were there, there was an abundance of gold leaf paintwork and beautifully scalloped edges framed the ponies within. Bouquets of flowers had been intricately printed upon its surround with an array of oil paints, and each section sported a detailed rendition of a scene from around the world. There was the Taj Mahal, the Eiffel Tower, gondolas over the Grand Canal, the Red Square and many more which were continued around the reverse. Flashing white lightbulbs decorated both the exterior and interior of the fairground ride and a swathe of red velour fabric had been pinned around the central pillar supporting the canopy, giving it an almost regal air. Everywhere Jenny looked there was lots of gold paint, sparkling and glinting fiercely as it caught the light. None of the above would have stopped Jenny's heart - it was the poles inside the contraption that were causing palpitations.

A normal carousel would have featured lots of brightly coloured, often gaudy animals, which would ride up and down upon a single pole. The carousel in front of Jenny featured several alterations that were going to make her life very interesting, thrilling, and somewhat hair-raising for whatever the duration of her ride would be. Unable to take her eyes off the spinning merry-go-round, watching as the other human horses were being 'fitted' upon the various poles that decorated the ride, Jenny listened with only half an ear to what was being said behind her. Her jaw was wide open and her head was whirling so fast it made the ride appear slow in comparison.

'Did you know the earliest carousels were thought to have been created by the Arabians?' This was from the elegantly attired gentleman holding her reins; she recognised his lilting Irish brogue.

'Bet they'd roll over in their graves if they saw this beauty here.' The second voice was a little rough around the edges, but Jenny couldn't accurately pinpoint its origins. He was English, probably from around the South East, but where exactly she could not guess.

'Probably, but maybe not. Did you know the original rides were made for adults? In France the wooden horses would be turned by a series of servants and some used real horsepower to propel the ride. Although many different animals have been used to decorate the ride throughout the ages, the horse is still the most popular, and we'll not be straying from that tradition today.'

There was a snicker of laughter from the other gentleman. 'That much is obvious, Sir. How will you make sure they keep moving, though?'

A smart slap to Jenny's buttocks brought her swiftly back to the here and now. 'There's a reason their delightful rumps have been left pink and paint-free, Connor. It makes them an easy target for a whip, paddle, or a frantically twitching palm. The more spanks these horses receive, the redder those backsides will become and the easier it will be to aim at them. I don't think they'll be slacking in their exercise pursuits this evening,' another firm smack caused Jenny to yelp, 'unless I am much mistaken.'

'You rarely are, Sir,' said Connor deferentially. 'Did you want me to go fit her in now, or should I wait for the last one to finish up?'

'Better get her fixed in now; we're on a schedule here. If things aren't ready to go in fifteen minutes his highness will have a fit, and we wouldn't want that, would we?'

'No Siree,' said Connor, and caught the gold reins neatly as they were thrown at him. With a sharp tug he had Jenny scrambling forward, and even though it was with the utmost reluctance that she set foot on the ride, she was also aware she didn't have a choice in the matter. Even worse than that, disobedience might result in a forfeit a damn site worse than the one the carousel had in store for her.

'Just wait there while I get your pole, Petal. I'll have you screwed in before you can blink.'

Gee thanks, thought Jenny, who was all for a good screw, but less inclined to be attached and imprisoned upon a steel pole. Paying no further attention to Connor, who'd shot off behind her somewhere, she began to look around her ride with a good degree of trepidation.

The gentleman in the pinstriped suit turned his attention back to her and smiled. 'You're one of the lucky ones this evening, Petal, if that's the appropriate word. There are four horses that will pull the carousel along and four horses that will "ride" it, so to speak. You get to ride, and I should think that's the more preferable option, although I may be wrong.' With a swift slap to her buttocks, and an amused spurt of laughter at her shocked expression, he turned his back on her and walked away, shaking his head.

Jenny barely noticed. Her attention was already elsewhere. There were two things giving her grave misgivings. One was a series of large black dildos protruding vertically from the floor that wobbled up and down as the carousel span. As her backside was already plugged, it was clear which hole it would be aimed at, and it was both exciting and terrifying. People were going to be lining up to take pictures of her, naked and being impaled on a thick black cock. Problem number two was that it wasn't going to be the only hole under fire. Above her head, resting beneath the beautiful landscaped frescoes that decorated the upper rim, there was a row of bright orange carrots dangling from little green stems. There was no question that these were intended for your mouth. Each carrot had a carefully rounded tip and tapered design, but the top of the vegetable sported an impressive girth which would involve quite a workout if they intended for her to suck the whole thing. Interestingly there were also indentations in each carrot, for teeth presumably, and she had to wonder why they were there. All would become clear in good time, she guessed. At the moment they were too high up for the ponies to reach, but she guessed they would be lowered as the 'guests' arrived. Looking around for Connor, and finding him nowhere in sight, she sighed.

This was an evening she should probably be dreading, and whilst a thread of fear ran through her body, it was anticipation that was the main emotion running amok inside her. Whatever happened, she guessed her body was going to enjoy itself, and she'd come to the conclusion that her mind wasn't offering up a whole load of objections these days. Her bottom loved being spanked, her skin craved the lightest of touches and all of her greedy little holes enjoyed being filled on a regular basis. Since starting at Albrecht her sexual appetite had shot off the scale. They had turned her, oh-so-very-easily, into a wanton little pleasure slave that lapped up all of their attentions and begged for more. Did she still want to leave? Yes. Could she give up the incredible sex? Hopefully, she wouldn't have to. Life with Mark Matthews would be just as kinky and depraved as life at Albrecht, unless she was much mistaken.

Deciding not to get lost inside that particular daydream again, she examined the horses that had already been fitted onto their fairground poles. It was clear that the human horses would be riding in vertical manner, in contrast to their plastic/wooden counterparts who always had four hooves pointed towards the floor, and they would not be spun around in circles by a motorised machine. The ponies that had already been installed were trudging along in their hoof boots and their legs were being worked hard, judging by the muscles twitching and rolling as they moved forward. She was glad she'd snagged a riding position. Her energy levels were already dwindling and the afternoon had barely begun.

Looking at the 'riders' in more detail, she saw that their fore-hooves had been clipped into stirrups that hung from the top of the carousel, rendering their hands completely useless. It was overkill, because covered in the thick leather mitts that were colour-matched almost perfectly to their body paint, they weren't going to pose much of a threat. Bright orange, cerise pink, aquamarine blue and brilliant purple were only some of the colours on display and all had been decorated in a similar fashion to Jenny, with beautifully detailed brushwork around their saddles, backsides and breasts. The frames the paint had made around the girls' major assets were screaming 'spank me' as loudly as they could, and she thought they all looked pretty delicious. She could only hope hers looked as good, and then cursed herself for the ridiculous vanity. What was she thinking?

Feeling the dressing upon her back itch under her saddle, she moved a hand up to try and reach under the blanket and give it a scratch. No such luck. Her hoof mitt bumped against the thick leather and she wanted to bang her head against the floor. Why was everything so difficult these days? Even the simplest movements were more often than not denied her.

'Sorry to keep you waiting, love. Got your pole, got your gag, and a pot of something wet and squishy for you and the intruder over there.' Connor grinned and angled his head towards the large black cock. 'You should be feeling mighty pleased with yourself, you know. You ponies get the best gig. Some girls get tied up, some get imprisoned, but few get the kind of ride you're about to have.' He winked at her. 'You guys get the works. You get to have all your holes plugged, some by moving parts and you get to be spanked, touched-up and teased. There isn't a woman in this entire place who wouldn't swap her position to be in yours right now, unless I'm much mistaken.' There was another leering grin. 'Right, guess we'd better get you strapped in and properly positioned then.'

And from then on in it was all business. Connor was quick and very efficient. Threading her chained hands and feet through the long gold post, he snapped it into the relevant slots with ease. Jenny was positioned midway up the pole by use of the stirrups up above her, which were clipped on to her hoof mitts and a set of lower hanging stirrups were fastened under the steep heel of her boots, before being similarly locked into place. This forced her into a squatting position, if she wanted to balance with any semblance of decorum. Flatting her stomach across the pole and flipping her hooves out behind her was another option, but even less comfortable than the first. Tipping her head over her neck and spying the large black cock resting beneath her, Jenny wasn't sure if she wanted to start the fun and games now, or wait until later.

Connor must have read her mind. 'Go ahead and try it, Petal. See if it's a good fit for you.' The look he wore was suspiciously mischievous and did not bode well, but Jenny was intrigued enough to test the theory. Squatting as far as her four stirrups would allow, it was to find that the most she could achieve was a gentle graze of the large cock's surface. No matter how she squirmed and tried to contort her body the dildo was too far down for her to reach. After a few more pitiful attempts she ruefully gave up and directed a sour gaze towards Connor, who was unashamedly laughing at what must have been a very entertaining couple of minutes.

Pushing a stray tendril of sweaty blond hair out of his eyes and trying, unsuccessfully, to put a lid on his amusement, he waved a large plastic pot in front of her face. 'Orders are to lube you up before the fun begins. We want you bouncing up and down and sliding around nicely, don't we?'

Jenny was inclined to agree with him, although she never would have admitted it. Feeling her face flush with heat she wobbled around on her stirrups and waited for the touch of his fingers. Would they be rough, gentle or just frustratingly hurried? She could cope with either of the former, but she longed for him to take his time with her. Two orgasms today and counting, yet already she hungered for her third. As his fingers reached between her legs they caressed her gently and slid between the soft folds of her labia, depositing something slippery and wet in their wake. She hissed quietly as they were withdrawn.

'You'll get plenty of touchy-feely later, which is why the lube is going everywhere, but you're not going to be enjoying yourself until the punters get here, Petal, so settle down and hold still.' A mewl of disappointment greeted that statement, but she did as asked and held herself as still as she was able. As his fingers reached inside her pussy, liberally smearing the cold liquid around, she tried to concentrate on anything bar his very competent hands. She needed to think about something else, and quickly.

Looking downwards, sure that was as good a place as any to start, she noted that the floor of the carousel was a metal grille sprayed gold, in keeping with the most prominent colour theme of the ride. As her eyes rose she examined the glittering pole she was attached to, admiring the little coils which made it appear rope-like, swirling forever upwards as the ride spun them around and around in circles. Staring at it quite hard for a few seconds made her stupidly dizzy, so she tried to focus on the other horses again, but it was difficult when someone had three fingers inside you and was pumping them up and down.

Knowing there was no point in pleading for an orgasm, Jenny tried to keep her mind busy on her surroundings. The knowledge might come in useful later, and in this peculiar world it was always best to pay attention to every little detail. So focus, Jennifer, she reprimanded herself, as the fingers continued on their quest for higher plains. The orange horse in front of her captured her attention for a moment, and her eyes zeroed-in initially on her pale pink buttocks, jiggling gently as her feet propelled the carousel around, and it was clear that the effort required was not a small one. When Jenny managed to catch a glimpse of her face it was to see little globules of sweat, running freely from the woman's forehead, and she shook her head from side to side on a regular basis to clear them. With her hands immobilised above her, in a similar fashion to Jenny's, there was little else she could do. Listening to the heavy thud of her horseshoes, which were fed between a square hole that went beneath the metal grille, the orange tail swam from side to side and swished over her rosy buttocks. Jenny wondered if hers would look so good, swinging around as she was. Her ass cheeks immediately clamped around her plug and she was punished for her troubles with a sharp slap.

'Stay still, Petal. Nearly done.'

Connor's fingers were applying more lubricant around the outside edge of her butt-plug, and she just managed to hold in a violent squirm. Blinking slowly and trying to redirect her thoughts back to her friend in front, Jenny examined the orange wig and headdress. Most of her additional accoutrements were exactly the same as Jenny's, just a vivid hue of orange in colour. The sound of bells, from every direction, indicated that all the horses had been clamped and decorated in a similar fashion.

Concentration began to prove difficult. The orange tresses and tail in front of her wavered in and out of focus as Connor's fingers found her clit. The touch was so frustratingly light it could have been nothing more than a flutter of silk across her sensitised flesh, and as quickly as they had appeared, they swiftly disappeared. She wanted to scream, but the collar around her neck was enough to ensure she remained mute.

'Now for your gag. I suspect you've gotten used to these beasties, being a pony-girl, but I don't think you'll have seen one like this yet.' He licked his lips almost reverently as he came to stand in front of her and after a brief rifle through the pocket of his sweater, there was a glint of light upon brushed steel. He brought it up to her face, so she could examine it more closely, but all she could see was lines of metal. How bizarre! Blinking in incomprehension, she was rewarded with a dark look. By using his fingers in a pincer motion he worked the ratchet up and down. It didn't take long before realisation dawned Not only was she going to be gagged, but also her mouth was going to be permanently prized open for the duration. It looked like she would be sucking the plastic carrot above her, whether she wanted to or not. To be fair, she wasn't sure what she wanted any more. Everything was moving too fast, nothing made sense and the hormones crashing through her body had her whimpering in need.

'I'm just going to slide the metal bars in between your lips, Petal. They're going to feel a bit cold, but in a few minutes there'll be plenty of people around to warm you and various parts of your body up.'

True to his word, the thin tubes of metal slotted past her lips and she found herself opening up automatically to accept them. The metal then sank behind her teeth and her jaw was being levered wide upon, spreading her lips so wide apart the yawning cavern of her mouth was on prominent display. Feeling warm fluid between her legs, she was immediately surprised at how aroused being gagged made her.

As if he could read her mind, Connor's hand went back between her legs and there was another dirty laugh. 'You're going to fit in perfectly around these parts,' he said, as his fingers tickled her clit with another of his infuriatingly light touches. Connecting two leather straps with karabiners to clips at the top of the carousel and drawing them down to attach them to metal eyelets angled around the jaw of Jenny's bridle, the new position forced her to look up towards the dangling carrot. The result was that she could only face forward now, because there wasn't enough leeway on the tight leather straps to turn her head.

'You're all set,' was accompanied by an impressive crack upon her backside. It made her jump, which sent her swinging wildly backwards, but he was ready for her and had already sidestepped out of the way. 'Show starts in five minutes. Hang in there, Petal.' Laughing so hard he nearly choked, the man jumped off the moving carousel with an impressive leap and hit the floor running. He didn't look back. Neither did Jenny; for one, she was physically unable to, and for another, the room was somewhat frighteningly being plunged into darkness.

'Five minutes and counting,' rang out, the sound issued over a loudspeaker by a very elegant female voice. The sudden announcement induced a fit of animated commands, running and hand waving. Last minute knots were tied, costumes were carefully adjusted and several of the bondage models were prepped with last minute touches for their curtain call. This continued until the two minute warning came up and then there was a flurry of feet, sprinting in all directions, but each pair was leaving and the general hush that spread across the room was disconcerting.

As the carousel turned slowly, Jenny felt the heat of a large spotlight upon her back and with her head held fast, she was forced to watch the continuing flicker of the lightbulbs around the top of the ride as they blinked their way around in circles. Swinging lightly, her tail sliding softly around the curves of her backside, she could only wonder at what was going to happen next. Her mouth was filling with annoying saliva, her hands and feet felt cramped in their tight leather mitts, her ass prickled from its earlier spankings and her clit was on fire. All she craved now was sensation and pleasure, and as the one minute warning mark was issued she wondered if she would be lucky enough to experience them both. She could hardly cross her fingers in hope, but the thought was there.

Counting down in her head, silently from sixty, she hit zero, only to find that nothing had changed. She was probably a little on the fast side, she reassured herself, feeling nervous as hell. Five long seconds went by before anything noticeable happened, but when it did, it all happened at once.

CHAPTER TEN

Spinning

It had become so quiet in the room that Jenny could almost have heard the splatter of her saliva as it dropped to the floor. Time had frozen into slow motion and even the carousel had appeared to stop spinning and merely made a slow, grand sweep of its garish contoured edges. The sudden darkness of the room had blinded her, and when added to the glare of the flashing lights above it made her feel vulnerable. Not knowing what was about to happen was always the killer, and the first flutters of panic began to take flight. Snakes coiled in her stomach, heavy and writhing, while her skin erupted in goose-bumps, although she was not cold. The tension in the room was a living, breathing entity and there wouldn't have been a knife big enough to cut it. Her own laboured breaths and those of the work horses seemed to merge into one until it was all she could hear. It took on a musicality all of its own and she swung on her stirrups to the invisible beat. Her fingers twitched inside her mitts as her body ached for the party to begin. Trying desperately to close her legs together, anything to get a little friction upon her clit, she found herself rocking wildly in and out of the shadows. Every asset she possessed was on display, and not only that, it had a bloody spotlight directed upon it, as if to scream 'Look at me!'

This could only end badly, right? She didn't even want to think about the tank. Gallons of water, a thin covering of latex and a body immobilised from head to toe did not lessened her heart palpitations. 'Get the party started before I go crazy!' she pleaded inside her head, listening to her heartbeat get louder and louder until it threatened to burst right though her chest. Her tongue waggled ineffectually in her mouth, her throat emitted little whimpers of anxiety and her nipples had hardened into tight little pebbles that were almost begging to be pulled. Her mind begged, 'Now, now, now, please now!'

Thankfully someone must have heard her for the double entrance doors swung open at exactly the same time and the room was swathed in a dim, dirty grey light. A gust of air whistled around the vast walls and it was yet another torment that all the waiting participants had to bear. The prickling upon her skin became more pronounced and she felt her pussy clench tightly in expectation. It was clear that the onlookers were as eager to begin the festivities as she, for they wasted no time in traversing the great hall in their droves, and there were literally hundreds of them. After the previous silence the stampede of elegantly shod feet sounded like thunder in her ears.

The men outnumbered the women three to one, but the women made up for their minority presence with some of the most amazing costumes Jenny had ever seen. Red PVC outfits, thigh high boots, elegant evening gowns, sparkling diamonds, black lace, crimson lipstick and so much more flittered across her vision. They all looked utterly beautiful. There was not a hair out of place on a single one. These women were from money, immaculately groomed, tanned courtesy of their very own island retreat and dripping with confidence. The men were a little more uniform in their appearance, keeping to suits, or at the very least slacks and a dress shirt. All came armed with implements of ass destruction and that just made the proceedings ten times more exciting.

Paddles, crops, whips, hairbrushes, wooden spoons and floggers erupted from designer leather handbags and sequinned purses. Some of the women even had special slots on their clothing or boots in which to install their implements of torture. The men simply held theirs loosely in their hands as they awaited their turn to use them, more than a few tapping their tools against their palms as a warning to all around. For Jenny it served as nothing more than delicious anticipation.

The slow motion blur of earlier finished with a definitive snap and now everything sped up with frightening clarity. Using her peripheral vision to its fullest extent, she watched as the visitors almost ran towards the moving fairground ride, bringing with them their big smiles and animated faces. It was an exaggeration inside her head, but she couldn't stop the feeling of being crowded and hemmed in as the room began to fill. One moment the little glass bubble she was in was almost empty, and in the next it was bursting at the seams. The models were being descended upon from every angle as the tide of people swamped over each corner of the room. Hands snaked around legs, arms, breasts and torsos. Fingertips scraped gentle paths of fire, soft words were whispered in ears, and strands of hair were coiled tightly and pulled. Lipstick was smeared, mouths were opened, cheeks were cupped, faces were caressed and bodies were tasted. The room was being devoured with lips, tongues and teeth, and Jenny inhaled the potent scent of seduction in shaky little gulps as she waited for the onslaught to reach her. When it did, the room spun wildly out of control and for a moment it almost felt as if the earth had not only spun off its axis, but plummeted a million feet to a neighbouring galaxy below.

A storm of people stampeded the carousel and they hopped onto its moving surrounds, like wasps swarming around a pot of strawberry jam. The other ponies disappeared from her sight, surrounded by eager onlookers who were anxious to discover each little detail of their uniforms, and she was no exception. Hands reached and covered every spare inch of flesh they could find. They slithered and glided around the inky black planes of her body, traced patterns around the raised, faceted gems and lingered over the bright gold scrollwork that appeared almost three dimensional, but was nothing more than an optical illusion. They dipped into all the secret, hidden, and velvety wet contours that her form had to offer, and they went back for more, greedily.

Her tail was yanked, bridle pulled, and enterprising hands even managed to climb up the pole so they could examine the thin metal lines of her gag, and the silky lining within. The delicate waves of her wig were caressed, her headdress was shaken, and the tiny little bells that decorated her body were being spun around in circles as fingers reached for the pretty little gold baubles, ascertaining their purpose.

All this happened within the space of five seconds. She was granted just five tiny seconds of the softly softly approach as the crowd examined their prey. Then, they *really* got to work.

Her breasts were weighted and her nipples pulled, yanked and flicked with the edge of a fingernail or worse. Her tail was pumped in and out, while inquisitive fingers explored the concave, delicate flesh of her underarms and stomach, just beneath her blanket. Palms stroked up and around her neck and faces were pressed so close to her body they appeared to be actually inhaling her scent, their lips opening and closing in a kind of sensual daze. Fingers plundered her pussy, and when they had tested its warmth there was a queue of others waiting to take their place, with the occasional end of a wooden spoon, or other equally hard implement being thrust inside her for good measure. Her eyebrows were stroked, the cerulean blue of her eyes admired, and the curve of her buttocks slapped as they commented on her 'colour' and 'resilience'.

The seams of her leather hoof boots were traced, the stirrups examined, and her saddle was patted in an almost affectionate manner. The bright orange carrot above her and the big black dildo beneath were remarked upon, and there were giggles and snorts in response. There were nips, pinches and bites all over her, and she couldn't have said where one ended and another began. They were everywhere. Like seething, tiny ants homing in on their next meal, they dominated her entire being. Dangling upon her glittering perch with her feet so far off the floor they could have been on Jupiter, her mind swung from side to side and threatened to break free of its casing. Were these people nuts? She was flung back and forth, kissed, tongued and fondled. Even through the awkward confines of the gag they managed to find her lips, and her pussy was much easier prey, which they worshipped freely. Some took a little more time than their fair share and were briskly reprimanded, while others came in for only a fleeting touch, as if afraid she might explode.

Their fears weren't entirely unfounded; Jenny was beginning to wonder if she might do exactly that. The lights flashed above her, bright circles of incandescent colour, and she began to lose herself in the moment. Her anxiety melted in what felt like thirty-degree heat, and with it, her body began to liquefy.

Tight coils of heat began to expand inside her and radiated outwards with a fiery intensity. The tongues became stronger, rougher, and more determined. The fingers pulled and plucked, turning her body into a unique instrument of pleasure that could be played by many pairs of hands. Slaps and pinches abounded, as well as the sucking sounds of kisses, groans, moans and growls. If any of the noises were hers they weren't obvious to her. She felt like she was humming from the tips of her toes up to the fine ebony hairs on the top of her head.

It was a crushing crescendo of hands and lips that forced her to erupt in such a painfully short period of time, but erupt she did and in spectacular fashion. She took one of her onlookers out as her perch flew madly in all directions, and watched his body out of an almost disjointed mind as it fell off the moving steel floor and tumbled to the floor below. Thankfully he hadn't hurt himself and got right back up again, mounting the carousel with a wry little grin. She suspected he'd be a little more careful this time around, but then again... maybe not. He was already fighting his way back to Jenny's side, knocking others out of the way as he tried to forge a path through the writhing bodies.

Watching all of this from the corner of her eye, she couldn't be entirely sure if she was dreaming or not. The room flew about her head in bizarre, multi-hued fractals that all merged faultlessly into one another before creating another pattern, even prettier than the first. Her grip on reality was shortly about to fade, and at this particular moment in time it wasn't entirely a bad thing. Swinging to and fro as the intense paroxysms of her orgasm tried to subside, she welcomed the sliding hands as they soothed her path back into the land of the living. Gurgling cooing sounds of pleasure, she wondered if they'd be able to bring her back to orgasm shortly, exactly like that, if she begged nicely enough.

She never got to find out. The lights above snapped on in a blazing fury, illuminating everyone and everything in painful, harsh lines that had her eyes smarting with a rapid frenzy of blinking.

'Ladies and Gentlemen,' intoned the well-defined female voice of the loud speaker, 'please put your hands together and give a warm welcome to your host, Leyland Forbes.' Just like that the animalistic crowd, who had been scratching and biting only moments before, settled down like meek little lambs. They all stood up straight, gave one another a little breathing space and clapped their hands delicately together in a polite fashion. Their heads turned discretely from side to side, and there were murmured whispers as all eyes searched the vast hall for a glimpse of Forbes.

Jenny's field of vision was severely limited with her head pushed up high, but she was lucky enough to be one of the first few that spotted 'his highness', as he had been called on more than one occasion. It wasn't a bad description. He had a regal manner about him with his upright carriage and the straight set of his shoulders. His dark black hair had been neatly slicked close to his head and he sported sleek, black leather gloves upon his hands. His grey suit looked ridiculously expensive, and the tie he wore was clearly Charmeuse silk. A crisp blue shirt and a gold watch finished the ensemble. He was strangely attractive, in a gloriously dark way. Jenny got the impression that here was a man she should run from screaming, and yet as per usual, her body had other ideas. He didn't measure up against Mark, for that would be like trying to compare a Greek God with a mortal, but there was a gleam in his eyes that called to her. It should have worried her, but she had far more important things to worry about at this moment in time.

The reason she was one of the first to spot him was that everyone else had assumed he would walk in through the same door that they had. As the carousel spun towards the rear of the room a hidden portion of the white wall appeared to move. Leyland Forbes had decided on a much more discreet entrance and was striding through a single door buried in the opposite direction of the main doors and still partially shrouded in darkness, with the aid of a couple of giant Chinese windmill palm trees. When the light found him it still took several seconds before his audience managed to turn around and pinpoint his whereabouts. Silence had returned to the room as they eagerly awaited their benefactor and nothing more than a muted hum could be heard across the sea of rabidly aroused faces. Pupils were large and black, lips wet and shiny, chests heaving with excitement, and clothes decidedly ruffled. As soon as a couple of heads turned, however, the Mexican wave effect began, and it wasn't long before Mr Forbes was being serenaded by a thunderous round of clapping hands.

The man smiled serenely at the attention as he walked further into the room, inclined his head politely, and used his hands in a downward sweeping motion in order to dispel the noise. It took a few moments, but it wasn't very long before Mr Forbes had the rapt attention of the room upon him. Clearing his throat, he made to deliver a speech.

'Ladies and gentlemen, can I offer my thanks to all of you busy people who have made the time to attend this little soiree of mine this evening.' Another round of applause began, but he nipped it in the bud by clearing his throat loudly once again and placing his palms outward. 'Thank you kindly, but we're on a schedule here so I had better be brief. There are not many rules to tonight's proceedings. All of the models you see artfully strung up and displayed are for your pleasure. They are to be admired, touched, teased and tormented as you see fit. Their pleasure is not a prerequisite for your enjoyment. You may grant or withhold their release - whichever amuses you more. All I ask is that you do not mark them permanently in any way, and if you see my photographers in passing, allow them enough space to take pictures. For those that have admired my erotic artwork in the past, there will be a grand unveiling of some of my more recent works in the gallery later, with some canapés and champagne for light refreshment. Now, are there any questions before I let the games commence?' He let his head sweep slowly from one corner of the room to the other and his confident, arrogant gaze missed no one in his brief assessment. There was a small, almost sly smile, and his eyes took on a devilish twinkle. 'I see you are as eager as I am to get your fingers dirty. Well then, don't let me hold you back, go forth and amuse yourselves.'

He strode off, slicing a path down the middle of the room where the waters parted like the Red Sea to allow him access. The power he carried in the room was absolute. No one was going to risk their place by offending him on a night of debauchery such as this. There probably wasn't another party like it on earth, although Jenny was swiftly coming to realise that more people enjoyed the 'kink' scene than she had previously given credence for. There must have been at least five hundred bodies in the room, and probably several more. Movement then caught the corner of her eye and she turned to examine a string of people coming through the back exit.

Hot on Leyland's heels, rubber soles squeaked as the photographers filed past the potted palms, carrying large black nylon bags and an array of cameras, lenses, flashes and strobes. They had obviously been prepped for the scenes ahead, because they had an agenda and did not stop until they had reached the airborne mobile of flapping organza and stretched limbs. They then began snapping continuously, greedily soaking up every single detail with a symphony of differing clicks and flashes. This captured the attention of the audience for a few seconds, who seemed transfixed on the flickering lights. Whereas before the angled orange spotlights had made them seem as if they were on fire, the additional flash of the cameras made them appear to sparkle and glisten, as if they were divine beings not of this earth. The effect was quite startling, and when reflected upon the many mirrors around the room it created a current of movement that seemed to ripple downwards and outwards towards the guests.

Jenny eyed the glittering mass of bodies as best she was able and then stared at the glossy carrot above her head. She wanted that carrot. Being suspended in mid-air was all very well when there were fifty hands upon you seeking to pleasure you in every way possible, but just hanging there, watching and aching for another orgasm when the last one had barely left your body was almost impossible to imagine. She had come such a long way in a week and she could only wonder where the journey would end. Another long line of drool dripped down her cheek, leaving a wet, sticky trail that glistened upon her ebony body and she felt the stainless steel collar weigh heavy around her neck.

Snap, snap, flick, flash. Touch me, her body pleaded. *Click, click, flash.* The carousel continued to turn, the ponies in front and behind trudging along in their heavy boots, straining uncomfortably as they performed their duty. She should be grateful she had a moment's respite, but she ached for the touch of a hand, the sting of a paddle, anything that would provide stimulation and contact on her tingling flesh. As if her prayers had been heard, the anonymous female voice began again.

'Ladies and gentlemen, please remove yourselves behind the white lines of the moving exhibits. This is for your safety. Thank you in advance for your co-operation.'

Her beautiful voice was loud enough to be heard by all the milling participants and they obediently formed a ring around the carousel, standing just behind the white line that had been drawn upon the floor. Jenny guessed things were shortly about to get interesting, and as it happened, she wasn't wrong, but she had most certainly underestimated the word 'interesting'.

CHAPTER ELEVEN
The Carrot

Although nothing immediately appeared to change, the atmosphere around the carousel heated up considerably. The men had managed to attain a certain gleam in their eyes and the ladies pursed their lips prettily and searched through their handbags. The floggers, crops and wooden hairbrushes of earlier began to appear fisted in several palms and everyone looked eager to use them. There were a few who were already testing the strength of their spanking hand out, displacing the air in front of them with violent swishes and swashes.

If this was meant to frighten Jenny, it fell far short of its mark. She couldn't wait for the real antics to begin. Her body had now progressed to an animated knot of nervous energy and the sound spanking she was about to receive was going to release it. This was going to be a purging, cathartic experience, and she needed it, to get through whatever might lie ahead for her after this evening had ended. For now, she wanted to live in the moment, swing from the chandeliers and forget. She did not want to think, but she needed to feel. Every last sensation would be relished and they were going to make her fly. For tonight, she was going to hold on for dear life and see where the rabbit hole led. If she wasn't much mistaken, it burrowed far deeper than she had originally thought.

A whirr of noise above caught her attention, but she could not turn her head to examine it further. It was clear that some sort of machinery was in motion. As the carousel was powered by foot, she guessed that it wasn't going to be used to turn the ride. When the bright orange triangle of the carrot began to lower itself towards her mouth and the rounded tip of a dildo began to nudge for entrance between the folds of her sex, she knew she was in trouble.

Watching absently as the pony in front of her tried to dodge her intruder, she mentally constructed the game inside her head. The dildos were balanced on long steel poles and were a glossy black plastic with delicate veined ridges upon them. They were thick, impossibly strong and well lubricated. Avoidance for any length of time was going to be difficult, but she managed to deflect its first invasion attempt with her left buttock. The big black cock didn't take it personally, diving down towards the floor before quickly gearing up for another visit. Meanwhile, the smooth tip of the orange carrot lowered itself to her waiting mouth, and there was no avoiding that. With her lips peeled open wide by the shiny steel lines of the gag, it glided in easily. It was cold, marble-like in texture, and only dipped a couple of centimetres inside her jaw before it began to disappear upwards again. The machine was going to wear them down gradually, unless she was much mistaken.

Batting her eyelashes a few times, as if trying to figure out whether the fairy-tale bubble she was in was going to pop if she moved, she felt the dildo angled between her legs come up for round two. The attempt at penetration was once again avoided, but it took a good degree of wiggling and her black tail swished back and forth, tickling her buttocks. A few sniggers from the gathered crowd told Jenny that this was exactly the show they were hoping for and she realised that if she kept this behaviour up she'd be giving these people the performance of the century. The trouble was, she found it impossible to stop herself. It was instinctive. As the dildo and carrot came at her a third time her mouth accepted the swooping orange phallus, whilst her sex shied away from the impossibly big black boy beneath her. Perhaps it knew something she didn't... in any case, Jenny wasn't silly enough to realise she was fighting a losing battle, but fight it she would until she was forced to surrender. When the first smack of a wooden hairbrush hit her firmly on her left thigh she knew that time would not be long in coming.

Smarting painfully with a bite that surprised her, she knew that if her skin hadn't been painted black there would be a blossoming red mark at the impact point. As soon as the heat of the smack had faded away she instantly craved another. The participants were only just getting into the flow of things, though, and aiming objects at moving bodies took a little practice at first. The tip of a riding crop managed a good lick at one of her clamped nipples and she yelped in protest as the rouged tip shot forth like a freshly fired bullet.

On the next spin of the merry-go-round the flat of a paddle caught her firmly across the butt cheeks. She slammed into her twirling pole with the impact of the strike and clenched her ass as tightly as she was able, to lessen the spiralling sting. Heat pooled between her legs, hot and sticky, and she had an urge to close them tightly to prevent any leakage. This was not possible, of course, and as the dildo bounced up yet again the slick path leading towards the apex of her thighs allowed its tip a gentle dip within her sex. She gurgled through her gag and witnessed the laughing faces, out of the corner of her eye, as they pointed at her and unleashed their comments.

'Can't wait to see them all impaled.'

'I want to see all those white bits turn a vivid red.'

'Do we get to fuck them afterwards?'

'Gonna pull that tail, hard.'

'Do you think they'll be able to take all of those carrots?'

'Do you think they'll be able to take all of those black cocks?'

All these comments and more flitted upon the air as she turned around in ever increasing circles. They ranged from a seductive French purr to a harsh and grating European accent that she couldn't place, but for the most part the comments were spoken in English. But of course they would be. They were only uttered to torment her and her equine friends.

Tuning out most of the snide remarks, mainly because it was becoming far too difficult to dodge the oversized monster beneath her, Jenny felt herself blush. No one would be able to see it, which was one blessing of the black paint job, but her face felt hot and uncomfortable. Already she could see herself with the carrot lodged deep inside her throat and with her pussy firmly squashed over the big dildo. The two of them together would pin her in place quite neatly, making sure she could not move a muscle. Then the spanking fiends would have a grand time, for each of their swats would easily reach its mark. She shuddered at the thought.

The dildo pushed upwards again, sliding and skidding across the 'V' of her upper thighs far too easily and she needed all of her attention to escape it. Using her legs to propel her body upwards she just managed to avoid full penetration, but over half of its length had now found its way inside her. It gave her a rather tingly 'full' feeling, and she let out a gasp of pleasure. It wasn't going to last, though. She knew it was only a matter of time before her thighs tired and she found the whole of her bodyweight impaled upon the thick black beast. She was going to evade that moment for as long as possible, because she had a suspicious feeling it was going to hurt, and far more than the slaps and spanks she was currently receiving. That wasn't to say the heat building upon her backside and outer thighs didn't hurt, because when the paddles, spoons and floggers found their mark, they packed quite a punch. With each new round of paddling she felt the resulting smarting sting increase, and knew that the two poor globes of her ass were already burning bright red, beautifully encased in their heart-shaped frame. Her hands itched to grab the pole and scramble up its golden length until her head hit the roof, but her hoof mitts were clipped firmly in place and her movement was severely limited. Another whack slammed into her ass and she felt the indentations of her pole compress into the soft flesh of her stomach. On the next sweep the dildo shot up another inch in its quest to find her cervix.

By this time the carrot had managed to make some impressive progress. She did not have any wiggle room with which to escape the happily bobbing gag above her, and each time it descended towards her mouth it went a fraction deeper. Initially the tantalisingly light dips had been nothing short of frustrating, but after a few laps the carrot was beginning to compress her tongue against the back of her jaw.

'Isn't that the most beautiful thing you've ever seen?' A sturdy, middle-aged gentleman let the soft thud of a flogger land within inches of her clit. He ran his hand through the greying lines of his salt and pepper hair and blew her a cheeky kiss.

The next pelt of his flogger caught her firmly on the ass and had her yelping. Well, it would have had her yelping, had her mouth not been full of a very thick carrot. 'Unnghh,' was the phrase that actually left the corners of her lips, and nobody bar Jenny managed to hear it.

There was a throaty chuckle from beside him and a seductive little purr whispered, 'She's adorable isn't she? But I think there's room for improvement. Her ass cheeks are nowhere near the fiery red I usually require, sweetheart.'

Muted laughter accompanied that comment, but thankfully Jenny was already spinning away from it. The blows rained down harder after that though, and each new spank became a trial that had to be borne and endured. Her thighs were beginning to wobble with the exertion of holding herself up, and she knew it wouldn't be long before she collapsed on the big beast below. As a riding crop caught her once again on the side of her breast she shuddered and howled. This time the carrot was thankfully on its upward surge. A flurry of paddles then caught her ass cheeks and imparted such maddening fire that Jenny rattled her chains, hoof mitts and boots in protest, trying to swing her body out of harm's way.

Peals of laughter followed her pathetic antics. 'I give her two minutes before she gets spit-roasted,' said the same gentleman as before. No one took it upon themselves to disagree with his prediction and as Jenny's thigh muscles took a turn for the worse, going from a wobble to a full-on trembling fit, she knew she was shortly about to make several people very happy.

A band of photographers chose that moment to arrive, and they proved a welcome distraction from her abject torment. They were clad in an army of denim, and the biggest cameras she had ever seen obscured their faces. Tripods were set up, lenses adjusted and then they went about the business of taking the perfect shot - several hundred times over. They lit up the carousel brighter than a set of twenty floodlights would have managed, and that was saying something. Jenny went dizzy with the continuous pops and flashes being aimed all around her. Everything changed instantly from colour to black and white, and it made her eyes roll. If it hadn't, the thought that her naked body was being photographed from all angles to decorate Forbes' house would have done the trick. Oh God. She had now been caught on camera for all eternity dressed as a pony-girl with a large carrot sinking down her throat and a big plastic penis trying to dismember her insides, not to mention the swishing black horsetail that twitched every time someone walloped her backside. How utterly humiliating... and how hideously arousing.

A sudden jolt behind her had her head trying to turn around, but of course that was impossible. The sound of paddling and spanking immediately ceased, and she couldn't help but wonder what was going on. If she wasn't much mistaken, someone had jumped on the carousel behind her and it made her strangely nervous. The patrons had been told to stay behind the lines, so could it be an enterprising photographer? That might make sense, she supposed, if they were gearing up for more 'personal' shots. Her face flooded with heat again. She could just imagine a snapshot of her ass, tail proudly fluttering, as she descended towards the dildo below. That was probably the least of her worries. Imagine if they got headshots! Whilst she was somewhat disguised in black paint, if the newspapers got hold of one of those babies her social standing would be history.

'Ahh, Miss Redcliff, isn't it?' A hand reached out to caress her upwardly stretched arm and she jumped at the contact, which caused her strained legs to shake even harder. 'Still jittery after a week of training? You are quite the surprise, my dear. We had bets you'd be sobbing your little heart out by now.'

Jenny couldn't answer the question for several reasons. Her collar was still in place, the steel bars of the gag made forming words difficult and her mouth was currently stuffed full with a rather solid carrot. Had she been able to, though, a sharp retort would have been forthcoming. If she wasn't much mistaken this was the disreputable Leyland Forbes and she was curious to know what he wanted.

'I give you two minutes before you collapse onto that teeny, tiny *massive* pole beneath you. Your legs are already shot to bits. They'll have to work on your endurance training back at Albrecht. The other girls here will manage another five minutes at the very least,' his hand slid back down until his fingertips rested on the curve of her shoulder, and to add insult to injury he added, 'I make sure all the girls who work for me stay in tip-top shape.' He slapped her right buttock and she felt it bounce, but managed to keep her gasp from spewing out of her mouth. 'There's not enough muscle tone here, yet, but there will be. His finger circled her butt plug tail and she nearly impaled herself then and there.

Keep it together, Jenny, she told herself firmly, but guessed his earlier assumption was probably correct. She had minutes left in her at most.

'Do you know why I brought you here?' Two hands snaked over her back and reached up to stroke the underside of her breasts. 'Well, the reason is twofold.' His fingers brushed against her nipples and the resulting gurgle or arousal could not be supressed. 'Firstly, I knew how much Mark Matthews wanted you, and I like to annoy him on occasion, and secondly, if I grant him a favour he'll owe me. It's always good to have favours of the high calibre variety Mark can deliver, especially when you like the kinds of things I do.' As the dildo reached up again it buried itself two thirds of the way into her insides and it was all Jenny could do not to scream. It was big. Much bigger than she had thought at first glance, and if she was going to be made to take the whole of it the experience was going to be quite the eye opener.

'It will fit.' Forbes chuckled away as the dildo made a long, slow, sucking pop as it left her body once again. Apparently Matthews and he shared the same mindreading ability, which was just wonderful.

'I wouldn't concern yourself with size. You'd be surprised how much you can take when given plenty of foreplay and lubrication.' Jenny contained her reservations on that score, not that she had much choice. The carrot was once again filling her mouth and becoming very determined in its downward pursuit. 'What I would concern yourself with, is that when your legs go out from underneath you, due to exhaustion, the whole of your bodyweight will be resting on your hanging arms and that dildo. I'm not letting Matthews in until your eyes are begging for mercy and your body is pleading for relief.'

As Jenny's body jerked upright at the mention of Mark's name, Forbes' fingertips flicked the little nub of her clit lightly, making her groan.

'Yes, that's right Precious. Your protector is now charging down the motorway on his silver steed, a Mercedes if I'm not mistaken, and he's coming to rescue his princess. After I'm finished with you, of course, and that won't be for quite some time. I have a great respect for Matthews and find him a reasonably likeable fellow, but I also love toying with people. He knows this, so I suspect I won't get too much of a show from him, but I think you're going to be the highlight of his evening here tonight - and just so you know, he has never dropped everything to rush down and save a damsel before. So I'm curious as to what he sees in you, although I'll probably never find out.'

The words were wasted on her because as his hands went to work on her body her mind disintegrated into dust. His finger depressed her clit lightly, once, twice and finally three times before he stepped back. Jenny found herself on a knife-edge plateau and she would have said or done anything that was required of her in order to get her hands on an orgasm.

'No orgasms yet, we'll save that for later.' A smart swipe of his right hand across her butt cheek snapped her out of the aroused haze she found herself in, although her clit was still pulsing painfully, and she was again firmly in the here and now. Unfortunately her legs chose that moment to buckle as Forbes had previously predicted. She rammed herself down on the black monster with considerable force and it made her eyes water, although amazingly the thing had slid in easily enough.

'Does it feel good, Petal?' Forbes' words dripped with innuendo and his grey eyes flashed with malicious glee. Jenny grunted in reply, but if she was honest the thing felt rather heavenly. It filled up all the parts that Mr Average couldn't usually reach. 'Thought it would. Most of the girls around here seem to like it. The catch is that you're going to find yourself a little sore, hanging like that whilst being bumped up and down. We'll give you a minute or two, so you can see what I mean.'

The annoying man came around to stand in front of her and gave her a sly grin. Wetting his finger, he traced it around her areolas so they puckered from the cold smear of saliva, and then he pinched each nipple in turn. With the dildo pounding into her from beneath, with a steady and uncompromising beat, Jenny mewled pitifully, but Forbes was not paying attention. He'd turned around and was talking to his guests, who were watching his progress with interest, to the point that they'd stopped all their shenanigans with the paddles and crops, and the rest of the ponies were getting a little break, for the time being.

'Do you think you can speed things up around here for me, ladies and gentlemen? Petal here, would like to be shown a good time.' Instantly Jenny's eyes closed and her whole body trembled in horror. She knew exactly what Forbes was up to and it wasn't going to be pretty. The man then pulled out his cell and barked into it, 'You can send him in now. Things are about to get interesting.'

Forbes then caressed her cheek with two fingers, winked and hopped off the carousel without another word.

Her brief respite, if you could call it that, ceased immediately. The sound of spanking, much louder than before, began to make the previously trudging ponies turn their plodding hooves into a slow canter. The direct effect of this was felt upon Jenny's poor behind and there was no escaping the extra and much more vigorous blows. They were being doled out with fast and furious abandon. The sting each smack created was now enough to make her eyes water, and that wasn't the worst of her ordeal. The increasing speed of the carousel, in turn, pumped both the carrot and dildo up and down with far greater enthusiasm, and the effect was startling. It felt as if she were being launched into the air when the dildo fired itself upwards and sucked down into the floor when it receded. The result was a jarring movement that made her feel like a trampoline gymnast. No sooner had she been sucked down than she was being thrown back up again. Placing a lot of her bodyweight against the dildo was not an entirely pleasurable experience either. The spot between her thighs wasn't going to take too much of the 'bumps' before it began protesting in earnest. To make matters worse, the carrot was nearly stopping her breath on each downward plunge as it was ramming itself so far down her throat. She should have been miserable, but the result was that the shortage of air was making her muscles spasm in the most sublime way. Her clit was bursting to cream against the long plastic intruder and the warm, pleasurable sensation flooding through her body made her forget all her woes and embrace the spanking paddles and floggers. She had never felt anything like it in her life. It was as if a great ball of nervous energy was expanding inside her and the pressure was so great, if someone had taken a pin to her she was sure she would have burst. Little black spots began to appear before her eyes and the room began to blur in a confetti of bright white circles that danced with the precision of a ballerina. All she needed was for someone to take a crop to her clit. Just one tap, that was all it would take. One tiny, tiny little tap. She would have got down on her hands and knees and begged for it, had it been an option. Alas, her torment was set to continue.

The horses moved faster and faster as the spanks increased, and bells jingled everywhere. The pounding that had at first been uncomfortable got considerably worse as her whole body was being tossed and turned around so much that she began to resemble something in a Punch and Judy show. She didn't care about the bouncing and she couldn't have given two hoots about the pain; all she craved was release, although a large lungful of air should have figured a little higher on her priorities. Her mind was a little fuzzy around the edges. She felt drunk, lightheaded and almost a little euphoric. That was when she knew she was dreaming.

Sky-high on excitement and drunk on pleasure, whom should she see running across the great hall's floor? Why, Mark Matthews, of course. Her head lolled between the leather restraints that held her up and Matthews' eyes creased in concern, causing him to expend a further burst of energy as he ran as fast as the packed room would allow, his arms swatting milling people out the way left and right. As the carousel turned Jenny caught a brief glimpse of his profile before he disappeared from view. He was wearing a cream linen suit, a starched white shirt that was open past the hollow of his neck and a thick brown leather belt. Oh, who was she kidding? The state her head was in right now it could have been Batman running to save her and she probably wouldn't have known the difference. Her dream vision abruptly vanished and the dark and light within her head were warring for supremacy. It was touch and go for a moment on which was going to win, and then the carousel's metal grill dipped sharply beneath her. There was a wild growl of annoyance before someone began shouting in her ear.

'Stay with me, Petal. For God's sake don't faint on me.' The carrot was tugged roughly from her mouth and suddenly her body was desperately trying to suck in air. A rough voice barked at her, 'Little breaths at first, else you'll choke. Keep calm and take it steady. I'm undoing your gag.'

Jenny's vision had gone black, but the voice she heard was Mark's. Could it be him? Hadn't Forbes said something about him being here? Slowly precious air flooded her body and though it took a few seconds for her vision to return she knew without doubt, that the man in front of her was indeed Mark Matthews. She recognised his smell. It was a tantalising mix of lemon, sandalwood and something else she couldn't quite put her finger on. Something spicy, she thought. As she mulled over the possibilities she felt the ratchet on her gag loosen, and suddenly her mouth was free. Stretching it from side to side to loosen some of the tension she felt there, she heard Mark bark at the gathering audience.

'Stop gawking! This little pony is mine, and Leyland's just having some fun with me.' He smiled widely for their benefit. It was the smile redolent of a big bad wolf. 'I suggest you put away the spanking implements for the time being, and get out the tickle sticks and airguns Leyland has thoughtfully provided in the large vase around the corner. First person to get a pony to orgasm wins £50,000. How's that for a wager?'

Clearly the game was on, because the few spanks that had carried on throughout Mark's rescue attempt immediately stopped and everyone scurried off to find some new toys to play with. With their backsides free of torment the other horses slowed to a crawl in order to recover their breath and the dildo beneath Jenny took on much slower intrusions, which gave her a measure of relief, but not the kind she wanted, unfortunately.

'Are you OK?'

Jenny wanted to roll her eyes at the ridiculously stupid question. She'd been spray-painted black, someone had wired her jaw open and forced a plastic carrot down it and, oh yes, there was a massive black dildo in her pussy and a butt plug in her ass. She was A-OK, hunky-dory, top-of-the-world, absolutely-over-the-moon *not* OK. She carefully pointed her eyes downwards, trying to indicate the collar around her neck, which would not allow her to answer his question. He seemed to get the message for his eyes looked down and then immediately snapped back to hers.

'Your collar and plugs have been switched off. You're about to be dunked in a large vat of water, I hear.' Jenny narrowed her eyes and looked at him darkly. He held up his hands, 'Hey, I'm just the messenger. Anyway, feel free to exercise those vocal chords.'

Jenny gave a loud growl, which was an instinctive response to his teasing, and then slowly sighed. She croaked, 'Yes, I'm OK. I think.'

'Good. We haven't much time before the muppets come back, so listen up. You weren't supposed to be wearing a gag. Leyland's just trying to piss me off. The idea is that when your legs tire you grab the grooves of the carrot between your teeth and hang off it, to give them a rest. It's not a whole lot more fun, but it will save the pounding your insides will take if you don't. Focus and get yourself through the next ten minutes or so, and then you'll be moving along to the next exhibit, I believe.'

No sooner had Mark finished his sentence than a horde of people came back into the picture. They were armed with what appeared to be large, fluffy feather dusters in every colour of the rainbow, peacock and ostrich feathers, and bizarrely, long black rifles with cylindrical silver canisters attached to the top of them. What the hell were they? The word 'airgun' rang in her head, from Mark's earlier comment, but seeing big black guns everywhere was one sure way to freak a restrained girl out.

'Relax. There's nothing more than pressurised air in there,' said Mark, and he sported his first real smile of the afternoon. 'Leyland might be nuts, but he'd be foolish to kill off all of his models before the fun has even begun.' His lips twitched.

'I loathe you,' Jenny whispered, and her blue eyes flashed fire, framed beautifully by her charcoal-shaded eyes and the gold and silver swirls that decorated them. There was a slight pause, and she wondered if she would regret her outburst.

'I know and we're going to work on that. I won't be happy with anything less than "hate".' Another twitch. He turned his head smartly as something was thrown at him and neatly caught one of the large rifles in his right hand.

'You ready?' came an overeager male voice from behind him.

'One second,' he replied, and bent to murmur in her ear, 'is there anything you need before we begin?' His hand cupped her sex, which was currently free of the dildo, and rubbed itself backwards and forwards, before it speedily left to allow the black beast room for penetration.

'An orgasm,' she whined pitifully, shaking and rattling her hands in protest at the short visit of his warm hand.

'What the fuck do you think I've had them get airguns for? Target practice?' Mark shook his head. 'Wait your turn young lady, and you'll get yours.' He tutted to himself. 'Such a greedy little thing.' There was a brief tap against her ass, and then he leapt from the carousel, landing with two feet on the floor.

'Well, what are you waiting for?' Mark said to the bystanders as his head slowly turned to assess the group. Then he smiled and said, 'Let's get this show on the road.'

What began after that was sheer and utter chaos. A mad hailstorm of tickle sticks, feather dusters, and blasts of ice-cold pressurised air was directed at the ponies - and Jenny could only be grateful that, for the most part, their aim sucked. Although the moving horses were trudging slowly, it wasn't the easiest thing in the world to aim at a moving target. It was a bizarre sight to behold, however.

Long-stemmed peacock feathers, in the most beautiful iridescent blues and greens she had ever seen, were now being waggled in front of her nose, across her breasts, down her arms, along her back and basically anywhere they could get at. Some patrons used flouncy little wiggles, and others preferred a long and unending stroke, which sent shivers down her spine. The ostrich feathers were worse. Although they looked much plainer, in shades of white and black, their fluffier texture did wonderful, *horrible* things to Jenny's skin, especially the areas that had been previously reddened.

Take a pair of fiery, stinging, freshly paddled ass-cheeks and run an ostrich feather down them. Nerve endings she hadn't known she had flew out of her body, did somersaults and then attempted backward flips. Goosebumps erupted all over her flesh and she couldn't stop herself from shivering, though the room was a comfortable, if not balmy temperature. The airguns were by far the worst, though. The short sharp bursts of air they delivered at freezing cold temperatures had her body flinching wherever they hit, and she had little room to avoid them. In a matter of a few seconds it felt like little needles of ice were trying to force their way inside her skin and she fought against the pole that imprisoned her tooth and nail to escape them. Well, tooth anyway, because nails weren't available commodities. On the plus side, it had given her the impetus to use her legs again and she pushed herself back up on her weakened muscles to do as Mark had previously instructed.

When the carrot came down she searched for the groove, and using her teeth she bit down tightly. This raised her and allowed the dildo far less penetration, which was a good thing, wasn't it? Her mind wasn't really able to answer the simple question. All it cared about were the feathers caressing her skin and the blasts of air that were mauling it. Those little spikes of icy air got everywhere, but the worst areas were her bright red backside, where they stung like hell and her nipples, which were now auditioning for the role of porcupine spikes. This was made even worse by the tiny gold clamps she wore, as the greater her buds swelled the more painful the clamping sensation became. No one had managed, as of yet, to get a burst of air near her clit, but plenty of shots had misfired between her legs, and the flesh there quivered rather anxiously.

As each pony was tormented in a similar way it didn't take long before hormones got the better of the group. Grunts, moans, groans and frantically jingling bells could be heard from each pony as the feathers and airguns did their worst. Jenny was fairly certain she could not have been more aroused had the Marquis de Sade, Don Juan, Casanova and 007 had their tongues and fingers all over her at the same time. All she needed was that little something to tip her over the edge, but tickle sticks and feathers were not going to cut it. She needed just a tiny bit of pressure on her sweet spot and she'd be exploding, much like Beethoven's symphony number five that had started to burst from all corners of the room.

She had to give it to Forbes. He timed his musical pieces well. Her body had never felt so in tune with notes of angst that were pouring from the speakers. Her legs twisted and turned to try and avoid the fluttering's of the brilliant peacock feathers, her thighs gripped the golden pole in front of her in an effort to prevent entrance for the fluffy ostrich plumes which seemed to take a special interest in her sex, and as for the airguns... they simply weren't aiming the things in the right place. If she could let go of her carrot for a moment and scream loud enough, she'd tell them what she thought of their lacklustre technique.

As the carousel slowly spun she kept catching Mark's eyes and the devilish light inside them seemed to glow with each pass. He didn't bother with the feathers, just aimed the odd blast of air here and there. It was enough to annoy her, little more. The low slant of his eyebrows told her all she needed to know. He intended to make her wait. She would suffer and simmer until her boiling point was reached, or until such time as he saw fit to bestow his benevolence upon her. The dildo pounced, dipping in and out of her now swollen sex, the carrot filled her mouth tightly, and the leather saddle hung heavy around her midriff. Her whole body throbbed with painful intent. The long black tendrils of her wig flapped against her back and the clamps on her nipples were biting with a punishing and relentless pinch. Her backside stung madly, having being driven mercilessly insane by the cruel onlookers as they applied their various weapons upon it. She was positive that a single second more of the torment would drive her mad. And she was wrong.

As the music drew headlong into its finale with a deafening crescendo of sound, the screams of the pony in front of her could be heard. An enterprising gentleman had run two quills through her labia simultaneously and then squeezed her clit hard between them. Her body flew apart in an instant and she landed on her dildo with a vicious backward thud. It was the beginning of the end. The next pony could be heard yelling at the top of her lungs barely three seconds later. Repeated blasts of air had been directed at her clit until she came undone and her fate was a similar one to the pony before her. There was a round of laughter as her chains jangled, her legs flew sideways and her pussy shot straight down on the impaler beneath.

Jenny could not see what had happened to the rest of ponies, but she could hear their screams. Picking them off, one by one, she knew she was the only one left. Biting into her carrot as if it were the real thing, Jenny wanted to howl in defeat. Would Mark leave her desperate and shaking, the only one not to be allowed to come? Could he be that mean? Hell yes, and worse, she thought, as drums filled the sound of her head. His face flashed by once again and this time there was a wicked smile upon his face.

Please, please, please, please, please, she pleaded silently. Another turn of the carousel and still the man was standing with his arms by his sides, although he was looking at her fixedly. The ride slowly ground to a halt as the momentum of the ponies' hooves left it and she felt herself close to tears. The frustration she felt was indescribable. Seeing the wide smile of satisfaction that now crept over his face, she thought her fate had been sealed. Then there was a quick flick of his right arm and she found herself screaming and floundering as all of her friends before, but there had been no quick burst of air for her. No friendly feathers or squeezing quills. Mark Matthews had simply brought the butt of the rifle up between her legs with a moderate degree of force. As her body initially tensed each nerve, sinew and fibre strained to be free of her body - and then she fell apart. Or to be more exact, her legs flew out from under her and she speared herself heavily on a very thick and very long dildo. The resulting scream of pleasure was her longest to date.

'She's quite beautiful, isn't she?' Leyland, who had sprung out of nowhere, sidled up to Mark and gave him a supportive tap on the shoulder. 'Don't worry, it happens to us all. You'll get through it, old chap, take my word for it.'

Mark, who was having a hard time prizing his eyes away from Jenny's body, resplendent in the aftermath of orgasm, was listening with only half an ear. 'Hmm?'

Leyland took it upon himself to play a little. 'I was just saying that your bride-to-be looks rather wonderful, does she not?' He nodded his head as if to confirm his thoughts.

'Ha, bloody ha,' said Mark, not at all amused, but spoiled it when he followed up with, 'How soon can I get her out of here?' Worryingly, he meant it, because the thought of her with hundreds of eyes upon her and being photographed from every angle was doing funny things to his equilibrium. He would have paid just about any amount of money at that moment in time, to pick her up and whisk her away somewhere safe. What the hell was wrong with him?

'She's not going anywhere until she's acted out her starring role in my aquarium centrepiece,' said Forbes, smiling broadly.

Two men, snappily dressed in smart black suits, hopped onto to the now static carousel and began to free Jennifer Redcliff from her various restraints, one by one, finally managing to take down her pole.

'If they harm a hair on her head, so help me God, I'll...'

'Relax. They're just delivering her to the cleaning crew and then she'll get sprayed up for act two.'

Both Leyland and Mark watched the departing figures as they carried the exhausted pony-girl between them.

It took all of Mark's willpower not to go roaring off after them, but he knew it would do little good, and he had no wish to fuel Leyland's amusement further. Reigning in his temper and sliding his hands in his trouser pockets with a deceptively casual air he asked, 'So what is act two, exactly?'

'Underwater bondage, submergence play and a few little games I have devised entirely from my overactive imagination.' Leyland inclined his head to talk in a conspiratorial tone. 'They'll be breathing from artificial gills,' he said, 'which will make the aesthetics for my photos so much more pleasing.'

'There's no such thing as an artificial gill,' said Mark, hands now out of his pockets and fiddling with his tie.

'There is now. An enterprising fellow in the Middle East has developed the technology. It's going to revolutionise the diving industry. People will be diving to depths previously unknown with one of those little babies between their lips.'

Mark did not share Leyland's enthusiasm. His temper wanted to explode and he could feel bile bottling at the base of his throat.

'Let me get this straight. You mean to tell me that you are going to use experimental technology on ladies and gents who will be firmly restrained in bondage gear and dropped into a large vat of water?' The tone of his voice suggested that Forbes tread with caution.

'Yes,' said Forbes. 'That pretty much sums it up perfectly.' Unfortunately, either Forbes had missed the warning tone in Mark's question or was completely oblivious to it.

'Then let me tell you something,' said Mark, his tone dangerously low and laced with illusory amounts of saccharine. 'If I have to get into that tank and ruin my five figure suit, you will be responsible for the cleaning bill. That will hardly matter though, as I will make damned sure to shove one of those devices between your lips, chuck you in at the deep end and nail the top of the tank shut. I hope we understand each other.' His smile was tight but deadly.

Leyland's answering smile was just as tight. 'I believe we do, Matthews.' It was now Leyland's turn to adjust his tie and the merest tremble was evident in his fingertips. 'Do not worry. This is going to be the biggest event of the year and everything will be perfect.'

'It had better be,' snarled Mark, and Forbes could only imagine the look on Mark's face, because he was already striding away from him.

Leyland's eyes narrowed at the rigid set of Mark's shoulders and a sly smile reached his eyes. 'That man's in love,' he murmured to himself with an incredulous look, before allowing himself a small chuckle. Taking a moment to draw in a deep breath, he found himself very thankful that he'd had the foresight to test the gills himself before tonight's event. They had held up splendidly in all his extensive tests, and he would just have to hope that they would do the same this evening. Though it had to be said that Mark's threat had dampened his spirits a little.

Chapter Twelve

The Aquarium

Jenny was quickly whisked away from the great hall and led down a maze of endless corridors until finally the creak of a thick wooden door indicated that her journey might be at an end. Dumped unceremoniously on a large white plastic sheet again, all she could think about was trying to get her breath back. Goddamn. The man had smacked her clit with the butt of a rifle, and what's more, she'd loved it. She'd never come so fiercely in her life. The resulting fall and rather hard but infinitely delicious orgasm had her screaming the walls down. It was utter madness and enchanting depravation. And it was only going to get worse!

Mark Matthew's dark brown eyes swam before hers and she wondered if he'd managed to talk to her father yet. It might only be a couple of hours before she was living with him permanently... at his beck and call, and enslaved for the foreseeable future. What a wonderful, but oh-my-god-am-I-ready-for-this thought? He would test her to the absolute limit and beyond, but if tonight's antics were anything to go by, she might have one hell of a fantastic time on her hands. If his earlier words were true she would be continuously needy, and hopefully constantly in demand for sex. How could that not be an enchanting vision? Imagine waking up to him every damn morning? It would be kind of like winning the lottery, only to discover you couldn't keep the money. Matthews was a prize catch, but no one had managed to capture his interest yet and it would be foolish to hope for anything more than their proposed 'arrangement'. Still, she was prepared to accept the consequences for now and see where the road ahead might take her.

When a team of ladies and gents trailed into the room armed with buckets, sponges, cloths and brushes, she paid them little attention. Even when they began scrubbing at her black skin in earnest she remained oblivious for the most part. There was no pain. The endorphin level in her body made her oblivious to the fact. Even when they vigorously scrubbed her upper thighs she didn't make a murmur because her mind was still far, far away and daydreaming about her first night under Mark's care.

'Drink.'

She blinked her eyes lazily, not wanting to re-enter the real world quite so quickly. When a striped red straw was firmly pressed against her lips it snapped her out of her head-trip in double-quick time, and as three fingers threaded the straw into her mouth she guessed she had better play nicely.

'It's a protein shake. You'll have to eat on the go, I'm afraid.' Jenny ended up snorting her first mouthful of the foulest tasting chocolate concoction she'd ever had the privilege to imbibe. Eat? Since when did you call a drink food? But she sucked it all up, mainly because she was ravenously thirsty and there didn't appear to be anything else. It wasn't the easiest thing in the world to drink, when your body was being roughly scrubbed all over, but somehow she managed to get most of the stuff inside her.

'Good girl.' The inevitable pat on her head followed and Jenny wished she'd saved a mouthful of her shake for the pair of shoes in front of her face. 'Len and the gang will be in shortly to respray you, but you'll be pleased to know all the black paint is gone.'

Several pairs of feet filed out in short order and Jenny had just realised that she hadn't set her eyes on a single face. She'd been far too absorbed in herself, for the most part. It was unlike her. Not being absorbed in herself per se, but she was used to observing people in meticulous detail. Apparently huge orgasms and the dreamy sting of a scrubbing brush did funny things to her insides.

'Well, well, well. What do we have here?'

Jenny didn't need to look up to see who had just entered, but she did anyway, and lo and behold her two tormentors had come back to haunt her.

'I hear the carousel was star of the show out there,' said Len, chuckling. 'Not only did you have Forbes admiring my delectable artwork, but you managed to attract the attention of Matthews as well. The others will be horribly jealous.' He laughed at her expression. 'There's no point frowning at me. I'm doing you a favour. Upping your price, isn't that what this is all about? Don't worry. By the time I'm finished with you and the liquid latex you'll be playing a starring role in the next round as well.' Jenny looked at him sideways and couldn't decide whether his threat was a good one or a bad one.

His right-hand man got to work mixing up some tins of coloured paint in the corner, and began plugging in a couple of airbrushes while Len placed a thick white napkin in her hands. 'Hold tight, close your eyes and use this to cover your mouth and nose. You don't want it going anywhere near your face and you certainly don't want to inhale the stuff.' That was all the warning she got. Her breasts, sex and chains were covered with the familiar sticky plastic of before and then they began spraying her all over in earnest. The first coat was a chocolatey brown and they painted her from the neck downwards a total of four times before they were satisfied. The smell of ammonia assailed her nostrils and it wasn't pleasant, but she guessed it could have been worse. Each coat required a couple of minutes to dry and Jenny could only squirm in torment as the stuff began to set. No one had mentioned that when liquid latex dried it tightened quite considerably. Her breasts were feeling somewhat squeezed through the form-fitting circles of fabric around them. It felt like having a second skin. She was quickly covered from head to toe in wet, sticky goo. As the paint began to harden it moulded the contours of her body perfectly and no little lump or bump escaped unnoticed. When she was turned over they covered all of her bar a small oval shape around her sex and anus. Jenny was long past the embarrassment and humiliation stage. She didn't care if they wanted to stare at her privates all day long, but it would be nice if they'd get a move on.

To be fair to the pair they didn't drag their heels. As the brown coat dried they quickly brought out their paint brushes and covered her body in white stripes, making her look every bit the part of a zebra-esque marine fish. Their artistry was incredibly lifelike and drawn in three-dimensional, textured detail. The speed in which they accomplished the feat was nothing less than astounding, and as soon as they'd finished things began to get *really* interesting.

They had already prepared a hood to go over her head and this had slots for her eyes and mouth. It matched the colours of her body perfectly and fitted just as snugly as the liquid spray paint had. The hair from her wig was carefully pinned and tucked high inside so it wouldn't interfere with the neck seal. Then they brought her arms up to her stomach and encased her hands in plastic tape, before inserting them in a colour-coded rubber muffler, which was wound around her body. Webbed fins were attached by means of Velcro to her arms, and flippers had been made for each foot. The first knot of worry began to take root. She was going to be dropped in a tank without the use of her arms and her feet, even though webbed, would not be able to move far due to her chains.

'Ah, I see you're coming to terms with your predicament,' said Len, fiddling with a small, clear-plastic cylinder and what appeared to be a handheld pump. 'If you want to move through the water you're going to need to flip your feet really fast in order to make up for your lack of range, and tilt your arms from side to side to steer. It'll take a little practice but I think you'll get the hang of it. You'll have an incentive to do so, I suspect.'

Jenny did not like the sound of that, but there was no time to consider the matter further because Len was coming at her with a thin tube and a pair of scissors, of all things. 'Have you ever heard of cupping before?' Jenny shook her head and narrowed her eyes. Unless 'cupping' was some fancy word for overenthusiastic coffee drinking she had no idea what the word meant, but she had a nasty feeling she was about to find out.

'This type of cupping is called "vacuum cupping" and I'm going to be attaching your spines via these tiny cylinders, placed strategically all over your body. I just need to snip a little nick in the latex, get a seal on your skin and then pump all the air out of the tube and attach your spines. Leyland wanted to try it this way, because then you'd feel them moving as you swim through the water. They'll tug and drag at your skin, and hopefully sensitise your body for pleasure.' He paused, letting his words sink in before continuing. 'There is a downside to the procedure, I'm afraid.' Jenny's eyes, which were looking almost Siamese in origin, narrowed further. 'You'll be left with a series of little red marks all over, or *hickeys* as you probably know them. They'll disappear in a few days of their own accord, so you needn't worry about them.' Seeing her dark expression, his mouth quirked. 'Look on the bright side, Petal. You'll have a delicious reminder of your torment for several days to come. You submissives like that kind of thing, right?'

Jenny wanted to roar at him, but knew it would do little good. Clearly he had no idea of how she came to be here, and why would he? It wasn't like they were going to advertise the fact, and her bleating about it wasn't likely to get her released, unfortunately. She wondered if she should try though, for old time's sake. If she was headed back to Albrecht, and heaven help her if that was the case, using her voice to plead for release would not be an option. She decided to give it a shot.

'You know I've been kidnapped, right?' Both Len and his friend burst into fits of tear-inducing hysterics. She had never wanted a brick wall so badly. If there had been one in the near vicinity she would have smashed her head into it. 'My name's Jennifer...'

Len was the first to catch his breath back. 'Whatever gets you horny, Petal. If that's the way you wanna play it, you go ahead.' The Siamese eyes were back, but she wisely kept her mouth shut. She'd tried, and that was that. Watching as the rim of the first tube was smeared in Vaseline and pressed against her back, she felt the pump being attached and sensed, rather than heard, the subsequent suction. It was a strange feeling, having your skin sucked upwards into a small tube, but not entirely unpleasant. The pressure Len used was not too intense, and the slow tingling burn it created almost made her groan. It wasn't too bad though. She could handle it. A walk in the park, compared to the rest of the things she'd faced so far today...

She was wrong. After Connor had applied twenty or thirty of the things she was a dribbling mass of seething, wailing hormones. The men were now attaching feathery striped spikes to each cylinder in turn, and checking that each was anchored firmly to her skin by giving them a gentle ping. Jenny wanted to scream. After she'd screamed she wanted the use of her hands back so she could get herself off not just once, but several hundred times over. The sensations those little tubes were producing were getting horribly intense.

'Coming along nicely now, Petal. Don't worry, your time with us is nearly up. Just need to do a couple more things and you'll be good to go. Next up we're going to pop a couple of nipple suckers on you and, boy oh boy, are you going to like these monsters. 'Cupping is all very well over your back and thighs, but when you place them somewhere really sensitive they'll have blood rushing up to the surface. Your tits aren't going to know what hit them after you've been wearing these babies for a few minutes.' That was all the warning she got. The suckers were applied, the plastic knobs twisted and her nipples pulled forcibly forward, almost filling out their little tubes. A few seconds later, after their feathery brown and white stripes had been attached, they began to throb in earnest. She gave up all pretence of being stalwart and began wriggling like a baby. 'Relax. You'll get used to the pressure in a minute. Just focus on your breathing. In and out, easy does it. We've got your clit and asshole to do next, so this is the least of your worries.'

'What? You have got to be joking,' Jenny seethed. You're going to attach spines there, too?' Her breaths were coming in little pants, and she was barely able to control the vicious arousal flooding her body. Any more and she'd be experiencing internal combustion of the worst kind. Or should that be the best kind?

'Don't worry, no fins down there. They'll be needed for... other things. All we're doing is drawing blood to the surface and letting them redden and swell a little, so the photographers can get a good shot. Leyland's very particular about these things.' He grinned and hauled her to her feet.

'I'll just bet he fu...' Jenny was cut off abruptly as she was bent over and a large suction cup placed over her sex. It was pumped up excruciatingly tightly. Her eyes began to disintegrate in their sockets. Having come such a short while before, the suction was unbearably pleasurable and powerful. Then a smaller cup was placed around the ring of her anus and the same treatment applied. Jenny's whole body began to shake. She was so close to climaxing she could feel tears of frustration leaking down her cheeks. Again. They'd reduced her to this again and so damn easily. Of course there was no way she could come, because the tiny bit of pressure she required to finish the task would not be forthcoming. She was becoming well versed in the art of torture.

The insertion of a fresh butt plug, complete with a striped fanned tail, was the last straw. When the sleek, tempered glass diving mask was placed securely over her eyes tears were flowing so freely they left a small puddle along the tight rubber seal.

Being carried aloft by six suited and booted volunteers and dressed as a tropical spiky fish was probably something she was going to remember for the rest of her life. Namely because they had to carry her face down because of the array of spikes festooning her back and ass. She'd managed to stop crying, realising how futile that was, and was now concentrating on the differing floors as they sped past below her. Wooden floorboards, marble, terracotta slabs, and seagrass matting were only some of the options that appeared to float by. As each new surface flew into view she wondered if this would be the one to lead into her underwater prison, but it was clear there was quite a trek ahead to reach their destination.

When the six pairs of feet did enter the room Jenny would always remember as The Aquarium she knew instantly. The tiles below her were mosaic, and a shimmering pearlescent green in colour. Judging by the faint lingering smell of brine on the air, there was water inside the room and lots of it. Wavelike ripples were reflected on a curved wall and she guessed that miniature camera's all over the room were projecting the image of calm and tranquil seas. For a moment she could almost imagine herself sailing... a lone boat upon the water. That was before her eyes took in the hundreds of people milling around the room's centrepiece. By some impressive feat of engineering a massive tank of jade green water resided in the middle of the room. Easily six feet in height, it could have been up to thirty metres in length and twenty metres in width. It was a beast. No expense had been spared in its creation, either. Lined with edges of brushed steel, it had been scalloped around the tank's edges to form etched art-nouveau waves, creating a frame for the play that was about to unfold.

Jenny was not the first 'fishie' to have arrived for a swim. A platform had been suspended above the tank and a couple of divers, their wetsuits stripped to their waists, were stationed on it, displaying an impressive set of abdominal muscles and biceps. They were currently dealing with a bright blue fish, who wore a large black stripe down her side and a bright yellow tale which had an anchor point much the same as Jenny's. She was treading water as they waved a long boomerang-shaped piece of apparatus in front of her and it was clear by the nodding of heads and waving of arms that they were explaining the use of the artificial gill. They then placed the device inside the girl's mouth and its two ends poked out on either side of her face. With a thumb pointing downward they indicated she should go below the water, and that's what she did. Twenty seconds later she'd popped back up and when they gave her the thumbs-up signal, she nodded. Then she was off and it was Jenny being led up the stone steps to the tank and gently but firmly immersed in the water, feet first.

The first surprise was that the water was bathtub warm; a good thing because Jenny was feeling rather cold. Whether that was due to the panic of being submerged in a large aquarium with nothing more than a little tube to breath from, or due to the sheer excitement of the evening so far, was anybody's guess. When she began to dip below the surface too quickly she spat out a mouthful of water and began to waggle her feet furiously.

'You'll need to move those legs, quick as you can while we explain the gill,' said one of the divers, who'd approached the edge of the platform with one of the boomerang devices. Pointing to the black edges of the design he said, 'These are the motorised parts of the gill and they'll whizz round extracting oxygen from the water. Make sure you don't block them. This,' he pointed to the plastic mouthpiece, 'will fit inside your mouth and all you need to do is breathe normally. Remember to bite down hard on the mouthpiece, and for God's sake don't drop it. If you do drop it, go lightheaded or any kind of safety issue occurs, lie on the bottom of the tank with one arm up. We'll be watching everything down below from our platform here, and will bring in scuba tanks to get you to the surface if there are any problems. Nod if you understand me.' She did so. 'OK, I want you to test this out. I'm going to place it in your mouth and I want you to go under the surface and count to twenty before coming up again. Take normal breaths, as many as you need, and then kick your way to the surface. When I ask if you can breathe normally and give you the thumbs-up, if everything is OK nod your head. If you have problems, shake it. We clear?'

She nodded, but it was a lie. Nothing was very clear at the moment. Being tied up was one thing, but being reliant on a tiny piece of plastic for the very air you breathed was another entirely.

'Remember, what doesn't kill you makes you stronger.'

Another weak nod. She hoped that was it for the pep talk, and thankfully his next words confirmed it was.

'Down you go then.'

So down she sank. For a minute she was overcome with blinding panic and all she wanted to do was spit the gill out and scream. Green water filled her vision and muffled all sound. It was quiet, overwhelming and ridiculously scary to be dropped in a deep tank of water with no arms, limited movement of legs, and a stick to breathe out of. Remembering the diver's words *what doesn't kill you makes you stronger* was of precious little comfort in her terrifying new home.

Down and down she went. Then the years of training as Redcliff's daughter came into force, and the *you will succeed no matter what* mentality snapped back into place. Kicking her legs gently she took a cautious breath. One. It wasn't the same as scuba diving. There wasn't that hard tug of air you had to suck into your lungs. Two. She could feel the arms of the gill spinning as it sucked air from the tank water and deposited it into her lungs. Three. At the moment there was only one other fish in the tank other than her. Seven. She wondered how many more there would be.

No expense was spared in the tank's decoration, for there were coloured pebbles at the bottom, plenty of foliage in the form of grasses and ferns, and even a stretch of coral reef could be seen, complete with live anemones. LED lighting had been filtered upon the colourful marine flowers and they glowed in hues of oranges, purples, reds and yellows. Twelve. Breathing in oxygen from a gill wasn't anywhere near as dry as the air in a scuba tank, so that was a plus. Fourteen. Was she counting too slowly? Perhaps she should start kicking again? Seventeen. Swimming in warm bathwater was actually quite pleasant, if you took things slowly. Nineteen. She broke through the surface of the tank and was surprised to find herself quite a way back from the platform. Her steering would require some work. Looking up she saw her diver with his thumbs in the air, mouthing some words at her. She nodded her head; she didn't need to hear what he was saying. When he pointed for her to go back down into the water it was almost a relief, because it was far less effort swimming underwater than trying to keep her body afloat on the surface.

Figuring the smart idea would be to explore the circumference of the tank and see what was where, she began to propel herself to the outer edge. Jenny had no idea how long she would be down here, but they weren't going to go to all this trouble for a ten minute swim, so she might as well get comfortable. Figuring she had little to worry about at present, as there were only two of them in the tank, she took it slow and had a good look around. As it happened there was more than enough to keep her occupied.

Angling her feet upwards, and flipping hard to plunge her body towards the bright green and white pebbles at the bottom of the tank, she realised that 'human fish' weren't the only fish that inhabited the tank. There were shoals of brightly coloured orange fish with little white stripes swimming alongside her; Clown fish, if she remembered correctly. There were also Angelfish swirling about the sponges and coral, with bright yellow bodies and neon blue stripes. The rest of the marine life that floated past her was a mystery, and she just hoped none of it was poisonous.

Flicking her flippers along slowly, she began to feel the first effects of her suit as the pull of the water took its toll. Each little spine attached to her back pulled at her skin as they were dragged forward. If she tried to move fast it became almost painful and did rather strange things to her libido. The biggest culprit was the large fantail that protruded from her plug. It felt like the water was trying to rip it out of her if she moved too quickly, but she knew that the beast inside her was far too big to be dislodged in that way. So she quickly learned to swim slowly. Tiny movements that helped her to glide through the water, giving her enough momentum to stay afloat, but very little speed. It still produced a tingling effect throughout her body, but it was the best she could hope for.

Hearing a loud splosh from above she craned her head up to see another fish, once again female, entering the tank for her twenty second taster. She had been outfitted as a puffer fish, and the poor girl would also have to contend with spikes, although they were a good deal shorter than Jenny's and wouldn't pull anywhere near as badly.

Rounding the corner of the tank she tried to peer out, wondering if Mark would be out there waiting for her, but the lights inside were too bright and all she could see was a dark blurry mess. She guessed she didn't need to see outside to know what was waiting for her. A small platoon of photographers and a mass of leering sex-fiends who would probably be preparing to masturbate to the antics that were shortly about to unfold. What sort of games might be played out down here? What was the worst that could happen?

Jenny's thoughts stopped in their tracks as she rounded the corner of the reef. Stuck to the wall of the tank was an array of glowing pink dildos, each differing in length and girth. The sight was so surreal that Jenny almost lost her gill, before remembering to clamp her mouth down tightly shut upon it. With the LED lights angled all over the tank, and those housed inside the dildos, she was beginning to wonder if she'd entered the most bizarre nightclub in the galaxy. When a shot of bubbles erupted from beneath her she knew she had. They tickled her latex-clad body and fluttered over her naked sex, and when another volley shot off behind her she couldn't help a groan as her fins twisted and turned with the vibrations. For a moment she considered trying to angle herself directly under one of the jets, with the hopes that if she sat right on top of it, it just might bring her to orgasm - but knowing there was a room full of hungry people, waiting to see something exactly like that, she took in a slow breath and continued moving forward.

A large splash alerted her head towards the top of the tank again, and she expected to see another brightly coloured fish floundering away at the top. As her eyes caught a blur of movement, and muscled legs giving powerful kicks downwards towards the bottom of the tank, she quickly discerned that this was a predator. For one, he was dressed all in black and that never boded well. He also had the use of his arms, and that was more than anyone else she had come across thus far. If in any doubt there was also the matter of a bright white rifle attached to his back. What the hell was that for? Firing bullets could be checked off the list, unless they wanted to kill their source of entertainment and break the tank, and firing bursts of air wouldn't be much use underwater, surely? The mind boggled. What was it with the guns this evening, anyway? Forbes must be a firearms nut in real life or something.

Watching Mr Wetsuit race off to chase after the blue fish, Jenny made more of an effort to keep her wits about her and eyes all around. The spiky fins beneath her stomach trailed backwards and tormented her sex relentlessly, but she was not going to be a victim to hormones again. She was damned if one of those divers was going to get a free ride from her without a fight.

Rounding the back of the tank, trying to look for a suitable hiding place,

Jenny's breath nearly caught in her throat. More dildos were scattered everywhere, like flickering lilac candles, but this time there were also pairs of large clear plastic suckers, connected to various sizes of plastic strapping, and they could have only one purpose. Restraint. There were also a couple of black hoses with silver nozzles and she didn't particularly fancy finding out their purpose. As another loud splash could be heard from above, Jenny flapped her feet with renewed vigour and ignored the protestations of her fins as they screamed in protest. She needed to get away from this side of the tank as quickly as possible. A quick flick of her head confirmed that there was another diver above and this time he had his sights firmly fixed on her. Oh God. Jenny wasted the next ten seconds battling with her rubber muffler as she struggled to free her hands, but it was a useless endeavour. These guys weren't amateurs. They knew exactly what they were doing and her bindings held fast.

Speeding along as fast as her shackled legs would allow she watched mushroom corals, resplendent in shades of cerise, peach and cyan, flapping gently in the wake that her frantically flapping body left behind. Tiny fish flittered through her legs and her heart made such a racket inside her head it was worse than one hundred and twenty decibel heavy metal in a teeny tiny room. She was a small fish in a very small tank, and there was no escape really, was there? So what was the point in trying? She almost berated herself for the defeatist attitude, but it was a good question. Why tire yourself out if you didn't have to? The restraints and dildos chose that moment to flicker in front of her eyes. Then again, why give these bastards any longer to play with your body than absolutely necessary? And the chase was on.

Little exaggerated flicks with her fins and steering by means of shoulder-blades enabled her to traverse the length of the tank without getting caught. The little blue fish hadn't fared so well. She was currently caught under the arm of a diver and headed for the back wall. Good luck with that, Jenny thought and kicked her legs faster, feeling the chains between her feet rattle. Her whole body was on fire, but she didn't care. All she wanted to do was prolong her freedom, such as it was, for as long as possible. Rounding the corner she risked turning her head to discover he was just three or four feet behind her and she knew it was game over. Using up the last reserves of her energy she gave one almighty furious blast with her feet, hoping to knock his gill out - but in the next moment she felt an arm snake around her ankle and knew her lot was up. Kicking for all she worth she felt her flipper connect sharply with his shoulder, but his grip didn't falter. In the next instant he had an arm around her waist, crushing her fins painfully close to her body, and he began steering her around in a circle - exactly where she didn't want to go.

Quickly moving up her body, he dug his gloved fingertips around her shoulders and used his powerful legs to make short work of the ride that had taken Jenny several minutes to complete. As his limbs were unencumbered by fetters he used long, economical movements that he probably could have kept up for hours. Twisting and wriggling in his grip achieved nothing except a good deal of uncomfortable pulling against her spiky fins. A black finger waggled from side to side in front of her mask and tapped her hard on the nose. Jenny figured she was being told off, but she didn't care. She did not want to be plastered up against that wall with all those people watching. Unfortunately, it appeared to be a foregone conclusion.

No matter what she tried the diver was one step ahead of her. When she let her body go limp and dragged her flippers along the floor he moved his arms back around her waist and pulled her upward, so she couldn't disrupt his journey. When she kicked her flippers as hard as she could to break free he easily caught her up and tightened his hold, which was now beginning to feel like the tightest of rubber bands. After several thwarted attempts he grew tired of her antics. Tearing the gill roughly from her face he threw it to the floor. As her eyes widened and she struggled to race for the top of the tank he held onto one of her legs, watching the slow ascent of bubbles as they left her lips. When the bubbles ceased and she began struggling in earnest he came face to face with her and waved the gill around airily. His eyes were black. Deep dark pools of obsidian and they held a gleam of menace within them. He wanted to let her know he was not someone you messed with. Feeling scarily lightheaded, her lungs stretched to bursting point, she wondered if she was going to pass out, but then he finally relented and shoved the gill viciously back in her mouth. She got the message though. The warning had been served. Do not fuck with me.

The rest of the short journey was accomplished quickly, with little interference on her part. She gave up all resistance and when she was shoved up against the tank, face forward, fins bending sharply underneath her, she remained meekly in place while plastic belts were fastened around her body and the suckers adjusted. Her mask was flat against the side of the tank and the gill rested awkwardly, slightly bent in her mouth, but her grip on it was ferocious.

Even though the light was bright within the tank and the room outside had now been reduced to darkness, Jenny was sure she could detect movement out there. She wondered how many people would be watching her torments in avid fascination. All three fish were now pressed up against the glass, tightly restrained and awaiting their fate. Jenny's skin prickled all over with anticipation and she clenched the heavy butt plug deep inside her, feeling the large fantail behind her flap as she did so. *What can they do to you in the water?* The sentence played over and over in her head. There would be no electric shocks down here, thankfully, but she guessed there were plenty of other tricks they could employ.

Bracing her body tightly for the worst, she was taken by surprise when she felt an ice-cold jet of water being directed at her. It was the pressurised hose she'd laid eyes on earlier and the diver behind her was directing it all over her body. The first burst took her by surprise, but it wasn't long before she and all the other fish were struggling in their plastic wrapping, trying to avoid its vicious sting as it assaulted various body parts.

A flash of blinding lights popped off in front of her and Jenny groaned in comprehension. The photographers. All of this would be captured on film. The thought was utterly mortifying, but she had little time to dwell on it for the jet was now being directed at the fins upon her back and one by one it tried to burst them from her body. It succeeded on a couple of attempts, but for the most part the tiny little cylinders held - although they protested at the treatment, and quite loudly. Each little fin was worked over as she rattled her body helplessly against the glass and the swirling, arctic currents around her had her tense and tightly on edge, wondering where the next jet of freezing water would attack next.

The diver upped the pressure setting and aimed the hose sideways in order to target her breasts. Jenny had pressed them up close against the glass in order to protect them from just such a manoeuvre, but the vicious onslaught gave no quarter and she was thrashing within her plastic bonds in a matter of moments. Trying to crouch her body in on itself, which was no easy feat without the use of arms, she tried her best to lessen the damage, but Mr Wetsuit was determined in his pursuit. When the first cylinder pinged from her left nipple she let out an agonised yell. The blood-engorged teat was then given frostbite and the resulting heady stab of pain was delicious, electrifying, and utterly unbearable. The blood in her body shot straight down to her sex and had the craziest dance party alive. As he moved around to set his instrument of torture on her right boob she was ready for him and immediately turned away, shielding herself. It made no difference. The force of the hose wouldn't let her stay still and before long he had added another cylinder to his tally.

Screaming underwater wasn't the easiest feat, Jenny reflected, as both of her freed nipples pulsed and throbbed with a fiery heat that could not be ignored. For starters, you really needed to inhale through your nose to scream, and that wasn't an option currently available to her. You also needed to hear the noise for it to be of any type of cathartic benefit, and the water muffled the sound in such a way that Jenny almost wondered whether the effort was worth it. She was about to find out.

Mr Wetsuit's next destination was her ass and her reddened backside protested vehemently at such treatment. It flattened the globes of her butt, pinning her to the glass like a sodden butterfly seeking shelter in a thunderstorm, and when the full force of it was directed on top of her plug it felt like her tormentor was trying to do some internal damage. She shrieked into her gill and a stream of bubbles shot out of either side of her mouth. The volume might not have sounded as impressive as it should have, but the venting of her anger helped to lessen the brutal sensation. He then swam up close and let his gloved hand stroke her hooded cheek. The gesture was unnerving. In the next moment his back covered hers, he'd pressed her cheek firmly against the glass, and the hose was being slid up the inside of her leg, although it was now only a dribble of its former glory.

Violet rays were being directed down upon her, illuminating the white bands of her costume until she glowed with an eerie halo that would have been more at home on a ghost. The glow increased in intensity and she knew they were setting her up for her big moment. The flow of the hose was gradually increasing in strength and while it hadn't reached any particular tender areas yet, she knew exactly where it was headed. The guy behind kept a firm pressure on her neck, determined to keep her face to the glass. He wanted a good shot for the cameras, she thought wryly. Damned if she was going to give them their 'shot'. They were determined thoughts, with conviction, yet utterly meaningless. As he swished the hose from side to side beneath her legs, catching her sex, she knew she would give them everything they wanted and more. Her body was already so ridiculously revved up she wanted to burst, and the game would be to make her wait. They would play with her, torment her, drag her up to her last breath and then capture every little movement on camera. Her life was about to become a photo storybook event.

The pressure increased by slow increments, and for the most part he kept it to the band of her upper thighs. The spray teased her sex every now and again, but he made sure the flicks were few and far between. That was when she began wriggling in earnest to catch it. One moment she was determined to avoid the icy blast, and the next she was actively seeking her own destruction. Of course he didn't let her get away with a thing. In the next instant a knee was pressed into her back, and when added to the hand around her neck and the restraints already encircling her body she was left to anticipate the whims of her captor. He let the water gurgle at the entrance of her pussy, but the pressure wasn't intense enough to excite her to any great degree. When he began to insert the end of the silver nozzle insider her, however, that was a different matter entirely. She nearly crawled up the walls of the tank. The tapered end of the hose slid inside the sleek wetness of her pussy so easily and she even bucked her hips involuntarily in order to welcome it. When he began to thread the thicker rubber of the hose inside her he was met with more resistance, but he dipped his finger in some kind of thick unguent and used it to grease the tube before easing it slowly forward a couple of inches. Jenny was not going to lie and say it didn't feel good. The vibrating, humming thing inside her felt amazing. His gloved fingers then found her clit and he'd obviously lubricated them, because they slid over her little bud effortlessly. He wasn't going to make anything easy for her though. In between his slippery circles he pinched and tweaked her poor clit mercilessly. In front of hundreds of people Jennifer Redcliff, destined to be one of the richest women in the UK, floundered like a Houdini experiment gone terribly wrong. No manner of twisting and writhing would allow her to escape those fingers, and no amount of straining on her part would give her the powerful depressions she required for release.

Her tolerance for such game playing was increasing. Whereas just a week ago she'd have thought she couldn't stand a single second more, now she gritted her teeth and endured. Her head was already in the clouds, or to be more accurate, in Mark Matthews' bed and they were working on breaking the thing. She had her fingers wrapped around his neck, her tongue inside his mouth and she was on top. *Yeah, like that'd ever happen...*

116

She came out of daydream-land with a bump, because the neoprene gentleman behind her had switched on the hose full blast and it shot out of her nether regions with impressive force. It hadn't hurt, but the wildly swishing hose beneath her was giving its added torment to an already hungry clit. Banging her head repeatedly upon the glass, indicating her frustration and displeasure, probably did little but amuse her antagonist and audience, but she didn't care. She had few enough outlets for her emotions and she intended to use each and every one she could find.

And then, all of a sudden, it happened. The mother-of-all-orgasms. The bastard behind her had turned on the hose full force and fired it directly at her clit. The blinding white lights in front of her went supernova.

Jenny was only partially aware of being released from the plastic strapping. She was floating, quite literally as it happened, but her frame of mind was on another planet and it was going to take a while to come back down to earth. Mr Wetsuit was pulling her over to the corner of the tank, and rigging up another one of his dastardly games, no doubt, but she had neither the inclination or will to care. It was so damn pleasant on cloud nine that she wondered how long you could reasonably expect to spend there if you took up this kind of life. Several hours a day, perhaps? With each day that passed things became more and more intense and greater reactions were being consistently wrenched out of her. The body had an amazing capacity for pleasure, if worked over in the right way. Who knew where she might be, a few weeks or years from now? The idea scared her because it meant she was coming to terms with her predicament, and she couldn't be sure if that was a good or bad thing.

Her musings were cut short. She was hauled upright, an inch-thick metal bar was threaded through her legs and one of the glowing purple dildos was being gently eased inside her pussy. Unfortunately she was hopelessly wet and it didn't require a whole lot of pushing. All she could do was watch as the large plastic suckers attached to the ends of the bar were attached to opposite ends of the tank, enabling it to be firmly secured in place. The bar was then adjusted a little higher until it cut into her tender and swollen sex. The dildo's rear end suction cup was attached to the bar, pinning her firmly in place, and a further rope was wound around her midriff and fastened a little higher up the tank walls to help keep her upright. She mewled pitifully through her gill. This was not going to be fun.

Struggling upwards to avoid the bite of the metal, she realised the attempt was useless. Trying to do anything with flippers on your feet was virtually impossible at best. Her bodyweight would rest on the bar, most of it borne by her clit, and there was little she could do about it. And time would be her enemy; the longer she rested the more intense the pressure upon her bud would be.

Mr Wetsuit came around in front of her to admire his handiwork and the smug bastard pulled his gill out and gave her a grin. That was when she checked him.

His eyes. Now her vision had adjusted to the dark she recognised those grey eyes and that self-satisfied smile. The diver in front of her was none other than Leyland Forbes and she would have happily bet her life on it. A sinking feeling, akin to swallowing around three tons of cement, began to settle in her stomach. This was not good. This was not good at all. And when the gill went back in his mouth and the white gun, which now glowed violet with the UV light, was pried slowly off his back, things got worse. Much worse.

He aimed it at her for the longest time, his eyes locked on hers, looking for signs of weakness. She didn't give him any discernible ones; though her heartrate stuttered and every last wisp of oxygen solidified in her body, she held that cold stare. If the bastard was going to kill her he could damn well watch as the light faded from her eyes. *It won't be a bullet*, the sensible part of her brain whispered, but since when were these lot sensible? And what if it was? A one-shot death, point blank in a tank of water was not a great way to go.

It was then that she spotted the twin pinhole cameras on either side of his mask. She inhaled. He just wanted a reaction. Well, she'd give him one. She gave him a long and flirtatious wink.

Leyland rolled his eyes in annoyance. An animated look transformed his features and she knew the battle was on. His finger moved imperceptibly on the trigger, degree by degree, until finally she braced herself for the worst and closed her eyes. He'd won the first round.

Bubbles. Goddamn bubbles. Jenny wanted to swear. The infernal man had taken ten years off her life for bubbles? The gun spewed forth a geyser of sparkling, perfect spheres, in all manner of different shapes and sizes. Reflecting all the colours of the rainbow they looked so pretty and innocent. What harm could a bubble possibly present?

She would have cause to rue that comment, again and again, in the next few minutes.

When the thought crossed her mind the bubbles had not touched her skin. Leyland had been far enough away that the surrounding water simply absorbed their gentle caress. But the man had other plans. He inched forward slowly, but with purpose. When the first flurry hit nothing more exciting than her lower leg she had reason to be optimistic. This was going to be a walk in the park, no less. The flutter of bubbles was pleasant and produced a gentle ripple of pleasure upon her skin, but nothing more solid than that. Another sigh of relief. What she hadn't realised was that Leyland was still a long away from her and the closer he got, the more the pressure would increase.

It didn't take long for her to realise the outcome of her latest challenge. With each step forward he took the bubble gun addressed different parts of her body. It started with the less sensitive areas, the backs of her calves, her shoulders, her abdomen and outer thighs. When he got to within three feet of her the ante was upped somewhat. He focused on her breasts and nipples, and ran the gun up and down her inner thighs. The sensation would have been intensely pleasurable except for one thing: her clit was suspended upon a line of thin metal that bit into her with each tiny movement she made. Moving around to her side he focused the gun on her ass and fired short bursts at her pink flesh repeatedly until she was wriggling helplessly. The metal began to slice painfully into her labia and she had to work hard to strain her body upright to lessen the pressure.

Leyland had only just started though. The bubbles caressed the crease of her ass, tickled her anus and dived between the 'V' of her legs to deliver a long cascade of popping, foaming bliss. She worked to keep herself as still as possible, but it was no easy task. Leyland was relentless in his pursuit of her erogenous zones and he worked over each part of her body with fanatical intent. Trying to avoid his aim in the predicament she was in was like trying to function without air. He knew just where to place jets and for how long. She swore she was going to saw her clit off on an inch-thick piece of steel.

He made her wait before he placed his bubbles where she really wanted them. Her sex may have been screaming from the torment of being suspended on a thin line of agony, but it still hungered for gratification at every opportunity. When he first flooded her clit with bubbles she thought she was going to come then and there, but he knew exactly how long to hold it for and then the wondrous steam of air disappeared. The gun was then returned to his back.

Jenny wanted to stamp her feet and scream in indignation, but moving was not an option. She was in too much pain. The blood in her body had dived to her clit and was making itself known as her little bud swelled into proportions previously unknown. It felt terrible and amazing, all at the same time. Leyland left her there, motionless in abject torment for several seconds while he did nothing more than stare at her. She barely noticed. Her whole being was focused on keeping her body upright and putting the least amount of pressure on her clit. The throbbing organ was becoming unbearably painful now that the stimulation had stopped. Sucking in laborious breaths she felt a single tear escape from her lashes and knew that was what he had been waiting for. He wanted that moment of angst and a solid piece of emotion on film to draw from.

A single tear was all he was going to get. She raised her head up and let her eyes bore into his, burying the pain deep inside her. It was a look that said, 'This is all you're going to get.' In the pit of her stomach, however, nerves knotted into a tight ball that bounced around with frenzied agitation.

Clearly satisfied he would get no more out of her for now, the man took three long strides forward and slowly peeled the black neoprene gloves from his fingers, letting them drop to the floor. What was he up to now? Flexing his digits in the water, knowing her eyes were upon him, he stretched out the moment of anticipation. They stared at each other, and you could almost hear the brain cells ticking over upon the quiet currents of the water. Leyland wanted something, and was probably gauging the best way to attain it. Jenny just wanted to make it out of the tank in one piece without giving too much away for the infernal cameras. Her skin prickled as the pair of stone-grey eyes in front of her slowly blinked, and then refocused.

He had decided upon a course of action and began walking towards her. Jenny braced herself for the worst. Another two strides and he slung himself over the wire she was suspended on, and with a distance of just ten centimetres lowered his mask until they were face to face. Then he really threw down the gauntlet.

His hands were all over her. They traced around the remaining tiny cylinders decorating her body and circled the smooth latex beneath. He ran her feathered fins through the palm of his hand and tugged sharply at them, but whether it was to examine their tenacity or simply to watch her squirm upon her tightrope was unclear. His fingers burrowed beneath the little nicks in the latex, anxious to discover the soft flesh beneath, and the soft scrape of his nails made her shudder. Just when she thought this might not be as bad as she'd previously thought, he reached out on either side of her, grabbed the bar and hauled it upwards.

Her gill flew out of her mouth in shock, but he was ready for it and easily caught the floating triangle before placing it back between her lips. Tapping the side of her head, as if to warn her to be careful, he reached back and she felt her tongue thick and fuzzy in her throat. Please no more bubbles, she prayed. As it happened she got her wish, but it wasn't necessarily a good thing. In his hand he held a shiny steel implement.

The first thing she noticed was its vicious appearance. There was a little circle at the top of the long thin base and the wheel must have featured fifteen or twenty sharp steel points. It looked like a fork, but where the tines should have been was a miniature Ferris wheel, complete with spikes. The spikes looked sharp and as he brought the device towards her she immediately shrank away from it. So much for not showing fear, she thought.

When the two inches of leeway she had were used up he let the wheel hover in front of her face. She was not amused. His baleful stare did little for her equilibrium, either. It wasn't an idle threat. She hadn't taken a breath since he'd begun waving it about.

When the first line of spikes crawled up her upper arm it wasn't quite as bad as she'd feared. It produced a prickling sensation that might almost have been pleasant, had she not known the bearer of said implement, and realised he was using a very light touch. If Leyland decided to sink those suckers firmly into her skin there was a good chance there would be screaming and shouting involved, water be damned.

Trying to relax as the spikes scored the thin latex of her suit, she watched as the pinwheel pirouetted all over her body. He trailed a path of fiery spikes up the curve of her breast and skirted the edge of a nipple, watching her shudder in panic. She quickly learned that the initial pressure he'd used was not one he intended to keep up. The pressure and tempo were varied constantly, keeping her on edge. One moment it would be a gentle bristle that had her body humming a tune of excitement, and in the next it felt like someone was trying to drive the point of a needle through her. He worked the tool skilfully and kept her body beautifully tensioned, but when he reached her ass he had some fun with her. As he drove the points down with some considerable force she shrieked and shot up into the air, waggling her tail feathers furiously. Landing heavily on the harsh metal bar was not an experience she cared to repeat, but Leyland had other ideas. He ripped through her thin latex covering effortlessly, tracing a pattern that was neither regular nor recognisable. For the most part the spikes whizzed along her flesh, but when he wanted a little entertainment he slowed things down to a crawl, angled the pinwheel lower in his hand, pressed a little harder and found the most sensitive areas of her flesh. Her ass, her inner thighs, her neck and her breasts were all recipients to his peculiar brand of torture. When he traced it along her pussy lips she jumped so hard she wondered if she'd mutilated herself on the landing. Blood thundered in her ears, and everywhere else for that matter. There was a whole lot of noise going on in her head, possibly silent screams, or possibly something else, but there was no time to examine them. Leyland had his fingers diving inside the latex of her suit and he was ripping the rubber from her body. Zebra stripes were plucked off her skin, piece by piece. Sometimes it was virtually painless and other times the recoil could be likened to that of a slingshot, depending how large a piece of material he had in his hands. The man worked with fervent enthusiasm. It wasn't long before there was a shimmering cloud of latex swirling all around her and her torso was almost naked.

He didn't stop there though. His fingernails worked under the little cylinders that covered her body and popped them free, one by one. He took his time. His fingers explored every inch of her flesh, running their gentle textures along the sculpted contours of her body.

Jenny's legs were once again shaking. The effort of holding herself upright while her body was being slowly worked over was bad enough. The slow increments of pain released with each fin torn from her were going to be her undoing. The first few produced a bearable throbbing that she could contain quite comfortably. After seven or eight things began to change. It felt like someone had turned up her core body temperature by about ten degrees. Things began to simmer and burn out of all proportion. When the last fin had been roughly snatched from her body she resisted the urge to scream. There were seething, burning hot spots all over her body and the warm water that cocooned her did little to improve the situation. Giving Forbes a glowering look she hopped from one flipper to the other, trying her best to alleviate the weight pressing cruelly down upon her clit.

Leyland pulled the gill out of his mouth once more and gave her a dark smile. It was not reassuring. He licked his upper lip and gave her a wink. Jenny wanted to knock him upside the head, but the chains rattling around her wrists suggested otherwise. Even had they been free she would have found herself faced with problems, for Forbes had decided to employ his talented mouth on her person, to great effect. The voices in her mind came back and began roaring once more. His warm tongue began to circle her hotspots, caressing and laving each one in a soothing manner, before letting his teeth give them a sharp nip. That was the trouble with Forbes. You never knew quite where you were. Soft whispers of heat were followed with the biting sting of his nails raking down her back. The soothing caress of his fingers was chased away by another circuit of the pinwheel. It began to drive her crazy. Watching him at work, breathing every now and again through his gill that he kept in a mesh pocket at his side, she knew he was just as dangerous an adversary as Mark. She wouldn't want to cross him. She wondered if Mark knew who it was inside the tank with her. Half of Leyland's face was covered with a thin neoprene hood, and the tinted lens of a diving mask hid his eyes. He wouldn't be easily recognisable at a distance, but perhaps that was part of the game.

When Forbes hooked himself back over the rope that held her upright, in order to bend himself double and attach his mouth to her clit, all reasonable thought left her. Life did not get any more surreal than this. She was being tongued and fingered by a millionaire several times over, six feet underwater, while she was watched and photographed by hundreds of spectators.

The pressure on her clit was excruciating, the slightest movement along the metal bar agony. Forbes was not at all concerned with her distress. He was pulling out all the stops to give his audience the best show ever. From her ankle to the top of her head he stroked, caressed, licked and bit. He interspersed this with lines from his pinwheel and shots of bubbles all over her body. He even had the audacity to wrench her gill from her mouth and kiss her, wrapping his hands around the back of her neck before he sharply pulled off her mask, letting her hood swiftly follow. He wanted everyone to see her. He wanted his perfect shot and he wanted it full of emotion.

Jenny wanted to hate the man in front of her, but the beast was too damn good at what he was doing. Her body was humming a brutal tune, but it was a melody of the finest order. Blood skipped in her veins, thrummed in her ears and throbbed in the parts that were currently suspended in mid-air. The current rocked her, the silence inside her head was overwhelming and Leyland Forbes was a force that could not be denied. Holding on for dear life, when she had no hands to speak of, was no mean feat. Another swoosh of the pinwheel tore off more of her costume and she was beginning to feel like the remains of a shipwreck. Was there anything left to salvage? Her clit felt so bruised that an orgasm would be nigh on impossible, but there was Leyland's tongue on her neck again, his teeth finding her earlobe and she began to wonder just what she might have been capable of, given half a chance. The gill was out of her mouth again, and he drank her in, probably knowing that the lack of breathable air would only serve to arouse her further. Her body was already in fits of spasms, due to his unceasing style of torment, and each second strung itself into a year. Her head had never felt so heavy on her shoulders. Forbes must have known, for his hands kept wrapping around her, supporting and holding her upright. She knew it was all an act. Designed and engineered to annoy Matthews in the most acute fashion possible. He was playing for the crowd and the photographers. The man was probably going to have a picture of her up on his wall with his hands all over her. He could invite Mark round to dinner and have him admire it. Wheels within wheels sprang to mind. Where did this mess end? She was just beginning to realise that she was a very small cog within a massive machine, and her status in life was now little more than a pawn.

A vicious spurt of bubbles, on maximum setting and directed straight at her clit, had her throwing her head back in the throes of ecstasy and blowing her own stream of bubbles. The bubbles below felt like hailstones as they connected and the powerful burst had her foaming at the mouth as she danced around like a bird on a wire. Her plugs were being twisted firmly out of her ass and pussy, and the convulsions all over her body were so tight and so hard she thought she might shatter. Her neck arched back, her hair flew out in a pretty cloud of tangles and everything went blank.

Unable to keep a hold on her gill it floated to the floor yet again, and though her eyes were closed the tank was filled with a bright white light that seemed to go on forever.

CHAPTER THIRTEEN

Chocolate

It could only have been seconds, but one moment she was underwater and in the next there was a large steel hook in her ass that reeled her upwards so damn quickly her ears popped. When she broke the surface the two divers grabbed a hold of her and hoisted her up to the platform. Opening her mouth to suck in a great big gulp of air the room went wild with the sound of camera shutters. She wasn't even aware of her now almost complete nakedness, but a glowering man with his arms folded tightly across his chest was.

'For God's sake get a blanket over her,' he bit out, and when none was forthcoming he tore off his own jacket and draped it over her. 'Tell Leyland his fun is up and if he wants a matching set of black eyes he can discuss the matter with me outside.' Mark hoisted the nearly comatose body of Jennifer Redcliff over his shoulder and strode purposefully from the room, not waiting for a reply. She was nearly asleep in his arms and trailing a river of water along the mosaic tiles. Thankfully someone had put some fluorescent lighting back on, so he could see where he was going, as the room had been swathed in darkness for most of the scene. What a scene it had been, though. Watching the chase had been entertaining enough, and there'd been no sexual antics back then at the start. He'd had another chance to admire her feisty spirit, and he'd actually laughed out loud when she tried to fight him at the beginning with her amusing antics. He hadn't been laughing when the jerk had taken out her gill, though. He'd been mentally rolling up his sleeves and preparing to take a running leap into the top of the tank. Watching her eyes pressed up against the glass as she battled off the force of a pressure hose had done some interesting things to his trousers, and he certainly wasn't the only man in the room who'd had his eyes trained solely on Miss Redcliff. The other girls in the tank weren't from quite such venerable stock and it was clear from the outset that everyone wanted to see the little rich kid brought low. Or high as the case might be.

When her mask was ripped off the exquisite torment on her face as she'd sat on the makeshift wooden pony had been a moment of crowning glory for Forbes. The photographers went crazy, so had Mark for that matter, but his kind of crazy was the kind that wanted to smash every single lens in the room, dive in the tank and haul his girl outta there. Shit. His girl? Had he really just thought that? There was no point going there after the ultimatum Redcliff had left him with. Wouldn't. Couldn't. It might be more than his sanity was worth.

Amusingly, no one stopped him as he strode out of the building with a wet naked girl carried sack-like over his back. Everyone swiftly cleared out of his path, so he figured he must have been glowering more fiercely than he thought. He didn't care. He just wanted out of there.

Jenny was in a state. Tired, hungry, exhausted and damp, she had bits of latex falling in awkward lumps all around her body. Her steel restraints rattled loudly as he carried her, which reminded him that fastening her into a seatbelt was going to be an interesting experience. He refrained from breaking into a run when his feet hit the ostentatious marble steps that framed Leyland's mansion, but the urge to sprint was strong. Forbes wasn't stupid enough to try and stop him, thankfully. Hearing the click of the release lock on his Mercedes he flung open the passenger door and battled with the belt until he managed to feed it through her chains. He then raced over to the boot, got out a blanket and draped it over her, before firing up the engine and turning up the heat full blast. He then depressed a button that lowered her seat into a more comfortable resting position. As he pulled out of the drive with a squeal of gravel underneath his tyres, he saw Jenny's eyes stir and had a moment to rue his impatience.

'How do you feel?' He whispered the question softly, not wanting to disturb her if she was going to go straight back to sleep. There was a long moment of silence and he was confident she'd gone back into the land of nod. Turning his attention back to the road of ahead of him, she made him jump when her voice groggily made an effort to speak.

'Like I've been tied to a railway crossing, run over by a Land Rover, and then had the London-Birmingham express finish me off.'

'That good, huh?' He chuckled. Turning his head to look at her he asked, 'So I'm curious. Did you enjoy yourself out there or not?'

It was her turn to laugh. 'Christ, you need to ask? I should think my face was a picture just before they hauled me out.' Another slow giggle left her lips. 'I am a little pissed, though.'

Mark turned to quirk an eyebrow at her. He wasn't surprised to find out she was pissed, more intrigued that it was 'a little pissed' rather than a whole lot of. 'I'm waiting,' he said.

'That bloody wall of the tank I was attached to had a world of dildos that I worked really hard to try and avoid. Swimming without your arms is nearly impossible - take it from me. So when he took me back I assumed that was what he had in store for me, but no such luck! I only got five minutes with one of the smaller ones right at the end.'

'So you're feeling put out that you didn't get a round with them, huh?' Mark was trying hard to keep a straight face. 'You'll be pleased to know that the other two ladies had lots of fun with them.' Not that anyone noticed, he silently added.

'Typical. I get the heavy-handed treatment, while everyone else gets to play nicely with the vibrators, huh?' She sighed and snuggled down into her blanket, thankful that the car was now warming up rapidly.

'No, you got the Forbes treatment, while everyone else got the standard affair, I believe.'

Jenny, who had been about to nod off once again, snapped open an eye. 'How in the hell did you know that? He was dressed from head to toe in black rubber.'

'I don't, not for certain, but my suspicions are usually correct. Judging by your response they are, which leads me to ask: how did you figure it out?'

'Leyland has very distinctive cold grey eyes and some of the longest eyelashes I have ever seen. It was definitely him.'

'It would have given him an awful lot of entertainment to know he had his hands all over you, while I was watching. He was watching me, too. There were cameras all over, waiting for me to go berserk.'

There was a sleepy yawn, and Jenny couldn't find her hand beneath the blanket in order to cover her mouth. Her limbs were not co-operating as they should, but she guessed it was the tiredness taking over her body. She gave up trying. 'And did you?'

'Fuck no, not till right at the end where I stormed up to the top of the tank. That man has a sixth sense where I'm concerned. You were the first one released from the tank, and there's a reason for that. His days in the land of the living were numbered if I had to get wet.' Mark grinned and took his eyes off the road for a moment in order to examine her. 'How's the back? Did they treat you gently?'

'Mmm, you'd warned them, hadn't you? They were very careful with me. I think I might even have enjoyed myself in a few places.'

He laughed. 'I noticed.'

'So, did you manage to work something out? What's happening now? Am I going back to the stables?'

Mark nearly winced at the question, but managed to keep his face neutral.

'Who do you think is responsible for your stay at Albrecht, Jenny?' He needed to know if she understood who she was dealing with and whilst fairly certain she did know, he had to make sure. He sure as hell wasn't going to be the one to break it to her if she didn't.

'If you think I didn't recognise his voice over the loudspeaker as he chose Kyle for the victor, you are nowhere near as intelligent as I've given you credit for.'

Mark snapped his teeth shut. Women. Narrowing his eyes he couldn't help saying, 'You're forgetting that I'd had no contact with Redcliff and absolutely no idea what his voice sounded like.'

'You didn't then. You have more than enough means to have discovered who the mysterious owner is by now.'

Mark pursed his lips and resisted the urge to smile. This one was nowhere near as foolish as she would have led him to believe.

'You do the stupid act very well, don't you? Socialite bimbo without a care in the world bar when her nails are going to be painted or when her back is about to be massaged. It is an act, though, isn't it?' He stared up at the darkening sky thoughtfully. 'The question is why?'

Jenny debated answering his enquiry, which was littered with cerebral landmines, but decided she was going to have to trust someone and Mark was her last resort. 'I do what is expected of me and I act accordingly. I learnt a long time ago that if I play the fool I learn a whole lot more than if I offer up a whiff of intelligence. I get into a lot less trouble if I'm the clueless daughter, with no hope of understanding the logistics of the oil business... or other things.'

Mark narrowed his eyes as he cast a sidelong glance at her. 'Doesn't keeping up an act like that on a daily basis drive you mad?'

'It keeps me out of the limelight for the most part, and these days that's all I care about.' Even as she uttered the words, Jenny knew them for a lie. That had been then. Now she was faced with a whole different ballgame and she had goals. Big goals. She turned the conversation back to him. 'So what did he say when you offered to buy me?'

He nearly knocked the transmission into reverse after that remark. Here was a girl who clearly knew her game. He guessed there was no point beating around the bush. 'He said no.'

'What did you offer?'

Mark felt rather uncomfortable as he answered, 'A lot.'

'Ten million? Twenty? I can help you get some of the money. I'm not entirely useless.'

'I offered fifty and then asked him to name his price. He still said no.' Mark felt an edge creeping into his voice as he remembered his conversation with her father.

She whistled and gave him a wan half-smile, fighting the heavy drag of her eyelids as they formed a determined path downwards. As her eyes shuttered themselves for sleep she managed one last sentence. 'Then he wants something else, and whatever it is, you'd better watch out. He's a man who always gets what he wants and he fights dirty.'

Jenny's head lolled awkwardly to the side and it was clear she didn't expect an answer, which was just as well, because Mark's reply would have been something along the lines of, 'There's no fucking way he's getting it this time.' Instead he drummed his fingers against the steering wheel and turned up the stereo. Beethoven's *Ode to Joy* thrummed through the speakers, which he found highly inappropriate and immediately punched his finger against the control to fast forward the annoyingly upbeat tune. Beethoven's *Descent into Madness* replaced it and that just about fit the bill for his current and most dark frame of mind. The road ahead was not impossible, but it was proving a good deal more challenging than he had anticipated.

Jenny had no idea how long she slept, but when she awoke the world had gone black. A couple of hours would have been her best guess. She seemed to have managed a lot of sleeping today, whether synthetically or otherwise. This time she seemed a little more alert than before, so natural sleep had to be the way forward.

'You snore and you dribble.' Mark's voice held a note of amusement within it.

'And I suppose you wake up smelling of daisies without a hair out of place?'

'Yes, that's exactly it.'

As she glanced at him she saw his lips twitch.

'Liar,' she whispered.

'You'll pay for that later, young lady. And I'll have you know that for the most part it's true, mainly because I don't sleep.'

She snorted, clearly disbelieving, but let the matter drop.

'So,' he continued, changing the subject, 'what lengths would you be willing to go to right now for a bar of chocolate?'

Jenny rubbed her eyes with the blanket and gave the matter some grave consideration. 'I'd probably commit murder for sugar, and as chocolate is even higher up my list of things I've missed most in captivity, let's just say I'd do an awful lot.'

'Oh,' was all he said, and Jenny found the 'oh' particularly annoying. The infernal man mentioned chocolate as if he'd had some, and then went silent on her. This was chocolate they were talking about. Chocolate! Life sustaining, sugar-rush, mouth-watering treat type material. She hadn't had any in a week and she'd had serious withdrawal symptoms, to say the least. She glowered at him, which amazed even herself, because it proved she wasn't intimidated or afraid of him, and she probably should have been. The man was dangerous to her. Forgetting that fact would be a mistake.

When a few seconds of silence had passed he said, 'It's a shame, you know, because I have a bar of Bernachon chocolate here, reportedly some of the finest French chocolate in the world, but I'm not really interested in being murdered, so I guess I'll just have to eat it myself. Pulling a bar of decadently dark chocolate from his glove compartment and removing the gold-edged wrapper, he broke a single piece off and let it melt slowly on his tongue.

'Oh God, I can smell that.' Jenny took a moment to suck in the most pleasant scent she had smelled in a long time. Then her attention was focused solely on him. 'You have no idea how much I have missed chocolate. Please can I have a bit? I'll do anything you want, and I mean anything, but don't torture me by making me watch you eat it.'

Mark closed his eyes and appeared to savour the chocolate, before he replied,

'I can smell you. You smell of sex and brine and sweat, and whilst that shouldn't be a particularly hedonistic scent, it seems to be doing funny things to my libido. If you can find a way to scratch the itch, then I might, just might, give you a bite.'

'A bite? A single bite? You want me to give you a blowjob for a bite of chocolate?' Jenny looked incredulous.

'Well, that's not exactly the way I would have phrased it, but yes, in a nutshell, that's exactly it.'

'Are you nuts?' Her mouth was still hanging open.

Mark broke off another large piece of chocolate with his teeth and sighed with apparent ecstasy. 'Yes, walnuts. There's a lovely crunch every time you sink your teeth into...'

Jenny didn't want to hear any more and squeaked, 'Are you really going to sit there and make me watch you eat the whole thing, without sharing a single piece?'

Mark thought for a couple of seconds. 'Pretty much, yes. Obviously I don't want to force you into doing anything you don't want to do, but I'm afraid I'm not the sharing type. Now if I was distracted, you could probably wrestle the bar of chocolate out of my hands and I'd hardly even notice.'

'But you're driving,' she said slowly, as if talking to a small child, 'and it's highly illegal.'

'Only if you get caught,' said Mark, flashing her his trademark bright white smile and adding a wink for good measure. 'Besides, I'd blame you. You viciously came at me, while I was minding my own business driving my car, and though I tried really hard to get you off me there was nothing I could do. Did I mention the *really hard* part?' He crumbled another piece of chocolate upon his teeth and used his fingers to scoop the messy debris into his mouth. 'Mmhmm,' he said, closing his eyes and plastering a blissful smile upon his face. Then through a full mouthful of sticky coco solids he continued, 'Id I ention, is is eally ood.'

Jenny screamed as he finished his mouthful and looked on in horror as the bar was now half-finished.

'I'd get to work quickly if I were you. One, I close my eyes an awful lot when eating chocolate, and that's never a good thing when you're on the road, and two, there isn't going to be anything left for you to eat if you don't hurry.'

Unfastening her seatbelt Jenny reached to grab the offending bar out of his hands, but he was too quick for her. Waggling it against the driver's side window, well out of the way of her grasping fingertips, he said, 'That just earned you a spanking, young lady.'

'Like I wasn't going to get one of those anyway,' she grumbled, already trying her best to unfasten his fly.

'That just earned you another, smartass.' The sound of a rasping zipper could be heard and it was all Mark could do not to punch his fist through the roof of the car. At last! This must have been the longest he had waited for a blowjob in the history of ever. As her mouth hovered over his crotch, her hot breath already making him jump, he found his tongue stuck painfully in his throat. It already felt amazing and she hadn't got anywhere near him yet. Here was a woman who might almost be worth tangling with Redcliff for. Almost.

She made him wait for her throat. Her two slim hands had a little fun with him, as best they could while wearing thick steel cuffs, and her tongue teased up and down the length of him. The oh-so slight pressure was exquisite. While she was working on getting him good and wet, teasing him around his glans and dipping her tongue into his urethra, he did his best to keep himself as still as possible. No point in letting her know she was any good just yet, he thought. She kept up the light teasing for a minute or two, but he was lost as soon as her lips hovered over him. It felt like steam was pouring out of her mouth and after the colossal evening his cock had been faced with, watching her being brought to orgasm again and again from the sidelines, it deserved a little attention. When she finally did close her lips around him and locked her jaw down tightly, he couldn't help an, 'Ah, fuck me,' but he cleverly countered it with, 'this has to be the best chocolate in the world.' It got the desired response, because she growled and then she really went to work on him.

Mark had no recollection of when he dropped the rest of the chocolate bar, but it must have slithered through his fingers silently on its descent, for Jenny did not stir from her ministrations. She was most adept at what she was tackling, and though the edges of her manacles bit rather painfully into his thigh, he was content to leave her exactly as she was for now, because to remove that deliciously tight mouth from his cock would be more painful than he could bear.

Using her fist along his shaft, she squeezed with just the right amount of pressure to make him shudder, and somehow a couple of her fingers made their way to his perineum, that wonderful spot right below his testicles that most of the newbies had never heard about. Miss Redcliff knew her subject, and she knew it well. She gently rolled his balls in her hand with a deliciously light touch and she alternated between long, pounding, deep throat spears, and then gentle little nudges which did nothing more than cover his glans before she bounced right back up again.

It was a struggle to contain himself. If he'd have let go he'd have come within perhaps a minute, but intended to savour the moment he had worked so hard to achieve. If this was the only twenty-four hours of his life that he was going to have the undivided attention of Jennifer Redcliff, then he was going to make every second count, so he gritted his teeth and held out. There wasn't much willpower left in him though. When she went back to fisting him and using her mouth on the sensitive little line right at the front of his cock he nearly went insane. There was no holding back after that. Three, two, one and a full engine blowout.

'Fuck, I've lost the wheel,' he yelled, as he felt himself squirting into the back of her throat, feeling her jaw bear down on him as she swallowed. He closed his eyes in bliss as he continued to pump inside her. The wait had been endless, but the result was nothing short of a miracle. The girl gave head with expert precision and finesse, and for a trainee, that was pretty impressive.

After his words, though, Jenny almost leapt off him in her haste to grab the wheel and get her face angled towards the road. She nearly dismembered him in the process, damn the blasted woman.

He shifted a little underneath her and tucked himself back in his pants. 'Relax. We've been stationary for the past ten minutes. I figured you might have noticed.'

Jenny's head snapped back towards him and her eyes narrowed. 'I was a little preoccupied and you just scared the hell out of me, you... you...'

Mark sat there quietly, a little smile playing around the corners of his lips as he began to lick his fingers clean, one by one.

'Oh my God,' screamed Jenny, 'you've eaten my chocolate!' Her eyes took on the murderous hue her previous comments had hinted at.

'Actually, it was my chocolate and it was very good chocolate. You're watching your figure, aren't you?' He raised an eyebrow at her cheekily.

'Right, that's it, Matthews! I am going to bite it off,' and to give the girl her due, the expression on her face as she lunged for him would have scared off a Mafia Don.

'Relax. You've got a fresh bar in the glovebox,' he said, laughing his head off as he tried his best to battle her head away from his crotch. 'Can't give you the rest of mine as it's gathering fluff on the floor somewhere.' He winked at her.

Scowling, she settled back against her seat and waited while he battled with the catch. In no time at all he'd wrested a fresh bar of sweet-smelling chocolate from inside the dark confines and offered it to her.

'Want to eat it here or do you want to go inside?'

'Here.' Jenny's fingers were already frantically tearing the wrapper off. Having been denied any form of sugar for the past week had been absolute hell, and she was anxious to remedy the fact. She practically stuffed the first bite into her mouth cellophane and all. It didn't help that she was also starving hungry, the joys of several intense hours of sexual torment having taken its toll.

'Go slowly,' he cautioned, 'or you'll make yourself sick, and if you make yourself sick, you'll be in for three sets of spankings which your backside will not be able to handle. Take my word for it.'

Jenny scowled at him from under her dark lashes, but she did take the threat seriously and slowed her almost animalistic behaviour down. As the first square of chocolate began to melt on her tongue and its sweetness saturated her mouth, she groaned, squirmed and closed her eyes. 'This is better than sex,' she whispered as her teeth bit through the delicate, nutty tang of walnuts.

'You haven't been doing it right in that case,' he said, raising an eyebrow provocatively.

Jenny flicked her eyes sideways at him and grinned. 'You'd best show me the error of my ways in a bit, then.'

'Oh, I intend to,' he replied, 'but first we're going out to dinner, so hurry up salivating over that chocolate bar, and then I can get you inside and showered for your big date.'

Jenny snorted. 'That's not even funny. I have my hands and feet cuffed in restraints you cannot remove and I'm naked. Think again, hotshot.' She took another bite of chocolate and mewled in delight.

'Young lady,' said Mark, in a much firmer tone that had her sitting upright immediately, 'this is where we are going to have problems. If you're determined to come and live with me and serve in the capacity of a submissive, then what you think is irrelevant. You don't get to think. All that needs to be in that pretty little head of yours is the willingness to obey.' He had no idea why he was spouting off, because it was unlikely that Jennifer Redcliff was going to be his in any way, shape or form, but for some reason he hadn't given up hope just yet and intended to see if the girl could, in fact, do as she was told.

'Fine.' Popping the last tiny morsel of chocolate into her mouth, and then licking her lips carefully to catch the few errant smears that remained, she threw off her blanket and made to open the door.

'Wait,' barked Mark, who immediately pressed the central locking switch just to be on the safe side. 'I would prefer it if we didn't scandalise all the neighbours in my apartment block, so I'm going to carry you upstairs in your blanket. We'll work out something a little better for this evening, but don't worry; you won't be naked.' You'll be squirming, you'll be wet, and you'll be drunk with desire, but you won't be naked, Mark added mentally to himself, the possibilities already spinning wildly inside his head.

'Spoilsport,' uttered Jenny, with a wicked gleam in her eyes.

That was when Mark knew for certain that he'd have a whole bunch of trouble on his hands if he took the feisty girl on, and damned if it didn't make the prospect a whole lot more exciting. Unbelievably his trousers were dictating that he was ready and rearing to go again. He almost sighed. He'd just regressed fifteen years of his life in an instant, and the feeling was intoxicating.

'Miss Redcliff, it appears that your smart mouth needs addressing.' He gave her a dark stare, which wiped the smile off her face in an instant. Climbing out of the car and taking his time as he went to open her door, he pulled it sharply towards him and gave her another long, hard stare. 'We can play this one of two ways,' he said softly, and from his chilling tone it was abundantly clear who was once again in charge. 'Either you can cover yourself back up with that blanket, apologise profusely and meekly, and come into my arms willingly, or I'm more than happy to do things the hard way.'

'Out of curiosity, what is "the hard way"?' Jenny asked, not able to resist goading him, before immediately regretting her question. His tall frame was suddenly all over hers and his face was mere centimetres away, causing her to sink deep into her seat. She cast her eyes downward, to avoid his penetrating glare.

'The hard way involves you crawling on your hands and knees naked, firstly on tarmac and then on stone, before riding up a busy public elevator to my penthouse suite. If you'd like further humiliation I'm happy to lead you around by your collar and leash, and I'm sure I can find a pretty pink bow for your hair and a matching tail for your ass. I could spank you along the way and we could also make sure a couple of my neighbours get their cell phones out and email the pictures to their friends. So what's it to be?'

Jenny wrapped the blanket around her body tightly and the light that had been within her eyes a few short seconds ago died. Mark almost regretted his harshness. It wasn't that she didn't need to be put in her place, for if she were to live with him there would be plenty of rules she would have to abide by, but he found he didn't entirely mind having an opponent in which to battle wits with. The girls in the office had been far too well trained to question any of his instructions, but once in a while the challenge of dealing with a recalcitrant sub was something to relish. Jennifer Redcliff wasn't going to be preparing for war at this moment in time though. She struggled out of the car as best she was able, mummified in a blanket and still chained from head to foot.

Standing before him, eyes downcast and her forehead furrowed in lines of misery, she whispered an apologetic, 'Sorry.' It was convincing enough. He bent down to swoop her up in his arms and it didn't take him long to march through a set of automatic doors, which opened outward to admit his entrance. The concierge proffered a greeting and Mark met it with a smile and an incline of his head, but he didn't stop his brisk pace. Heading straight for the lift he contained his sigh of relief that the thing was empty. He didn't bring women back to his apartment. If he did, they would have been on two feet to save awkward questions later. Had Jenny defied him, however, he would have made sure that she enacted his punishment in full. If he threatened a punishment he meant to go through with it, whatever the cost. In this case it would be either a new apartment, which would be somewhat inconvenient, or several sets of new neighbours, which might be even more inconvenient. One way or another, his level of control would be maintained.

At level ten the lift did a stomach-dropping lurch and proceeded to slow down. Mark debated pressing the alarm, with the hopes of scaring the interloper off, but decided against it. The action would probably be more trouble than it was worth. Instead he bent to whisper to Jenny, his hot breath tickling her ear as he murmured, 'Screaming for help is not an option right now.'

CHAPTER FOURTEEN

Kegels

When Mrs Esslemont entered the lift Mark wanted to roll his eyes and growl in frustration. Here was perhaps the only busybody in the building, and he had to meet her, today of all days. Watching Jenny's eyes as they darted over to the newcomer, he wondered if she would try anything. She'd be foolish to, because he'd already waved the remote control for her shock collar in front of her eyes and the blinking red light indicated that it had been switched on. If she talked, she wasn't going to talk for long. Explaining why she couldn't talk to the lovely Mrs Esslemont would be another matter entirely, though.

He smiled weakly at his neighbour and hoped the art of conversation was dead.

'Evening, Matthews.' Mrs Esslemont sniffed delicately and looked pointedly at Jenny. 'Is your lady-friend OK?'

What Mrs Esslemont actually meant was: I need as much gossip as you can give me, so I may liberally spread it in every corner of the world I can reach.

'Lady-friend?' repeated Mark absently, because the term was a new one and he needed to roll it about on his tongue.

Mrs Esslemont tucked a stray grey curl back into her plum hat and adjusted her agate necklace. Staring at Jenny once again, finding no help forthcoming from Mark, she waved her fingers over in her direction, as if Jenny was something unmentionable.

'Oh, you mean my sister,' said Mark, whose brain had once again caught up with the proceedings. 'She's been in hospital, poor dear. Had a bit of an accident and now her husband is away for a week, so I'm going to take care of her until he gets back. It'll be lovely catching up, won't it, Liz?' He looked down at Jenny and gave her his most avuncular, tender smile. Jenny nodded weakly.

'What's that big silver thing around her neck?'

Mark gritted his teeth and almost wished he'd had Jenny crawl in here on her hands and knees, as she'd offered. At least the old bag would have been too shocked to say a word.

'She's a fashion student,' said Mark, wrinkling his nose as if that explained everything, and apparently it did, for Mrs Esslemont uttered no further questions. Her gaze did start straying along the whole length of Jenny's body, though, and Mark nearly had kittens as he wondered if any loose 'chain' was dangling around. Thankfully, the lift chose that moment to swoop to a stop and Mrs Esslemont had her appearance to consider, because she turned her attention back to the stray strands of hair around her face, which she then began to tuck back into her hat.

'Have a very pleasant evening, Mrs Esslemont,' Mark said, as she stepped out onto the fourteenth floor.

'Thank you most kindly, Mr Matthews, you too,' she sang, as she waddled off in the direction of her apartment without a further glance back, her voluminous paisley-printed skirt billowing around her in all directions. Mark breathed a gigantic sigh of relief and couldn't help but laugh as Jenny glared at him. He tapped her collar pensively. 'I think I'm going to enjoy my peace and quiet for just a little bit longer,' he said wickedly.

Punching in his entry code, Mark took in a deep, calming breath as soon as the door had shut firmly closed behind him. Depositing Jenny on the floor without further ado, he strode off towards the kitchen and turned the coffee machine on. His body required caffeine in the worst way. Sleep had been even more elusive than usual, and a shot of Italian coffee beans would give him a new perspective on the world, hopefully. Looking briefly over his shoulder, to see what his captive was up to, it was to find her clambering up the length of his door, trying to examine the keypad.

'The door's locked and cannot be undone without a six numbered code. If I find you near that keypad again we'll forgo the hand spankings and move straight to the riding crop and a selection of whips. It would be a crying shame to have you squirming all through dinner, unable to enjoy your meal, wouldn't it?'

Jenny gave him a look of loathing, but obediently moved away from the door.

He didn't pause for breath. 'When in my house I expect you to crawl at all times, unless you've been granted permission to do otherwise. You must not speak unless you're spoken to, although that won't be a problem with your collar at the moment. You are not to wear clothes or any other garment for that matter, unless I personally place it upon you. To make things abundantly clear, you have absolutely no rights in this household. You give them all up when taking on the role of my submissive, and crossing the threshold of my apartment door signifies as such. You are even required to obtain permission to go to the bathroom. If in doubt, you need permission. All rules are non-negotiable. Failure to comply will mean your immediate return to Albrecht stables, where I suspect Mr Levison cannot wait to get his hands on you. Nod your head if you have understood the rules. If not I am more than happy to repeat them.'

Jenny gave him a level look, met his hard gaze, and dipped her eyes to the floor. She did not doubt the sincerity of his words, apparently, for she quickly nodded her head. Pulling the Albrecht card might have been mean of him, but it saved wasting time. If they only had the next twenty-four hours together, he was going to make every millisecond count.

Giving her a blank stare he said, 'You may crawl into the bedroom and bend over the edge of my bed to await my displeasure at your earlier disobedience. I will be with you shortly.' He abruptly turned away from her and busied himself with dispensing a steaming stream of bitter Italian coffee.

The smell of intense, aromatic coffee made Jenny's mouth water. Like chocolate, it was another of the things she had missed horribly. When used to drinking five or six cups daily, the withdrawal symptoms were none too pleasant, but to be fair, she'd had bigger problems to worry about at Albrecht. Sighing dejectedly she crawled quickly along his spotlessly clean kitchen floor, and tried to hold her breath until she reached his bedroom. Spying two doors in front of her, one obviously leading into a bathroom, she pushed the other open with her nose and found her knees greeted by a silky-soft charcoal carpet. Her eyes feasted on a king-sized double bed outfitted in shockingly bright white linen. Well, she was about to mess that up big style, but that wasn't her problem. She'd been ordered to smother herself into it, and if he wanted little pieces of brown and white latex smeared all over the place, that was his problem.

He made her wait, but she expected nothing less. Teasing her with the scent of caffeine was almost as bad as waiting for the inevitable smack of his hand. Interestingly, she no longer feared him, but also knew she could not push him. She needed to keep Mark Matthews on her side, because she had to get out of Albrecht. This might be her only chance, and whilst life under Matthews might be demanding, it wouldn't be unbearable. The trouble was that she had a hard time controlling her impulsiveness and temper on occasion. She guessed that was about to change. Feeling a sudden current of airflow over her body she felt herself bristling in anticipation.

'Your collar is off. You may speak.' He was directly behind her.

Her sensible brain cells were immediately overwritten by her outraged ones. 'Your sister?' she squeaked.

'I had a feeling I should have left that on,' Mark said. 'Yes, my sister. Obviously I could have said I'd like to introduce you to my new kinky, live-in lover, but that would have probably involved the press at my door this evening, and it would be mightily inconvenient. Now that you're my sister, you're rather boring and mundane. It won't be very exciting gossip for her to pass around.'

'So I'm to answer to Liz and look adoringly at you, that right?'

He laughed. 'I chose Liz because it's one of the most common names I could think of, just in case she decides to Google a Liz Matthews, although I should think that kind of technology is beyond her. As to the "look adoringly" part, that won't be a problem in a few minutes, I assure you.'

Jenny buried her face in the starchy, smooth material of his bedlinen. She couldn't smother a snort, but at least she managed to bury her pithy comeback. The next thing she knew Mark was pulling a long piece of her ragged latex suit away from her ass. He let it snap back sharply.

'You'll need to control those unladylike snorts, little Miss.' It was accompanied by the firm slap of his hand, before he traced a single finger up the spine of her back.

She couldn't help a shudder. Being spanked was one thing, but being spanked by a man who could turn her on by the touch of a single fingertip was something else entirely.

'We need to work together, you and I,' said Mark, and his lips descended to nuzzle her neck, 'because I suspect we want the same thing.'

'You want ten tonnes of sugar and a three litre vat of coffee?'

She was rewarded with a sharp nip for her troubles. 'Don't go vampire on me,' she threatened, 'I've already got you down as the big bad wolf.'

He laughed. 'Because I can see you, smell you and eat you better than anyone else you've ever known?'

'No, it was a "who's afraid of the big bad wolf" thing, but you've been replaced in that department. Anyway, tell me what we're working together on.'

'You're not afraid of me any more? Hmph. We'll have to work on that.' He ignored her question and let his lips travel along the line of her jaw as his fingers gently kneaded her buttocks. The feeling was electric on her bright pink skin.

'I'm never especially comfortable around you,' she yelped as she received a backhander on her left butt-cheek, 'but I'm not afraid of you, no.'

'Good.' Her right cheek was subjected to the same treatment and it felt divine. He then pressed something cold and hard against the entrance to her pussy, and she instinctively moved upwards to avoid it.

'Relax. It's just a set of Ben Wa balls. They'll help improve your pelvic floor muscles because you'll have to squeeze tightly to keep them inside you. Lots of squeezing makes my fun in the bedroom infinitely more entertaining.' Another slap on her backside, but the first ball was already being worked inside her and it felt sublime. It was heavy, smooth and almost certainly made of some kind of metal. Her money would be on stainless steel.

'These are some of the heaviest ones I can find, mainly because I don't like to make my games too easy for you. If you live under my roof you're going to have to work for everything, and I mean *everything*, but that's all part of the fun. If you can figure out a way to please me I'll make your life bearable.' He stroked the line of her throat and tongued the unbelievably sensitive spot just behind her earlobe. She shuddered.

'Does bearable include unlimited amounts of coffee and chocolate?' There was another petulant yelp as he increased the strength of his swats, but she didn't wiggle out of the way.

'No, and never tell me stuff like that, because now I'll ration both coffee and chocolate until you're begging for the stuff. I like watching women beg. There's something amazing about watching a woman beg, especially for sex.' He winked at her. 'I'll remember to cover you from head to toe in chocolate body-paint frequently, in order to torment the hell out of you.' The second kegel ball was slotted into place, as deep inside her as his fingers would go. There was a pause as her body took a moment to spasm all over. Matthews aroused her just by speaking, dammit, all the rest of the stuff was just overkill in her opinion. Biting her tongue sharply she managed to get a hold of herself.

'That might be OK, as long as I get a chance to lick the stuff off,' said Jenny thoughtfully.

'Oh no. I'll be painting your chocolate rations somewhere far more interesting.' Mark pulled her away from the bed and stood directly in front of her. Jenny was trying hard not to laugh. She couldn't help it. The image of Matthews with his cock covered in chocolate was doing strange things to her libido.

'Now I'm curious. Would you like your chocolate rations orally or as a suppository? I'm sure the sugar would hit you quicker if we...'

'Nooo,' Jenny bit out, and the man had successfully wiped the smile off her face in an instant, which she guessed was his goal.

'Right, enough distractions. The name of the game is this... I have a pair of bolt cutters that will make moving and walking far less embarrassing for your restaurant visit. You keep those balls inside you for the next ten minutes, no matter what I do to you, and I'll see what I can manage with regards to your restraints. You'll still have the cuffs on, of course, but you will be able to move - a little bit of freedom for a little bit of effort. What do you say, Miss Redcliff?'

'Game on,' came the reply.

The pressure of the heavy metal balls inside her had seemed fine at first. Mark made her crawl around the floor a bit, and introduced a flogger to the proceedings, but it was not particularly hard work to keep them securely inside her. She had to squeeze the muscles of her vagina tightly together, but the initial effort required to do so was sustainable, or so she'd thought.

Moving around proved difficult, not because of the chains, she'd almost become used to those, but when the balls vibrated and bounced together they sent shockwaves of pleasure radiating through her body. The flogger drove her this way and that throughout his apartment, and each twist and turn was murder on her insides.

'I've waited a long time to fuck you, Jennifer Redcliff.' His voice echoed in her ears but she didn't fully comprehend their meaning until a few moments later. 'Whatever I want is usually delivered immediately to me, with no questions asked. I guess that's one of the perks of being me. Having to wait over a week for something I really want is unheard of, and yet here I am still as excited by you as the first day I laid eyes on you. Scrap that, even more so. I want to pin you to the wall like a fucking Van Gogh, Miss Redcliff, and just like the Van Gogh, I wouldn't mind if you graced my wall for several years or more. Does that scare you? Do you want to serve, Jenny? Do you want to serve me? Or are you, perhaps, just telling me the words I want to hear so you can run out on me at the first opportunity?'

To prove his point, Mark had scooped her up off the floor and slammed her backside against the bright white wall behind her. He obviously preferred the minimalist look, because not a single painting adorned it, which was probably a good thing when your head was being slammed against it. Not that she cared. Her body was buzzing with an intensity that had little to do with the vibrating balls inside her. Just one look from the annoying man in front of her and she was reduced to speaking gibberish. He had his flies undone and his cock nudging for entrance at her pussy, which might explain her inability to articulate words, but then again those smouldering brown eyes could produce naked flames if one weren't careful. When he thrust himself inside her and smacked into the two balls she nearly exploded on the spot.

There was no question that she was wet. Dripping wet. These days she was always soaked. But having two heavy vibrating balls slammed into your cervix was an experience she was not going to forget in a hurry. Finally she got a grip on her tongue. 'So,' she said breathlessly, feeling his mouth hovering above her nipple, 'where are the Van Gogh's?' Bathing in the hot air from his mouth her nipple pleaded for more, and finally he teased it with his tongue. Small licks and flicks was all it was treated to, but it cried out for more, stretching and straining its little self until it could grow no more.

'I already told you, *you* are the Van Gogh, and if you don't shut up I might decide to hang you here permanently for my own personal use.'

His strokes were blunt but fierce. He worked the balls inside her as deep as they would go, cupping her reddened ass in his hands and tilting her towards him. Grinding against her clit, she was once again mute, so his threat had been a pointless one. Her head was in another place entirely and it was a happy place. Each thrust knocked the balls about inside her and they played a decadently wonderful tune.

'Madam, I am at your cervix for the entire evening,' Mark whispered, barely holding back a chuckle. Jenny didn't care. She was almost at the point where she was hoping his earlier threat might come true. Being pinned against his wall for this kind of regular treatment wouldn't be a hardship. Au contraire. It would be fucking amazing. But before that thought had a chance to be examined he pulled out of her.

Two heavy metal balls plummeted downwards and she did her best to slow their descent by clenching her PC muscles as hard as she could. Her face twisted as the effort of gripping them took hold.

'I'm not going to make this easy on you, Pet. You're going to have to work to keep those balls inside you. Grabbing her wrists, one at a time, he slammed them into the wall above her head. 'Tell me what you want,' he growled.

But she wasn't going to give in that easily. If he wanted to play nasty then so could she, and the chocolate episode was still fresh in her mind. 'I want,' she breathed in sexily and fluttered her eyelashes in great swoops that Cleopatra would have been proud of, 'the largest cup of coffee that you can find.'

He grinned evilly, and she knew instantly that she'd made a mistake, but controlling the things that flowed out of her mouth had never been one of her strong points and even less so in the heat of the moment. His cock slid between her legs and gently stroked the edges of her labia. Moving back and forth he teased her gently and she groaned in arousal. 'There goes your "before-dinner-orgasm" darling, and you'll be lucky if I don't take you out to dinner stark naked and wearing even more chains than you are already. Does that appeal?'

'No,' she mewled, swiftly curtailing anything else that might have threatened to spill out of her mouth. She had more important things to worry about. The heavy balls inside her were slipping. If she'd behaved herself she would barely have had to work for her bolt cutters, but now, without his help... things were getting difficult. Clamping together her tiring muscles, the lines of strain became evident upon her face.

'So let's try that again. Tell me what you want.' His eyes tunnelled into hers, his body pinned her to the wall so that she could barely breathe and his cock continued to stroke her. It took her several seconds to get her lips to move.

'I want to erase last week. I want to bury my father in a shallow grave. I want to feel safe again. I want a decent meal. I want another orgasm. But most of all, right at this moment in time, I want to watch you explode. I want to know if those dark eyes before me have ever known a moment's peace and I want to watch you let go.' There was honesty in her eyes and they were most beguiling.

There was a pause as he digested each of her words. 'You do amuse me, madam, but your wish is my command.' He uttered no word of a lie. The metal balls clanged inside her as he hammered against the wall, and she took a moment to wonder where he was trying to bury the damn things. Higher and higher she edged up the wall, and with each grind of his cock she desperately tried to wrench herself forward, in order to get just that little bit of friction her clit needed to plunge over the edge, but he was on to her. One hand held her neck, his body pinned the rest, and there was little hope that he'd change his mind. The vibrations of his thrusting flooded through her and she opened her mouth to scream, but he was ready for her. His thumb pressed sharply against her windpipe and it died in her throat.

'I have neighbours and as Mrs Esslemont thinks you're my sister, it might be wise to keep the noise down.' She nodded her understanding, but was more interested in watching his face, which was already twisted in a grimace of pleasure. She knew he was close. Another thrust and then another, and finally he let out an animalistic grunt, driving his fist into the plaster. 'Fuck, I needed that,' he said, as he let her slide gently down the wall.

When Jenny had recovered her breath, at least a minute or so later, Mark had already walked out of the room. There was the sound of running water and then the unmistakeable flush of the toilet. It appeared she had been casually dismissed. Not willing to take such a snub lying down she yelled, 'Permission to crawl through your house and pee, Sir?' She was fairly sure that would generate a reaction.

'Permission granted, and keep the noise down or I'll turn your collar back on.'

It was not quite the reaction she'd hoped for. Frowning, she got up on all fours and clenched her now enormously heavy Ben Wa balls deep inside her. Hearing his footsteps recede down the hall she admired the stark stripes of the pristine black and white rug below her. She hadn't even noticed it was there. Mark's bedroom was pretty unremarkable. White furniture, white walls, black carpet, and on the east elevation there was a floor to ceiling white drape, which he'd drawn. The view below must be really bad, she thought. All in all, it took the word 'minimalist' to the extreme and was probably one of the dullest room's on earth. A rabbit hutch had more character. There wasn't a stray magazine to be found, the odd sock or even a robe hung on the back of the door. Hell, there wasn't even a wardrobe to be seen. What did the man do with his clothes?

Padding along the floor until she found the bathroom Mark had recently vacated, she was greeted with a white ceramic suite that didn't have a colour in sight. Whoever cleaned this place must love him, she thought sourly. Propping herself up as best as she could on the toilet, thankful for the small comforts his apartment afforded if nothing else, she sighed and relaxed. Just before she relieved herself two metal balls clanged loudly into the toilet bowl.

Jenny smacked her forehead awkwardly with her hand and hoped to hell she'd made it past the ten-minute mark.

CHAPTER FIFTEEN
Wined, Dined and Electrified

An hour later and Jenny had been whisked away to a private salon in the Dorchester Hotel. Mark had been ever the attentive host. He gently bathed her in his six-foot claw tub and scrubbed away every last remnant of latex from her body. Then he had towelled her down, carried her to his bed and given her a sensuous but brief massage, liberally covering her in scented oils with notes of citrus, coconut and sweet almond. She had almost fallen asleep under his talented hands, almost but not quite. His wandering fingers had found every single one of her body's sweet spots, and worked the oil into her skin with skill and speed. He had lingered for a few minutes on her pussy and ass, sliding the oil deep inside her, but had given her clit nothing more than a token rub. So alas, sleep was not going to be an option until that itch was scratched.

'Did you know that Forbes very kindly gave me a present before we departed for home? Can you guess what it is?' The soft skin of his wrists had begun to work out some knots in her upper back, rolling up and down her ribcage, and the feeling was blissful. He was careful to avoid her lower back, which was still extremely tender. Just as her body once again disintegrated into liquid and lazy, there was a cold hard feeling at the entrance to her sphincter. She squeaked and tried to shoot upwards, but as usual he was ready for her, with a palm against the flat of her back. 'He returned your plugs to me. He figured I might need them later, and indeed I do. How else will I keep you in line over dinner?'

Jenny couldn't help a groan. It was partly due to the fact that the evening's events had taken a downturn for the worse and partly due to him rimming her tight hole with the tapered point of the steel plug. She needed to come, so very badly.

'So, I thought we'd charge up your little beasties and have some fun with them over our Chateaubriand and a bottle of Nuit-St-Georges. Obviously you'll be having much more fun than I, but I'm sure I can derive some form of entertainment by watching that delightfully expressive face of yours.'

'Which will obviously be swearing at you, loudly, embarrassing you in front of all of the guests,' she said.

He smacked her oiled ass, hard, and the neat slap had her begging for more of the same, though none were forthcoming.

'Ah, but that's where you're wrong. Firstly, we'll be in a private salon, so there will be no one's eyes on you but mine, and secondly, you'll be wearing your collar, which I fully intend to turn up to the max. You utter so much as a squeak and you'll light up the room.' He bent over her shoulder and chuckled in her ear, as his hands worked the soft curves of her breasts beneath.

'That doesn't sound like a particularly fun evening,' grumbled Jenny, who couldn't be too mad when her nipples were being slowly squeezed, tweaked and gently pulled.

'Oh I assure you it will be, for me, and that's all you need concern yourself with. That's what your life is all about now. Showing me your utter devotion and absolute capitulation in every task I may choose to set for you.' He moved back down her body and the plug was once again pressing at her rear. 'Relax for me, sweetness. It will go in much easier if you relax, and we need to loosen you up for later. This is a kindness, believe me, because you have a hell of an evening ahead.'

So, here she was, sitting in a private dining room at the Dorchester, having been dressed up to the nines by none other than Matthews himself. After the oil had dried he got out the bolt cutters as promised and chased her halfway around his apartment, before cornering her and promising he would do no permanent damage with the brutes. He was true to his word. The chains had been severed and while she could now walk, the weight of the steel cuffs at her wrists and arms reminded her that she was still a prisoner with every step she took. It could not be helped.

To disguise her chains, Mark had encased her feet in the most exquisite pair of designer boots known to man. Italian red nappa leather, wedge heels and peep toes created a stunning contrast to the black outfit she wore. He had painted her toenails in bright red polish to complete the effect. Every time her floor-length skirt moved a splash of colour leaked from beneath. Mark had been assiduous in every detail, as he had prepared her for the evening ahead. The undergarments he'd chosen were a bodice in sheer tulle, embroidered with arabesques. The ribs of the garment were subtly contoured and covered in soft black velvet, whilst black satin half cups encased her breasts. Her panties were made of the same material but virtually transparent, bar the thin strip of velvet that covered their waistline. Thankfully they were tight enough to hold both plugs in with little effort. A mermaid-style floor-length gown in midnight black had completed the effect with a plunging V-neckline and an appliqued back of swirling scrolls that hugged the curves of her ass like a long lost lover. Featuring full length batwing sleeves, and a fishtail skirt, it successfully managed to hide all her cuffs. Mark had tied a thick silk scarf around her neck in the same shade of crimson as her boots, and whilst it probably wasn't a perfect disguise - she looked relatively normal at a distance, providing you weren't looking too closely.

The trouble was, nearly all eyes were upon her as she crossed the threshold of the three Michelin starred restaurant. For once she didn't even notice. Her eyes were solely on Mark as he went to chat with the Maitre'd. Dressed to perfection in a dark-blue wool suit, she was openly drooling at his back. This probably had something to do with the state he had left her in at his place. The short drive to the hotel in his Mercedes, sitting right next to him, had done nothing to dampen her ardour. Oh God. It was already happening to her. For the past couple of hours she had thought of nothing but sex. It was all about her next orgasm and how she was going to achieve it. Was this going to be her life from now on? The trusted pet of Mark Matthews? Her body voted yes, while her mind had a quick waver before it, too, said 'oh yes, please.'

'What do you think of the Table Lumiére? It's stunning, isn't it?'

Jenny had no idea what he was talking about until she nearly ran smack into the thing. The 'table of light' was a circular table surrounded by thousands of floor to ceiling strands of sparkling fibre optics. It would allow the guests within to eat their meal almost screened from view of the entire restaurant. When Mark had said 'private dining' this wasn't quite what she'd envisaged.

'Oh no,' Jenny whispered, expecting the worst.

'Your face is a picture right now, my dear, but don't worry, that isn't for us. I prefer the privacy of closed doors.' Taking her arm he led her away from the bustle and buzz of noise, and into a private dining room that was far too large for just the two of them. Flowers were everywhere. Arrangements of pale pink roses, Stargazer lilies and gypsophila were strewn above the fireplace and at intervals along the table that would be able to seat at least twelve people comfortably. Their beautiful scent filled the room in a sensual haze. The cutlery glistened, the porcelain shone and the Saint-Louis crystal was almost blinding.

'Are we expecting guests?' she asked weakly, looking along the length and breadth of the table.

'No, it's been set for two. Pay attention, pet.' He took his place at the head of the table and tucking her skirt behind her, Jenny sat at the place laid out to his left.

'You're always on the left, pet. You're never right. Remember that, and you'll do well.'

Jenny wanted to groan out loud, but he waved her tiny black remote control in the air, and with a single finger to his lips she knew better than to test his command. It looked like the fun and games were about to begin.

There were a few tense minutes of silence, where Jenny wanted nothing more than to cross and uncross her legs several times. Unfortunately the dress prevented all such movement. She got to sit there as still and silent as a statue while she watched Mark peruse the menu. Picking up her own leather-bound volume seemed like a good thing to do with her hands, so she began to run her eyes down the delights on offer. Lobster, langoustines, crab, sea bass, pigeon and more flowed up from the soft cream pages, and with a protesting empty rumble from her stomach, she had a feeling she might be able to eat them all. French cheese, exotic fruit, tasting menus of seven courses with flavours that were foreign but sounded divine all vied for her attention, and it was almost impossible to choose.

When the door quietly set-to with a tiny squeak, and an immaculately dressed waiter stood ready and waiting for their order, no notepad in sight, he almost made her jump. The silence that had been absolute had finally been broken.

'Has Madam made a decision?'

The waiter, with his soft blond curls and twinkling blue eyes stared at Jenny directly and raised his eyebrows in question.

Jenny looked at Mark, who smiled encouragingly, no doubt enjoying her discomfort. Placing a hand at her throat and rubbing it gently, she looked pleadingly at Mark. This seemed to have little effect, bar make his smile wider. Jenny tapped her foot on the floor and stopped the action almost immediately upon hearing the leftover chain rattle against her cuff. Looking up at her waiter she smiled awkwardly and cleared her throat. If Mark really wanted her to scream in front of an audience, then so be it. As soon as she opened her mouth, though, the annoying man immediately butted in.

'We'll have the usual, Christoph,' he said, 'but this time I think we'll probably want the dessert menu as well.' He plucked the menu out of Jenny's trembling hands and handed it back to Christoph with his own.

Christoph nodded a couple of times, smiled, and said brightly, 'Of course, Sir. We'll be with you in just a couple of moments. Is there anything else I can bring you? Some aperitifs, perhaps?'

Mark shook his head and Christoph uttered, 'Very good, Sir,' and disappeared as quietly as he had entered.

Jenny, however, tapped her foot on the floor angrily and glared at her tormentor. Mark laughed out loud.

'If you thought that was mean you're not going to enjoy yourself very much this evening,' he said, openly grinning at her furious expression. Jenny wanted to throttle him. She also wanted to direct a whole stream of invectives upon him, but didn't particularly fancy frying herself in the process.

'So, do you want to know what you're dining upon this evening, or do you prefer surprises?' Jenny continued to glare at him. 'I like surprises too,' he said, nodding, and suddenly her whole body began to vibrate. She jumped off the seat in shock at first, before she realised he must be playing with her ridiculous remote beneath the table. She gave him a dirty look, because the glares didn't appear to be working.

'That's just the vibrate setting. I'll pop some current through those beasts later and then we'll really have some fun.'

Sitting down gingerly upon her seat and listening for any discernible noise, Jenny could only be thankful that the fabric of her dress obscured any sound. Internally she felt like someone had buried her electric toothbrush halfway to her stomach. It was not a gentle vibration that had her plugs jiggling and dancing inside her; it was a full blown juddering war.

Jenny gave up looking at Mark and found an interesting spot on the floor, about three centimetres away from the table leg. She found herself annoyingly gripping the edge of the table, worried that she might orbit into space at any moment.

'You look stunning, by the way. That dress makes you look far more edible than any plate of food ever could.' Mark ran his eyes appreciatively up and down the length of her and stroked the soft velvet of her sleeve. 'How does it feel to be my mute dinner prisoner?'

Jenny's glare returned. She was perfecting it into quite a satisfactory scowl.

'You shouldn't do that, Princess. One, because it deters from the beauty of that exceptionally sculpted face and two, I will punish you for adding frown lines to your features.'

She tapped her fingernails on the table in response and notched up the intensity of her gaze.

'You're playing with fire, darling,' he whispered. The tone of his voice was deadly and immediately removed the frown from her face. In the next second current flowed through her body, tingling in tight little waves as it spiralled through her nether regions. It was startlingly pleasurable and she let out an involuntary groan, her hand immediately going to her throat where she expected a nasty shock. Thankfully none was forthcoming.

'I lied about the collar. I just wanted to watch you squirm a little. It was nice to have a little peace and quiet to properly appreciate my menu, though.'

Jenny wanted to scream at him, but the current shot up a notch and if she'd thought the previous vibrations were bad they were nothing when compared to the million or so little snakes that were writhing all over her body. Parts of her had just come to life that she never knew existed.

'It's quite a unique feeling, isn't it?'

It certainly was, Jenny thought, and she wasn't sure if it was intensely pleasurable or horribly uncomfortable. Time would tell, she guessed.

'So, I think we'll play it like this. If you're good I'll turn the setting down a level and if you're bad, I'll turn it up. The higher I turn this dial, the more likely it is that you'll have a forced orgasm or orgasms, depending on how cruel I'm feeling.'

Jenny swallowed numbly. The current flowing through her was already melting down her insides and she didn't realistically think she could take much more, which meant that...

'You will have to do everything I say, or Christoph is going to catch quite an eyeful, I think.'

Christoph didn't see girls writhing on the floor of his restaurant every day wrapped in chains? What a positively boring existence the man must lead! Jenny swiped back a tendril of her artificial hair that had been tamed into a glossy knot at the nape of her neck. She could already feel droplets of sweat beginning to form between her breasts and a slow tremor ran through her fingertips. The evening was not going well.

'Now I'm going to test the theory, Princess.' He threw a small black object in the air and she instinctively caught it. 'Nice catch,' he said with a grin. 'Your task is to get that in the front of your panties before Christoph comes back with your amuse-bouche.' He put his folded hand under her chin and looked at her with pure devilment in his eyes. Jenny wanted nothing more than to knock the stupid man senseless, but her brain was anxiously trying to process the elements of the game. *Tick, tock, tick.* He wasn't going to say a word to hurry her along. He wanted her to get caught and the man must know that his grin was as distracting as a naked Adonis. He'd probably been here a million times before and knew exactly how long it would take each course to get to the table, so that meant she had very little time to work with. To make matters worse, the gown she wore would have to be hiked up to her waist to get the task done and it would require two hands, which meant she would need three.

Knowing she had already wasted enough time she stood up, gathered her skirts and frantically pushed them as best as she could into one hand, whilst trying to search for her panties with the other. The dress was extremely tight and it was no mean feat trying to get the thing around her waist. Hearing the footsteps of the waiter echo in her head, though she was sure she was imagining things, Jenny fumbled around with the small black square, almost dropping it in her haste to shove the thing between her legs. Trying desperately to find the waistband of her panties she heard the tell-tale squeak of the door opening. Several things then happened all at once. The little black box flew out of her hand and landed on the floor under the table. With her skirts nearly over her head she shot down with as much force as she could muster and flew after it. Successfully retrieving the thing she let out a relieved sigh and closed her fist around it, before thrusting it deep inside her waistband and pushing her skirts back down again. She then cracked her head on the table as she struggled to get out again. How very elegant.

'Are you OK, Madam? Here, let me help you.' Christoph held out an arm and helped her up, while she was torn between rubbing her head and smoothing down her ruffled skirts. The head won. 'What happened?' he asked quizzically.

Jenny felt his gaze upon her and was almost paralysed for a moment. Telling him the truth was obviously not an option, so she looked to Mark for help. He raised his eyebrows and the light dancing in his eyes told her he would be of little use. 'Umm,' smoothing her skirts to stall for time she frantically tried to think of a good excuse for diving under a table at a restaurant. She knew exactly what the man would be thinking and her cheeks were already flooding with unpleasant, scalding heat. Smoothing a non-existent wrinkle in her skirt with a trembling hand, finally something came to her. 'I was looking for my contact lens. My eye is a bit watery this evening, so I rubbed it without thinking and it shot off on the floor.' Her voice held just the right tremor of shock and panic and she was reasonably pleased with her performance.

'Can I help you look for it, Madam?' There was no sign of laughter in his face, but Jenny knew he hadn't believed a word of her lie.

She tightened one hand into a fist and shook it at him. 'No need. I found it. Thanks for your help, though.' She smiled tightly as his lips twitched.

'Would you like me to escort you to the restroom?'

When she looked at him strangely, he pointed to her fist.

145

'Oh,' she squeaked, shooting upwards, for a blistering current was now throbbing through both her plugs and to add insult to injury, the little black box was vibrating happily against her clit. Nearly climaxing on the spot, she gritted her teeth tightly and let out a helpless little moan. Looking back over at Mark, it was to find him trying his best to smother a laugh, and he wasn't trying all that hard in fairness.

With her brightest smile she turned back to Christoph and said, 'No need. The view isn't all that amazing across the table. I'm sure I'll survive.' Ignoring his shocked expression, she fell into her chair as both the current and vibrations, impossibly, managed to shoot up to new levels of acute discomfort. She was going to embarrass herself in about thirty seconds, if she wasn't much mistaken. Letting out a quiet keening wail of distress she gripped the bottom of her chair tightly, as if afraid she might fall off it.

'It's OK, Christoph,' said Mark with a wink, 'you can tell them to bring in the first course. Hopefully the food will improve her mood and... her view,' he said, pursing his lips together.

Christoph cleared his throat and said, 'Very good, Sir,' and marched out of the room with impressive alacrity.

Just as Jenny had resigned herself to a much needed orgasm the current and vibrations stopped abruptly. She wailed again, this time with much more force and thumped her fist against the table. 'I hope you're enjoying yourself,' she spat venomously.

'Immensely,' was her only reply.

Thankfully, the first course was then served in a delicate porcelain egg and it proved a distraction that no sarcasm or funny business could touch. Unearthing the contents of her egg, and spooning the mixture into her mouth, Jenny could do nothing but close her eyes and savour the rich taste and texture, bemoaning her week of abstinence.

'You're eating celeriac veloutee with green apples, I believe.'

Jenny didn't care what it was called; the main thing was it tasted divine. It took a good degree of willpower to stop herself picking up the egg and chucking the contents down her throat, but she paced herself with her small spoon and relished every single drop.

'You look adorable,' said Mark, as he watched her scrape up the last remnants. 'It's nice to see someone who enjoys their food so much. Most of my dates tend to eat rabbit food and pass up anything that looks as if it might contain sugar.'

'You have no fear of that this evening,' said Jenny. 'I'm not leaving a single bite and the sugar part is the one I'm most looking forward to.' There was a faraway, dreamy look in her eye and it was clear she was remembering sweeter times.

'Tell me about your relationship with your father.'

Jenny nearly choked upon nothing more deadly than air. Thankfully she was given time to chew upon the command, because the egg was whisked away and a small plate of langoustines now resided in its place. The buttery scent that wafted upwards had her salivating so much the question was completely forgotten. She was instantly reminded of it when current began to flow through her once more. Gritting her teeth and looking longingly at the langoustines she said, 'Turn it off and I'll talk.'

Mark barked out a laugh and popped a morsel of the succulent white shellfish into his mouth. 'And since when do you think you get to bargain with me?'

The current increased another notch and some powerful vibrations joined it. Jenny could only look at her dinner miserably as she tried to sit still upon her chair. Trying fiercely hard to concentrate on peeling her plump little langoustine she wanted to stamp her feet and fling her arms about, but she knew that would only bring further torment, so she began talking. If he wanted conversation, then the man was about to get more than he bargained for.

'My father and I share a tenuous respect for each other, or we did,' she said acidly. 'When my mother was around the man was all sweetness and light, but when she left he deteriorated quite quickly. I'm talking massive, mean mood swings and plunging into weeks of dark depression that no one could rouse him from.' The current ebbed down a notch, allowing Jenny to eat without quite as much distraction as before. As the butter and seafood swirled about in her mouth she took a sip of the bone dry Chablis that accompanied it and decided that heaven was indeed a real place, and it was right down on earth.

'Should I be playing the violin?' Mark raised an eyebrow sardonically, but clearly wanted her to carry on with her story, motioning with his hand for her to continue. She was tempted to defy him, but there was always the chance that this might be the last decent meal she ate for some time, and it would be a shame if she couldn't appreciate it, so swallowing her delightful, creamy mouthful, she did.

'Yes. His depression at her leaving was channelled into a hatred for me. His eyes would follow me everywhere and even the slightest indiscretions were punished harshly, although not personally by himself. Finding ways to make my life miserable became his mission in life, and up until about fifteen years of age, I'd say he succeeded. I ran in fear of everything in our house. For a while I ended up as a recluse, frightened to go out, socialise or utter a word.'

Spearing a forkful of asparagus into his mouth Mark appeared to take all of this in, but made no comment. He clearly hoped his silence would urge her to continue, but she'd had to cope with more than her fair share of the stuff in her life and if he wanted more he was going to have to ask for it. She concentrated on the plate in front of her and didn't give him so much as a glance. Wondering how he'd retaliate she kept her eyes downcast as the waiters came in to remove their plates and serve up the main course. He'd been waiting for them, and the brief respite she'd been given was over, because everything suddenly buzzed, tingled, throbbed and vibrated at the same time. Jenny nearly came on the spot and beads of sweat popped up everywhere, while a hard line furrowed across her brow.

'Is everything OK?' Christoph asked her, looking concerned.

147

Finally she could hold herself back no longer. Shoving her fist into her jaw she screamed into it, somehow managing to stem the bucking and rolling that her body desperately wanted to publically perform. There was only so much that could be quashed, though. A red stain seeped upwards from her neckline, quickly covering her face, and the heat that flooded through her most unpleasant. As her body internally convulsed and threw out waves the likes that Hawaii would be proud of, she looked up at Christoph helplessly, her mind at sea and her body adrift.

Several seconds ticked by before he felt the need to repeat his question, and it was clear that ignoring it was not going to work. She opened her mouth, but no sound came out, and she looked at Mark, imploring him to help her again, but a shake of his head instantly killed that option. At a loss she came up with the only thing she could think of. Smiling sweetly at Christoph, she purred prettily and said, 'He asked me to marry him.'

After the necessary looks of surprise and words of congratulation had been spoken, the room was again silent and as soon as there was just the two of them once more Mark wore a thunderous look upon his face.

'Wouldn't it have been easier just to have said "yes"?' he barked. 'Now I'm going to have to employ damage control, because even though you're booked in here as a Liz Layton-Lovette, there's a good chance that snippet might hit the papers tomorrow and it won't do my reputation as the world's most eligible bachelor any good if that kind of news gets loose.'

'Excuse me while I go and find my violin,' came the acerbic reply.

'You really don't know when you're beat, do you young lady?' Picking up his cell, Mark punched a few digits in and issued a few terse instructions into it. Unless Jenny was much mistaken his problems were going to be taken care of very swiftly with rather large sums of money. If only hers could be solved that easily...

As soon as the phone was returned to his pocket, she shot off the chair and her body nearly had a seizure with the force of electricity that was currently flowing through it. It took her about ten seconds to orgasm and she had a feeling that the next one wouldn't take much longer.

By the time the Chateaubriand arrived she had climaxed exactly four times. Her body felt as limp as a week-old lettuce and all the fight and aggression she had harboured over the last week had dissipated swiftly into the room's now very frigid air. Mark hadn't uttered a word and Jenny was beginning to realise that her chances of being returned to Albrecht were increasing with each passing second. As the fifth orgasm hit her she nearly smeared her face in the beef before her, and could have cried because there was no way on earth she could eat the stuff now. Stifling the tears that wanted to flow waterfall-style, she looked up at her antagonist and thumped both fists upon the table. She had his attention. Pushing her plate roughly to one side she closed her eyes and bit down on the scream that she couldn't utter, mostly because she was too damn exhausted.

'I'm sorry,' she managed to hiccup, and the effort of holding her tears back was almost too much for her. She knew her eyes would be shiny and that her lashes were wet. Her hands were shaking upon the rim of the table and that was nothing compared to what the rest of her body was doing. She also knew that this wouldn't matter a whit to the man in front of her.

'You'll need to do better,' was all he said, before returning his attention back to the meal in front of him.

'So let me talk,' she whispered, as a single tear tried to meander its way down her face, only to be brushed away abruptly. It was a weakness she could no longer afford. Raising her face she used her eyes to implore his forgiveness. He gave her a hard look in response, but the voltage dropped to a more manageable level.

'This had better be good,' he said.

And so she began to recount tales of her childhood. 'You've remarked that my tolerance for pain is quite impressive, haven't you? Well, there's a reason for that. I've been used to being beaten from a very early age.' When he gave her an incredulous look she smiled. 'Oh, not by my father. He was far too smart for that. But he'd have my governess or tutor do it, and he'd make sure I knew he'd instructed them to do it.'

'He abused you?'

'By proxy, yes. He would never sully his hands with the dispensing of my "discipline" but it was clear that he actively encouraged my chastisement among the staff and I was punished for the tiniest misdemeanour, which meant I spent most of my childhood walking on eggshells. He wanted to create a timid little beast that would be afraid of her own shadow. He also didn't want to run across me unless absolutely necessary, and he achieved both aims with reasonable success.'

'I'm not sure I can believe a word you're saying. The tigress that currently sits opposite me is a world away from that girl you're describing. You'll need to fill in the blanks, Princess.' Mark's expression had narrowed, but his interest was clear.

Jenny placed a forkful of tender beef inside her mouth and closed her eyes. 'I love beef,' she sighed. Seeing Mark's dark expression, she frowned. 'You want to know how I went from mouse to lion, I suppose?'

'The thought had crossed my mind,' he said.

She uttered a bitter laugh. 'That took years and was the culmination of several different things. All you need to know is that I studied his business affairs in great detail, took a few covert shots of what he and his current mistress got up to on a fun evening back at home, and, just to nail the coffin firmly shut, I reported his abuse of me to the relevant authorities.'

'Fuck,' Mark whispered slowly. 'You're lucky he didn't ship you off somewhere far flung and throw away the key.'

'Oh, he wanted to,' smiled Jenny, 'but that's the beauty of the reporting system. Police, social workers, therapists... the man was then watched night and day. Of course, he denied everything and told them I was crazy, but I'd taken photos of the stuff they'd done over the period of a couple of years. There was no explaining away that. He then had to change tack and say he'd had no knowledge of it, sack all of his staff, act horrified and cuddle me affectionately whenever he was being interviewed. So no one was ever sure if it was me who was nuts, or him. Unfortunately they gave him the benefit of the doubt, but I had enough on him to make sure he never stepped a foot out of line with me again, and I pushed every little aspect of my newfound independence to the limit after that. You have no idea how hard-won that freedom was.'

'So you spent the next several years in rebellion, getting your own back?' Mark tilted his head to the side and matched up this new information with that which he had already collected.

Scooping up a pile of fluffy mash, laced with some of the most heavenly gravy she had ever tasted, Jenny sighed. In her mind, to ruin a meal such as this with talking was sacrilege, but it wasn't as if she had much choice. 'Not exactly. Some of it was rebellion, I won't deny it, but most of it was calculated with some form of goal in mind. I've wanted to bring my father down for years, but it was only just recently where I'd nearly gathered enough information in order to do so.'

Mark had a pained look on his face from across the table. Using his napkin to wipe the remnants of his half-eaten meal from his lips, he closed his eyes and whispered, 'And just where did you store this information that you were going to use for his downfall?'

'On my Mac. It's password protected and I've never shared the code with anyone.'

Mark visibly winced. 'Oh, Jenny,' he said, shaking his head. 'You may think you're smart, but you've got such a lot to learn, young lady.' His previously healthy pallor was now tinged with a sickly yellow. 'It does explain a few things, however.'

Over dessert, Mark explained exactly how easy it was for computers to be hacked, even Mac's, to Jenny's absolute horror. He also went on to explain that as her father had probably bought her the computer, it probably hadn't even been necessary. He could have set up monitoring that would have allowed him to access every piece of information she came across, with very little effort on his part. It was now Jenny's turn to look ill, and pushing her gooey chocolate fondant away from her, which was a crime in itself, she covered her mouth with her hands and looked aghast. 'How come I never knew any of this?'

'You've barely ever had any peers with whom to talk with your private schooling, and I'm guessing your television has probably been censored. In all probability he has your room bugged and an operative following your every move.'

'Shit,' whispered Jenny, 'he'll want to kill me.'

'You've made it impossible for that to happen without serious repercussions, I think,' said Mark, who softened the blow with, 'and you're still his daughter.'

Jenny did not look as if that held much weight in her family.

'So what do you think he wants?'

'I know what he wants,' Mark said softly, swirling his Nuit-St-George around in his glass and gently inhaling the powerful aroma. 'Me.'

Jenny swallowed hard and her look was far too astute.

'He wants to play with you, doesn't he?'

Mark smothered a sardonic, bitter laugh. 'That's one way of putting it. He wants to mess with me and then see if he can break me, and then he'll get down to what he really wants.'

Jenny's eyes had taken on a faraway look. 'And what was your response to that?'

'What would your response have been?' he countered.

'No way in ten thousand hells,' she replied bleakly.

Chapter Sixteen

Don't Forget the Safe Word

Dinner was a rather reserved affair after that. Mark picked Jenny's brains for information and she gave him whatever she could. The tone of the meal had gone from screams to hushed whispers, which was a shame, Jenny thought absently, as the conversation had turned serious and gloomy. Thankfully she'd been allowed to enjoy her coffee and mignardises in peace, with no threat of electricity present, but it was a shallow victory. Her inevitable return to Albrecht and Kyle Levison was not a thought she wished to dwell upon and the chances of a fairy-tale ending were looking slim, if not nigh on impossible.

The drive home was completed in contemplative silence. Each party was lost in their own thoughts and none of them were particularly pleasant.

'I can try and reason with your Father,' offered Mark.

'Don't bother,' replied Jenny, shaking her head, a dark look on her face. 'You can't reason with Michael Redcliff. You either do as he says or you beat him at his own game. It's not a particularly fun game, either, I've heard.' She smiled wanly.

'Maybe we can ship you off somewhere safe. Blame it on Leyland, or something.' Mark looked helpless as his hands gripped the wheel ferociously tight, trying to process every option available to them.

'You and I both know that's not going to work,' she said, shaking her head.

Mark rubbed his temples, trying to soothe the knot of tension that was threatening to turn into a full-blown migraine as he rapidly tried to search for a plausible solution. It was rare for him to be at a loss, and he hated the feeling of helplessness that accompanied it.

'What would you like me to do?' he asked, in a defeated tone of voice, wondering if she could come up with anything better than the meagre offerings he'd been sorting through.

Jenny already knew exactly how everything was going to pan out. Turning her head towards the passenger side window and watching the bright lights of the oncoming traffic light up the night sky, she took a deep breath as she debated her next words. In the end, she figured she had little to lose. 'I want you to show me a good time, Matthews. You've got one night to show me how it could have been between us, so give me a glimpse into your world that I can take with me. Make it so damn marvellous that I can file it away under "fucking incredible" and no one can ever take that kind of thing away, right?'

Mark didn't need any further encouragement to take her at her word. He didn't want to think any further ahead than the single night looming before them, and if she wanted to go through with it as planned, then he was more than happy to grant her last wish.

Back in his apartment, Mark felt his phone vibrate in his pocket. He ignored it. Work could wait. The chances were he had only one evening to last him through the next few years, and he intended to make it count. That didn't mean he wouldn't pull out all the stops in order to rescue Miss Redcliff, but he wasn't about to do it on the old man's terms.

Pouring two cups of steaming black coffee, knowing there was little chance either of them was likely to get much sleep, he offered an elegant black mug to Jenny and smiled when she did nothing but savour the fumes. 'It's alright, there's plenty more where that came from,' he added gently. He didn't need to add *but you'd better get your fill this evening, because you're not likely to see it again in the near future.*

She must have caught his thought though, because she clutched the mug the way a dying man would grab a life preserver.

Inwardly he was squirming. How bad would it be to submit to Redcliff for just one evening? He had the power to rescue the woman before him with a single phone call. Twelve hours should be a piece of cake. He'd been through hell and back before. Just how deranged was the man? Then he thought of Kyle, and shuddered. The panic of being at the mercy of another was nothing when you compared it to the horrors of what Redcliff was capable of. He made Lyle look like a pussycat, and that was saying something.

'Look, try not to worry. It might take a few days, but I promise one way or another I'll get you out of there. There is always a way,' he said determinedly.

Jenny took a big slug of her coffee and did nothing but issue a timid smile in return. The coffee had just been brewed and was nuclear, but the scalding heat seemed to have no effect on her throat and that alone was telling enough. The girl was finally in shock and it was no real surprise. 'Look, if you want to go straight to bed, that's fine with me. You've been through enough lately. I'm more than happy to sleep on the couch...'

'No. You're not getting out of this that easily. You cannot put me to bed and pretend this has nothing to do with you. I know this is not your fault, but neither is it mine. I respect your decision to keep yourself as far away from this as you can, and believe me in your place I would be doing the same thing, but I need something from you this evening. I need you to fuck me so thoroughly and completely that I'm too exhausted to think. I want you to wrap your arms around my spent body and leave me no option but sleep. I want the comfort of another's arms for one evening and I want to feel like a normal human being, because I have no idea when the next opportunity might present itself. You can do this for me. It's not too much to ask, is it?' The tears were back in her eyes, but she blinked them back fiercely.

Mark growled, but a pained expression was reflected in his eyes. He thumped his hand against his cream leather sofa and said, 'No, it's not too much to ask, but I can't be gentle with you. I don't do "making love", which is what you're asking for this evening. I do rough, nasty, hair-pulling, biting, whips and chains. I can't change that part of me. It's what makes me tick and what turns me on. So for your sake, you might want to take the safe option and hit the sack.' He tried to push his short fingernails through the thick Italian leather of his sofa, but thankfully it resisted his efforts.

'Safe is an option that's no longer available to me, if it ever was,' said Jenny, swigging the rest of her coffee in a large molten gulp, 'and it's come to my attention that I like it rough, so show me what you're good at, Matthews. There's lots of talk in the stables that you're the best there is. "He can do this with his fingers, he can do that with his tongue",' she mimicked in a high-pitched voice. 'I need convincing. Show me more.'

Mark couldn't help but smile as it became clear she was goading him, for what was, in essence, a sure gone thing. He could have left her alone, if that had been what she wanted, but he would have suffered for the concession. He'd had an almost permanent erection for the last four hours, not to mention the last few days, and he wanted nothing more than to bury himself inside her and forget the world existed. Why she was so appealing, when he had so many other women to hand, was a mystery, but the fact remained. It was probably because he couldn't have her. Had she been readily available he'd probably have been bored of her within the week.

Feeling his phone vibrate once again in his pocket he inwardly cursed. Whoever it was would have to wait until tomorrow. Looking straight at Jenny he said, 'You want to play my game, fine. You've got five minutes to strip yourself naked and await me kneeling at the foot of my bed with your arms wrists to elbows, behind your back. Hold the position, head dipped down, until I'm ready for you. Any failures will, of course, be punished.' He gave her a hard stare, to let her know that Mr Nice Guy had officially left the building.

The teary look was instantly gone as the fires of arousal leapt back into her eyes. Her lashes lowered as her head already bowed towards the floor, and she murmured, 'Yes, Sir.' She immediately began crawling, and he wasn't sure whether her sprightly gait was due to fear or her eagerness for the night's activities to commence. Women were such fickle creatures.

Heading into his spare room, which doubled as an office, he shrugged off his jacket, flipped the light switch and slotted his phone into its charger. There was only one message, which was a relief, but it was from an unknown number. That was slightly odd because his secretary, Cecilia, fielded his calls first and would only send him those that were urgent. Tonight he couldn't have cared less. It could have been the Prime Minister himself, and he'd still have had to wait until tomorrow. He had a big night to plan and it was going to be quite something.

Undoing the top three buttons of his shirt he breathed in deeply, threw his head back and closed his eyes. Jennifer Redcliff was in his bedroom, kneeling on the floor and waiting to be fucked. Actually, she'd be begging to be fucked shortly, but it was a moot point. They'd work up to that. Tugging his shirt up and over his head he kicked off his shoes and ran his fingers through the short spikes of his jet-black hair. He needed a few minutes away from her to think. Not about the events of the evening and the little gems of information she had revealed; those he would chew over tomorrow. Now he wanted to concentrate on what he'd need for the bedroom scene that was about to unfold. That was as far ahead as his mind could focus right now. He tossed some ideas around quickly, and as a plan came together he began gathering his inventory. The standard bits and pieces he could find in his room, but this scene was going to be a little bit different. He wanted to give her something to remember, just in case he couldn't work her out of the impressive mess she was in. There'd never yet been a problem he couldn't find a way of solving, but everything took time and these days, he found himself an impatient man. He wanted her, and he was going to have her, one way or another.

Striding back to the kitchen he grabbed a bottle of Sambuca, a bucket of ice cubes, a penknife, a piece of ginger, a shot glass, a lighter and some coffee beans. Dumping them all on a tray, he carried the items silently to his room and nudged the door open with his elbow.

His little princess was kneeling at the foot of his bed, arms wrapped behind her as instructed, and her head was dipped towards the floor, but she was not naked. How interesting. 'Don't tell me you're in need of a spanking so soon after the theatrics of the carousel, my pet?'

'I couldn't undo the zip,' she whispered miserably, not daring to look up.

He smiled to himself. 'Then you should have ripped the thing off from end to end. Disobeying instructions is a very serious business between a Master and a submissive, and you should endeavour to obey each and every command to the letter.'

In truth, he'd known she wouldn't be able to get out of the dress without his help, and that gave him a reason for what he was about to do next - not that he'd really needed one, but it would certainly help instil a future eagerness for obedience. Bending down and placing both hands around her neck, watching her shudder helplessly beneath him, he whispered, 'Stand up.'

She got to her feet so quickly she nearly head-butted him in the process. Grabbing the little red penknife from the tray behind him, he held it out on his open palm in front of her eyes. 'Do you trust me?' he murmured softly, and knew she would be thinking about the mess Kyle had made of her back.

There was a moment's pause as she swallowed thickly and then a single, 'Yes,' managed to leap from her lips.

'Good.' He bent down and used the penknife to slice up the centre of her dress, stopping about an inch short of the juncture between her legs. She sucked in a breath, but otherwise remained as still as a statue, which was just as well all things considered. 'Pick a safe word.'

'A what?' Jenny had a look of utter confusion upon her face.

'You're not an animal any more. You're in my house and you're a willing submissive. You asked to be fucked and I'm complying with your wishes, on my own terms of course. You need a safe word that can put a stop to any of the proceedings that are about to happen. When things get out of control and you can't take any more, you utter your safe word and everything stops. I stop, the scene stops, we pack up for the evening and you go to bed. It's there to protect you, not me. So pick something you can easily remember.'

Jenny thought for a moment and then gave him an impish grin. 'How about, *bastard?*'

Mark's lips twitched. 'You, young lady, have just earned yourself yet another thrashing. I won't have submissives swearing in my presence. So be aware that each time you utter your safe word your bottom will be earning some damage. OK, you also need to pick a signal, in case I choose to gag you. On second thoughts, as you seem so bad at this, I'll pick it for you. Three nods of your head or three consecutive grunts will suffice. We'll practice in a minute. Right now you have ten seconds to rip that dress apart and get yourself naked.'

'But that's sacrilege,' she moaned. 'This is a designer dress and probably cost thousands.' Looking down at the long tear in front of her, she shook her head at the horror of what he wanted her to do.

Mark gave her a flat stare. 'Maybe we should call it a night. I'd only give you ten minutes, tops, till your safe word was being yelled at the top of your lungs.'

'Ooh, you arrogant bast...' Jenny's voice trailed off as she realised the evening might just prove harder than she thought. Mark was grinning widely and she couldn't help but splutter, 'There's no way I'll safe-word under you.'

He raised an eyebrow in challenge. 'Oh, ho ho. Fighting talk. Get to it then. Five seconds and counting. I'm happy to practise my knife work, if needed, but you should know that will add to your spanking tally, and as that delightful arse of yours is shortly going to be stuffed full of ginger, you're going to feel the force of each of every one in a really rather unpleasant way. Before this evening is out I'll hear that safe word uttered, or my nickname is not Mark-the-most-amazing-bastard-in-the-world-Matthews.'

She snorted. 'You do your worst.'

He grabbed her from behind and brought her up tight against him. 'Oh I intend to, darling, and now as your ten seconds is most definitely up, it's time for me to show you just how nice I can be.' Pushing her head down in front of her, he lowered her back and felt for the edges of the square strip of plaster he knew was under her dress. He took a moment to judge where his fingers would do the most damage and dug them gently into her raw skin. She shrieked and bucked against him.

'Take that fucking dress off now,' he whispered dangerously, 'or I might just finish up what Kyle has begun.' It was an outright lie, but you wouldn't know it by the tone of his voice.

Jenny obviously took him at his word, for her hands rushed to finish the split, a loud ripping noise confirming this as she frantically tore at the ends of her dress. The jagged tear finally reach her neck, where after a few frenzied attempts the whole garment split itself in two. She was about to wriggle out of her bodice and panties when Mark stopped her.

'I've changed my mind. Leave them on. That way I can have the pleasure of tearing them off you, later,' he gave her a predatory smile that was full of carnal intent. 'On the bed,' he ordered gruffly, 'lie on your back with your arms and legs outstretched in an X-shape.'

Mark could barely control his tightly supressed hunger and if he wasn't careful all his hard won years of experience would be for naught. His cock wanted a party in his pants, and it wouldn't necessarily require a warm, tight and incredibly inviting space in which to do so.

Flexing the fingers of his right hand, he made himself busy locating four of his silk ties. They would probably be unusable after the evening's events, but the thought didn't bother him overmuch. At least he could keep them as souvenirs, if things went the way he planned, and he was more than confident that they would.

Approaching her wrists first, he secured them to hidden eyebolts just behind the front of his bed. He'd normally have used rope, but found he couldn't bear the thought of marking her skin after what had happened back at Albrecht. The girl would have to be completely healed before he could even consider leaving something as minor as rope burns upon her alabaster flesh. Thankfully he had no problems with darkening the pink flush that still remained on her buttocks, and he intended to make sure it resembled a good fiery hue before he was finished with her. At least she'd have something to remember him by for the next few days.

Satisfied that her wrists were held tight he picked up the next two ties, which were a bit of an incongruous mix of polka dots and stripes. Ah well. He suspected neither of them would notice, much less care about such trivial details in less than five minutes' time.

'Put your legs up in the air.'

Jenny gave him a puzzled look. 'If you're going to tie them to the foot of the bed, why do you want them up in the air?'

'Who's in charge here? You? You look like the one tied up to me. Now put your legs in the air before I gag you and then bite your clit for kicks.' He rolled his eyes. 'I'm not going to say this again. You don't get to ask questions. You just obey each and every word. It's really not that hard once you get used to it.'

As her legs were thrust up in the air, holding her X-shape, he wrapped each in a silk tie and tied them to further eyebolts that were located about a metre higher than the previous ones. Now all he could see were ass cheeks and panties and it was a truly mesmerising sight. Standing tall at the foot of his bed, he couldn't help but admire the view.

'If I had you here, as my very own personal submissive, I think I'd have to put eyebolts all over the house. I can think of nothing more delicious than to have you hanging scantily clad, or preferably naked, in whichever room I choose to be in. That way, if I want to torment you,' he moved to bend over her and cupped her sex in his palm, 'you'll only ever be a few mere inches away.' He smiled at her answering groan and withdrew his hand. 'I wouldn't even have to get up, if I used something like my riding crop.' A sudden crack lit up the air as his crop swished down to connect with her inner thigh. She yelped. 'Maybe I'll have them made in impressively long lengths, just so you'll never be out of my reach.

'Anyway,' he drawled, 'where was I? Ah yes, an after dinner liqueur, I believe.' He sat down on the edge of the bed and stroked her thigh, noting that it sent little tremors running though her. 'Have you ever heard of a Flaming Sambuca?' He continued to stroke her and it must have been quite the distraction, for she took her own sweet time in answering.

'Isn't that where you put a couple of coffee beans on top of the shot and set fire to the thing?'

His eyes danced. 'Great, you've heard of it. I thought you would have, being the ardent little socialite that you are, but just wanted to check. Anyway, that's my drink of choice for this evening.'

Jenny's mouth moved, as if to ask a question, but then she thought the better of it and snapped her teeth shut.

He exhaled slowly. 'You may ask, though I suspect you're not going to like the answer.'

'And how do you know what I'm going to ask?' she said, a little put out.

'The answer is, that I'm going to be drinking it between your legs,' he returned.

Whether that answered the question Jenny had been intending to pose was never clarified, for her eyes widened into bright white marbles and her lip quivered. 'You're intending to set fire to me? I asked for a distraction, not a trip to the A&E department,' she whispered.

'Oh yea of little faith. I'm going to insert my shot glass into that deliciously sweet little hole between your legs and you're going to be a good little sub and clamp your muscles around it tightly, while I fill it with Sambuca. I'm then going to light it up and roast my coffee beans.'

'Between my legs?' Jenny's voice had taken on a panicked tone. 'Hang on a minute, let me get this straight,' she said, closing her eyes in disbelief. 'You're going to pour alcohol inside me, place a naked flame between my legs and set fire to me? Have you at least done this before?'

'That is a very good point, well made,' he said, and disappeared off to the kitchen. When he returned he was carrying a large fire extinguisher. It had been a mean trick, for when she saw it she looked like she might expire on the spot.

'You have no idea how much I'd love to have the use of my hands right now,' she said through gritted teeth.

Mark put his fingers inside her panties and, pulling them away from her skin, used his penknife to cut a large hole in them. Pulling out the large steel plug in her pussy with slow half-turns, he ran his fingers along the silky smooth skin nestled inside the sheer material and smiled as her body pulled towards him. Ignoring the bucking of her hips, he then began twisting his shot glass into her pussy through her panties. He was entertained that even though she appeared outwardly scared, she was still very much aroused.

'Out of curiosity, what would you do with them?' He sank the glass as deep as it would go, and it still left at least an inch of glass outside her lips.

'I'd flatten you,' she wailed, and there were tongues of flames in her eyes as anger began to war with fear. It was a beautiful combination.

Laughing, he said, 'That, I'd love to see, but maybe some other time.' Satisfied that his glass was correctly placed, he began searching for the Sambuca.

'No, no, no, no, no,' she whispered. Twisting her arms this way and that she struggled to free herself from the makeshift bonds. Unfortunately for her he was very good with knots, and she wasn't going to get out of them unless he chose to help her do so.

He gave her another little swat with his crop, to centre her attention. 'Don't move an inch. When I set fire to that liquid the last thing you're going to want is for it to be sloshing all over the place.' That stopped all movement smartly in its tracks. 'And be gentle with that glass inside you, too. Don't break it.'

He was teasing her. The shot glasses were made of sturdy stuff and on the odd occasion they'd be dropped, they bounced, thankfully. She didn't need to know that though. Giving her a moment or two to start begging, he was surprised when she remained mute but suspected it wouldn't last for long.

Circling his finger around the rim of the glass he watched her tremble, even though she tried hard to control the motion.

'Am I distracting you yet?' He was being flippant, but there was an undercurrent of something else in his voice, too. It was worrying. There was a good chance the little minx was beginning to grow on him, and that would not be a good thing. Her eyes stared back at him between the stretched 'V' of her legs and if they were able to shoot daggers, he'd resemble a rather nasty pincushion about now.

'You aren't seriously going to do this, are you?' Jenny appeared to be most unamused by her current situation.

'I'll have you know I take my drinking and eating very seriously. I'm quite the connoisseur, wouldn't you know?' Searching out the liqueur bottle once more, this time he grabbed it and flipped it over three hundred and sixty degrees in the air by its neck. He felt the liquid slosh around inside the bottle and took a seat beside her as it finally began to settle. 'One of my first jobs was as a barman, so don't worry, you're in safe hands.'

He unscrewed the cap and began pouring the liqueur between her legs.

'Why does that not reassure me?' she squeaked, as the shot glass sank even lower between her legs, the weight of the liquid dragging it down.

Placing a handful of coffee beans in the centre of the glass he said, 'Remember what I said about remaining perfectly still?' Flicking open the top of his French, S.T. Dupont Lighter, he waved the flame about for effect.

'You're evil. You do know you'll rot in hell one day, right?'

Mark snorted in response. 'Much better than having to listen to all those dreary harps and flapping wings. You're welcome to it. Now, did you want your coffee beans lightly toasted or completely incinerated with the delicate flavour of charcoal?'

Jenny let out a frustrated scream. When she had her lungs back under control she spat, 'Seriously, you are going to burn.' Her eyes never left the wavering flame in his hands.

Holding the lighter between her legs, he slowly lowered it. 'You first, sweetness, I think.' He looked at his watch. 'Want to use that safe word yet by any chance?'

'If I end up in hospital I am going to sue!' Her lungs were once again out of control and the pitch of her voice was rather unpleasantly high.

He debated on whether to give her another 'get out' or not. Clearly he was in softy-mode, because when he was about five inches away from the shot glass he murmured, 'You haven't forgotten it, have you?'

'No I bloody well haven't,' she yelled furiously, 'and if it wasn't the safe word, don't think I wouldn't be using it right now.'

'Ah ha, so I'm curtailing that naughty little mouth of yours already, huh? That's encouraging, my dear.'

'Ooh, you bas...'

He laughed as her sentence came up short. The naked flame was now an inch away from the lip of the glass and he decided that he really was going soft in his old age. Clearing his throat he said, 'Last chance. If you're going to say it, say it now.' Her eyes were cloudy with indecision and it was clear she was having an inner battle about the use of ladylike language.

'Too late,' he said, solving the dilemma for her, and with no further delay he set the glass on fire.

Jenny stared at the flames licking up between her legs and opened her mouth into the most amazing 'O' he had ever seen. It would have been the perfect deep-throat pose, but unfortunately the girl had other things on her mind. Her scream was ear-splitting. He had an idea on how to shut her up though.

Mark had to raise his voice to deafening pitch to be heard over the racket. 'We never did ascertain whether you wanted lightly toasted or char...'

'Lightly toasted! Lightly toasted,' she yelped, trying her best not to struggle as the flames flickered higher.

He raised an eyebrow. 'Manners, my dear, are very important when we're talking about the lifespan of one of my submissives.' He gave her a dark look.

'Please, Sir,' she whimpered, and he knew the glass was beginning to heat up inside her.

Snuffing it out quickly with the palm of his hand, feeling the suction of the glass as it clawed at his skin, he efficiently extinguished the flames. 'Spoilsport,' he muttered. Dipping his fingers into the glass, he swirled them around and then drew out a handful of rather warm coffee beans. Placing them in his mouth he bent his head forward to take a small sip of the liqueur, before stretching his body out over hers. Threading his hands underneath her shoulder blades, he brought his lips down on hers.

Initially wondering if she'd bite him, now that the shock of his stunt had worn off, he was pleasantly surprised when she practically tried to inhale him. Whether it was the effect of his monumental charm and good looks, or whether it was because she had a thing for liquorice and coffee beans remained to be seen. Deepening the kiss, and feeling her respond in kind, he found himself quickly lost in a delicious haze of hormones. He really needed to get on with things and fuck the living daylights out of his newest little protégé. His cock was practically crying 'enough is enough'. When she suddenly stopped kissing him back, though, his eyes snapped open and his lips formed a worried frown. Then he discovered that she was happily crunching his coffee beans.

'Mmm,' she sighed, looking up at him and fluttering her lashes beguilingly, 'more please?'

'Can I assume your request is for beans and not my sexual prowess?' His reply was dry.

'Your assumptions are correct,' said Jenny in a matter of fact tone, adding, 'but I'm happy for more of the other as well.'

'More of the *other*, hmm?' His dark eyes were glittering, and it wouldn't take her long to realise that the beast was back if her eyes were focused on him, and not daydreaming about the flavour of coffee upon her taste buds. He'd do what he could to make sure of the fact. The soft rasp of his zipper did not go unnoticed by the coffee addict in front of him and her beautiful blue eyes seemed to turn black in an instant. Kicking off the rest of his clothes he got naked in short order and pressed up against her, growling when she tried her best to break his ties in order to get closer to him. The lust in her eyes rivalled his own and he was aching with silent agony to bury himself inside her and thrust himself away to oblivion, but that would be over far too quickly and he wanted to draw this night out for as long as possible.

'If you want me to utter that safe word, you're going the wrong way about it,' she breathed, still struggling to rub her body against his.

He barked out a laugh. 'Oh you'll utter your naughty little word before the night is out,' he whispered, nuzzling his lips against her neck, 'but at the moment

I want to lick, bite, nibble, pinch, tweak and chew every inch of you. Then I'm going to spit you back out and start all over again.' He laughed when she made a face at him. 'Relax, you'll enjoy it.' She narrowed her eyes. 'OK,' he amended, 'you'll enjoy most of it.'

Whatever Jenny's reply to his comment might have been was lost, for his mouth descended quickly upon her sex and employed every trick in the book to get her to panting level in record time. When she'd reached the ten-seconds-to-blast-off point he abruptly stopped and moved on to other 'less sensitive' body parts. She made lots of funny gurgling noises, and some interesting Kung Fu moves against his knot-work, but ultimately she just had to wait and endure. He planned to cover her entire body with his tongue-work and lips, and he started high, tracing the delicate lines of her cheekbones, the ridge of her lips, the line of her nose, and the arch of her neck. Nipping at the tightly pointed buds of her nipples and palpating the soft flesh of her abdomen, he then moved to bite the tender inner flesh of her thighs and tongue a wavy line of worship down to her ankles. He sucked toes, pretty little red-tipped toes that were stretched high in the air, and then he got down low and traced a path around her plugs with his tongue. Under her arms, over her shoulders, down to her tight little waist, he suckled, blew, kissed and even hummed tunes against her skin. She smelled divine. She tasted better. It was a shame she was not edible, for he could have eaten her whole. When he had covered her body from top to bottom at least twice, only then did he return to his shot glass.

With his long fingers he gently pried the glass loose from the tight confines of her pussy, not able to contain his smile of satisfaction when she groaned at its removal. 'You like being filled.' It was a statement, not a question, which was just as well, because he didn't get an answer. 'Do you like being stretched, I wonder?' Inserting the middle and index finger of his right hand into her dripping wet channel he began to stretch the soft wet walls of her sex. There was another groan. 'I guess I'll take that as a yes,' he murmured.

Making slow scissor motions with his fingers, he began to stretch the tight flesh of her pussy, opening her up. 'Can you guess what I'm going to do next?' With his fingers still slipping and sliding inside her, he held up his shot glass and twirled the remaining liquid around. 'You only get one guess, Princess.'

'Oh God, please tell me you're not,' said Jenny, who spoke thickly and with stilted pauses. His fingers appeared to be quite the distraction.

'Oh,' breathed Mark happily, 'I'm afraid I am.' Tilting the glass to a forty-five degree angle he let it hover for just a second, and as soon as Jenny grimaced and closed her eyes, he slowly began to pour.

'It's still warm,' she whimpered in a pained voice.

'It'll be nothing compared to the temperature I'm about to rocket you up to, given a couple of a minutes.'

'How are you going to get that out again? You can suck it out, surely?' Jenny opened one eye at him and gave him a nasty look.

'We'll have to hope, for your sake, that I can. Otherwise I'll be searching the apartment for a straw, and then I might get distracted and feel the need to blow bubbles.'

She gave a horrified shudder beneath him, but then his mouth was upon her and it was all about pleasure. He flipped the stereo on with his spare hand and the shuffle function found the *Flower Duet*, from the opera *Lakmé*, which usually reminded him of an airline commercial, but tonight he had other things on his mind. It was a strangely appropriate piece, but he hadn't the time to consider the intricacies of opera at the moment. He was focused. He had his goal in sight and he was nothing if not an overachiever.

He suckled, tongued, stroked, slurped and sucked. Light trickles of Sambuca ran into his mouth, flavoured with her unique, spicy essence that made the subtle hint of elderflower and the strong tang of liquorice seem like nectar from the gods. Speaking of gods, she tasted heavenly. Earthy, musky, flowery, and there was a hint of sweetness he couldn't quite put his finger on. She seemed to have a particular scent and taste that drove him wild, and tonight, he intended to indulge himself. She wouldn't be getting a sip of this particular vintage. This was all for him and he savoured each drop. When her thighs began trembling beneath his hands he increased the suction of his mouth and captured her clitoris. In a few artful flicks he had her screaming and then he could wait no longer. He was inside her. With long, tortured thrusts of urgency, he finally found solace within her body. She squeezed him tightly, somehow remembering what she had been taught, and as he ran his fingers up and down her body, caressing and stroking her arms, breasts and thighs, he lost himself. One moment he was a sensible control-freak style dominant and in the next he was a rutting beast. He needed to pull himself back and rein it in, or this session would not end as planned.

Pulling out of Jennifer Redcliff's body was one of the hardest things he had ever done. Considering how long it had taken him to immerse himself inside it, it was hardly surprising. Breathing hard he withdrew his aching cock, and it was clear she felt the same way for her body tried desperately hard to hold on to him. 'They've taught you well, I see,' he said with a sardonic smile, as he finally gathered his breath back.

'Oh God,' she moaned.

'I'm that good, huh?' He fumbled for the tray that had been pushed to the edge of the bed, and reached for the penknife and ginger.

The sarcasm didn't even register. Upon her face were the markings of euphoric bliss, but even though he had let her come, her body knew it wanted more. And it would most certainly get it, but not for a few minutes or so.

With shaking hands he peeled a thin layer of skin away from the ginger and fashioned the tubular root into two makeshift plugs. Then he neatly sliced a few thick circles, once again removing the outer layer of skin, and laid them all back down on the tray. He intended to hear her safe word uttered, and a pared finger of ginger inserted into the anus was as reliable a method as any. After insertion it would take up to five minutes to reach maximum intensity and produce a burning sensation so intolerable she would be quickly reduced to begging for mercy. If that wasn't bad enough, he intended to crop her delectable backside at the same time, which would give her added inducement to utter her naughty little word. If his bartending skills weren't quite as good as they could be, he had a feeling his vegetable peeling and spanking skills were more than up to the task.

When satisfied with his handiwork he began to tease the steel plug out of her ass in order to make room for her new best friend.

'You're going to be begging for me to fuck you in the ass tonight, darling, you know that, right?' He'd intended to snap her out of her post-orgasmic stupor and the words did the trick, for she blinked her eyes, lost the look of loved-up wanton and gave him a sneer. Hooray - his titan was back.

'I'm also going to be screaming safe words, but so far you're all talk and no trousers.' She glared at him. The woman actually had the audacity to glare at him, not just once, but several times this evening. She was incredible. Here he was, a dominant who could usually reduce females to tears with no more than a few sharp words, and it appeared he'd finally met his match. He had a feeling that no matter how many torments he decided to heap upon her, there would be no quelling that intensely fiery nature. What fun it would be to find out though! He suspected it would take years, rather than days, for him to discover all of her secrets.

'Oh, you'll be uttering your safe word alright, and a few other swear words besides,' he said, finally managing to pry the rigid plug out of her. Sliding it back and forth a few times, purely to see the look of pleasure on her face as he did so, he pursed his lips thoughtfully. 'When are you going to admit you enjoy anal, my little virago?'

'I'm not,' she moaned, rattling the eyebolts that held both wrists and ankles and eyeing up the large finger of ginger in his hands.

'You're not enjoying anal or you're not going to admit that you enjoy anal?' he queried, sliding the sweet smelling ginger along her clitoris and then down her labia. There would be no real burn from it yet, because it took several minutes for the oil to take effect. Sliding the first root gently into her pussy he twisted and twirled it around and around until he had her panting.

'How does it feel?'

Jenny squirmed. 'It tingles,' she whispered, 'but it's not that bad.'

Mark made a noncommittal sound. He wasn't about to tell her it would burn like hell very shortly, so he progressed with plug number two. Plunging his middle and index finger into his mouth, he coated them with saliva and smeared it liberally around her sphincter. Although the ginger was wet, it would still require a little help to ease its insertion. Repeating the action several times he began sliding a single finger inside her, before quickly replacing it with two and then three. Her previous plug had done a good job of loosening her up and the ginger, unless he was much mistaken, would slide in quite easily. Rubbing the soft head of the root against her anus he slowly pushed, and sure enough it popped inside her with little effort and took only a few seconds of work to slide the long root deep. Finishing up by placing the neat slices of ginger between the folds of her labia, butterfly-style, he then took a step back to admire his artistry.

'Still feel fine?'

Jenny rolled her eyes back at him. 'I have no idea what all the fuss is about with the ginger. It's a little warm, but it's nothing I can't handle.'

Mark's lips twitched and he set the dial of his Rolex for five minutes exactly. At that point there should be tears, screams and more than a few expletives, one of which would be her safe word.

'You do remember the safe word, Precious?'

'I'm hardly likely to forget oh-delightfully-depraved-one,' she said with a flourish. He had to bite the inside of his cheek to stop from laughing. To distract himself from the lovely view of her nether regions, which he would be unable to fuck for a least a few minutes, he went in search of the black leather crop he'd dropped earlier. A good cropping session would improve his mood and give him some focus.

'Why is everything in your apartment black and white, and why do you have floor to ceiling curtains covering one end of your room when you have no windows.' The tone of her voice suggested that the ginger needed considerably more time to work. Trust his luck to find himself with a sub that had a high tolerance for pain. Giving up his search for the lost crop, he found another flexible beast with a fibreglass shaft from his inbuilt and very white wardrobe. He stroked the small leather keeper with his fingertips as he considered her questions.

He decided to indulge her. 'In answer to the colour scheme, I like to keep things simple, I guess,' he offered. 'And black and white are my favourite colours. You know where you are with them.' He nodded his head, lost in thought. 'As to the curtains, there is a window. I have a blackout blind fitted beneath them.'

'Oh,' said Jenny, and it was not in response to his answer, but rather her first taste of heat from the ginger root. She wriggled a little bit, but then relaxed herself and seemed to be able to contain her reaction. Looking at his watch, he saw they were two minutes in to his little experiment. Things were looking promising.

'So why do you keep the blinds closed?' she pressed.

'It's dark outside.'

'It's London outside. There's lots of lights and it's beautiful.' There were tells upon her face now, a wrinkle here and there as she tried to prevent herself from moving. The heat was spreading.

'I'm not much one for heights,' he offered.

Jenny was beginning to lose the battle with the ginger, for she began to move and once the movement began, there was no stopping it. It didn't prevent her from speaking her mind though. 'You live in the penthouse suite and you're afraid of heights? Please tell me you're kidding. This place must have one of the best views of London and I'll bet you keep it permanently shuttered.' At the narrowing of his lips she added, 'Why on earth did you buy it?'

'Because it's the best. Best area, best view, best location, and it even has parking.' He primed his crop for contact. It was high time she stopped talking. In future he would have to remember to gag her, but the sound of her voice did strange, liquid things to his internal organs and he was enjoying the sensation.

'So basically you're nu...' She didn't manage to finish her sentence. The crop made contact with the soft flesh of her lower buttocks, and in the rigid position she found herself in, it had to hurt. The ragged remains of her panties wouldn't offer any hindrance to the bite of the leather tip and damned if she didn't look sexy as hell. He fired off a volley of five quick strokes around her outer left thigh and watched her face redden.

'That's it, pet, tighten those ass cheeks. Feel the burn.' He grinned.

'It's not that bad,' she gritted out through her teeth, but her words were becoming a little stiffer and the expression on her face belied the glib words.

'Of course it isn't,' said Mark, running his hand up and down the curve of her right thigh, examining her flesh and planning his next course of action.

'So, let me get this right. If I safe-word, we stop and I go to bed?' Her breath was coming in little pants now and he could tell that things were beginning to hot up.

'That's the name of the game, I believe, yes.'

'Welllll...' she said, drawing out the length of the last letter to unusual proportions, 'at least that means you'll go to bed without having any fun too, I guess.'

Wrong, he thought, but decided it was best not to divulge the inner workings of his private life to Miss Redcliff at the moment. If she did manage to become a permanent feature, he'd probably have fun explaining his office away. He let another five strokes of his crop fly and they made satisfactory whistling and cracking noises. The crop made such beautiful music.

Sighing in pleasure he looked down at his watch. Four minutes had passed. Jenny's insides had to be at combustion point right about now. Little pink spots had bloomed all along her outer thighs and he intended to make sure they had plenty of friends to join them.

'The safe word is "bastard", darling,' he purred, as he renewed his efforts on the far more sensitive flesh of her inner thighs.

'I know what the safe word is,' she yelled, her hands straining against the soft silk of his ties, 'because I picked the fucker!'

'Tut, tut, tut,' he said slowly, and each reprimand was accompanied by a vicious swat from the crop. 'We've already had a chat about swearing, but I'm happy to have another.' Rubbing the tip of his crop along her clitoris he paused it there for effect. 'Care to try my patience, Precious?'

But either Jennifer Redcliff didn't hear him, or she had more important things on her mind, because her face had turned the colour of puce and she was shaking her head from side to side. Still no safe word, though.

Letting the crop fly in his hands, he decorated the seat of her ass in varying hues of pink and red. He was aiming for a Caribbean sunset - more reds than pinks with any luck, and red on a pert backside happened to be a very beautiful colour. He watched her inner struggle with amusement. It was obvious the girl wanted to scream her safe word from the top of her lungs, but still something was holding her back. He was curious as to what.

Laying down his crop he got up on the bed and sat astride her, one knee on either side of her ribcage. He used the crop to trace a path down her cheekbone. It annoyed him when she winced, but then, she really didn't have a clue how the normal submissive/dominant relationship went, and if she only had Albrecht with which to base her experience, then perhaps he shouldn't be surprised.

'I would never, ever crop someone on or around the face, so relax.' He let his eyes burrow into hers and wished to hell he could fathom what she was thinking.

'Relaxing is kind of hard when your knees are tied up around your ears, and your ass is on fire,' she growled.

'So safe-word.' The crop pushed against her lip and skewed it sideways.

'No.' There was a look of bitter determination in her eyes, and damned if it didn't turn him on something fierce.

He sat back on his haunches and chewed on his lip as he considered what to say next. 'You are a stubborn one, aren't you?' He tilted his head and narrowed his eyes. 'So what's stopping you? You hate losing?' She shook her head. 'I'm not going to send you to bed if you safe-word, if that's what you're worried about. Things have gone past that stage. You're getting fucked whether you like it or not. Is that it?' Again she shook her head. 'Then what?' he asked, exasperated.

She smiled at him, and considering the party that must have been going on in her pussy and ass, he thought it was quite an achievement. She cleared her throat to speak and it was several seconds before she managed to push the words past her lips.

'I guess I want to see how much I can take. It's no secret I'm going back to Albrecht, and if I'm going back things are going to get a hell of a lot worse before they get better. So I'm going to need to toughen up, but I need to tell you... if you untied me right now, I'd probably kill you.' She sniffed, and then began squirming like mad, unable to help herself.

As far as guilt trips went, it had the desired effect. He, the man with no conscience, or not much of one at any rate, felt decidedly guilty. It was just possible she might be worth enduring a night of purgatory for. One night of anguish was probably a bargain price for around ten years of entertaining fun - and let's face it, Jennifer Redcliff was far more amusing than the rest of his very obedient ladies back at the office. Clearly he had been seeking out the wrong form of entertainment for the past few years.

'IImpfh. It'd be fun watching you try.' The smile that accompanied his words was lacklustre though. Deciding to torture his thrashing submissive no longer, in this way at least, he gently eased the large fingers of ginger from her body and removed the cut slices from the lips of her sex. It wouldn't ease her suffering for the time being, the damage had already been done, but there were a few things he could do to help. A bit of olive oil and his cock would dilute the fierce burning, and as a distraction technique it was top notch. He hadn't given up his quest, either. There was more than one way to get a safe word out of his girl, and he intended to see this mission through to the end. If he had to wring the damn thing out of her kicking and screaming, so much the better.

Padding barefoot into his kitchen he wasted no time in locating a strip of condoms and a bottle of oil. Whilst he knew there was no risk of getting her pregnant, he wasn't prepared to suffer with the heat of the ginger if it could possibly be avoided. As an afterthought he also got another tray of ice out of the freezer. If the woman wanted to be distracted he could ensure she didn't know left from right, up from down or right from wrong, and in less than ten seconds. He was that good. Striding quickly away from the room he almost winced at his last thought, but it wasn't arrogance on his part. It was years and years, *and years* of practice.

Hopping up on the bed again, he tore the condom out of its packet and smoothed it down his swollen cock. The thing was once again throbbing like the meanest of migraines, and if he didn't put it out of its misery soon there was a good chance he might burst a blood vessel. At least he knew that Viagra wasn't an expense he was going to have to contend with any time soon.

'So, do you want slow and easy or fast and hard,' he asked, knowing the question was ridiculous, because she was going to get fast and hard whether she liked it or not. Eventually.

'It's... hot... down... there,' came the strained reply, 'is this... going... to hurt?'

'No baby. I'm going to make it all better. I'm going to heat you up and cool you down, and all at the same time. Am I amazing or what?' Cracking an ice cube out of the tray, he placed it between his teeth. He then unscrewed the cap off the bottle of oil and liberally coated his cock in it, keeping the open bottle in his hand, as he would soon need some more.

'Brace yourself,' he whispered evilly, and her body immediately tensed, but when his cock pressed for entrance it was a gentle push that slid him forward and a slow rock of his hips. Placing his elbows up near her neck he waited for the first drop of freezing cold water to drip down on her skin. Bang! At least, that's the noise you'd have thought Miss Redcliff had heard, judging by the way she reared up and tugged against his crude rigging.

'It's only water,' he mumbled between clenched teeth, nearly laughing as her head reared up and her teeth made to bite him in response.

'Now, now, now. That's hardly friendly, is it?'

'And it's only blood, which I will draw when I get the chance to bite you. I didn't put you down for a coward, Matthews.'

Mark snorted and nearly dropped his ice cube. 'I can see you're not with the program yet. Let me work on that, a bit... lower down.'

Staying away from the vicious end, Mark drove his cock into her eager little hole again and again. He took his time at first, careful to grind each move upon her clit and draw out each stroke for as long as possible. It took considerable restraint to keep the pace up, when he wanted nothing more than to smash himself inside her and make her vision go stellar, but he would drag this out to the limits of his ability, and he had reasonably impressive staying power. Besides, he had the urge to watch her suffer in a thousand and one differing, pleasurable ways and he was just getting started.

The oil kept coming. He slowly fucked every last morsel of the ginger out of her, stroke by stroke. He wasn't even sure she noticed, for while his cock had being doing one thing his mouth had been doing another entirely. The ice cube had flowed all over her body, finding each sweet spot she owned and making it his. He drew patterns along her stomach, her legs, her arms, and all over her face, until her body was a river of melting ice. There was no question that her wrists were going to be red raw tomorrow, even though they were encased in the softest silk. The one little word he was looking for was still trapped inside her though, and no matter how far his tongue prodded or how deep his cock plunged, his woman was going to take being stubborn to the next level. Unfortunately, she wasn't going to like the next level much.

'I'm going to fuck you in the arse now, my tenacious little pet, and repair the damage the ginger has wrought. Just remember to relax. We'll take it as slow as we can, and I promise you'll enjoy it. Almost as much as me.' He stretched out over her and let the warmth of his body soothe her, although the ice didn't seem to have done much to cool her ardour. Her face was flushed, her breath was coming in short, heavy pants and her eyes were glazed and lidded.

Oiling up his cock up once again for the finale, he also coated his fingers in the stuff and began with a single digit, sliding it inside her tight hole as slowly as he could, meeting little resistance as the plugs had already stretched her. With the other hand he drizzled a bit more oil on his fingers and began manipulating her clit. He knew she was nearly at breaking point, but it didn't hurt to keep her on the edge.

'I'm... going... to...'

'No, you're not. You're not going to do anything unless I tell you to, got that?' One finger became two and they pumped inside her mercilessly as his other hand concentrated on tormenting her clit.

'Oh God, oh God, oh...'

'Don't you fucking dare,' he whispered dangerously, and two fingers became three. Staring down at her, his dark eyes fierce with hunger, he stretched her open and worked the oil deep inside her. He could feel the heat of the ginger on his hands, even with the lubricant, but he didn't let it bother him. When he was good and satisfied she was ready for him he slowly withdrew the triangle of his fingers and reached for the ice tray.

He tipped the thing on its head and a barrage of cubes scattered across the white linen of his bedspread. Picking up one he traced it slowly around her lips and laughed as she tried to bite him again. 'You never give up, huh?'

'Never,' she growled and the words dripped from her lips, accompanied by a venomous look.

He shook his head, amused. 'You do realise, if you were mine I'd keep you tied up permanently. Are you sure you don't want to go back to Albrecht?' He didn't wait for a response. He inserted the melting ice cube into her pussy and managed to insert another three behind it. His mouth then bent down to take a nipple in his mouth as his cock slowly slid forward, but this time into her ass.

'Oh my fucking God,' he whispered, taking her nipple between his teeth. You're so damn tight.' He inched inside her gradually, letting her adjust to his length and thickness, taking his time. It wasn't long before his eyes were nearly rolling in his head and he was beginning to wonder just who had control of things here. Right now, it most certainly wasn't him.

'It doesn't hurt,' whispered Jenny, who wore an expression of utter amazement on her face.

'Not if you do it properly, no,' groaned Mark, who chose that moment to tweak her nipple. He almost smiled at the resulting gurgle of pain, before his hand tilted her head forward and their eyes connected squarely. 'But those ice cubes inside you are going to be unbearable very shortly.'

Having said that he thrust with his cock, surging as deep inside her as he could go while his teeth bit down upon her tender flesh. Squeezing his hand between their bodies he found her clit and mashed it down hard.

'You asshole!' she screamed at the top of her lungs, and he winced and hoped to hell all his neighbours were asleep.

Bucking back and forth, unable to stop himself, he slammed into her ass with a force that was unholy. Listening to her ragged, torn sounds of pleasure, he couldn't help a moment of smug satisfaction. Feeling his balls implode in the most spectacular fashion he slammed his fist into his headboard, startling her, and ground out, 'Still not the word I was looking for, pet, but thankfully we have all night.'

CHAPTER SEVENTEEN

The Scoville Scale

It was well past midnight when Mark left Jenny to sleep off the after effects of their session. She'd been so exhausted she was snoring before he'd managed to finish untying her. Finding a spare duvet, since the previous one had been soaked with his ice play and other various fluids, he'd cocooned her gently inside it and turned the lamp down low.

Her face was completely innocent in sleep. There was not a wrinkle to mar her beauty, nor a flaw to be seen upon it. Just looking down at her swollen lips,

169

ravaged from his kisses, made him want to inhale her and suck her so deep inside him that she could never get away. Goddamn. Another crazy thought, and the trouble was, they were getting more frequent. Could he whisk her away somewhere out of Redcliff's grasp? Would he be able to deal with the consequences? The answer was unequivocally 'no'. It didn't matter; his brain was furiously deciding the ramifications of purloining Miss Redcliff and hiding her somewhere safe. It was a nice idea. It would have severe penalties. He forcefully steered his thoughts away from that path.

Thinking back to the past couple of hours, he pursed his lips and then couldn't help a smile. It had taken four orgasms to get little Miss Stubborn to utter her safe word. Four. He'd been beginning to wonder if he might need Viagra after all, when finally she caved. She'd been babbling incoherently at the end. Begging him to stop, and then begging him to continue, before pleading, cajoling and demanding her last climax. He'd dragged it out in a painfully slow dance that had been almost as bad for him as it had for her, but finally... she'd given in. Never had the word 'bastard' seemed so sweet on anyone's lips. All he'd had to say was 'come' and repositioning his pelvis, he pounded her clit against him and drew out her orgasm until she'd been sobbing with pleasurable exhaustion. She would be a joy to train. A pain in the ass too, but ultimately he'd have such fun with her. Damn.

Easing himself out of the bedroom, he slowly closed the door. He'd go back and leave a glass of water and something to eat in case she woke up in a minute, but he just wanted to check his phone calls first. His OCD tendencies were beginning to show. Walking into his office and picking up the telephone, he keyed in his code and began listening to his voicemail. Taking a seat on his comfortable leather recliner he noted he was on edge, as if a sixth sense was telling him to be careful.

When a disembodied voice appeared on the line Mark knew his gut instinct had been correct. Without having heard the first word spoken, he knew it would be Redcliff and he knew that whatever the old man had to say, he wasn't going to like it much. When a slow and menacing message began his eyes squeezed shut. Pressing the telephone tightly to his ear, he felt his hand tremble against the handset and a cold, hard feeling of dread settled like a lead bowling ball in his stomach.

Hello Matthews. I seem to have acquired a friend of yours. I believe she will need rescuing, or I'll have a certain sadist I know peel her to ribbons. You know how an orange looks when you peel off its skin in a single go? That'll be the look he'll aim for unless I see you back at the stables tomorrow morning by ten a.m. Oh, and bring the girl with you. You're a naughty boy. You weren't supposed to get your hands on her just yet. You will, of course, be punished.

The speaker then went silent, which would have been a relief, but the sound of Isabelle's screams, present throughout the whole speech, became much louder until there was a sickening crunch and then the sound stopped dead.

Mark, who had been pleasantly relaxed after just having fucked all the tension out of his body, was now wound up tighter than a very small G-string on a very large ass. Shit. He'd been expecting this, hadn't he? The answer was no. All his thoughts had been centred on Jennifer Redcliff and he hadn't been thinking ahead, nor had he even been trying to consider damage control. How utterly stupid! He should have foreseen this. What the hell was the time anyway? Looking down at his watch with shaking hands, the luminous dials told him it was nearing two a.m. Shit, shit, shit. He had no more than two hours before they had to be in the car, in order to get them there in time. Think, Matthews, think!

Storming off to take a cold shower, his blood bubbled dangerously hot in his veins. Swinging the bathroom door wide open he didn't bother to close it. Redcliff junior would not be disturbing him. Marching over to the shower and turning the stainless steel spigots on full force, he stood under the icy spray and tried to get a perspective on things. Letting the frigid deluge of water slam into him, he tried to size up the situation as best he could.

Going to the police was not an option. The red tape was ridiculous, whether he would be believed was questionable, and Albrecht's security was tighter than that of Alcatraz. Hiding Jenny somewhere safe was also not an option if he wanted to get Isabelle out alive. Not that it had ever really been an option. He had no doubt in his mind that the old man's threats were serious. Hell, he'd seen part of what Kyle could do already and the thought of anyone hurting Isabelle made his fists clench. A cruel and heartless bastard he might be, but he couldn't let Isabelle take the fall for something he had instigated. He still had a conscience, somewhere, and while he didn't want to hear from it right now, Redcliff had him right where he wanted and the next part of this game was probably going to get messy.

So what was going to happen next? He'd go back to Albrecht, return his library loan, and hopefully they'd free Isabelle so he could get her somewhere safe. With any luck there'd be no permanent scars. He smiled grimly. He was stealing from Peter to pay Paul. That then left the problem of Jennifer Redcliff. Money was not an incentive, so what was? He could not sub for the old man. Not even to rescue a couple of girls. Christ, he'd be mad. You just had to look at Kyle's work to wonder what the other beast was capable of, and the chances were it wasn't going to be pretty.

Slamming the faucet shut, he grabbed a fluffy white towel and ran a basin full of hot water for a wet shave. He couldn't stand electric razors; they just didn't get the job done properly. Watching his hands shake as he reached into his bathroom cabinet for some shaving foam, he wondered if he'd manage to complete the simple task without taking half his face off, and then his thoughts immediately turned to Kyle. That piece of shit had better hope he was out of reach of Mark's fist, because he wouldn't think twice about flattening him. Calm down and get a grip, he thought. Two hours was more than long enough to get a couple of phone calls out, and it wasn't like he slept these days.

Taking a deep breath, he stilled the tremor in his hands and looked his reflection squarely in the eye. Redcliff might have won round one, but he wasn't about to win the war.

Seven hours and several cups of coffee later, both he and Miss Redcliff were greeted at the gates of Albrecht. She was quickly pulled out of the car and marched off, and he was firmly instructed by one of the security detail to make his way to the office. It hadn't been a particularly pleasant parting. The look on her face had been awful. Her eyes spoke of terror and defeat. He could only wonder what his were saying right now, and knew the look he wore wasn't an attractive one. He'd let her down, but he hadn't seen any way around it for the time being. She wouldn't be inside here for long, though. He had promised himself at least that much.

'Hello, Mr Matthews. How wonderful to see you again, young chap.'

Mark, upon entering the office, immediately winced at the use of the word 'young', but the smile upon his face belied the fact. 'To what do I owe the honour, Mr Redcliff? Don't tell me you're still lusting after my body?'

He smiled tightly. There was no getting around the fact that he wouldn't do what Redcliff had previously requested of him. The stakes were high, but he suspected nothing short of atomic war or death would manage to get him on his knees in front of another man.

'As a matter of fact, I am. Which is why you're here, as it happens. I thought I'd try and convince you I'm not the devil you think I am.'

Redcliff lied admirably well. There were no tell-tale twitches, blinking or fidgeting from the old man. 'So which devil are you then?' The wry smile upon Mark's face was blatant. Taking a seat in a large leather lounger, he crossed his legs and openly examined the man in front of him. Observing the sallow, sickly skin and the heavy bags lining his eyes, he noted his adversary's hair was grey and thinning, and his frame was slender and spindly. He did not look like a particularly well man and the years had not been kind to him.

Redcliff gave him a sly smile in return. 'Why, I suspect you'll find out in a few moments. The stable lads are just getting Petal ready and then we're going to give you a little show down in the dungeon. You've come all this way, after all. I couldn't let you go back without something to whet your appetite.'

Redcliff was about to pull a nasty stunt. Mark didn't need to be a mind reader to figure that much out. The only question was whether he was going to play nicely or throw his toys about. Judging by the look on his face, it was going to be toys and lots of them. 'Do I actually have a choice in the matter? Is this an invitation or an order?' Mark raised his eyebrow in question and propped his feet up on the desk in front of him, knowing it would antagonise his opponent. He knew exactly what it was, but he wanted Redcliff to acknowledge it as such.

Redcliff looked up at him, and adjusting the collar of his pinstriped shirt, gave Mark a veiled look. 'At the moment it's an invitation, and if you want to keep it that way I suggest you make your way down below.'

The man gazed directly at him, and if the chilling stare he was given was any indication of things to come, Mark decided he wasn't in for a particularly pleasant morning.

'Then by all means, lead the way, Michael.' Another stab was proffered and there was an answering tick in Redcliff's jaw.

'I think you can lead the way, *Mark*,' said Redcliff, tossing back the challenge. 'I'll watch your back.'

Getting to his feet, Mark hooked his fingers in the belt loops of his chinos and sighed. Stepping smartly out of the office and striding on ahead he said, 'Somehow I sincerely doubt that, Redcliff. Just try not to throw any sharp objects in my direction.' The door slammed in the distance and Mark's eyes glittered dangerously as he marched off to see just what atrocities were waiting for him. He decided then and there, that if Kyle was present he wouldn't be responsible for his actions. They had one hell of a score sheet that needed to be settled, and internal organ damage was probably the only way forward. Scrap that, multiple internal organ damage, and a fracture or two wouldn't go amiss.

When Mark's brogues tapped down the stone steps towards the dungeon everything was strangely silent. If there was a scene to be played for his amusement - or lack thereof - they were waiting for his presence in which to begin. He figured that loitering at the entrance wasn't going to do much for his street cred, so he barged straight in through the door and to the blackness beyond. He stopped dead in his tracks. Why on earth was it pitch black? A scene wasn't any good unless you could actually see the thing unfolding in front of you. The silent shroud of inky black velvet almost had him stepping backwards in his hurry to go back out of the door, but he managed to stop himself. He was not a coward. He would see what Redcliff wanted and negotiate terms. That's what men like Redcliff and himself did. They bargained for what they wanted, and the higher the stakes, the more they gambled.

When two hands clamped around each of his arms and propelled him forcefully towards an invisible chair he shouldn't have been surprised. After briefly falling through the air he landed on a firm wooden seat with a painful thud, and his jaw closed with an audible snap. The two hands remained around his arms, and they were heavy enough that he was not going to attempt to dislodge them. He scowled. He had not expected Redcliff to play fair, but clearly the man had no respect for him whatsoever.

'Call off the goons, Michael,' he said, in the most jovial voice he could muster. 'It's not like I'm going anywhere until I get the girl.' Eerie silence met his request and the hands stayed firmly where they were. Negotiations were already looking shaky.

After a few seconds had passed his vision managed to cut through the thick blanket of perpetual night. It seemed a stage had been erected at one end of the dungeon and two figures were huddled upon it. The image was still fuzzy to his unprepared eyes, but the figures were slowly coming into focus. Both were female. One was most certainly Jennifer Redcliff, for the wig had been removed and her shorn hair was an immediate giveaway. Back in full leather pony-girl tack, she was tied over the spanking horse by means of her four limbs. No doubt about it, the girl was a breathtaking site.

Opposite her was a shaking blonde, and it didn't take much to guess that she was the lovely Isabelle. Her hair was wild, she looked like she'd had a rough few days and if he wasn't mistaken, there were already tears running down her cheeks. Knowing Redcliff, he'd probably apprised the pair of what was about to happen to them in great detail, and poor little Isabelle just wasn't cut out for the stuff that went on in Albrecht. He knew she never stayed to watch the scenes played out, and if she ever had to enter the dungeon she left at the earliest opportunity. Unfortunately, her run of good luck was up. She was in for it big style this morning, if the hands around his arms were any indication.

'I trust everyone's seated and eager for the proceedings to begin?' The unmistakeable sound of Redcliff's rasping voice came over the loudspeaker and as it did so, the stage began to light up in slow degrees of soft grey until a vignette of light surrounded the bound pair, turning them into black and white portrait.

Mark was a little surprised, if he were honest. Full colour was usually more visually effective, but he was positive Redcliff had his reasons. Sure enough, when an arc of purple electricity shot across the stage and crackled loudly enough to make everyone in the room jump, he finally understood the gloom. Shit. His fingernails gripped the edges of his enforced chair. If he wasn't much mistaken, he was about to be treated to a violet wand display, and that was going to draw more screams out of the girls than a big dipper at a funfair. This was not good. This was not good at all. Several more arcs of electricity followed, sending beautiful purple lightning strikes across the stage and lit up the room with a soft neon glow.

'Have you ever tried the violet wand with the Wartenberg pinwheel, Matthews? If you get it just right, it feels like the steel spikes of the wheel are actually slicing the flesh. It's a masochist's dream, so I've heard. It's a shame that neither of these girls are masochists, but at least you'll get a pretty good idea of their pain tolerance level by the end of this number.'

Mark's fingers tapped agitatedly across the wooden arms of his chair. He'd seen rather too much of the pinwheel lately, and had no desire to see it again used thus, but there was little he could do about it. Listening to Redcliff's voice boom inside his head was an unpleasant experience, but he suspected it was nothing compared to what was coming next.

Isabelle, upon hearing Redcliff's intentions, struggled furiously upon her bench, but interestingly enough Jennifer remained perfectly still and composed. He suspected she had no idea what a violet wand was and assumed it would be no worse than a harsh spanking or cropping. She was in for a shock in more ways than one.

Music erupted on stage, for dramatic effect, he guessed, although none was needed. It was something irritating and modern; dance music at a guess. The beat thudded through the room and left an unpleasant vibration that seemed to throb through the base of his chair and rattle each of his bones. Get on with it, he thought.

A hooded woman appeared on stage in a black latex catsuit. With small slits for her eyes, the suit gave nothing away, but he would have dearly loved to know her identity. People who did this kind of thing deserved payback in the worst way. As she strutted about on stage he watched her gloved hands run up and down the girls' flanks, thighs and backsides. Redcliff intended to draw out the process, it seemed. Sighing, he had no option but to wait for the sparks to fly.

Eventually the woman got hold of a wand. She stood in the middle of the stage, facing him, and lit the thing up. They'd amplified the sound. When her fingers moved to stroke the outside of the clear glass tube a sharp buzzing and crackling sound could be heard. The sound went straight through him. Her fingers drew the current out and long lines of brilliant lavender arced around the stage. In her other hand she slowly held up a stainless steel Wartenberg pinwheel.

Mark had a great deal of respect for the pinwheel. The thing was originally designed for neurological use, with its sharp rotating spikes, but modern medicine found it a little 'unhygienic' for its tastes. He kept a couple at home in his bedside cabinet, for sensation play, but had never come across anyone that wanted to feel like they were being split open whilst using it. When electrified the cold metal would send a flurry of hot sparks across the skin and an intense feeling of pain. The girl who should be worried was little Miss Redcliff. They intended to fight nasty, it seemed.

The hooded figure placed her pinwheel on a heavily scarred old oak table located at the rear of the stage, and began her electric dance with Isabelle. Starting with just the wand she ran the glass tip up the line of her shaking back, leaving a gap of perhaps an inch with which to conduct the current. Several lines of snaking electricity appeared and crackled against Isabelle's pale skin. Although he knew the current probably wasn't all that painful yet, Albrecht's former secretary was less than impressed, because all four of her limbs were flailing and trying to work their way out of the thick ropes that encased them. To be fair, it was live electricity being directed at her body and the subtle smell of burning which the wand emitted, actually nothing more than ozone, would probably be freaking the poor girl out.

Next on stage was a hooded man covered in the same black latex getup as the woman, and Mark narrowed his eyes. He swaggered on stage with such confidence and arrogance that Mark knew almost instantly who he was. A scream began building in his chest. Immediately trying to shoot up off his chair, although he was firmly pinned down again before he even managed to get to his feet, Mark glared at the hooded figure who stared him down. He had no idea how he knew it was Levison, it could have been the swagger, the general build or the way he just stared at Mark before he began playing, but his anxiety level had just hit the roof. Breathe, he told himself. It could be worse. What the fuck was worse than Kyle Levison loose with electric current on his girl? Go back to breathing, he cautioned himself. A couple of breaths went in and out, and though they were painful, he tried to distract himself. OK, how could it be worse? He could be having open-heart surgery or something, he supposed. Jesus. He could feel his chest tightening and his airflow becoming restricted. Levison was a wild card. There was no telling what that freak show of a man might get up to.

Watching the proceedings with wide eyes, he saw Levison run the pinwheel down Jenny's back. She didn't move a muscle. Thank God. So, as he suspected, it wasn't painful yet. They were going to work them up, get them excited and then shock the living daylights out of them. If Redcliff thought he was going to negotiate in this way he was much mistaken. The girls would just have to endure the pain. It wouldn't kill them. Sitting through Isabelle's continuous screams might kill him, but he could examine his conscience or lack thereof later. He hoped to hell Jenny wouldn't scream. There was only so much he would be able to endure.

More women appeared on stage, this time with g-spot, curved dildo shaped attachments. They glowed a ferocious bright orange and made quite an impact in the dark. They were probably going to make quite an impact somewhere else in a minute, and the girls were in for a treat before the real nastiness happened.

Sure enough bottoms were slapped, wands buzzed and crackled over every inch of exposed flesh and the internal electrodes began to tease inside their victims. The neon gas trapped inside the dildos glowed like orange fire. They were almost mesmerising to watch and he couldn't take his eyes off the women as they slowly worked their humming instruments of pleasure deep inside the girls, pumping them back and forth. A corona of glowing hues of purple and orange formed upon the stage that twisted and streaked inside one another. It really was a shame that he had to watch the scene under duress, because it was incredibly beautiful.

Two more electrodes showed up, this time held by a pair of latex-suited men. To complement the effect, these were red. There was one for poor Isabelle's ass, and judging by the racket going on there it hadn't been used much, and another for Jenny's mouth. The stage was covered in colour and bright light. Both Jenny and Isabelle were moving now. Rubbing their hips up and down the horse, twisting their arms and legs in the bonds, edging their bodies down to try and get some contact friction on their poor neglected clits. Little did they know, but they wouldn't need it. Those g-spot probes would get them where they wanted to go soon enough, with a little help.

Without further ado the wands were retracted and covered in a condom or two, before being placed back into their respective holes.

The girls were going to be treated to a whole new level of fun: internal sparks. Sure enough, the groaning and moaning became much more pronounced as the dildos stroked the elusive little area directly behind the pubic bone. The tempo, which had begun as a slow and sensuous stroke, quickly increased to a frenetic pounding. Mark's eyes danced with lines of neon, and he could now barely decipher one colour from another. As their bodies coiled and writhed it was clear his girls were close. As soon as the stage appeared to be nothing more than a pumping, pounding, grinding array of coloured sticks, the first scream erupted from the practiced lips of Isabelle, but Jenny was only seconds behind her.

The men and women did not stop. They dragged out each contraction, but slowed the movement of their toys, making sure each bound girl was a shaking, dribbling, cursing wreck.

'Well, that's pleasure, Matthews,' came the smug sound of Redcliff's voice. 'Now, I think it's high time we showed you how pain plays out, don't you?'

Mark did not want to see how pain played out, but judging by the way the grip on his arms had tightened, he didn't think it particularly mattered. The only thing he could now do for the girls was watch on with stoic indifference. He had a feeling it wasn't going to be the easiest thing he had ever done by a long shot.

The various latex-clad crew began to walk with a little more purpose as they searched for new and far more devious toys. There was excitement in the air and the silence that surrounded them was broken only by the heaving gasps of the post-orgasmic girls. Then everyone turned the power up and the heat rating went off the Celsius/Fahrenheit scale.

They began with special Mylar floggers, and not just any floggers. These featured heavyweight, industrial grade tails and they were going to sting. Their handles were made of shiny orange copper and left unpainted to increase conductivity.

Kyle started on Jennifer first. The tails were run along her body from the ankle to the waist and then they returned back in a V-shape. Vivid blue sparks shot everywhere, the air crackled and burned, and Jenny wriggled and moaned under the agonising torrent. She took it well, considering the mess she was in. When they started on Isabelle she was much more vocal and the sound almost made him wince.

The floggers moved up and down with relentless precision and lengths of steel chain followed them. The wands had obviously been turned up to their maximum settings and the girls were writhing in torment in seconds. Even the jute rope that kept them tethered to their respective spanking benches had been specially chosen for conductivity. Indigo sparks danced in pretty lines upon it and very soon the bodies appeared to be covered in a relentless mist of neon lines.

'You can put a stop to this, Matthews,' said a sinister little voice that echoed around the room. 'You know what I want. All it would take is a little "yes" and this could all be over.' The 'S' at the end of 'yes' seemed to go on forever.

Mark knew Redcliff would be watching him, so he was careful to keep his facial expression neutral, but he could not contain the frantic tapping of his fingers. Managing to keep his voice low he uttered, 'And where would be the fun in that?' As long as Redcliff kept to the violet wand he was pretty sure the girls would survive. Isabelle might need a few years of therapy, but there'd be no permanent scars. Breathe, Matthews. Just Breathe.

The girls were turned around and instead of being faced with their profile, he got to see their faces. Two spotlights began to shine down on them so he would be able to see every little nuance. Oh fuck. Things were getting better and better.

When all of the above appeared to have no effect on him, the ladies and gents got out nasty looking medical grade scalpels and paraded them in front of the girls' faces. Jenny's eyes hardened and she purposely dipped them so as not to look at him. Isabelle took one look at the knife and could have then been admitted to the nearest psychiatric hospital. She went all sorts of crazy, all at once. It was all he could do to hold the impassive line of his face. She'll get through this, Matthews, he told himself. The scalpel is blunt. Yes, but she doesn't know that, he remonstrated with himself, and in a minute it will feel like they're trying to tear her insides out. But, he added to soothe himself, there'll hardly be a mark on her.

'Matthews, Matthews, Matthews,' his inner voice growled, 'are you really going to let them suffer in this way?' Images of himself naked, bound, kneeling, helpless, begging and pleading came to mind. His ass plugged... fuck no. He wasn't going there. Redcliff would want the works. So he held his head up straight and stared directly at the pair of them. There was no room for weakness.

The scalpels began to spark blue fire across their skin. Kyle's produced a grunt and a groan in one corner and there was more infernal screaming in the other. The artwork performed by the black latex crew was truly beautiful and had this been a normal demonstration, he would have thoroughly enjoyed himself. Little licks of blue lightning flew across their backs, in circles, in figures of eights, straight lines and curves. Jenny was drawn tight as a bowstring, trying to keep her noise and movement to a minimum. Isabelle was the opposite. She flailed about and squawked the place down. Funnily enough, Jenny's silence affected him more than Isabelle's caterwauling. It took a great deal of practice to hold in pain like that. He didn't want to think about how she'd learned to lock it all inside. He knew, the hard way.

After the scalpels had given him a good show, the pinwheels he had glimpsed earlier were brought into the fray. Things were about to get a lot more unpleasant. They began a slow and agonising path of purple sparks. Intertwining themselves with the lines of blue, the level of endorphins the girls were facing was notching up. Point by point the stainless steel pinwheels made their indentations into soft, responsive flesh. Isabelle's eyes were running with tears, red-rimmed and pleading. Jenny's were mutinous, but then, they would be. She knew who was responsible for all of this. Mark wondered if she knew exactly what he was capable of, and he suspected she didn't. Time would tell.

The ladies and gents kept the proceedings interesting by alternating between floggers, glass fibre canes, pinwheels and scalpels. The girls were being shocked left, right and centre, and their bodies were flopping around on the table like fish out of water one moment, and then as the current lit them up, flying about like headless chickens. It was not a pleasant sight to watch, but he couldn't take his eyes off them for a second. He watched them fight each stroke, he watched them suffer each pseudo slice and he watched as they struggled wildly against their ropes.

He continued to watch as all the fight died out of them. Kyle began tormenting Jenny's back with the sharp needles of the pinwheel and she arced upwards in agony. Kyle was lucky Mark was firmly pinned down, else he'd grab one of those blunt scalpels in the corner and no matter how long it took he'd sever each of his limbs, one by one. This time she couldn't supress her screams and they bounced around the room until they began echoing over and over in his head. Guilt tore through him like sulphuric acid, contaminating every pore, but he still didn't say the words that would put a stop to her suffering. He watched with eyes that felt like they'd been stretched permanently open and smeared liberally with sand. He wanted to tear each fingernail he owned off, and would have quite happily if it meant the antics on stage would stop, but he endured the show. When the fire in their eyes was gradually snuffed out and their bodies were too weak to put up more than a token struggle, Redcliff finally spoke.

'So, that's round one, Matthews, and I'm glad to see you're still standing, or sitting, as it were. You'll be pleased to know I haven't finished yet. Round two involves a little more intensity and we're going to turn up the heat. I'm going to narrate alongside this scene, so I think you'll enjoy this very much.'

The girls disappeared from view as everything went dark. Mark wanted to drive splinters through his fingernails as he waited to see what would happen next. Alas, the edges of his enforced seat were smooth and glossy. Keep it all inside, he cautioned himself. Push it down, stamp on it, hide it. Don't give the bastard any more ammunition than he already has. His world began to spin in the darkness. He could still hear Isabelle's sobs and they were going to haunt his dreams, and that was nothing compared to what Jennifer Redcliff was doing to his guts. Everything had twisted and knotted and if he wasn't careful his breakfast, which had consisted of nothing more than three espressos, was shortly going to be coming back up to greet him. Get on with it, he silently pleaded.

They made him wait. Then they turned up the heat in the room and he began to sweat. Before long the stuff was running down the back of his neck and soaking his collar. Whatever floats your boat, Redcliff, he thought sourly, whilst plotting revenge. The things he could do to that man and his son. Normally he was a pretty sane and rational being, but he could happily lose every single last shred of his conscience when dealing with the men of the Redcliff family. Buggered if he'd suffer a moment of guilt, either. The pair of them needed to meet a timely end. They were a menace to mankind. Before he'd had time to fully think through his plans of violent and bloody revenge, the lights erupted on stage once more.

Both girls were in the same place they'd been before the lights went out, but they now each featured a new addition to their meagre wardrobe. They'd been gagged. Large black balls stretched their lips and disfigured their jaws. Additional layers of rope had been applied to their bodies to hold them securely in place and while mindless, sheer panic could be read all over Isabelle's face,

Jenny had managed to recover her defiant look. Good girl, he thought.

'Silence is golden, isn't it?' The annoying timbre of Redcliff's voice permeated the room and Mark dearly wanted to smash his fist into the head it was attached to. 'We've had to gag them, because they're probably going to get a bit vocal for what we have planned next. Can't be helped, I'm afraid. Anyway, moving on, have you heard of the Bhut Jolokia chilli by any chance?' There was a short pause for Mark to digest this sentence and then he continued. 'Well, just to put you in perspective, let's talk Scoville heat points. Your average jalapeno pepper has about five thousand Scoville units. Boring. We like to push the boat out here at Albrecht, and the Bhut Jolokia has around one million heat units. It's four thousand times hotter than your average bottle of Tabasco sauce. Pretty impressive, yes? Did you know that around three and a half pounds of this particular chilli, if ingested all at once, could kill a person? Thankfully, we're not that mean. First we're going to spread it on their fingertips and toes, then we're going to smear some around the delicate membranes of their lips, both oral and vaginal, and finally, if you're still up for more, we're going to fill their asses up to the brim with mashed, fiery and excruciatingly intense chilli pepper. Sounds amazing, doesn't it? As there's likely to be lots of noise, even with the gags, if you want to put a stop to the proceedings just raise your hand, OK?' Redcliff sounded most pleased with his sarcastic quip.

There was then a bustle of activity on stage as the men and women readied themselves to carry out their tasks. Mark was frozen to his chair. He didn't think he was going to be able to sit through it. Trying to fathom things out rationally in his mind, he knew that whilst the chilli pepper would burn something awful, it would not actually leave scars or lasting damage. He'd seen salves and paste in action before, but never something as strong as that which Redcliff had indicated. Fuck. He felt his hands begin to shake and a large rivulet of sweat rolled down his back. He tried to calculate the possible damage in his head. Pepper spray. That would be of a similar intensity. What were the symptoms? Obviously it irritated the eyes to the point of tears, and was extremely inflammatory often causing the eyes to swell shut. It could also cause moderate to severe breathing problems, uncontrollable coughing, and had in some cases caused death. If used internally the pain would be horrific and the effects of the spray could last for hours. He also believed there were some reports of the stuff being carcinogenic.

Feeling his heartrate increase he tried to play this scene to the end in his head. If he made it through the chilli saga, would it end there? He suspected not. Redcliff would keep going. So he should just shout out now. At least he'd stop their suffering. Or would he? Redcliff might decide to hold him here regardless and watch as he played out his games to the end. How did you get inside the head of a crazy person? You didn't. All you could do was try to outwit them. He would try and limit the damage, but he didn't think it could be avoided altogether. Redcliff was a sadist with a capital 'S' and he would be thoroughly enjoying all that was being played out.

Inhaling a deep lungful of air, he braced his hands against his chair and watched as the first application of the monster chilli was applied. The screams were immediate.

'You see how it perks them up almost instantly? It's magic,' said Redcliff, and there was almost awe in his voice. 'This is one of my favourite torments. After they get an idea of what the nasty stuff can do you keep telling them where you're going to apply it next. It's one of the absolute best mind fucks.'

Mark sat completely still as it was applied to fingertips, toenails, wrists, elbows and knees. The screams were going around in his head, but somehow he managed to shut them out. He was just biding his time. He couldn't let the stuff go anywhere serious. It appeared he did have a conscience after all. Managing to sit through five minutes of extreme torment on his behalf, let alone the girls, whilst maintaining his bored expression as they bucked and tore at their bonds, he finally spoke.

'If you want a piece of me, for fucks sake have it. My eardrums might never recover from this shit, so here's an offer, asshole. You can have your night, but you release the pair of them now. Isabelle comes home with me. The other one is a pain in the ass and you're welcome to her. And by the way, this is a one-time offer. You continue trying to perforate my eardrums and I'm going to settle down for a nap, because this isn't anything I haven't seen before. What do you think I have an office full of submissives for?' Mark yawned and crossed his legs. 'You could always paint me with chilli; that might help lengthen my attention span.'

There was a low growl from the loudspeaker and it was clear that Redcliff was torn between continuing his fun or going for the big prize. Finally, he appeared on stage.

'Get them out of here and wash them up quickly. Bring Isabelle out in ten minutes,' he barked. 'And use oil, not water, you idiots.'

He faced Mark and the tick in his jaw indicated that he was furious. Gesturing to the two security guards that they could let their captive up, he bent over Mark and with effort, just managed to contain his fists. In a low murmur he managed to grind out, 'No, Matthews, I'm not the devil you think I am. I am far, far worse. You'll be discovering just how bad in another day or two. Chilli will be the least of your problems. Sweet dreams, darling. Now get the fuck out of here.'

Mark stood up and made a show of dusting himself down. He hadn't expected that Redcliff would let him go that easily. What was going on here? 'Are we doing this now or do I have to wait for an invitation?'

'You'll get your invitation. Now get the hell out of here before I change my mind and finish those girls off properly.' His face was less than an inch away from Mark's and they eyeballed each other, neither wanting to back down.

Finally Mark stepped back and ran a hand through his drenched hair. 'Well, you let me know when the ball is, Prince Charming, and I'll be there,' he said, smiling brightly, already knowing that after this little meeting there was no way Redcliff was getting him alone anytime in the next century.

'Oh, you'll be there alright,' said Redcliff, turning and marching stiffly away. 'You needn't worry your pretty little head about that.'

CHAPTER EIGHTEEN
Tell Me What You Want

Mark paced the length and breadth of his office. There was a sharp knot of anxiety in his gut that he hadn't been able to shift for three whole days. He could not get Jennifer Redcliff out of his head. Optimistically, he'd thought he might forget about her if he didn't lay eyes on her, but that wasn't the case at all. Each day that passed caused his thoughts to stray to her more and more often, and the not knowing was fucking miserable. What was happening to her? Was she still at Albrecht? Had they taken her somewhere else? Was she OK?

Isabelle hadn't been. He'd had her shipped off to therapy the second they'd got back in London and had provided her with a member of his security team to look after her until he was satisfied that Redcliff had finished with her. He hadn't told her that, of course. What he had done was deposit $500,000 in her bank account and the promise of more if she ever needed it. He suspected she wouldn't be working anywhere in a hurry. Good God. How did you shut a man like Redcliff down? He could teach the Marquis De Sade a trick or two, and before you knew it, people would be calling the dark arts *Redcliffism*.

He tried to focus his thoughts, knowing revenge was probably not going to be possible and that it would be useless to even bother contemplating it.

All he could do now was keep himself and everyone around him safe. Khalil had already culled his staff down to the bare minimum and all the girls that were left had been thoroughly checked out. The rest had been sent packing with a generous pay-off. He felt little regret at losing them. He still had more than enough ladies to keep himself happy and, if he were honest, at the moment he didn't feel like indulging himself with any of them. He had been given a brief taste of the sublime and to have it taken away before he'd fully had a chance to appreciate it was horribly frustrating, to say the least. Khalil was keeping tabs on the comings and goings at Albrecht, but so far had nothing to report. The scary thought was that she might very well be kept in that compound for years, where he wouldn't be able to get a shred of intel on her. It was probably best not to dwell on that, but distracting himself with work was impossible. He'd tried it pretty much 24/7 for the last three days to no avail. It was time to try sex. That usually worked when all else failed.

'Coffee!' he barked, to no one in particular. Never had his need for caffeine been so great, and that was saying something, considering he was an insomniac. Thankfully there was the sound of scuttling heels outside his office, so someone had got the message. Heaven help them if they fucked up his order, because he was in a mean and nasty mood this morning.

Trying to turn his attention back to his computer screen he found the symbols and figures blurring into one another before him. He had a board meeting tomorrow and it was important that he do some form of research before they hammered him with questions about his latest acquisition. Slamming his fist down on the desk he growled, refocused his eyes, and tried his best to concentrate.

Less than two minutes later there was a timid knock at the door and a pitiful sounding, 'Sir?'

'Come in Marianna. I don't bite. Unless you've messed up my coffee and then I still don't bite. I tear heads off.'

The silver platter bearing his delicate porcelain cup rattled a little, before being placed very gently on his desk, and the lovely Marianna got to her knees quick sharpish on the floor. Her panties this morning were frilly scraps of bright red silk and they obediently hugged her ankles. He couldn't help a smile. Taking a firm grip on his cup, he gulped a scalding hot mouthful of coffee and turned his attention to the pretty little thing on the floor in front of him.

'So tell me, Marianna, what is life like with your panties around your ankles?' He needed a moment of humour, and he had a feeling she might give him one. Peering down at her head, he braced his chin on his hand and waited eagerly for her response. She did not disappoint.

With her eyes still downcast to the floor, Marianna softly replied, 'Oh, just wonderful thank you, Sir. All the girls have taken it upon themselves to make sure that my choice of panties now colour co-ordinates with my work wardrobe and if I wear a particularly nice pair, I get to spend a half hour discussing where I purchased them and how they feel. I get the feeling it's been a long time since the girls around here wore panties - even around their ankles. Oh, and whenever I need to use the facilities, all I have to do is pick up my skirt and go - there's none of this ridiculous fussing around with panty elastic. It's so much easier and very liberating. You've also ensured that I need never run anywhere in the office, so if the mailman calls downstairs for a girl, I have no fear that I might be chosen. When you add that to the fact that my laundry load is so much lighter, due to complete lack of lingerie, then it's strawberries and cream all around, really. I mean, there isn't much point in washing them if I'm not actually going to wear them, is there? And you know what?' Her tone dipped to a whisper. 'I think I'm actually becoming a style icon around these parts.'

Mark's lips twitched. The girl was an absolute treasure. 'Who said you wouldn't be wearing them, Miss Morreau?'

'You said I wouldn't be wearing them, anywhere except my ankles, Sir.' Marianna sounded confused.

Mark shook his head. 'I said no such thing, sweetie pie. You won't be wearing them in the conventional way, that's for sure, but I have other places I might like you to wear them.'

Marianna looked up then, confused, before remembering herself and plunging her head back down to the floor. 'I'm not sure I understand, Sir,' she whispered.

'Then let me explain,' said Mark, smiling wickedly. 'Stand up and remove that ridiculous excuse for underwear, Miss Morreau. You may then roll them up in a little ball and place them inside your mouth.'

Her face fell as she began to understand what he meant, but she quickly rose to her feet and, kicking off her heels, stepped out of her panties and began them rolling them up in her fingertips.

'I think we should make very sure that you remember to wash your panties, Miss Morreau, don't you? Personal hygiene is not something we take lightly here.' He pushed his chair back from his desk and got to his feet, towering above her and giving her his most intimidating stare.

'No Sir. Of course not, Sir.' The panties were now in a little ball and she raised them to her lips, an expression of distaste upon her face, before she stuffed her mouth full with them.

'And once again we've found a way to silence that smart mouth of yours. This might become a habit, you know. You look most endearing with your cheeks puffed out like a hamster.' He pursed his lips to stop himself from laughing. 'OK, enough chatter. Bend yourself over my desk, remove those panties and give them to me. I think I'd better make sure they're good and dirty, so you won't forget to wash them, oh disgustingly filthy one.'

As she stretched over the smooth lines of his dark mahogany desk, the globes of her ass pressing tightly against the white fabric of her summer skirt, the anxiety of the moment was forgotten. Watching her remove the now damp panties from her mouth and pass them back to him, he was reminded of Khalil's warning regarding Marianna. A follow up of her original background check had proved inconclusive and James Entwell, her trainer, had been unavailable for comment. Mark had brushed away Khalil's concerns, saying Redcliff would have to be a madman if he was going to plant a brunette to get close to him, but Khalil had advised against keeping her. But Marianna, for all the fire in her belly, only managed to purge it by use of her voice. The woman almost physically jumped every time he was near, and if she could get away with it, he was positive she would hide in a corner somewhere for the duration of her service. His objection to her removal had been sharp and vehement, and he knew why. There was a little bit of Jennifer Redcliff in her and right at this moment in time, it was as close to her as he was going to get.

Squeezing the panties together in his hand and admiring the smooth silk as he did so, he trailed the soft material up the back of Marianna's endless legs. A shudder ran through her and as his hands felt the movement vibrate through them, he couldn't resist pressing his face up against the soft folds of her pussy lips and drawing a long line up and down them with his tongue. Then he tormented her with the panties, fluttering the silk up and down her sex one moment and pressing it tightly against her the next, so his fingers almost crushed her clit.

'What should I do with you, sweetness?'

He began threading the bright red silk into her pussy with his fingertips, inch by slow and torturous inch. His fingers probed inside her over and over again, filling her up, and all he could hear was little mewls of pleasure.

'Tell me,' he demanded, and grabbed both her ass cheeks and squeezed them tightly, so she'd know he was serious.

Marianna let out a breathy little moan as her hips bucked against the hard wood of his desk. 'I'm not sure you'll want to know,' she said on a whisper.

Having left a little tail of scarlet silk outside her pussy, he grabbed it and tugged it tightly, pulling her body backwards against him. 'I'm positive I will,' he growled, 'and if you don't fess up this instant, I'm going to take off my belt and have some fun with that far too pale backside of yours.' He gave it a sharp slap for good measure and smiled as it gave a little wobble.

Marianna wiggled it again and made sure she got his attention. 'Well,' she said throatily, 'there might be something I want, actually.'

Another growl. 'Are you teasing me, Miss Morreau? Because I'll have you know there's only one person who's allowed to tease around these parts, and it isn't you.' There was another tug of the tail and then his hand slipped underneath her sex and slid back and forth with a frustratingly light touch. 'Tell me,' he drawled seductively, and slowly began to unravel the length of panties back out of her pussy, smiling as her breath hitched.

'I want,' she paused and swallowed, as a thick wedge of material suddenly broke free.

'Yes,' Mark encouraged, pulling the last few centimetres of her soaked panties back into his hands. He brought them up to his face and inhaled deeply. Then he scooped them up and smothered them across her nose. 'Smell that, Miss Morreau. That is the scent of rabid lust. Yours.'

Marianna's hands stretched over the top of his desk and her body was incredibly elegant in supine repose.

She laughed at his statement, which was unexpected but not altogether unpleasant. When his body moved back from hers so he could adjust his fly she reared backwards into him with such force she knocked him over. 'What the fuck?' he spluttered, and then saw her hand.

'And this, Mr Matthews, is the scent of death. Yours.'

And just like that, someone pulled the plug out of his world and everything went black.

CHAPTER NINETEEN

Impending Doom

Marianna discarded the syringe that had been full of sodium thiopental and looked at the unconscious body that had crashed awkwardly to the floor. The stuff took around thirty seconds to kick in and the thought of getting a black eye had not been an appealing one. Thankfully Mark had been in shock as she'd directed the needle at his jugular and hadn't had the sense to try and knock her out. Straightening her skirt and smoothing her hair back, she removed her cell phone from the top pocket of her blouse and a series of bleeps went off as she pressed speed dial.

'It's done.' Her voice was brusque. Hanging up, she then strode over to the back of his office and broke the seal of the red fire alarm cover that had pride of place by the window. A piercing and unrelenting shriek immediately lit up the building. Counting slowly to twenty, she then peered around the door to see what the girls were up to. As it was only seven-thirty a.m. there was hardly anyone in yet, but it was important that they were all hoarded downstairs.

She barked at them, 'Mark says to assemble at the meeting point and don't bother waiting for him as he's going to investigate the problem. We'll follow you downstairs shortly.' The tone of her voice provided immediate results. Liah grabbed her beige leather handbag, and ran over to help her colleague Marguerite as they began to quickly pack all their things away. Marianna's orders were not questioned. The hierarchy in this building was such that orders were followed without question if they appeared to come from the right place.

As soon as the pair of blondes made swift their escape Marianna retrieved her bag from under her desk. Pulling out another syringe, she went back to give him a dose of something stronger. Pentothal would only keep him out for around five or ten minutes, and the clean up team might require a little longer than that, so she shot him with a sedative. He'd feel a bit groggy and lightheaded when he woke up, but that would be the least of his worries. As it was, she was tempted to get her own back for several long and arduous hours spent in his 'room for naughty girls' by giving him a swift kick to the groin, but he could thank his lucky stars that she was under a time constraint here.

Disposing of the syringes and the double-sided sticky tape that had been storing it in its discreet hiding place under the edge of Matthews' desk, she placed the incriminating evidence in her bag and draped a long cardigan around her shoulders. As an afterthought she also picked up her discarded panties and stuffed them in her pocket. She didn't need any more attention drawn to herself. Searching around in her bag one last time, she pulled out a pair of steel handcuffs and fastened Mark's hands behind his back, to ensure he didn't give anyone any trouble for the next few minutes or so.

Finally she propped open the fire exit door with a chair, so the team could get in easily, and then removed her shoes, carrying the straps in her hands. She didn't intend to loiter in the stairway. Her work here was finished.

When Mark came to his initial reaction was relief that he wasn't dead. His head was spinning ferociously, his vision was triplicate and in all colours of the spectrum, and all he could hear in his head were Marianna's parting words. Oh shit. The syringe. Where the hell was he? Fuck. Redcliff had managed to infiltrate his company, and with a brunette no less. Why hadn't he listened to Khalil? Always a good idea to hedge your bets, he guessed. He wondered how many girls Redcliff had managed to get inside Zystrom? Clearly he had been planning this for a while. Shit, shit, shit.

Trying to ignore the pounding in his head, he did his best to keep his groggy eyelids peeled back from their sockets. He needed to examine his surroundings. It took a few attempts and an awful lot of blinking, but eventually he managed to squeeze the jagged lines together and get some kind of perspective. The first thing he noticed was he was naked, and that couldn't be a good thing. The second thing that captured his attention was that his arms were in cuffs, separated by means of a three-foot spreader pole in front of him. He didn't take in anything else because his vision had finally managed to join the dots and he found himself somewhere very high above London. He instinctively grabbed for the rope around either side of his hands, and was rewarded with an amused snort.

'Good afternoon, Mr Matthews. You'll kick yourself in a minute, but you've just done all the hard work for me.' The voice was unmistakeably Redcliff's.

There was a sudden jerk and Mark's body shot forward forty-five degrees so that he was facing a large sheet of glass and the dizzying vista of a busy motorway below. 'Jesus Christ!' he spluttered, and tightened his grip around the rough ends of the rope. Looking up he found that the two ends of rope he held were threaded through a steel ring above him. He thought about using every swear word ever invented and then decided it would only entertain Redcliff, so he kept his mouth shut.

'Well, I hope you've got tempered glass,' was all he said.

'Actually, there's the thing. We recently had some of that Hollywood glass stuff installed. You know, the kind that shatters into a thousand pieces with the slightest impact. Costs a fortune, but you really can't tell the difference, can you?'

'I don't believe you,' said Mark, who was going all kinds of crazy as his head swam with vertigo. Wanting to look anywhere but down, he actually had very little choice in the matter. How the hell had Redcliff discovered his weakness? The only person he had told was... No. He refused to believe it could be her. She'd been abused in much the same way as he was about to be, give or take a few anatomical differences.

'I'll happily prove it to you, if you wish.' A stone came whizzing past Mark's ear, making him recoil sharply, and then shot through the window to the left of him. The whole thing disintegrated into dust in an instant, with tiny shards of glass spraying everywhere. It was a horribly sobering moment.

'Now, you're a smart man, Matthews. You've already realised that if you let either hand off that rope you're holding, you'll fall to your death below. You're tilted at such an angle that you'll have no way to stop your fall and your body will crash through the glass and disappear in an instant. It'll be a messy death, I suspect, and you'll probably break every bone in your body, but it will also be quick. So, you could take the easy way and go now before the suffering begins.

'Fuck you, Redcliff.'

'That's not on the cards, but who knows? If I find you endearing enough maybe we can arrange a little something another day. Now, where was I? Oh yes, you also have another option.' He paused and took his time examining Mark's body from head to foot. Mark gritted his teeth and looked away from the penetrating grey eyes, only to find himself swimming in the dizzying heights of downtown London, and he really wasn't sure which one was worse.

'And that is?' He was already running through every possible escape plan from the predicament he now found himself in, and none looked particularly pleasant.

Redcliff stared out through the broken window in front of him and ran his finger along the broken glass. 'Well, it wouldn't be any fun if I told you now, would it? You can beg for the opportunity to appease me later. Plead, beg, scream and sob too, I suspect.'

'Good luck with that,' snarled Mark as his wrists tested the strength of the spreader bar that held them. His mouth formed a hard line when he discovered it did not bend at all. Behind the rubber surround that covered it, it was cold hard steel. Redcliff was leaving nothing to chance.

'Luck won't have a thing to do with it, dear boy. Not a thing.' He used the back of his hand to swat Mark's ass cheek and then strolled casually away. 'I think I'll give you ten minutes to settle into your new surroundings and then we'll begin.' He smacked his lips together with a satisfied air. 'I wish you luck with Mistress Katrina. You'll be needing it.'

His receding reflection in the glass and the sound of a door slamming indicated his departure. Mark squeezed his eyes tightly shut. Katrina? Well, didn't that explain a few things? So they were fucking. What she saw in the old man could only be counted in figures. Ignoring the path his mind wanted to take, he began to analyse his surroundings.

Scrutinising the window in front of him, he wondered if Redcliff had been lying when he'd said it was the same type of glass as the pane he'd broken. All the panels would have originally been toughened glass and unless Mark was much mistaken, Redcliff had plans for him that didn't include murder. Examining the remnants of the pane to the left of him and then comparing it with the one in front did little to appease him. They looked exactly the same. If he wanted to test the theory he could very well be doing so with his life. Was the old man crazy enough to pull a stunt like this? Absolutely.

Pushing back and trying to place his feet flat on the floor confirmed what he already knew. They'd placed a long pad of spikes, nails perhaps, behind them. Investigating them more closely he found they were four-inch nails and the pads had been secured to the floor with four screws a half-inch thick in diameter. It would keep him off balance and on tiptoes. If he wanted to get rid of them in a hurry he was going to have to develop an allergic reaction to kryptonite.

So, how was this little scenario going to play out? At a guess, Katrina was going to do some of the things she had implied back in Albrecht stables around a week ago. He knew he was going to get the works. They'd torment and tease him to begin with. Then the effects of orgasm denial would kick in. When he began to flag and tire pain would be employed to keep him awake, and when his screaming back and arm muscles could bear it no more, he would beg. Then Redcliff would confront him and he would finally find out what this farce was really about. There would be no rushing the process. If he begged too soon they would simply ignore him and Redcliff's respect would dwindle rapidly. He needed to keep that at all costs. If Redcliff thought he had a worthy opponent, he would play the game. If he decided otherwise, there was no telling where Mark might end up and the thought didn't bear thinking about. He wasn't stupid, though. Redcliff would be aware of the resources Mark had behind him, and hiding him away somewhere wasn't going to be an option without a hell of a lot of noise. Khalil would at least ensure that much. It was a God-awful shame they were up so high, though. No one would be likely to find him up here in a hurry. Christ. *Think, Matthews, think!*

But there was no time for thinking. The clatter of stiletto heels filled his head, and it appeared that Katrina was far too eager for the proceedings to begin to wait her allotted ten minutes.

'Good afternoon, Kat. Beautiful day for a kidnapping and a spot of erotic torture, don't you think? If Redcliff's not careful this type of behaviour might become a habit.' His tone was deliberately goading.

The tread of the stilettos slowed and he immediately braced his body. Sure enough, the point of a very sharp boot found its way between his legs and up into his crotch. There was then a sickening crunch as she brought her toes up to his groin and crushed his testicles. He didn't make a sound. He'd had too many fucking years of practice, which she'd soon discover later to her great chagrin. So he bottled the intense, jaw-dropping pain, and ignored the fact that he might never sire children. Instead he turned his head and smiled at her.

'You'll have to do better than that, Princess. You do know I like this kind of thing, right?'

A set of five red nails, painted to a glossy sheen, gripped his chin. 'You will address me only as "Mistress". Failure to do so will mean that I have to punish you and I can get quite mean on occasion.' The fingers tapped against his jaw and then dug deep into his skin. His grin did not falter.

'Well get on with it, Kat. We're wasting time. Redcliff will be expecting a good show from all his hidden cameras dotted around the room, and I'd hate to keep him waiting.'

His head was wrenched violently to the right and for a minute he wondered if it was possible to dislocate your neck, because he could feel something tearing. Thankfully, however, there was no lasting pain.

'Mistress.' The word was virtually spat into his face. 'Each time you fail to say my name correctly the punishments will get progressively worse.' She lowered her face towards him and captured his bottom lip in her teeth. She bit. His eyes danced, and this time the pain barely registered. He was having too much fun.

Clearly she wasn't used to someone of his calibre.

'Is is all ery ice, ut can we ove on to the hard stuff?'

His lip was quickly released and the full weight of the blonde beauty's heavy stare was lavished upon him. Her eyes were mere slits, her elegant cheekbones constrained in hard lines and she ground her teeth together before muttering, 'I am going to enjoy making your life hell, Matthews.' She released his face to give him a vicious backhander across the cheek.

He felt his teeth rattle around his head. When the room stopped spinning he managed to get out, 'Well hurry up and stop messing about then.' He turned to face her and winked. The cheekbones, if it were possible, narrowed further and then she stormed from the room. He couldn't help a personal smile of victory and whispered to himself, knowing Redcliff would be able to hear, 'Round one to Matthews, Katrina nil.'

It took Katrina a while to calm down. Mark had no idea exactly how long, as they had removed his watch, but he knew it was considerably more than a few minutes. When eventually she did come back he knew she wouldn't be taking any prisoners. It wouldn't be anything he hadn't seen before, but that didn't mean he was going to enjoy himself much.

'Ever heard of a penis plug, Matthews?' Katrina had applied a fresh coat of lip-gloss and was advertising the fact by giving him a close up view of her pearly whites. In front of his eyes she dangled a small, tapered silver object and swung it to and fro.

His day, he decided, was not improving much. 'Yes. It's what's used to stopper the average female mouth when she begins to talk nonsense, much as you are...' He had to stop. Her long fingers had grabbed hold of his flaccid cock and began to stroke him, giving him a good squeeze in the process. She began to work him over, her eyes devouring every inch of him, admiring every line of muscle and sinew as she did so. Her face began to take on a delicate rose flush and he knew she found him attractive. The bad news was her feelings were not reciprocated. His cock had barely twitched in her fingers.

'You're supposed to insert those beasts while I'm less enthusiastic, but I'm guessing you want me hard so it'll hurt more. Unfortunately you're not going to achieve that unless you go down on me, and even then it's a fifty/fifty thing. I've gone off blondes lately.'

It was apparent that Katrina did not believe him. She'd probably never had a man refuse her before, so it was high time she had someone stand up to her - or not as the case may be - and tamp her ego back down.

'Mistress.' She squeezed his cock painfully in her fist, but it had little effect and he could see her getting frustrated. Coming around to stand in front of him, she let him cop an eyeful of her black leather catsuit and the thigh-high boots that accompanied it. Pushing her sleek blonde waves back over her shoulder, she reached to undo the zip that kept her nubile body neatly contained. He admired her spirit. She was not to be easily defeated.

The shiny silver zip was slowly drawn down across her chest and the globes of two perfect size 36D breasts came into view. They were pert, plump and had dark red nipples that stood up like little homing beacons. His cock thought about it, they were quite tempting after all, but he managed to keep a lid on things. She got a single twitch and nothing more. 'Hurry up and suck the fuck up, darling. I'm getting bored.'

There was a gurgled scream from Katrina's lips as her frustration at being thwarted grew. She was unused to defeat, it seemed. When she got herself under control she spoke and the soft purr of her voice indicated that he wasn't going to like what came next.

'Attractive as you are, Matthews, the chance of my lips coming anywhere near your cock is out of the question. So I figure we'll employ other measures. How about we get your little pony-girl in here, all naked and primed for action? I bet she wouldn't even need to suck, would she?'

His cock immediately thickened and he couldn't do a thing about it. Damn the woman to hell. 'Oh dear,' murmured Katrina, capturing one of her fingernails between her teeth and pulling. 'You're jonesing for that girl like a heroine addict who's gone a day without a fix. Maybe we should remedy that?' Katrina pulled his cock sharply upwards and he caught his breath. Squeezing the tip between her fingers she turned her head away from him and yelled, 'Bring her in!'

Mark directed his attention upward and swore silently. He did not want to look out of the window for obvious reasons, and he did not want to look sideways at Katrina. Most of all he did not want to look at Jennifer Redcliff. He did not want to see those big blues eyes and the pity they might now contain, or perhaps it would be her contempt? He wouldn't be of any use to her now. There wasn't the option of choice though. Katrina grabbed a handful of his hair and yanked it firmly downwards.

There at his feet was the naked pony-girl he remembered. In just a week the lines of her ribcage had become more pronounced and her figure had lost another few pounds of flesh, which she could scarcely afford to lose. Her body was tense, her face was once again devoid of make-up and the tight stretch of her corset around her midriff was obviously causing her some distress. Unable to help himself, he let his eyes travel up her body. They took in the thick tail plug and the long line of hair that fell between her legs, the lines of interwoven leather tack, and the tiny gold clamps that elongated the twin peaks of her nipples. The corset made her waist look impossibly small and he was sure his hands would easily be able to span the circumference. Her body had become considerably more toned, her calf muscles especially; they had obviously been working hard on her stamina. Raising his head, he watched her mouth chew anxiously on her rubber bit, a line of drool already trailing towards the floor. There was no help for it. Sighing, he searched out her eyes.

Pity. That's what he read there. In front of him were great big blue eyes anxiously examining him, probably wondering how the hell he was going to get himself out of this mess. Well, that made two of them. He guessed the emotion was better than contempt, though he didn't have much use for it.

'And we have an instant erection. How utterly charming.' Katrina's voice was laced with sarcasm. She paced up and down for a few seconds as she decided her next move. Mark hoped she took her time, because he was drowning in the vision before him. It was not to last. Katrina grabbed hold of his cock once more and the weight of a solid steel penis plug rested at the tip. It took his attention away from Jenny and refocused him.

'If Redcliff wasn't watching you'd suck me, right honey? It's this pretty face, isn't it? Women can't resist it.' He wanted her concentration on him and not on the pony-girl below.

The plug, thankfully lubricated, made its way far too quickly into his urethra. It felt thick and heavy. He'd learnt, from experience, that you had to be totally relaxed when they were being inserted. His urethral muscles initially fought it, but eventually the weight of the toy would drag it down inside him. It wasn't without pain and he had to clear his head and focus on keeping a straight face to make sure he gave nothing away.

'I know it hurts, pretty boy, but you're determined to be a big brave stallion for Mistress, aren't you?'

Mark winked at her. Talking was not an option at this moment in time in any case.

'I'm going to have your little pony-girl suck you off every half hour until you nearly shoot your load, and then we'll get a few friends involved for kicks when she needs a rest. When those arms and legs of yours are shaking I'm going to paddle, flog, crop and whip that beautiful body of yours from top to bottom until you beg me to stop, and then I'm going to do it some more. If I'm feeling really generous I might even let you have the odd retrograde ejaculation. That'll be fun, won't it?' Her hand smacked his left butt cheek and the contact jarred the plug now buried inside him. The sensation was intense and a heady mixture of both pleasure and pain. He suspected he'd be pissing blood for a few days after this mess, and that was the least of his concerns. What did Redcliff want from him?

Katrina moved around to unbuckle Jenny's bit and bridle. She then thrust her booted foot at Jenny's buttocks and pushed her towards his cock, barking out the command, 'Suck!'

His little pony-girl didn't even hesitate. Her head shot forward and her lips circled around the tip, teasing him immediately into ramrod stance. Obviously she'd been practising her skills in the past few days because her tongue flicked and caressed with expert precision, and the tight vacuum she created nearly made him come there and then.

Meanwhile, Katrina had found a riding crop and began to circle the tip over Jenny's backside. 'Make him squirm and groan for me, Pretty Pink Petals, or I'll decorate your ass with stripes and then find some of that chilli salve we played with the other day and rub it in the welts. You fail me and you won't sleep for the next couple of days.'

The crack of the riding crop came down sharply, and though Jenny balked at the contact her head did not stop moving back and forth across his cock. The stricture of her mouth was amazing. All sorts of fireworks were exploding in his head and he wondered if it was just because it was her, or because of the plug and the adrenaline flowing through him. It didn't really matter at the moment. What mattered was that his little princess had just made his life a whole lot harder, if you could excuse the pun. Katrina he could have dealt with. Jennifer Redcliff was going to unravel him piece by piece with nothing more than her mouth, and those big blue eyes and fluttering lashes were the icing on the cake.

Even though Jen did an admirable job of making his life the kind of hell Katrina had in mind, the woman did not go easy on her. Her boots made little jabs at the soft flesh of her thighs and calves when she believed she was flagging, while the crop worked its way over her body with unavoidable enthusiasm. This caused the poor girl to frequently gag upon him, and if anything it made the sensations even more intense. Her tongue coiled around him, her jaw tightened and she took the whole length of him into her pretty little mouth, over and over, flicking at the top of the plug he wore to increase his pleasure. Fuck silence. Fuck Katrina. Fuck Redcliff. He was going to come and there was sod all he could do about it. With his hands tight around the rope that rested either side of him, his back stiffened and he felt his cock jerk.

Jenny was instantly hauled off him while Katrina laid into his ass like a woman possessed, and the plug somehow managed to stopper all his fun. He felt himself spasm, once, twice and then nothing. Frustration tore at him. As the familiar pain of a good beating rained down upon his ass he began to feel his arms flag and he knew then that the outcome of this little soiree was inevitable. He would beg. He would plead. He would agree to whatever Redcliff wanted. When the beating stopped and Jennifer Redcliff's mouth was back upon him he acknowledged that round two had most certainly gone to Katrina.

Less than three hours later he was in agony. Jenny had been dragged off for a break, and a thousand and one hands replaced her lips. They were nowhere near as good as her talented mouth, but they did the job of keeping him miserably erect and ensured his brain was unable to function. His arms were now shaking painfully, jerking the rope all over the place, and the cityscape of London below swam in and out of his vision, almost causing him to hyperventilate. In and out, Matthews, he had to tell himself over and over. But his anxiety increased with each new pair of hands and each ferocious smack of the paddle. They'd gone from crop, to flogger, to paddle, and he knew without a doubt that the cane would be next. His eyes were watering from the overload of endorphins invading his system and he had never felt so helpless in his entire life. Even under Sophia he'd always had the power to say no. That was not an option available to him here. The only options here were death or do as he was told.

A set of pretty pink fingernails descended on him and tugged gently, to be replaced by a meaty hand that knew exactly what it was doing. He was so sensitive now that every touch was an unbearable agony.

'Going to beg me for an orgasm, pretty boy?'

Kyle's rough hand upon his cock almost had him in tears, but pride won out.

'Probably not, no,' growled Mark, 'but if I get really desperate, manage to go blind and am force fed several litres of alcohol there's always a chance you might get lucky.' He managed to keep his voice free of tremors, but it was a close run thing.

Kyle snorted, and it was clear his ego had not been bruised. 'I've loved fucking my little pony-girl this week. Petal and I have been working on the pain/pleasure barrier thing, and wouldn't you know, it's generally more pain than pleasure. She's been doing well though. I've taught her to suck with such enthusiasm you'd almost think she was a natural. How does it feel knowing that I taught the girl everything she knows? I'm such a lucky bastard. I get to play with her 24/7 and you've just had a single night in her company. It really is too bad, dearest.'

Mark couldn't resist a snort of his own. 'I don't believe for a second that she was completely green when she met you, Kyle, so leave off. All you've taught the girl to do is fear you. That's your choice. In any case, one night was enough. Love 'em and leave 'em. That's the way I like it. You're welcome to the long term stuff.' He gave a low moan as Kyle viciously tugged his cock and felt his hips rock forward, knowing he would inevitably come if he kept up the forceful motion. Thankfully, Kyle did not seem inclined to give him pleasure this afternoon, and with a nasty swat at his testicles he moved aside to let the next pair of hands do their worst.

Mark blinked back tears and thanked God that Kyle was behind him, and therefore could not see them. He was left with a parting shot though.

'I don't believe you, Matthews. Anyone who's offering to buy one of our girls for the money you were talking about has it bad, and we like to exploit things like that around here. You'll see.'

After that Mark couldn't have cared less what he said, because the pain was all encompassing and it was all he could do to control his screaming. The hands were ruthless. The queue of people was long and endless. Everyone wanted a piece of him, and to his mind they'd probably taken one because everything was breaking up inside him. The glue that held him together was slowly tearing apart and it wouldn't be long before he came unstuck in the worst way.

Katrina had informed him that they were bringing Jenny back out again after a couple of hours respite, and then she would begin again. There was no way he could endure another round of that. His mouth was already as dry as the Kalahari and his brain was fried. Sweat was pouring off him in rivers, and if he passed out there was only one way down, unless that pane was toughened glass. Could he test the theory? Was Redcliff insane? Because that's what you'd have to be, to pull a stunt like this. Was he, wasn't he? Could he get away with murder? Probably. Sweat dripped into his eyes and the salt stung, so he had to blink rapidly to clear it. It was nothing compared to the rest of his body, which was burning brighter than a bloody bonfire. More hands, then more fingers, pressing against him, vibrating the little plug that now felt like a scouring brush embedded deep inside him. Fuck, fuck, fuck. Concentrate.

A male fist, a tight squeeze and crippling pain. Mark felt his knees give way and his heels rocked back upon the nails. He wondered for a second if he'd drawn blood. He could feel the indentations of the spikes along his heel, but no, the pain wasn't enough for it to have broken the skin.

Jesus! Another heavy tug on his cock and the first bite of the cane. His head spun. Then his sweat-slicked hand loosened its grip upon the rope and for a moment he felt himself falling, before his reflexes managed to kick in and his fist, somehow, managed to tighten once more. His teeth sliced into his tongue, drawing blood, and his arms were now skewed at awkward angles in order to keep himself aloft. The pain was intolerable.

'What the fuck do you want, Redcliff?' he hollered as loud as he could, but his voice was a pitiful wreck. With no saliva he could barely get his tongue to move, but somehow Katrina heard him.

Everything in the room stopped. The cane, the hands, and the noise... it all abruptly ceased.

There was a pause and then a slow cough as Redcliff cleared his throat. 'Impressive stamina, Matthews. I believe we'll have to work on your manners, though.'

The cane flew down in a fury, the fingers and fists resumed and someone placed the tip of a thick dildo against his ass. Oh fuck, not that. Please, not that. His top teeth tried their best to grind the lower ones to dust as his face twisted in pain.

The penis plug was rotated inside him and the dildo gradually began to penetrate his sphincter, only a centimetre or so, but it was enough. His fingernails buried themselves in spiky shards of rope as his body bucked furiously to and fro. The plug made it feel like he was being masturbated from the inside out. It was exquisitely painful and pleasurable, to the degree that he did not know which sensation was greater at any one time. As the dildo behind him plied for greater depth he knew he had lost the battle for control. Throwing his head back and shaking the beads of sweat from his face he roared out his climax, and even that was painful. As the semen could not travel out of the traditional route he had a dry, retrograde orgasm and he knew exactly what he'd be pissing in a few hours' time.

Not five seconds after he'd come the fingers began again, but this time they were allowed free reign over his body, between his legs, tugging upon his nipples. He knew that now the floodgates had been opened Redcliff would see he orgasmed again and again, until he was too weak to stand. It was time to stop this madness.

It was an effort to clear his throat and open his eyes. As it was he blinked several times and gulped as the city blurred into lines below him. Don't look down. For God's sake, don't look down. As if that were possible when your body was tilted at a forty-five degree angle. Where else could he look? Trying to swallow, and unable to get enough saliva together to do so, he growled. What he wouldn't give for a cool blast of air, but typically it was a scorching hot afternoon and the shattered window provided no relief. His internal core temperature must have shot up at least five degrees and he was feverishly burning all over, not helped by a cocktail of drugs that had left him dehydrated and drowsy. As the thick head of the dildo began to penetrate he somehow managed to yell out and offer up what the old man wanted.

'Anything you want, Redcliff. I'll give you anything you want, but you need to hurry. I have about two minutes worth of grip left in my fingers, and if you don't want to clear up a gruesome mess down below I suggest you get to the point quickly.' As if to confirm his statement his whole body began shaking wildly. There was nothing he could do to stop it. His muscles were fatigued and at the limit of their endurance. The room went silent as his plea was debated again.

Redcliff made him wait, but finally there was a, 'Get him down,' and immediately several strong hands were placed under his arms as he was gently picked up, led away from the window and placed down on the floor. Then the men quickly stepped away from him as if he were a landmine, and a particularly unstable one at that.

He had news for them. He wasn't moving for the next ten minutes. He pressed his hot forehead on the cool linoleum floor and alternated his movements between breathing and shaking. It was just nice to be alive and not faced with a vision of two hundred metres of nothing but air followed by tarmac.

When the room went even quieter than it had been already, and even the little murmurs and scuffles of feet stopped abruptly, Mark guessed that Redcliff had entered. Sure enough his steely voice cut through the silent room and when he barked, 'Get him to his feet,' people rushed to obey.

'Touch me and I'll fucking rip your head off,' spat Mark, and his fist shot out and smacked the nearest heavy in the eye.

As hands rushed everywhere in order to restrain him Redcliff waved them off and said, 'Leave him be.'

Mark took his own sweet time getting to his feet. Everything hurt, but he was not going to be carried in front of this asshole. He wanted Redcliff to realise just what he was dealing with now. A fucking monster that would not stop until every last shred of the man before him was annihilated.

'So what do you want? Money, women, property, equity, gold, state secrets...? Tell me exactly what it is that has required around five hours of my life today.' The angry set to Mark's jaw could not be supressed.

Redcliff looked him up and down, but if he thought that would intimidate Mark he was much mistaken. As Redcliff's lip twitched, realising his error, he reached into his jacket pocket and pulled out a bundle of forms. 'This is an ante-nuptial agreement. It states that the division of wealth and property be split fifty-fifty on completion of marriage.'

Mark gave Redcliff a look of utter loathing as he was quickly beginning to piece together the puzzle. 'It may have escaped your notice, but I am not yet married,' he bit out.

'Ah, but you will be. Jennifer,' he called, and beckoned with his arm towards the doorway, 'come and meet your new husband-to-be.'

Mark's head swung towards the doorway and in waltzed Jennifer Redcliff, fully clothed and heeled. Her hair had been freshly cut around her face, giving her a beautiful, impish look, and her make-up had been professionally applied. Eyes that looked so big they almost popped out of their cocoon of eyeliner stared at him, and she smelled delicious, with notes of vanilla and jasmine flooding the room. Brilliant red lips and nails complemented the elegant cream shift dress she wore, and a gold belt accentuated her tiny waist.

Mark threw his head back and roared again for the second time that day, this time with a good deal more force. 'You have got to be kidding me. You two were in this together from the start?' Jennifer had the grace to lower her gaze, but neither of them spoke. Mark's jaw dropped open. If a giraffe had managed to climb up the twenty or so flights of stairs needed to reach this room and kissed him on the lips he could not have been more shocked. His head reeled. No, he didn't believe it. Yes, he did. Of course she would be capable of something like this. How horribly fucking clever. What an ass he had been. Then he doubted himself. Who would put themselves through something like that?

Damnit, why couldn't he think straight?

Turning the full weight of his stare upon her and letting her know exactly what he thought of the stunt, he quietly said, 'Just one question. Were you in on this or not? Just a yes or no will do, because I assure you if your answer is the former, that's the last thing you'll ever say near me.'

'Yes.'

She looked him straight in the eye and there was a single blink after she had spoken. Jennifer Redcliff spoke with conviction and the softest of smiles. It was just as well he didn't have any energy left, because right now he wanted to rip her head off its hinges. That 'yes' had just destroyed his world. It put a whole new slant on things. It meant she had been complicit in this whole farce from start to end. The bitch had been in cohorts with her father, and between them they had been working him over. His chest heaved in great gulps of air with the exertion it had taken him to withstand the last five hours of torture, but he carefully controlled the fury that wanted to erupt volcano-style.

Unfortunately, the balance of control was firmly in their court. So he put a lid on the all-consuming anger that would have had his bare hands annihilating the pair of them, right then and right there, and he smiled. He gave them a thousand-watt smile that belied his utter fucking exhaustion. More than one person could play at this little charade and he was more than conversant with the rules.

'Fuck.' Mark rocked back on his heels and then wished he hadn't. 'How?'

She looked at him and raised an eyebrow, compressing her lips tightly. 'You can speak just this once; my curiosity seems to have gotten the better of me,' he got out tightly. He had an inner battle with himself to stop his hands forming into tight fists.

'I was told to imagine myself as a victim, from start to finish, and that's exactly what I did. I played my part.' She emphasised the word 'part', but it was lost on him. He couldn't see past his fury. Right now he didn't see her red-rimmed eyes, the trembling hands that were clasped tightly together or the ghostly pallor of her skin. All he saw was red. As he was passed a clipboard with an array of documents upon it he barely looked at them as he signed each form that was required of him. He had been neatly and cleverly outmanoeuvred. There was no way out of this.

His head swivelled back to Redcliff and things began adding up very quickly. 'All of this is on tape, in case I decide to change my mind, right?'

Redcliff's eyes sparkled. 'Of course. It makes for very lovely viewing. If you ever feel the need for a divorce I think I could possibly make it into a nice YouTube video and have it go viral. You are awfully pretty, after all.'

Mark nodded his head. 'Then let the games commence.' Five words, softly spoken, and the smile was wiped off Michael Redcliff's face in an instant. Here he was completely naked and vulnerable, but already the ball was firmly back in his court.

His mouth forming into a grim line, he calmly walked up to the window that had plagued him for so long and thrust a closed fist at it. It shattered around his hand instantly and he nearly fell over. Holy fuck! Mark bottled the now all-consuming rage and turned around to smile. 'You're just as crazy as they say you are. Absolutely cuckoo and nuttier than a KP peanut factory. I think I could kill you with my bare hands right now.' He could, but with the all the others around, he wouldn't live through the experience.

'Remember I have this on tape, Matthews,' Redcliff bit out. 'I will happily destroy you if you push my buttons.'

Mark's grin got wider but he reined in his tongue. 'Excuse me if I don't wish to lay eyes on my future bride before the nuptials,' he called over his shoulder as he brushed past them both, 'but I'm a firm believer in tradition, you understand.' He turned his head and winked at the old man before proceeding to walk from the building, uncaring that he had not a stitch of clothing to his name. At this moment in time he couldn't have cared less had the Queen herself copped an eyeful. He had his revenge to plan. It would keep him warm as nothing else could. Oh yes, he would allow Jennifer Redcliff to marry him. She could pick a white dress, get herself a lovely bunch of flowers and whisper 'I do', but he'd put money on the fact that she'd be screaming for a divorce inside of a week. An awful lot of money...

He didn't even cast a glance in his bride-to-be's direction as he sailed out of the door, but he did ensure it slammed noisily behind him.

Thus endeth the Pony Tales Series

The Pony Tales

The complete series is available for you to order online now...

The Riding School

Hetty turned her attention back to her subject's face and was quite surprised to see a meek little submissive, almost ashamed of the orgasm she was about to have, panting and heaving for breath whilst nearly foaming at the mouth. Indeed she looked quite tortured in the throes of passion and any Master would be extremely pleased with that particular look during training. Hetty's fingers found their final rhythm and with a measured pressure, they would send the pony girl off to 'O' land in a few seconds...

Meet Jenny. She's rich, spoiled, rude and obnoxious. She's also just been signed up for the BDSM ride of her life - without her consent. An intensive training course at the Albrecht Stables is not what it appears to be and training to become a human pony was not on Jenny's to-do list.

The trouble is, how do you escape when you're tied up, gagged and constantly sexually aroused? Which Master or Mistress do you turn to for rescue? And what do you do if you suspect you might actually be enjoying yourself?

This is Jenny's adventure into the world of BDSM and pony play. She's about to find out just how much effort it takes to become a pony girl and that she has no choice but to excel in every aspect of her training or she may never stand a chance of being released from her bondage.

Book One features Jenny's abrupt induction, where she finds herself being stripped naked, medically examined and intimately measured for her new uniform - as a pony girl.

Learning the Ropes

Finding a suitable four inch collar, he released the leather restraint around her neck. Gently bunching her long black hair into a ponytail, to ensure it didn't get trapped inside, he quickly fastened the two silver buckles at the rear that would hold it in place. Mark decided that was quite enough of the softly-softly approach. He tugged her hair sharply to get her attention and was rewarded with a grimace of pain. Her glorious blue eyes looked at him and widened like saucers as he spoke...

In Book Two of Pony Tales, Jenny finds herself in the capable hands of Mark, her guide and tormentor for the day. She becomes accomplished in the art of crawling, gets an eye-opening tour of the facility and suffers regularly with the pain of orgasm denial. Finding herself at the mercy of his fingertips, when he demonstrates the complexities of breath play, she panics that each gasp of air may be her last.

Displayed, touched, fondled and at the mercy of others, Jenny begins to discover what life as a pony girl might entail, especially when faced with the wicked tongues of several pony boys! Getting acquainted with the rather aptly named Red Room and finding herself subject to a thorough spanking is her first discovery into the delicious world of pain and pleasure that awaits her.

But there are far more devilish torments than spanking to be found at the Albrecht stables...

Hot to Trot

Jenny remained where she had been told and eyed the dildos in the room with trepidation. She then made a point of staring at the floor and not looking in the direction of Mr Big. The man wasn't a monster, surely? Looking at the various sizes of toys on display, she felt her breath catch. Would they really fit... there? Her buttocks clenched tightly in panic and she was immediately reminded of her predicament. Was this going to hurt? Adrenaline was already beginning to flow through her veins at the anticipation of what might come next, and the silence in the room was unnerving...

The viciously attractive Mark, with the unfaltering smile, has a day of endurance planned for Jenny that the devil himself would find challenging. His artful temperature play has her screaming, his anal dilators have her howling and a ride in the sybian's saddle leaves her virtually unconscious, but the day is far from over. A group of ladies, with wandering fingers, are given the task of transforming Jenny into a sweet, submissive pony girl who will be left looking 'hot to trot' in no time at all.

After an exhausting day of training, Jenny has only escape or rescue on her mind. Alas, escape is rather difficult when you're naked, dressed in thigh high pony boots and have your hands immobilised in leather mittens which are clipped behind your back. Besides, escape isn't all that important - not when you're desperate for your next orgasm, it isn't.

Named and Shamed

Gritting her teeth Jenny grimaced and gave him what he wanted; the lewd sight of her backside jiggling this way and that as he continued to spank it. His hand now felt like sandpaper on the sensitised flesh. How much longer would she have to endure this? The clamps continued to bite into her tender nipples, and as she swayed to and fro she could feel them moving with her, the ache increasing with each passing second...

If Jenny thought life was hard under the expert tutelage of Mark, being faced with a stable full of sex-starved pony girls poses several more challenges. For instance, how do you bring eleven young women to orgasm in a timely fashion? But to her surprise, tackling the problem with experimentation and enthusiasm, she finds herself enjoying the experience.

When training begins it is anything but enjoyable, however. Harnessed in pony girl tack, her body is encircled with leather, rubber and steel. It nips, chafes and rubs cruelly, especially when she's faced with a morning of naughty games in the exercise yard.

In Book Four of Pony Tales Jenny earns herself several punishments, and is subjected to some very thorough sex indoctrination she has to submit to the whims of her groom, trainers and even the stable-hands. Will rescue arrive or will she have to beg to be released, with nothing more than her body as currency?

A Rough Ride

Left with nothing more than two small slits for her eyes and two round holes beneath her nostrils through which to breathe, she haltingly turned her eyes to witness the damage he had wreaked upon her.
She immediately recoiled in horror, for reflected in the mirror before her was a human horse, complete with perky rubberised ears. Hoof-mitts were being worked up her hands and she knew it wouldn't be long before her boots followed suit. Not content with having taken her speech, liberty and free will away, now they wanted to make her look like an animal too!

Who will have the pleasure of training Petal? By rights, the honour should go to Mark Matthews, but the cowboy has other plans. The matter is not settled until the stable owner is brought into the fray.

It is to be a monumental first week for Albrecht's newest trainee. The pony girl will have two days to find a way of coping with her new latex bodysuit and the rigorous buzzing and pumping of the never-ending 'device' which torments her every waking moment. She will then find herself shipped off as a sex slave, chained and caged, to the mysterious high-bidder from the auction.

It doesn't take Petal long to realise that her chances of escaping from Albrecht are slim at best, but her defiant nature won't let her give up hope just yet. There is a way out for her, but she may have to give up more than her sanity in order to achieve it.

Also by C. P. Mandara

The Velvet Chair

"Oh, darling. You're going to be so fucking easy to conquer." His finger reached under my chin and pulled my face back to meet his. "I can't wait to strip you out of that dress and watch you crawl around my home naked. I'm going to spank that delectable ass with every damn pervertible I can find. Hairbrushes, wooden spoons, spatulas, and I might even try a damn baking sheet. That ass of yours is always going to be prettily pink and perfectly swollen while you're under my roof."

My name is Mark Matthews. I own half of London, and the part I don't own, I'm working on.

Life was all going swimmingly well until Michael Redcliff entered my life, demanding that I marry his daughter. Actually, swap demand for blackmail. He's got goods on me that I want no one else to see, so for the time being I need to be his little lapdog.

I'll marry his daughter. I'll give him all the status, money and power he can handle... for as long as it takes me to get a divorce. You see, I can't renege on our little arrangement - but she can. I give her a week. One week and she'll be screaming the place down for her legal counsel.

I am never wrong.

www.chimerabooks.co.uk